Scarlet Wilson wrot[...] and has never stoppe[...] service for more thar[...] as a nurse and a heal[...] in public health and lives on the West Coast of Scotland with her fiancé and their two sons. Writing medical romances and contemporary romances is a dream come true for her.

Kate Hardy has always loved books, and could read before she went to school. She discovered Mills & Boon books when she was twelve and decided that this was what she wanted to do. When she isn't writing Kate enjoys reading, cinema, ballroom dancing and the gym. You can contact her via her website: katehardy.com.

Discover more at millsandboon.co.uk.

SLOW DANCE WITH THE ITALIAN

SCARLET WILSON

A FAKE BRIDE'S GUIDE TO FOREVER

KATE HARDY

MILLS & BOON

First published in Great Britain 2024
by Mills & Boon, an imprint of HarperCollins*Publishers* Ltd,
1 London Bridge Street, London, SE1 9GF

www.harpercollins.co.uk

HarperCollins*Publishers*, Macken House, 39/40 Mayor Street Upper, Dublin 1, D01 C9W8, Ireland

ISBN: 978-0-263-32132-6

06/24

This book contains FSC™ certified paper and other controlled sources to ensure responsible forest management.

For more information visit www.harpercollins.co.uk/green.

Printed and Bound in the UK using 100% Renewable Electricity at CPI Group (UK) Ltd, Croydon, CR0 4YY

SLOW DANCE WITH THE ITALIAN

SCARLET WILSON

MILLS & BOON

This book is dedicated to my fellow author
Kate Hardy, who always motivates me to work hard
and write better stories.

PROLOGUE

DARCY HELD HER hands in her lap, twisting one of the green leaves in her bouquet. 'Where is he?' she asked again, knowing that her voice sounded awkward with strain. She could see the sweat at her dad's collar.

The chauffeur gave a difficult smile. 'I'm sure it will just be a few minutes. Most brides aren't as organised as you and are usually running way behind. We're here dead on time. It's almost unheard of.'

He tugged at his jacket and Darcy looked down at the gold watch on her slim wrist. She could see the hint of pale green near the church's main doors. Her sisters. The bridesmaids had gone ahead as planned. But it seemed that they too had arrived before the groom.

Darcy took a deep breath. She was already worried about Laura. The pale green colour that had looked so beautiful in the early planning stages of the wedding had washed out her already paler than pale sister, making her look sicker than she wanted anyone to know she was.

It was a mild summer's day, but would Laura be cold? The bridesmaids' dresses were strapless, and Darcy didn't want her sister to have to hang around the church entrance—getting more chilled by the second—because Damian couldn't organise himself enough to get to his own wedding on time.

They'd often joked about how chaotic he was—the polar opposite to Darcy, who planned things to perfection. They drove each other to distraction, but opposites attracted, didn't they? That was what people always said, and Darcy assumed they must have been fated to meet.

A brisk breeze caught the jacket of the chauffeur and Darcy made up her mind. 'We're getting out,' she said to her father, who started in surprise. 'I'm not having Laura stand in the cold. We can all go inside and wait in the foyer. I'll get Fizz to call Damian and see where on earth he is. The other car has probably broken down or something.'

Her stomach gave an uncomfortable twist as she gathered up her skirts and opened the car door, stepping out onto the road outside the church. She waved her hand at the photographer, who tried to stop her as she strode up the path towards her sisters, her father hurrying behind her.

Her mother was sheltering in the foyer, her pale pink hat perfectly positioned on her head. 'What's going on?' she asked Darcy.

Darcy looked from side to side. The minister was hovering in the background, clearly as unnerved as the rest of them. The chauffeur appeared beside Darcy. 'Can you give my sister your jacket for a few minutes, please?' she asked.

He looked surprised, but after one glance at frail Laura he immediately nodded and slipped his jacket off, and around her shoulders.

Fizz—who had been missing for a few seconds—appeared from the side, a phone in her hand. 'Darcy—' she said in a croaky voice '—come here.'

Darcy's stomach plummeted. She knew. She knew

what was about to happen. But she didn't actually believe it was about to happen to her.

Fizz had gone ahead with a few family items in the bridesmaids' car. Just normal things, like touch-up make-up, phones, emergency snacks and safety pins—because you never knew when you might need a safety pin. The overnight bags were already at the reception hotel.

But Fizz was currently holding a phone in her hand. It was silver. Which meant it was Darcy's. Fizz had the same phone in pink, and Laura in green.

Darcy handed her orange gerbera and dark green leaf bouquet to her mother and walked over to Fizz. She spoke in a low voice. 'What is it?'

Fizz looked pained. 'I heard your phone pinging. I think you have some texts.' She blinked, and Darcy knew her sister was blinking back tears on her behalf.

She calmly took her phone from her sister's hand.

The screen was still lit and the first few words of the message were clearly visible. I am so, so sorry.

Darcy licked her lips. Her throat was instantly dry and her skin prickled uncomfortably. She slid the message open with her finger then blinked at the length of the message. Damian had never been known to be long-winded. But it seemed today he'd made an exception.

Her eyes scanned the message as tears she didn't want to shed blurred her vision.

'I'll kill him,' came the voice of her father behind her, who had obviously read part of the message over her shoulder. 'I'll find him, and I'll kill him.'

And Darcy knew that in that second her father, the most placid man on the planet, meant every word. He adored his girls. She knew he would lay down his life for any one of them.

Every part of her body was shaking. But she was determined to be strong. She didn't want her family to see her break. Not after everything they'd been through together. The last few years with Laura's illness had taken its toll on every one of them. Her mother and father had aged visibly. They didn't need any more stress. Not when Laura was still at risk and only part way through her treatment.

Darcy lifted her head. This was her mess. No one else's. Her heart squeezed when she thought of all their family and friends currently sitting in the church, waiting for her and Damian.

A braver woman would walk in, tell them that he'd changed his mind and invite them all back to the hotel for a party—after all, it was already paid for. That was what other brides on social media did, wasn't it?

But even though Darcy knew her family and friends would put up a good front on her behalf, she knew that wasn't what she wanted. She wasn't that kind of person.

She took her phone and did a search. It took a few seconds to pull up a hotel that she'd looked at in the past but was always out of her price range. A few presses of some buttons and she'd booked herself in for the next five nights.

She kissed her sisters and her mum and dad on the cheeks. 'Thank you all. But you know that Damian isn't coming.' She shook her head, trying to pretend her voice wasn't trembling. 'I know I should go and tell people, but I just can't do it. I need some time to myself.' She tilted her chin up, feeling a little braver. 'I've booked a hotel. Please invite our guests back to the reception, some of them have travelled a distance. Look after them.'

'Darcy,' Fizz said, her arm immediately on Darcy's. 'I'll come with you. You're not going by yourself.'

Darcy pulled Fizz in tight. 'Look after Laura,' she whispered in her ear. 'Her next round of chemo is two days away. Look after her for both of us.' She pulled back now, not trying to hide the tears streaming down her face. 'We're the Bennetts. We'll get over this,' she said, the family motto they were all familiar with. 'I love you all,' she added before she gave a nod to the chauffeur. 'Will you take me where I want to go?'

The man gave an immediate nod and Darcy turned and started walking away from the church, not wanting to look back at her family.

She couldn't. Not now.

Not when her heart was breaking.

Not when she had no idea what might come next.

CHAPTER ONE

THE TWO SISTERS held hands as they sat down in front of the solicitor. His invitation to them had been like a bolt out of the blue. The date was seared on both of their hearts. It was the date that Laura had died. Today was the five-year anniversary.

Darcy felt as if a lump had settled directly in the centre of her chest. She was conscious of Felicity's hand in hers. Her fingers were cold. Had she lost weight? Darcy wasn't sure.

They'd spent the last few years living in different parts of the country, her in Edinburgh and Fizz in London. Where once all three of them had been in constant contact, since the loss of Laura, things had changed. There had been no fall-out, nothing dramatic. But the miles between them had enabled a distance to form in their relationship—almost as if they lived in separate bubbles. They still chatted on occasion, and texted, but their connection had changed—as if something was missing between them and they both felt it hard.

Fizz was usually effervescent, occasionally flighty, and jumped from one thing to the next. She had bags of energy, but today seemed a little more subdued. Maybe Darcy was overthinking things? It could be that Fizz was just as nervous as she was about being called to the solicitor's office.

'Ladies.' Darcy jerked at the deep voice. Mr Cochrane's slim frame filled the doorway. 'Thank you for coming.' He shot them a warm smile as he crossed the room and sat down behind the desk.

He was in his late sixties, with a neat grey beard and carefully trimmed hair. The last time Darcy had been here was when he'd spoken to the family about Laura's will. She'd still lived with their parents but had owned a car and had some savings and a few treasured possessions. They'd all been surprised she'd made a will, but had carried out all her wishes once her small estate had been settled. So why on earth had Mr Cochrane invited them back to his office today?

He gave them both a nod and opened a file on his desk. 'It's nice to see you both, and I am conscious of the date.' He paused and took a breath. 'But today's meeting was intentionally called on this date.'

Darcy glanced anxiously at Fizz, who seemed just as bewildered as she was.

Mr Cochrane clasped his hands. 'It's Laura that asked me to invite you both here today.'

'What?' said Fizz quickly, her brow furrowing.

Mr Cochrane held up his hand. 'She gave me some instructions, and it is those instructions that I'm following.' He glanced at them both, and Darcy could sense something.

'The truth is,' he continued, 'Laura was worried about how you would both cope once she was no longer here. She described the three of you as the Terrible Trio.' As soon as he said those words Darcy couldn't help but smile.

'She left some instructions that if in five years' time

neither of you were settled with a partner or had a family, she wanted to leave something else for you both.'

He slid a paper across the desk towards them. Both of them instinctively reached out for it then gave a nervous laugh. 'Go on,' Darcy said to her sister, waiting as Fizz lifted the paper and held it in front of them.

Fizz started reading, her voice trembling. *'Time has passed and I hope both of you are happy and healthy. I'm not sure where you are in life right now, but if you're both here today it's because I've left you a final task to fulfil for me. Although Mr Cochrane handled my will and distributed my millions to the masses...'* Fizz's voice broke and she wiped a tear from her face. She gave a little laugh and turned to Darcy, who had the biggest lump in her throat. 'I can just hear her voice—hear her saying these words.'

Darcy nodded and brushed a tear from her own face. 'Me too.' She swallowed, even though the lump was still there, and took over the reading from Fizz. *'I kept a little something back. A policy that Mum and Dad had for me as a child, and has remained in the bank—on my instructions, under the care of Mr Cochrane. I wanted to keep this little pot of money for something special. My bucket list.'*

Darcy dropped the hand that was holding the paper. 'Her bucket list?'

It was an expression she hadn't heard in years.

Mr Cochrane gave a gentle smile. He nodded to her to continue reading.

Darcy took a breath and lifted the paper. *'I want you to take the money, split it between you and fulfil the items on my bucket list over the next month. I want to push you both to maybe do something you haven't. I want my sisters to have fun. Have fun in my memory. Know that I am right by your side when you do all these things. I love you girls, Laura.'*

Darcy turned the paper over. There was no writing on the other side.

Fizz spoke first. 'Where's the bucket list?'

Mr Cochrane handed over two sealed envelopes, the names on the envelopes were in Laura's handwriting.

Now the tears did start to fall. Darcy reached out quickly and held it to her chest. Holding something that her sister had written for her a number of years ago tugged every emotion she had. She was glad she was sitting down right now because she wasn't sure if her legs would carry her.

After a few moments Fizz spoke. 'Why two envelopes? Are we doing the same things? Have we to do them together?'

Mr Cochrane held up both his hands. 'The instruction I was given is that you can both interpret your lists the way you think best—so I'm not entirely sure if they are identical or not. What I do know is that she wanted you to do these things your own way. So you've to do the bucket lists separately.' He raised one eyebrow. 'There was a mention you might need a companion or friend for some things.'

Darcy sat back in her chair and breathed out. This was the last thing she'd expected. A bucket list? She hadn't had one of those since she was a child—or a teenager at least.

He handed over a further item for each of them. Darcy blinked at the figure. 'This is the amount of each share of Laura's final gift to you both. If you give me current bank details the money can be transferred to your accounts.'

Fizz said the words out loud. 'It's more than I would have expected.'

Mr Cochrane gave a nod. 'Laura trusted me to invest it for the last few years on her, and your, behalf.' His smile was sincere. 'I think she would be happy with how things have worked out.'

They left the office in stunned silence, Darcy still clutching the envelope with the bucket list to her chest.

The connection to their sister was still there. It always would be. The Terrible Trio. Her heart ached at those words. Sometimes she'd wondered what nickname their father would have given them if there had only been two. The Dangerous Duo? Even the thought felt like betrayal.

She swallowed again. She'd never got over Laura's death. It always felt as if a part of them was missing. How could she go on and live a happy life when her sister had never got that chance? Those feelings of guilt had never left her, no matter how hard she tried to rationalise them. It was all just so unfair.

She glanced sideways at Fizz. They'd grown apart over the last few years. Not deliberately. But with Darcy living in Edinburgh, Fizz in London and both of them adults with their own life, it seemed inevitable, even if it did make her heart twist and turn.

She'd already lost one sister. And this event just gave her the harsh reminder that she couldn't take her other sister for granted.

'What do you want to do?' Fizz asked before Darcy had a chance to speak.

She glanced around her, unsure of what to do next. Both of them had to be feeling a bit strange—how could they not?

'Let's go for a coffee,' suggested Fizz.

'No.' Darcy shook her head in a way that was very unlike her. 'Let's go for a drink.'

Fizz blinked, and then followed Darcy as they walked down the road. It didn't take long to reach a fairly reasonable-looking hotel and they made their way to the bar.

'Something to toast our sister,' murmured Darcy as she scanned the bar.

'It's a cocktail,' said Fizz without a second's hesitation. 'It has to be.' She swiped the cocktail menu from the bar and scanned it as the bartender approached. 'Porn Star Martini,' she said.

They sat in comfortable silence as the bartender made the drinks. Darcy knew that her sister's brain was spinning just as much as hers was. But in some ways she and Fizz were very similar. Laura had been much more practical. She would have wanted to talk things through. But Fizz and Darcy both needed time to process things. To sort them out in their own time and in their own way.

As he slid the drinks towards them, Darcy picked hers up, knowing that they would drink them in entirely different ways. As predicted, Fizz downed her prosecco shot first, then held her glass with the mango cocktail. Darcy gave a small laugh and mixed her prosecco in with the cocktail—as Fizz shook her head—then lifted her glass to her sister's.

'To Laura. We loved her and miss her every day,' she said.

'To Laura,' Fizz agreed. 'And whatever she has in store for us with this bucket list.'

CHAPTER TWO

DARCY TURNED THE letter over and over in her hand. She was back home in Edinburgh, trying to make sense of what had just happened.

The aroma of the tea drifted towards her and she poured some from the teapot, cradling her cup in her hands as she looked out at the Scottish countryside.

For a bride who'd been stood up at the altar, things had actually turned out okay. The hotel she'd booked into in the city for five nights had given her a taste for Edinburgh. She'd been able to look at career opportunities that would allow her to rent a place on the outskirts. Her cybersecurity degree had led her from one job to another, with salary increases along the way, with much of her work being done remotely.

Her increase last year had allowed her to buy this cottage on the outskirts of Edinburgh, and although all the original features and stonework had been kept at the front of the cottage, the extension at the back had a glass wall that looked out onto the rolling green countryside and trickling stream nearby.

The farm next door had some fence gaps that allowed a chicken or sheep to occasionally appear in what was supposed to be her back garden. But Darcy didn't mind in the least.

She loved her peaceful countryside view, who needed a TV? She had neighbours close enough to not feel isolated, but far enough away to give her the space she desired.

Her life was settled. Her life was simple. Her life was quiet.

Which was why the bucket list from her sister was giving her so much trouble.

The four items listed for Darcy were:

Do something that scares you.
Grab a friend and have a mad twenty-four hours in a European city that you've always wanted to visit.
Make a lifelong commitment to something or someone.
Find somewhere peaceful—a space to share—to reflect on what you want out of life.

These were just the rough notes. Because alongside the typewritten page were scribbles in Laura's handwriting. Darcy was pretty sure that the notes Laura had written for her would be entirely different than the notes she wrote for Fizz.

Across the top of her page, in writing so familiar it made her heart ache, were the words:

You need to learn to connect with people again, Darcy.

She hated that her younger sister, five years ago, had known Darcy better than she knew herself.

Laura had never really been a fan of Darcy's fiancé Damian. Darcy had dated him for three years, and been engaged for one before their almost-wedding. They'd met at university—he'd been studying geography—and they had settled into a comfortable relationship. He'd struggled with Laura's illness. He'd never been nasty, but had sometimes clearly been frustrated when Darcy had cancelled plans at short notice because Laura was unwell.

At one time he'd accused Darcy of always prioritising Laura over him. She'd denied it at the time, but now, looking back, she could see that she clearly always had—and wasn't the least bit sorry about it.

The fallout from her never-to-be wedding hadn't been extreme by any means. Darcy had taken herself to Edinburgh for five days, walked around the city, ate room service, joined a night-time ghost tour and spent an hour talking to a lonely elderly man in a café one day. Arthur had lost his wife of fifty years and was heartbroken. Darcy was the first person he'd spoken to all week.

She'd reached out and held his hand in hers, wary of his paper-thin skin. She'd told him about being left at the altar, and he'd decided it was his job to cheer her up. His strong accent had thrown her at first, but she'd concentrated, and her ear adjusted quickly. By the end of the hour, just having that short-term connection with someone had given her hope and she'd left with his phone number in her pocket and called him every week since.

She'd headed home, sold the house she'd bought with Damian and started looking for another job—one that meant she could get even further away. There had been no shouting or screaming. Damian had been level with her, telling her that even though they'd been in a relationship, she'd never really been 'there' and he didn't want to spend the rest of his life like that. The words hadn't stung at the time—she'd still been numb about being left at the altar. But in the years since she'd understood them a little better. He'd been right. She hadn't been invested the way she should have been. She hadn't been wildly in love. She'd been comfortable. She'd never pined for Damian after he'd ended things with her. Yes, she'd been sad, upset and unsettled. And everything about that event had bled into her present-day life. Whilst she'd dated over the last few years, she'd never found anyone that she'd wanted to go all in for. Something always held her back.

Darcy closed her eyes for a second, imagining Laura looking down on her and hearing her voice in her ear.

You've isolated yourself. You have to get back out there. What's happened between you and Fizz? Yes, you have a beautiful house, but what else do you have here?

Her computer gave a sharp buzz and she jerked, moving on automatic pilot to sit in her bright red ergonomic chair and click the button to take the video call. Libby's face flashed up on the screen and Darcy relaxed. Her friend from uni had moved to Australia a few years ago and was doing just as well as Darcy, except she had found a husband along the way and had a six-month-old baby.

'I've been thinking,' said Libby without pausing for a second to say hello.

Darcy couldn't help but smile and put her head in her hands. 'It's always dangerous when you think, Lib.'

Libby laughed, her blonde hair partly covering her face. 'I've been thinking about the photo of the list you sent me.'

Darcy groaned. 'Now, I *know* this is dangerous. I should never have sent you it.'

'Rubbish.' Libby smiled, her thick Welsh accent still present. 'You had a moment of madness as you were getting on the plane to come back home, and thought you would share the list with your best friend on the other side of the world.'

She lifted a glass of wine to Darcy. 'You also knew I'd be sleeping and you'd be safe from a response for a while.' Her smile broadened.

'Oh, no,' said Darcy, her stomach clenching. 'I know that look.'

'I had a baby who was teething. I was up most of the night rocking her back and forward. And while I did that, I found a whole heap of things I thought you could sign up for.'

Darcy looked down at her cup of tea. 'I don't think this is going to be strong enough to get me through.'

'You know Edinburgh's a great city,' said Libby. 'There's lots going on. All you have to do is look.'

Darcy leaned her head on one hand and held up the other. 'Okay, hit me with it, but just know, I'm not agreeing to anything until I've had a chance to think about it.'

'I want you to know I'm versatile,' continued Libby.

'Why do I have a feeling of impending doom?'

'Rubbish,' scoffed Libby. It really was her favourite word. 'I found things that you could use for either *"Do something that scares you"* or *"Make a lifetime commitment to someone or something".*'

Darcy had let her head slump back into her hands, but it shot up at this point. 'Tell me you didn't sign me up for something.'

Libby did her best to look innocent. 'So, hear me out. I found adult gymnastics—which could be scary, a church was looking for a Scout leader—that could come under a lifetime commitment.'

'I don't know a single thing about Scouts, don't you dare sign me up for that,' threatened Darcy.

But Libby wasn't planning on stopping going through her list. 'I also found pottery, painting, book clubs, curling, jogging, a netball team, a women's rugby club, but none of these seemed challenging enough.'

'How long was Charity up for last night? And why do you look so awake?'

Libby shook her head. 'I'm not really awake. I'm just in some kind of hazy, glazed state. Lack of sleep does things to your brain.' She held up one finger. 'But then I found something good.'

Now that Darcy looked closer, she could see a glint in Libby's eye. Libby had never done well with late night studying and lack of sleep, so she wasn't too sure she should argue with her.

'Do you remember years ago when we used to watch Saturday night TV as we were getting ready to go out?'

Darcy nodded slowly.

Libby tipped her head to the side and imitated Darcy's voice perfectly. 'And you always said there was *no way* you would do that.'

Her heart sank like a stone. There had been two Saturday night shows on rival TV channels. One involved intricate dancing, and one involved being on a stage and doing…something, as the judges buzzed contestants off for being… Libby's favourite word again—rubbish.

She couldn't quite find her voice right now. Either option made her feel sick.

Libby beamed. 'So, we know that Laura wanted you to go back out and meet people. What about this?'

The copied and pasted poster flashed up in the chat on her screen.

Carnival Ballroom Dancing
Variety Hall, Edinburgh
Every Monday at seven p.m.
Want to learn the quickstep? The samba? The fox-
trot? The Viennese waltz or the paso doble?
Come along!
Bring a partner or we'll find one for you!

'No.' All of Darcy's automatic defence mechanisms kicked into place. 'Not a chance.'

'Oh, come on!' said Libby, an edge of humour and scorn in her voice. 'I could have picked a parachute jump, abseiling, or diving off the top of a mountain.' She leaned forward into the camera and put her hand on her chest. 'But remember, I know you. I was there when you shuddered as the celebs had to learn to dance with their professional partner, then some stomped around the dance floor and others flew like butterflies.'

'And you knew I was terrified of it.'

'Just like I know that you're equally terrified of heights and deep water. I picked the lesser of the evils.' Libby looked decidedly pleased with herself.

Darcy took a long, slow breath. She'd been pondering the list for a few days and got nowhere. The truth was, she was scared to start. Scared to take the steps that Laura was pushing her towards. She wondered if that was the reason she'd actually shared the list with Libby. Deep down, she'd known that Libby would push her on.

'Okay,' she agreed, as something flashed into her brain. Those words: *Bring a partner or we'll find one for you!*

Arthur. Five years later, he was still in her life. They had occasional lunches together, or afternoon teas, or sometimes even met in the Princes Street Gardens. The last thing she wanted to do was be up close and personal with someone she didn't know. Arthur was a gentleman. Plus, he was eighty-five. They could sit out the vigorous dances and maybe just try the Viennese waltz. Would she be able to persuade him?

Something else pricked in her brain. She'd heard that some of these kinds of classes were full of older women. Maybe Arthur could meet someone?

'This might not be a bad idea,' she said, straightening up.

'Eureka!' declared Libby. 'So, will you sign up?' Almost instantly a link appeared in the chat.

'Did you plan this?'

Libby shrugged. 'Told you. I've had some time on my hands.'

Darcy looked at her friend again. Libby was always immaculate. It didn't matter if it was the middle of the night for her, or if she'd only had a few hours' sleep. But did looking good mean anything?

'Are you okay?' she asked carefully.

'Yes, why?' Libby's brow furrowed.

'It's just...you've said you hardly had any sleep. But you still seem so...well, great.'

Libby gave a nod of understanding. 'Remember I have my mum, dad and Charlie to help too. They all look after me. I'm fine, honestly.' She tilted her head to one side. Libby had always been perceptive. 'What about Fizz? How was she? You haven't said much.'

'Not much to say. We went for a drink afterwards. But neither of us opened our letters together. It just felt too... personal. She texted me later and I know that we have roughly the same things to do—but Laura suspected we might interpret them differently.'

'So, any day now I'll hear about Fizz joining a nunnery or taking a vow of silence for a year? I can't imagine there's much in this life that scares your sister. At least none of the outrageous stuff that scares the rest of us.'

Darcy rested back in her chair and let her shoulders finally relax. 'I think you'd be surprised. Fizz puts on a good face to the world, but she's not quite as brave as everyone thinks.'

Libby gave a slow nod and raised her glass. 'Well, I'm toasting you and your dancing. And I might send you a little surprise.'

'What kind of surprise?' Darcy was instantly suspicious. Libby could be wicked at times.

Libby winked. 'Guess you'll just need to wait and find out.'

CHAPTER THREE

ARTURO FABIANO WAS never nervous. He couldn't remember a single time in his life that he'd been nervous. Except now. And except here.

It was ridiculous. He walked past the unassuming entrance of the Variety Hall for the second time and shook his head.

He'd left things to the last possible second, hoping some kind of emergency might arise that would get him out of this. He glanced at the phone in his hand for the last time. *Ring!* But the phone stayed stubbornly unlit.

Giving his sister away at her wedding was an honour, of course it was, and after the death of their father, a few years before, he was delighted she had asked him. Delighted right up until someone had reminded him of the father of the bride dance he'd be expected to fill in for.

Dancing had never been an Arturo thing. While some of his friends had slid around the dance floor as teenagers, Arturo had charmed his way around the bar and the dance floor edges instead. For years people had complimented him on his looks, his business acumen and his family values. But no one had complimented his dancing skills, because he'd made it a rule not to embarrass himself.

Now? He stared at the panel outside the Variety Hall

announcing the weekly activities held there. Now, it seemed like he was going to have to learn some kind of dancing in order to not let his sister down.

'Coming in?' asked a petite older woman with white hair. She had one of those intense gazes that gave the impression people didn't normally argue with her.

'Yes,' he said quickly, holding out his arm for her to go first, then striding up the steps as if he hadn't walked past them twice already.

He gulped as he entered the large hall filled with chattering voices. The scent caught the back of his throat. Perfume, soap, dancing shoes and in Edinburgh, of course, the smell of wet umbrellas and damp coats.

'You're new,' said another older woman, moving closer, along with a few of her friends.

Arturo gave a weak smile, wondering if they pounced on all new attendees. His eyes scanned the room. At the other side was an older man with a woman around Arturo's age. She had blonde hair in a ponytail and a puffy red skirt. She looked every bit as nervous as he did, and kept tugging at the edges of her skirt.

A woman with her hair in a bun and a black leotard with a floaty skirt over the top approached him. She walked with an elegance that suited her. 'Arturo?' she asked.

He nodded gratefully.

'Margaret.' She held her hand out towards him. The woman he'd emailed about the classes. She ran her eyes up and down his body. 'You strike me as someone who doesn't usually feel like a fish out of water.'

'You could say that,' he agreed, his tense shoulders finally relaxing a bit. Margaret could be anywhere between fifty and sixty, her dark hair had streaks of grey and she had the lean body of a woman who had danced all her life. As she glanced around the room at the hotch-potch of dance fans, he could see the patience on her face, and he sent a silent prayer upwards.

'Maybe this wasn't the best place for me to learn. Maybe I should have asked for private lessons.'

She side-eyed him. 'You're that bad?'

He laughed. 'I could be.'

She tapped his arm. 'Let's wait and see. There are a number of newbies here tonight. Let's see how it goes.' Her smile was reassuring. 'I promise that I'll be able to teach you enough to glide your sister around the dance floor. You'll be fine.'

She walked away, her movements all long legs and graceful limbs. An hour. That was how long this class lasted. If he could get through this, he might have to take some time to rethink things. Thankfully, there was no one here he knew. His friends would be in hysterics if they knew he was taking dance classes.

And Arturo was determined to keep this quiet.

'This is a bad idea,' said Darcy to Arthur. 'I should never have asked you to come.'

Arthur straightened his shoulders as he looked around. Another woman nearby gave him a shy smile.

'Like flies around honey,' breathed Darcy. This might be a bad idea for her, but it didn't look like it was going to be a bad idea for Arthur. She could see the number of women in his age range who were already trying to catch his eye.

And she couldn't blame them. He was tall, trim, with a dapper beard and maroon waistcoat. Arthur knew how to dress.

'This might not be so bad,' he mused.

There was another guy at the opposite end of the room. He'd glanced in her direction a few times, and at first she'd wondered if he was one of the instructors. His dark hair and broad frame, as well as his impeccably fitted suit, would catch anyone's eye. But even though he looked like a man who turned heads, he didn't look like a dance instructor.

At least, he didn't seem to have the confidence she imagined went along with being a dance instructor. In fact, he looked every bit as uncomfortable as she was.

Margaret, the lady who'd greeted them when they'd first arrived, appeared in the middle of the room and clapped her hands above her head.

'Everyone. Get ready to start. We'll begin with some gentle warm-up exercises and stretches to get us all ready. Make sure you have some space around, and follow my lead.' She gave a nod to someone and some music started.

Gentle exercise. Darcy could manage that. She stared down at the red lightweight tulle skirt that had appeared in the post from her friend Libby. She hadn't even been sure she should wear it, but a quick text from her sister had encouraged her.

She followed the exercises, rolling shoulders, swinging arms, bending and stretching. It gave her a chance to look at the room around her. The Variety Hall in Edinburgh had been used for more than a hundred years. The wide, light wooden floor was deluged with sunshine that streamed through the central glass domed ceiling above them, with tiny insets of stained glass. It currently gave the illusion that it was a beautiful and bright day outside, whereas the wind tunnel known as Princes Street gave an entirely different version of the day.

The warm-up exercises finished quickly, and Darcy found herself face to face with Arthur, following some very simple steps. It was clear that at some point in his life he'd done this before and was a complete natural.

As she glanced around the room it was also clear that many of the participants had been coming for a while. Hardly anyone seemed as confused as she was.

'Move around!' said Margaret, clapping her hands above her head, and Darcy's eyes widened as she realised that everyone else was swapping partners. She'd only planned on dancing with Arthur, but he was swept away from her eagerly by another woman, and she found herself in the arms of an older grey-haired woman.

'Barbara,' she sighed quickly. 'I always end up as the man.'

Darcy couldn't help but laugh. She started to relax a little. The people around her were lovely. Some took things very seriously, but most were there to keep fit and have fun. A few were reliving dancing from their youth. All were patient with Darcy if she messed up a few steps. She kept her eye on Arthur and he seemed to be having the time of his life.

Her heart ached, remembering how lonely he'd been when she'd first met him. Since she'd moved to Edinburgh they'd become firm friends, but now she wondered if she should have tried some more sociable activities with him earlier.

Darcy twirled around and side-stepped straight into her next partner. His large frame filled her vision in the expensive cut of an Italian suit and a whiff of entirely masculine and woody noted aftershave. She caught her breath and looked up, just as he stepped on her foot.

'Yeow!' she said, hopping and catching her foot in her

hand. The soft leather shoes she'd been recommended for class certainly couldn't deal with the weight of his muscular build.

'I am so sorry,' he said immediately, but her ear didn't take in the words. Her ear took in the accent. The rich Italian accent that fitted entirely with the dark handsome man in front of her.

For a second, she wondered if this was all some elaborate game show. Libby and Fizz had concocted this whole thing together as a kind of 'gotcha'. The guy was actually some actor and was probably supposed to make this whole thing a nightmare, to see how much it would take her to flip.

She pushed the thought away almost as soon as it formed. That was the trouble with having an active imagination. It could take her down dangerous paths and ridiculous scenarios. Anyway, no one could really top being stood up at the altar, so what would be the point?

The man's hand was on her arm, his other trying to reach her foot as she hopped around. Heads had turned and were watching them.

She put her slightly squashed foot back on the ground and tried not to grimace. 'It's okay,' she said automatically. 'It will be fine.'

Fine *after* she'd raided her bathroom cupboard for some painkillers and probably sat it up on her sofa for the rest of the night.

His face was marred by a deeply furrowed brow and he spoke some rapid Italian that she didn't have a single chance of following. His words were musical, the language rich and smooth. It did things to her skin. Things she didn't recognise at first. Not until the skin prickles made their way directly to her spine.

The jolt was instant. Disturbing. And then strangely awakening.

It was a long time since she'd felt any kind of attraction to a man. It wasn't as if she'd lived like a monk—or, more appropriately, a nun, for the last five years. But everything had been very casual for her. She hadn't really allowed herself to be invested in anyone since Damian. Losing both her sister, and Damian in such a short space of time had made her wary of risking her heart again. It was so much easier to keep a protective barrier wrapped around herself and focus on other things. Like work or the renovations to the cottage. Both of which had been ultimately time-consuming.

Someone squeezed her hand gently and she jolted back to reality. It was him, of course it was him, and now he was looking at her with concern.

'Arturo,' he said softly, as if he'd already said it before. 'I am Arturo Fabiano. I am so sorry.'

She blinked. 'Darcy Bennett,' she replied, meeting his dark brown eyes.

He shook his head in disgust. 'I should never have come here. It was a stupid idea. How on earth can anyone learn to dance in a few weeks? I should have known better.'

Her interest was instantly piqued. 'You want to learn to dance in a few weeks? Why?'

He took a breath and sighed. She could tell by the expression on his face this meant something to him. 'My sister is getting married. Our father died a few years ago, and she's asked me to give her away.'

Something tugged at Darcy's heartstrings. Words could be simple but she understood the heartache behind them.

'I'm sorry about your dad.'

She watched him swallow, clearly surprised she hadn't just kept talking. He paused and met her gaze. For a moment they didn't move, held in place. *'Grazie,'* he said in a low voice.

The people around them had started moving again, and it was clear they were blocking the flow. Arturo looked around them and held out his arms automatically—one on her shoulder, one at her waist, for them to get back into the rhythm of those around them.

As she slid her hand into his, the warmth of his palm seemed intensely personal. As she tried to remember the steps that Margaret continued to shout out loud, Darcy took a deep breath. 'So, I take it giving your sister away also means doing one of the dances at the wedding?'

His expression was almost a grimace and she had to hide the smile that threatened to dart across her face.

'Yes,' came the short reply.

The furrow had appeared on his brow again and she could tell he was concentrating on the steps they were doing. Every now and then he glanced down, obviously trying not to step on her toes again.

'Is this your first time here?'

'Yes.'

'Mine too.'

Now, his eyes came up from the floor and locked gazes with her again.

'Why did you come?'

Her stomach twisted a bit. Arturo might be tall, dark and handsome, but he was also a complete stranger. She wasn't sure she wanted to share about Laura and the bucket list. A Variety Hall filled with a hundred other people just didn't seem like the place for that conversation. 'I have an older friend—Arthur.' She nodded in his direction. 'I persuaded him to come because I'm trying to get him out more.'

It wasn't the truth, but it also wasn't completely a lie. Her brain made a few more connections and she prayed he wouldn't ask how she and Arthur had met. Telling him the humiliating being left at the altar story was even less appealing than the personal bucket list story.

Arturo followed her line of sight. 'That sounds nice.' He gave a smile—the first one she'd seen from him. It had an easiness about it and changed his expression completely. His furrowed brow could be intimidating. But the smile? Well, that could make knees weak on the other side of the room. 'He certainly looks as if he's going down a storm.'

Darcy nodded. 'And I couldn't be happier for him. This looks like it's giving him the boost he needs and deserves.'

Arturo gave her a curious glance but she didn't fill in any of the blanks. Instead, she looked straight into those brown eyes with a renewed burst of confidence. 'So, Arturo Fabiano. What do you do for a living?'

He raised his eyebrows. 'Just call me Indiana Jones.'

She couldn't help but smile. 'You're an archaeologist?'

He shook his head as they took another few steps. 'I find hidden treasures.'

Now it was Darcy's turn to raise her eyebrows. 'What does that mean?' She wasn't quite getting the steps right, but at this point she didn't care. 'Don't archaeologists spend all their time digging in the dirt?'

'I've done that,' he agreed with a nod. 'I've worked on sites at Pompeii, Egypt, Turkey and the UK. Now, I do mainly retrieval. Mostly it's art—paintings, sculpture, artefacts.'

'So, who do you work for?'

There was a fleeting expression. Was that embarrassment? 'I work for one of the Italian national agencies.'

She felt a little tremor down her spine. It was the way he said the words. Was he like an art kind of James Bond? 'I get the impression you're not looking for new works— or new artists.'

He gave the smallest dip of his head. 'Let's call it a recovery operation.'

Darcy was intrigued. She'd heard of people trying to retrieve pieces of art that had been stolen during wartime. Was that what he did?

'How do you do that? And how do you know what to look for?'

He spun her around and she almost lost her footing because she was no longer paying attention to the instructions but more to the man holding her in his arms. 'Sorry,' he laughed.

She shook her head as a woman tapped her arm. 'It's time to move partners again.' She glanced pointedly at Arturo.

Darcy tried not to laugh and went to step back, but Arturo shook his head. 'Maybe it's best to leave us out of the swapping. We're both complete beginners and we don't want to spoil anyone else's dance experience tonight.'

He said it so smoothly but commandingly that the woman blinked, gave a half-annoyed look and moved away.

He leaned forward and she caught his woody aftershave again. 'Hope you're not offended. But I don't plan on being picked apart by all the experts here tonight. Plus, I don't want to stand on anyone else's toes.'

'Whereas mine are already flat?' she countered.

She could see the waver in his eyes—trying to tell if she was joking or not—but his face broke into a wide smile again. 'Exactly,' he agreed.

'So, you've interrogated me,' he said good-naturedly. 'What do you do?'

'Cybersecurity.'

'You're a hacker?' His eyes widened and it was Darcy's turn to laugh.

'Sometimes. It depends what the job is. I've worked with banks to improve their security systems. I've worked with private companies who've purposely asked me to hack into their systems in order to find any points of failure. Sometimes I'm just giving general security safety advice or training for staff.' She'd actually done a whole lot more than that but, thanks to contractual obligations, wasn't allowed to say.

'You must be a woman of many secrets.' He was teasing, but the comment hit a nerve, immediately causing her to tense. This attractive man was a perfect stranger. She really knew nothing about him. And she wasn't quite sure she was ready to admit the strange pull she felt towards him.

She was so out of practice with all this. In a flash of panic, her eyes darted to his hand, checking to see if he wore a wedding ring. Thankfully, his finger was bare. Relief. In years gone by, she would have always checked before continuing a conversation with a stranger, particularly one who seemed to be flirting with her.

As the music stopped, she dropped her hands from

his. 'I should check on Arthur,' she said quickly. 'See if he needs rescuing.'

Was that disappointment on his face? 'Of course,' he said graciously. 'Thank you,' he added.

'For what?' she asked as she stepped back.

'For making an evening I was dreading...' he paused and gave a hint of a smile '...not quite as bad as I thought.'

She could swear an army of butterflies just fluttered next to her skin. Darcy just smiled and headed across the dance floor towards Arthur. He gave her a knowing look as he glanced in Arturo's direction.

'Darcy, my dear,' he said with a twinkle in his eye, 'I think we need to talk.'

CHAPTER FOUR

ARTURO SPOKE IN rapid Italian to his counterpart. He'd been chasing this stolen artefact for years. It had belonged to a fellow Italian family over a hundred years ago and had been stolen in a midnight raid on their property. There had been no trace of the painting for years— meaning it had likely been stolen to order by another family. Now? He'd heard rumours of house clearances and basement sales, along with a few whispers amongst the antique dealers. He pulled up his screen and noted the next flight to Catania. With another few words, he completed the call and leaned back in his chair, looking out over the city.

Most people were surprised that he'd temporarily based himself in Edinburgh. Arturo had travelled the world with his job and stayed in many cities. But after an initial visit a few years ago he'd liked the charm and vibe of the ancient city. Some of the streets seemed to brim with history, and there were a surprising number of experts relevant to his field nearby. A flight to London was only an hour away and nowhere was ultimately out of his reach. Plus, after the death of his fiancée, followed a few years later by the death of his father, Italy had too many memories and reminders. Arturo had realised quickly that he needed a little space and some different scenery in order to move on with his life.

But had he moved on? Not really. Two big losses had made the usually steady ground shake beneath his feet. He wasn't even sure he was ready to. But at least in Edinburgh he was away from the microscopic glances of his family, their love, their opinions and their strong-armed influence. And the truth was, Edinburgh already held a little space in his heart.

His fingers moved quickly, booking his flights and accommodation. He could have asked his assistant to do all this for him, but he'd already sent her a piece of research work this morning and would rather she continue with that. He glanced at the return flight. He would be back in time for the next dance class.

His fingers froze on the keypad and he leaned back, staring out of his glass-walled office towards Edinburgh Castle. The thought had just slipped into his head, like a little seed secretly sown. Arturo's skin prickled. He couldn't deny that the woman he'd met the other night had piqued his curiosity. He was sure there was much more to Darcy Bennett than met the eye. He liked that.

It had been so long since a woman had sparked his interest. His American fiancée had held a role similar to his. They'd met first on a dig in Egypt, then again when they were both trying to retrieve the same piece. It had seemed like fate. The whirlwind engagement had surprised both their families. And even though Faye and himself could be like ships passing in the night, the spark hadn't died. At least not until she had.

She'd been in Japan at the time, at Shibuya, the world's busiest crossing. An investigation had shown images of Faye being distracted by her phone and not paying attention to a speeding car. Arturo had spent hours wondering if it had been he that had distracted her. She hadn't answered the phone, but pulled it from her pocket to see who was calling. If she would have answered or not, no one would ever find out, because things had happened in a flash.

He'd checked times around the world and was sure he'd been in a meeting at the time, but it had always stuck in the back of his head. Who had called Faye and distracted her at the very second she needed to be paying attention to the world around her?

That hadn't been part of the investigation because no one had cared. It was irrelevant. But thoughts about it still occasionally found a space in his dreams.

His family had encouraged him to date again, and he was sure at some point he would. He'd taken a few female friends to dinner, but he hadn't considered them dates because he'd had no romantic intentions.

The woman he'd met the other night—Darcy?—had thrown him. At first it was her fellow awkwardness. Then, when she'd spoken, he'd realised she was English instead of Scottish. He'd grown so adept at listening to the Scottish accent these days, another accent had thrown him for a second. He hadn't expected to look into a pair of blue eyes and feel a pool of warmth inside him. It had almost been like flicking a switch back on.

He was relieved that someone else with no experience had attended the class. When he'd realised just how pretty and intriguing she was it had sparked his interest. Arturo had spent a long time focused on work. It was all-encompassing, particularly when his team knew they were close to revealing some hidden secrets and finding a long-lost painting or artefact. Occasionally, his job was dangerous. People paid millions to own some of the pieces he'd come across, and not all had been originally sourced by legal means.

But his job was also a family legacy. His father had trained him, alongside his two degrees in Archaeology and Art History. Even as a child, he could remember tense moments when his father had clearly been threatened because of pieces he was pursuing. Arturo was almost sure threats had been made towards his family too.

It was part of the reason he struggled to connect. Attraction to women was never a problem, but connection… was an entirely different story. If he knew his job could potentially put someone at risk it would be fundamentally wrong to pursue anything other than a short-term fling. At least that was what he always told himself.

The thought had played in his mind around Faye's death. She'd had a similar job to him. But, to the best of his knowledge, Faye had never encountered any real threats. And there had been no connection between the driver that had hit her and any work she had been pursuing. Her death had been nothing but a tragic accident. But still the thought remained.

The fact that his personal family fortune meant that neither he nor his father had a real need to pursue the careers that they had didn't really feature in his thought processes. Both of them loved the job that they did. And Arturo couldn't see himself ever leaving this role.

But it made meeting a woman tricky. There had been the odd occasion in his life when he'd been targeted by a woman whose purpose was to entice details around his latest research. It had even come into his head at the first meeting with Faye. But Arturo had quickly learned to recognise those people. Darcy Bennett? An English girl, working in cybersecurity and dancing with an older man in the Edinburgh Variety Hall—on the exact same night that he attended—would be a feat that even a psychic couldn't have planned.

So he felt comfortable about thoughts of Darcy. Particularly when he remembered her little quirks. She'd been just as nervous as he was. She had a habit of biting her bottom lip or curling a piece of hair around her finger. She'd tugged at her bright red skirt a few times as if she'd had second thoughts about wearing it.

But there were also the things that she couldn't hide beneath her façade. The way she'd glanced over at her older friend on a regular basis, to make sure he was surviving. The fact she had no problem looking Arturo right in the eye and responding to his questions. She hadn't even pretended for a second that she was a good dancer, which gave him the sense that Darcy was straight down the line—honest, true and had a sense of humour. This was a woman he would be happy to see again.

Maybe this time he could ask her out for a drink? It might be a bit forward but, if he made it to the class in time next week, who knew what could happen?

His phone buzzed and all his thoughts went back to work. Darcy Bennett and her red skirt would have to wait.

CHAPTER FIVE

'BE COOL,' Darcy said out loud as she walked alongside Arthur, then wondered if she were saying it for him or for herself.

It was official. Arthur had a date after the dance class tonight. It was already prearranged at a nearby quiet bar with Connie, a woman he'd been texting since last week.

He was nervous. Arthur hadn't dated anyone since his wife had died, and said he didn't even remember what to do.

'Be yourself,' Darcy had reassured him. 'She's already met you and likes you. That's a great start.'

She glanced along the street, wondering if she might catch a glimpse of her tall, dark Italian. She'd had major regrets since last week, wishing she hadn't made an excuse to get away, and had instead continued the conversation with him.

Libby and Fizz had both been in touch about the dance class and she hadn't even mentioned him. She didn't want to be interrogated on someone she might never see again.

'Ready?' asked Arthur, tilting his elbow towards her. She slid her arm through his and they climbed the stairs.

The class was busy again, people were stripping off coats and outdoor shoes. Margaret was making a few introductions, then moved to the centre of the room.

'We're splitting into two groups this week. Anyone who wishes to try the quickstep and some swing, go on through to the Callaghan Hall next door. Anyone who wishes to continue with the Viennese waltz, we'll start with that in here, then move onto the foxtrot.' She clapped her hands above her head. 'Find a partner for the Viennese waltz if you are staying, and you'll be staying with that partner for the first half of the class to concentrate on frame and footwork.'

Arthur gave a nervous cough and Darcy gave him a nudge. 'Go on, go and find her.'

He'd barely taken a few steps when there was a tap on her shoulder. 'I'm looking for a partner for the Viennese waltz, are you taken?'

The accented words sent an unexpected tremor down her spine and by the time she spun around she knew she had a stupid grin on her face.

She put her hands on her hips and tried to be much cooler than she actually felt. 'You came back?'

'For a second round of torture. I'm actually going to come on Wednesday too. I need to up the ante here to get myself ready for this wedding.'

'You're deadly serious?' She was secretly impressed.

He raised his eyebrows. 'You haven't met my sister. If I step on *her* toes the way I stepped on yours...' He let his voice trail off but he was still smiling.

It was the easiest thing in the world to put her hands into his and join him on the dance floor. Margaret came around and sternly positioned them. 'Hips straight, head up, shoulders back, chest out.' The words were like commands, and she could see from Arturo's face he was trying hard not to laugh.

'We'd better concentrate,' she whispered.

His eyes stayed on Margaret as he leaned forward and whispered in her ear. 'I'll concentrate better if you agree to come for a drink with me afterwards.'

For a second, her mouth was instantly dry. The thing that had circled her dreams most nights this week was actually happening. She licked her lips. 'Well, it just so happens that Arthur has a date after class, so I am free.'

Arturo grinned. 'He does?' His head inclined to watch Arthur and his new female friend and she could tell his interest was genuine. 'That's great.'

She nodded and Arturo studied her for a few moments. 'I'm scared to ask, but do you want to go to the same place that they are? Just in case you're worried,' he added swiftly.

'What if I told you they were going to bingo?' she teased.

'I'd tell you that I missed that skill set in Italy. You'll need to show me the ropes.'

She laughed. 'You're safe, they're going to a pub. It might not be your scene either though.'

He shrugged easily. 'You've said yes. I don't care where we go.'

There was something about those words. While her stomach gave a little flip, she actually felt relaxed around him. Yes, they barely knew each other. But in this day and age he acknowledged the fact she might want to be around friends rather than alone with a relative stranger. It was considerate.

Margaret's voice cut through her thoughts. 'Music is starting now, get ready.'

They both straightened up, concentrating hard. One hour later, her back stiff from trying to keep both her posture straight and lean back the way she should, Darcy's legs were aching.

'I think I've got the natural turn and the reverse turn, but that's about it,' she admitted.'

He gave her an appreciative smile. 'That's two of the basic steps. We're doing good.'

'Why did your sister pick the Viennese waltz? Why not the normal waltz? You could probably have got away with just shuffling around the floor for that one.'

He nodded. 'I probably could. But she likes to be specific, and she's planned her wedding to perfection. She did offer to find someone to train me.'

'She did? From Italy? Wow.'

'Yip, she sent a list of instructors and was slightly annoyed when I told her I would find my own.'

Darcy somehow knew that 'slightly annoyed' was likely a toned-down term.

Arturo glanced across the room. 'Do you want to stay for the foxtrot?'

She laughed. 'You are joking, aren't you? Buy me a drink, please. Let me just tell Arthur that we're leaving.'

She moved around the edges of the dance floor and gave Arthur a kiss on the cheek. 'Good luck,' she whispered.

'You too,' he said in a low voice, while keeping his arms around his current dance partner.

Darcy collected her coat and walked out into the autumn evening with Arturo. Edinburgh could frequently see four seasons in one day, but the air was warm this evening, with the sun setting behind the castle in a brilliant array of oranges and purple. She stopped for a second and took a deep breath.

Arturo paused at her shoulder and looked in the same

direction she was. 'Stunning, isn't it? My office has a view of the castle and the sunrises and sunsets are the best thing about it.'

She gave a deep sigh of appreciation before turning to him. 'And in those words you've just told me that you spend entirely too much time in your office.'

He nodded in agreement. 'You're right, I do. But sometimes it's worth it.'

She gave him a curious look. Just how much was there to find out about Arturo Fabiano?

He glanced along the street. 'How about a drink somewhere special? I know a place that does lovely Italian wine.'

She raised her eyebrows. 'It had better be public.'

He laughed and nodded. 'Don't worry, it is.'

A few minutes later he took her into the best known and most expensive hotel in Edinburgh. She didn't even want to know what the prices were in the bar here.

But once they'd settled in comfortable leather chairs and there had been a few smiles towards her dance skirt, Arturo leaned forward. 'Do you have a preference between white and red?'

'If I was sophisticated, I'd say red. But the truth is I like white. Red always gives me a headache.'

He lifted his finger then shook his head, laughing at himself. 'I am saying nothing.' He ran his eye down the wine list and motioned to the waiter, who returned with a bottle of white wine.

He signalled he didn't need to test the wine, and watched as the waiter poured it into the glasses. She hadn't even taken a sip before the waiter returned with some bread, olives, oils and a bowl of nuts.

'Do you think we look hungry?' she whispered.

'Maybe,' he replied with a smile.

She sipped the wine and gave a sigh. 'Lovely.'

'I'm glad you approve.'

Darcy relaxed back in the chair, looking at the comfortable surroundings. There was a quiet ambience in the bar, with a number of the tables taken and low-voiced conversations taking place around them. 'This place is nice,' she said.

He pressed his lips together for a moment.

'What?'

He pulled a face. 'I should probably tell you that technically I've been staying here for the last few months.'

'Here?' She couldn't help but be astounded. People stayed here for one night, maybe two at a push. But months? What would be the price tag for that?

'Seemed like a central location.'

She took another sip of her wine. 'I guess you could call it that.' She narrowed her gaze towards him. 'I am not coming upstairs to your room.'

He held up a hand. 'And I didn't intend to ask—no, that might not have come out the way it should. I just thought I should tell you now, in case it came up later and you were annoyed I hadn't mentioned it.'

He looked genuinely worried and she decided to let him off easy.

'It's fine. Now I know why you knew there were good Italian wines here.'

He nodded through towards another room. 'There's sometimes a harpist playing in the gallery above in the room next door. It really is a nice place.'

She knew it was a really nice place. Most people who stayed in Edinburgh did—it just wasn't an everyday place, and that made her a little nervous. It wasn't as if money was a big thing for her. She made a better than average salary on her own, the private sector paid handsomely for people with her cybersecurity skills. Her cottage was her pride and joy, and she had some savings in the bank and was already paying into a pension. But she was beginning to suspect that Arturo was in an entirely different league when it came to money.

She raised her glass to him. 'So, tell me more about your sister's wedding. You said she was a planner.'

He smiled. 'Cara was born a planner, and I think in truth she's actually been planning her wedding since she was around six years old.'

'When is it?'

'In a few weeks. I don't have much time to perfect my dancing skills. That's why I said I would go to the extra class this week.' He gave her a thoughtful look. 'Are you a glutton for punishment—will you join me?'

Darcy gave a small gulp, a little taken aback by his straightforwardness. 'I'll need to think about it,' she stalled. 'Tell me more about your family.'

He paused for a moment, watching her carefully with his dark brown eyes before taking a sip of his wine and talking again. 'I only have one sister, and her fiancé is a man from another part of Italy who she met at university.'

'Do you like him?'

He gave a careful smile. 'It takes a special man to stand up to my sister.'

Darcy wrinkled her nose. 'What does that mean?'

'It means that I think he's up for the job. She's been very precise about her wedding details and he has on occasion told her no, and to be reasonable.'

She was amused at how wide his smile was. 'And you can't say no to her?'

He laughed and shook his head, 'Oh, I've spent a life-time saying no to my sister, with varying degrees of success.' He waggled his hand in the air. 'But things are different now.' His voice quietened. 'Her dream was for our father to walk her down the aisle. That can't happen now. So I feel as if I have to give her some—what do you call it—leeway?'

Darcy nodded. He took another sip of wine then leaned forward, eating up the space between them. 'So, tell me truthfully, Ms Cybersecurity, why are you really at a dance class? You like it as much as I do,' he joked. 'And it can't all be about Arthur.'

She took a breath, not sure how truthful to be. 'It is partly about Arthur.' And she did genuinely mean that. She just wished she'd thought about something like this a few years ago. 'He's really come out of his shell. If you'd seen him when I first met him five years ago, he was very different.'

'But he was still grieving then, wasn't he?'

The words settled over her like a comfortable hug. It was the combination of things. The way he said the words, the tone and the understanding. She knew he'd experienced the grief of losing his father a few years ago, and it was clear he comprehended what that did to a person.

'He was,' she said simply then leaned forward too. There were now only inches between their faces, but what she needed to say wasn't something she really talked about in public, or at all. She needed this space to feel private, as if it were just theirs. She said the words before the courage left her.

'The reason I'm at the class is because my sister left me a bucket list that she wanted me to complete. She died five years ago, and I was only given it last week. I'm doing it in her honour.'

She spoke so quickly that she was sure all the words ran together. Would Arturo even have picked them all up? His English was excellent, but Italian was his first language.

His eyes widened by the slightest margin, but she was close enough to see it. Was this too close?

He reached out and put his hand over hers. 'I am so sorry about your sister.'

There was silence for a few moments, and Arturo didn't try to fill it. His expression was sincere. He seemed to know that those few words would be enough.

Darcy sucked in a deep breath and just let it sit. Experience had taught her that if another human being had experienced grief then they seemed better at acknowledging it and understanding it in others. That seemed to be true this evening.

The warmth from his palm flooded up her arm. He couldn't possibly know how much this all overwhelmed her. Attraction. It had been a long time since she'd felt it. But attraction along with connection? She couldn't remember feeling like this in for ever.

Her past relationship with Damian was now a distant memory. He was married to someone else and had a family of his own. She strongly suspected he might have met his wife before Darcy and he had actually split. But suspicions and repercussions were not a path she'd ever wanted to go down. Once a relationship was over, it was over. She didn't dwell. She didn't dissect. At least that was what she told herself because, deep down, the hurt was still there.

But as she felt warmth radiate up her arm she was

asking herself a whole host of other things. While she'd dated and had a few casual relationships, she knew she'd built walls around herself.

It was her duty to protect herself from hurt. Being stood up at the altar, closely followed by the death of her beloved sister, meant she'd learned to shield herself from the outside world. Edinburgh, and her home, had become her protective sanctuary. Was she lonely sometimes? Of course she was. But being a bit lonely was nothing compared to having your heart ripped out.

She woke up to a beautiful view every morning. The flexibility of her job allowed her to live her life more or less as she pleased. All of a sudden, though, she was questioning if that was enough. If that was what she wanted. And the hot contact from Arturo's palm was doing strange things to her body.

He lifted one eyebrow. Did he know? Did he know the wave of panic that had just enveloped her? Or was this something else entirely?

That lifted eyebrow was enough distraction to centre herself again. He gave an amused smile. 'A bucket list? Hers, or yours?'

Okay, a normal question. She could handle that. Thank goodness he couldn't see all the places that her mind had just gone. Darcy leaned back, disconnecting their hands, and rested her elbow on the table, letting her head sit in her hand.

'Mine, I guess. But I had no say in it, and she wrote it.' She bit her lip and added, 'I should have said I have another sister—Felicity. Laura wrote a bucket list for us both.'

'Wow,' said Arturo, sitting back in his chair too and lifting his glass of wine again. He picked up the wine bottle from the bucket next to them and topped up their glasses. 'I'm settling in for the ride.'

She smiled. He was making this easy on her. And, for the first time in for ever, it felt nice to share.

'Okay, so are your bucket lists the same?'

Darcy pulled a face. 'So, I don't really know.'

'What do you mean?'

'We were together when we were given them, but we didn't open them together.' She sighed and admitted out loud what she'd been holding in her head. 'In a way, I'm glad we didn't. Because mine has little handwritten notes from our sister Laura, and that just made it way more special. I imagine Fizz's is the same.'

'You call your sister Fizz?'

'Yes, it's like a nickname. You have them in Italy, right?'

He gave a slow nod. 'Yes.'

'So, Felicity's is Fizz. She couldn't say Felicity as a child, so she called herself Fizz. It stuck. As for the bucket list, she likely has the same kind of notes that I have. And we were also told we could interpret the list of things any way we wanted.'

Arturo's brow furrowed. 'This is just getting curiouser and curiouser.'

She smiled at the common phrase.

'So she told you to go to a dance class?'

'Not exactly. She told me to…' Darcy paused for a second as she tried to remember the exact wording '…"Do something that scares you".'

Before Arturo had a chance to laugh, she waved her hand, 'Oh, I know, I know, it's not exactly as scary as a parachute jump, or diving with sharks, but—'

'No, wait,' Arturo said quickly, holding up his hand.

'I am right there with you. Dancing is scary. Particularly if you didn't spend your youth—' he smiled and she could see him trying to recall something '—the lady that cleans the offices calls it "jigging around the dance floor".' He gave a little shuffle of his shoulders as he said those words, and Darcy burst out laughing. Several heads turned and she put her hand up to her mouth.

'Sorry,' she whispered. 'But you tried a Scottish accent there and it was perfect.'

'Really? I'll tell Doris, she'll be impressed.'

'Was it her that told you about the dance classes?'

He nodded. 'She heard my sister on a video call to me. Told me she could find me a dance class instead of my sister.'

He tapped the side of his nose. 'And, let me tell you, I've done a parachute jump and I've dived in a shark cage. Those things have nothing on being in that dance hall, all eyes on you, and your feet, back, arms and body all doing entirely separate things.'

She lifted her free hand. 'See? You get it. You understand. I've never been a natural dancer. I never like all eyes on me.' She gave an awkward kind of shiver. 'And I don't really like getting that up close and personal with people I don't know.'

He blinked, his face deadpan. 'So if Margaret had suggested the rumba?'

She lifted her glass to him. 'I would have broken the four-minute mile getting out of that place.'

Arturo leaned forward and clinked his glass off hers. 'To us,' he agreed.

They smiled at each other, and that flip-flop sensation was in her stomach again. This guy was doing strange things to her. This didn't feel like the previous flirtations she'd had. This was just...different.

'So, why do you think your sister is telling—presumably both of you—to do something that scares you?'

Darcy's skin chilled a bit and she set her wine glass down and started pulling a few pieces off the bread. 'Our family changed when Laura was sick.' It suddenly occurred to her that Arturo hadn't asked what happened. 'Her death wasn't an accident. She had acute lymphoblastic leukaemia and had a variety of treatments over a number of years. Other things happened too.' She paused because she wasn't ready to go there yet. 'So there was a lot of strain on our family.' She gave a sad smile. 'Fizz and I are actually twins. Laura came along a few years later but we were all inseparable. My dad used to call me and my sisters the Terrible Trio. We actually all got on. We had our own friends and things, but there's nothing like having sisters.' She pressed her lips together for a second, deliberately not letting herself get lost in memories. 'Once one of us wasn't there any more, things just changed. Fizz is in London now, and I'm in Edinburgh. We don't see each other as much as we should.'

As she said the words out loud, she realised how true they were. She knew that right now her eyes were shining with unshed tears. 'I think Laura probably knew what would happen. She was kind of the linchpin—the steadying force. She knew we would probably retreat into ourselves. I guess her bucket list is to try and push us out there again.'

She sat back and took a breath, trying to sort things out in her head. It was as if she'd already known all that but saying it out loud made the difference.

Arturo was looking at her curiously. 'You have a twin?'

She nodded.

'Identical?'

Darcy shook her head. 'No. We do look like sisters, but we're not identical.'

Arturo gave her a few moments. 'A bucket list is an interesting idea. What else does she have on it for you?'

Darcy took a handful of nuts. 'Another three things. I haven't quite worked out what I'll do for them yet. One of them is to grab a friend and have a mad twenty-four hours in a European city somewhere.'

'That's a good one.' He reached over for some of the bread. 'What's your favourite city then? Barcelona? Vienna? Paris? Madrid?'

She shook her head. 'I've been to a few. But I'm toying with somewhere I've never been before.'

'You have a list?'

'In my head.' She tapped the side of her forehead. 'Pisa—do I want to stand and do the traditional tourist picture with my hand outstretched?'

She demonstrated and he shook his head. 'Oh, please, no.'

'Or Venice? I know that they're hideously expensive, but I might want to try a trip on a gondola and look at St Mark's Square.'

He gave a slow nod. 'Venice is a cool place, particularly at night.'

She raised an eyebrow. 'Not sure if I should ask questions about that or not.'

He gave her a smooth smile and she breathed in, trying to not let her body respond to just how unconsciously attractive Arturo Fabiano was. It wasn't just her. She'd seen the occasional glance from other females in the bar area. They probably wondered what Arturo was doing with her, sitting here in Edinburgh's poshest hotel with her silly dance skirt on.

'I considered Milan too, and Rome. I'd love to see the Colosseum.'

'Once seen, never forgotten,' he agreed. Then he looked up. 'All your cities are in Italy. Is that just a co-incidence?'

Her cheeks started to flush. 'Well, yes and no. It's a place I've never been. I did have plans to go there a few years ago and...' she looked out of the large window to the street outside '... I ended up here instead.'

'Edinburgh instead of Italy?'

She swallowed and spoke as lightly as she could. 'Don't ask. And I have looked at other places. But some of them I've been to—Paris and Euro Disney, Berlin, Crete and mainland Spain on traditional girl holidays or city breaks. My father took us to Switzerland and Denmark on family holidays years ago. But Italy—' she looked upwards '—it just slipped through my grasp.' She tilted her head and connected with those eyes again. 'Which part of Italy are you from?'

'Verona,' he said without hesitation. 'The city of love. *Romeo and Juliet* land.'

She put her hand on her heart. 'Oops, sorry I didn't mention it on my wish list.'

'You're forgiven,' he said. 'If the *Romeo and Juliet* play didn't exist, we probably could have kept Verona as Italy's hidden secret.' He held up both hands. 'Unfortunately...'

'Is that where your sister's wedding is?'

He nodded.

'In a hotel in the city?'

He took a few seconds to answer, stroking his wine

glass between his fingertips in a way that instantly dried her throat. 'Actually, she's getting married in our estate.'

'What?' The word came out before she could help it. But of course. A man staying at the most expensive hotel in Edinburgh, with a glass office that faced the castle and wore suits like he did? Of course they'd have an estate. Not your average house in a normal street. She was kind of feeling stupid right now for not even considering this before.

Arturo spoke carefully. 'We have an estate in the outskirts of Verona. My family have lived there for generations. The house is big enough to hold the wedding, and Cara has always wanted to get married in our home.'

He gave a soft laugh. 'I doubt I'll recognise the place by the time I get home. I can only imagine what she's been up to in my absence.'

'Are you worried?'

He gave the slightest shake of his head. 'Cara has impeccable taste. She won't have done anything long-lasting.' He pulled a face. 'At least I hope she won't.'

Darcy was still trying to get over the fact that Arturo had an estate. That, plus the good looks and the Indiana Jones-style job. She felt as if she could be in her own version of a film.

'How do you like the wine?' He leaned over and topped up her glass again.

'It's lovely,' she admitted, 'but no more for me. I'm a lightweight.'

'Will you join me at the next class?'

She lifted her glass. 'Ah, you've been bribing me.'

'Not at all. I just prefer learning with someone who is at the same stage as me. You know why I'm there and why it's important to me, so...'

Something rushed into her head. Darcy had never been impetuous, and even the second she had the thought, something told her she should check with either Libby or her sister before she proceeded any further. She took a slow breath, trying to calm her heart-rate that had instantly speeded up. Could she really ask him to join her on a mad twenty-four-hour tour? It was certainly playing on her mind right now.

She swallowed the last of her wine and looked Arturo Fabiano in the eye. When was the last time she'd taken a chance? When was the last time she'd done something spontaneous?

'I'll come on Wednesday with you, if you agree to have a mad twenty-four hours with me in an Italian city of my choosing.' She waved her hand. 'I'm paying, of course.'

He blinked. For a moment he just sat there, and part of her cringed, a tiny part started to die inside.

Her mouth automatically started talking again. 'Who better to show me around than a real-life Italian who can show me the best bits, and help me with the language?'

Silence, but only for a second.

Something flickered in his vision, then he blinked again and raised the rest of his wine towards her. 'It's a deal. But I'll warn you...'

His words dangled in the air. She was still getting over the 'deal' word and trying not to punch the air.

'You'll warn me what?' Her voice had a teasing tone that even she didn't recognise. This was what good Italian wine and a surge in confidence did for her.

'Once we've done your mad twenty-four hours, I might ask you for something in return.' His eyes were fixed on hers. He had a teasing look in them too. 'Only if you agree, of course.'

Her stomach twisted and she wasn't sure how she would explain this turn of events to anyone else.

'I do a favour for you, and you do a favour for me,' he said slowly, in a smooth tone that made her feel as if dragonflies had just fluttered against her skin.

This was convenience, certainly for her, and it looked like it would be for him too.

She lifted a few of the nuts into her palm. 'I guess we'll just need to see what the future holds then.' She smiled back, nodding in agreement, and told herself she must be out of her mind.

CHAPTER SIX

FOUR DAYS LATER, Arturo pulled up outside the cottage and gave a low whistle. When Darcy had told him that she lived 'somewhere out in the sticks' he hadn't expected a white stone cottage set against a splash of green hills. It looked more like a painting than a real home.

He also tried to take a steadying breath. His family home back in Verona was more than a hundred times bigger than this. He had to be careful not to say or do anything to overwhelm her. Particularly when he knew what he was going to ask her in return.

Darcy Bennett was intriguing. He'd done a little digging. Some people might say that was off. But Arturo was used to doing a little digging on any new person he came across. With his line of work, and his family wealth, it paid to know who you were making friends with. Darcy Bennett was exactly who she said she was. She had a good job, and was well regarded in her field. When she'd given him her address for the pick-up to the airport, council planning records showed that she'd done extensive renovations on her cottage over the last few years.

The bright red door flew open and she stood there with a smile. Her blonde hair was pulled up in a pony-tail, she was wearing black three-quarter-length trousers, flat shoes and a white shirt tied at the waist. 'Come in,' she shouted as she disappeared back inside.

He got out of his car, locked it—even though he hadn't seen another person—and walked to her doorway. A small bag was sitting just inside the door and he ducked his head as he stepped inside the cottage.

The whole place was much brighter and airier than he'd expected. To his left was a pale blue fitted kitchen with a large Aga stove that was popular in farmhouses. Through another door that was slightly ajar he could see a modern white bathroom. But the place that drew his attention was just ahead. As he stepped into what must be Darcy's sitting room, he saw a wall of glass that faced straight out onto the Scottish landscape. It was completely hidden from the road, out of sight from anyone else. The view was magnificent, and there was even a sheep wandering around outside, which seemed utterly uninterested in the new person through the glass.

It was six in the morning, and the sun was up with a little mist on the hills.

Arturo couldn't help but smile as he moved over and sat down on the cheerful multicoloured large sofa. Darcy was inside a cupboard, wrestling with some coats. She pulled out two. 'What do you think? Black or red?' She held them both up but he just laughed and held out his hands towards the glass wall.

'I think this place is amazing.'

'You do?' He could tell by the expression on her face that she was pleased. She obviously took pride in her home.

'Of course,' he said and nodded outside. 'You even have your own sheep.'

She laughed, 'Oh, that's Betty, and she isn't mine.

She's the farmer's next door. There's a small gap in his fence that he keeps meaning to fix and she likes to wander through.' She held up the coats again. 'Which one?'

He stood up and walked over, touching one and then the other. The black one was made of wool, the red one a lightweight raincoat. 'Are you absolutely sure you want to take a coat?'

She looked surprised. 'Of course.'

'Italy's a lot warmer than Scotland.' He smiled at her.

She shrugged. 'I know. But I can't go away for twenty-four hours without a coat.'

'In that case, definitely the red. The black one will be too warm for Italy right now.'

She beamed. 'Where's a handy Italian when I need one?' She hung the black coat back in her cupboard and put the red one over her arm. 'Want to know what city I chose?'

She hadn't told him where they were going, and he didn't want to break it to her that it wasn't hard to work out when they were flying from Edinburgh Airport, but he played along.

She held up the tickets. 'Rome! It had to be the Colosseum. I've even bought us tickets.' She waggled them at him. 'I hope you slept well last night—the rules are no sleep for the next twenty-four hours.'

'I think I can manage that.' He smiled, wondering what on earth he'd got himself into. Through his family and his work, he had connections in Rome that he could pull at short notice. He could have got them into anywhere she might have wanted to go. But Darcy didn't need to know that.

They took one last look at the view and headed to the airport. Arturo's normal domain was the first-class lounge, but Darcy had insisted that she was paying for things since it was her bucket list, so he contented himself with buying them some drinks from the bar.

The three-hour flight was over quickly, and because they had no luggage they exited the airport swiftly.

'Where to first?'

She pulled a face. 'I want to see the Trevi Fountain, the Colosseum and St Peter's Square and the Sistine Chapel at the Vatican. What will be the busiest?'

He glanced at his watch and lifted his hand to hail a taxi. 'We'll go to the Trevi Fountain, then stop and grab some lunch. The Colosseum and Vatican always have queues—even when you have fast-track tickets. It is too hot to queue right now. So, let's start the way we mean to continue.'

The taxi ride was chaotic. Darcy sat with her face pressed up against the window and Arturo pointed out some of the other parts of Rome they might not have time to visit.

The streets around the fountain were packed with tourists, just like Arturo knew they would be. As they exited the taxi, he slipped Darcy's hand into his. 'Stay close,' he whispered as he threaded through the crowds.

It was warm already and by the time they reached the junction where the fountain sat it was wall to wall people.

'Is it always like this?'

He nodded, keeping threading through the throng of people. 'It can be like this at six in the morning, and in the middle of the night.' Arturo scanned the surroundings and found a spot where they could stand that was a bit quieter.

He pulled her in next to him and let her stand for a few moments taking in the giant display. 'A large part of this was hidden for a few years while the renovations took place. People still came, but now they are gone, a lot of tourists are keen to come back.'

'It's beautiful,' Darcy breathed, her eyes fixed on the white baroque fountain with its central figure.

'It is,' he agreed, watching the water flow through the fountain. 'Do you want to know some facts about it?'

She looked up at him, her blue eyes shining. 'Go for it.'

'So, *trevi* means three. It dates back to Roman times when there was an ancient aqueduct called the Aqua Virgo that provided water to the Roman baths and fountains of central Rome. It was built at the end point of an aqueduct at the junction of three roads. This construction finished in 1762.'

'That long,' she sighed. 'And look how popular it still is.' She leaned against him and he wondered if she was already hot in the Italian sun. For him the weather was mild, but the UK was always colder than Italy, and Scotland even more so.

He held out a hand towards it. 'Even though it's white now, it's been black and red before.'

'No way!' Darcy looked genuinely surprised.

He gave an amused smile. 'Not for any period of time. It was turned off and draped in black when an Italian actor died who starred in the most famous film made here. The red, unfortunately, was vandals, but it was cleaned up quickly enough.'

'Vandals? Here?' She shook her head. 'It just seems so ridiculous.'

He nodded. 'The fountain uses a massive amount of water—and you wouldn't want to drink from it. But thankfully, the water is recycled, so there's minimum wastage.'

'But what about the coins?'

They were watching as lots of people stood in front of the fountain and tossed coins over their shoulders.

'Collected every night,' he answered promptly, 'and they all go to charity. It's a crime to steal coins from the fountain.'

'Has anyone tried?'

'Oh, yes, and been caught. The most famous by a hidden camera.'

He gave her a nudge. 'Want to be a tourist and throw a coin in?'

'Of course.' She smiled and they edged their way through the crowd. Thankfully, most people posed for a photo, threw their coin and moved on. As she readied herself in front of the fountain, she smiled up at him.

For a second, his heart stopped. He hadn't doubted his attraction to Darcy had been growing, even though part of him told him she was wrong for him. Arturo moved around the world. Darcy seemed very settled in Edinburgh. He had a large, opinionated Italian family. Darcy seemed quieter. He wasn't quite sure how she would fare against his headstrong sister or occasionally outspoken mother. He wasn't sure they would ever be a good fit, particularly with the type of job he did.

And all these thoughts made him a little uneasy. Where had they come from? He still didn't know that much about Darcy—nor she about him. She'd told him her bucket list, and he'd told her about his father. But he knew that wasn't all he should tell her. Not if he liked her, and not if he thought this could go somewhere.

His phone pinged and he looked at the text. It was an Italian antique dealer who always had his ear to the ground. He wanted Arturo to get in touch. He was based in Rome, his shop near the Colosseum. Arturo contemplated for a few moments. He'd promised these twenty-four hours to Darcy. Would it be fair to go along?

He switched to his camera and held up his phone. 'Know that the legend says if you throw a coin in the fountain, it guarantees a return trip to Rome.'

'I think I can live with that.' She grinned, holding up her coin before tossing it over her shoulder and closing her eyes for a few seconds, her lips moving silently.

'What was that?' he asked.

'A secret,' she replied with a smile.

He grabbed her hand again and led her down one of the long nearby streets. Tables from a variety of restaurants lined the length of the street, and Arturo picked one that he knew did particularly good pizza.

'Can I order for you?' he asked.

She nodded as she sagged into the chair opposite and let her hair down for a few moments. At least here they were in the shade and the waiter brought them water, before taking Arturo's order.

Forty-five minutes later, Darcy was clearly revived after pizza, wine and some water. Her hair was back in a ponytail and she launched into her plan of attack for the Colosseum. The fast-track tickets meant they wouldn't need to queue in the sun and could start on one of the audio tours as soon as they got in there. It would still be warm. Unless Rome was surprised by showers, she wouldn't be wearing her jacket at all today. He waved his hand and settled the bill before she could argue, then took her to a nearby street to find a taxi again.

He heard it. The moment that she caught sight of the Colosseum and sucked in her breath at the marvel of it.

People could look at pictures online, but no one really

understood the scale, size and beauty of the structure until they could actually see it.

Something about her reaction struck him deep inside. He was proud of his nation and its history. There was a real sense of delight that she thought the Colosseum just as fascinating as he did. What he would give to wave a magic wand and go back in time to see it in a past life. Once an archaeologist, always an archaeologist.

She tapped his arm. 'What are you smiling about?'

'Just wishing I had powers and we could go back and see this in gladiator times.'

'We can watch the movie,' she said with a face so straight he wasn't entirely sure she was joking. But then she threw back her head and laughed. 'I should have taken a photo. Your face was an absolute picture then.'

She started to climb out of the taxi. 'Please tell me you're not going to give me a list of all the historical in-accuracies in the film, and all the archaeological facts they got wrong.'

'Only if you really annoy me,' he quipped good-hu-mouredly as he paid the driver and climbed out of the taxi too.

They joined the fast queue, waiting around fifteen minutes for entry, the supply of their audio tour and a book with the history of the Colosseum. Arrows showed where they should start, but Darcy was distracted.

She left the headphones dangling around her neck in her haste to climb some floors and get the full feel of the structure.

It was busy but, because of its size, there was plenty of space to find a spot of their own. Arturo couldn't help but watch those around him. He pointed over at a tour group of schoolchildren.

'I was brought here with my school friends when I was seven. All of us just wanted to pretend to be gladiators and be down in the central arena.'

'Were you allowed?' asked Darcy as she stared down, then she frowned at him. 'But there's no central floor, it's all the dungeons underneath.'

'I know that...' He sighed. 'But we had overactive imaginations and wanted to pretend that the central floor was still there.'

Darcy just stood admiring the structure around her. 'How on earth did they build this more than two thousand years ago? The perfect arches. The symmetry? The details.' She kept glancing around as the tourists milled about, stopping to take pictures and admire different viewpoints.

'Want to go down to where the gladiators were held?'

She gave him a strange look, then shuddered. 'No. I can feel it.' She held out her hands. 'There's an atmosphere here. A...something. As soon as you walk through, it's as if a thousand souls are speaking to you.' She touched the stone. 'Every part of this has been here all this time. Even the colour. The grey, the pink, the flecks of white. What kind of stone did you say this was?'

'Travertine limestone, along with tuff—volcanic rock—and brick-faced concrete.'

'Even that feels of something,' she breathed as she continued to look around in wonder. 'Can you imagine the noise if sixty-five thousand people were in here? I really wish you had that magic wand.'

He nodded and they stood for a few more moments in silence. There really was no need to fill in the space. The Colosseum told its own story, and he could see how much Darcy appreciated. There were other people in here, videoing themselves and taking a photo of every step. But apart from a snap outside, Darcy hadn't got her phone out yet. She was just 'feeling' the place, and he liked that about her.

It was something that he'd always done at archaeological sites. Some people just couldn't wait to start digging or exploring in their enthusiasm to find something mind-blowing. But Arturo, and Faye, had liked to get the feel of a place. To sense the history, and the people who had gone before.

He had a flash of guilt for thinking of Faye when he was with Darcy. The truth was, Faye had faded from his thoughts with time. She would always be there. Particularly if he was doing something work-related that might remind him of past digs or conversations. But she'd moved from being a central figure to a pleasant memory. Was this why he'd started to feel the spark with Darcy? Was he ready to move on and think about someone else?

Darcy turned around, pulling his attention back to the moment, leaning back and looking upwards. 'Imagine being in the cheap seats,' she said with a smile.

Arturo looked up too. 'What? You don't imagine you would have been in the special boxes with the Emperor and Vestal Virgins?' He liked that she was so enthralled by the place she was imagining it back in the day.

She laughed out loud. 'And where would you have been? Would you have been a senator?'

'I hope so,' he said, then screwed up his face. 'But maybe not. If I'd been a former gladiator, I would have been banned.'

'So you would,' she agreed as she flicked through the pages of her book. 'You, and the gravediggers.'

They both laughed out loud, then she sighed at the

raincoat over her arm. 'Give me that,' he said, smiling. It was hot, and her skin was turning a little pink. 'I think you need some more sunscreen.'

'Really?' She rummaged in her bag. 'I'm wearing factor fifty. I just burn at the drop of a hat.' She rubbed some more sunscreen into her face, neck and arms, then handed it to him. 'You too,' she ordered, not giving him a chance to argue.

When he handed it back, she finally pulled out her camera. But before she even took a photograph she turned to him, her eyes squinting in the sun. 'Thank you.'

'For what?'

'For agreeing to come. For being able to speak Italian and keep control of the taxis.' She took a deep breath. 'For saying you would do this with me. I know I kind of pushed you into it. I know this likely wasn't your first choice—a mad twenty-four hours in Rome.'

He gave a little bow of his head. He knew her words were sincere. 'It's my pleasure.' And he meant it. Because it had been a long time since he hadn't focused entirely on work or family matters. Arturo couldn't remember the last time he'd taken a holiday. And even though this was officially only twenty-four hours, he was grateful for even that. He raised his eyebrows just a touch. 'You don't know yet how you're going to repay me.'

'Nothing dubious, I hope,' she replied quickly.

'Not at all,' he responded. 'Just know that I will likely need at least twenty-four hours of your time too.'

She frowned then smiled. 'Oh, go on then. Don't be all mysterious about it. Spill.'

He threw back his head and laughed. 'I will, on the way home.'

She shot him a mock angry face as she started to snap some pictures.

He hadn't realised how much he'd needed this until he was actually here. He took her phone and took some photos for her. 'Let's go for a coffee, and do you mind if we get out of the sun for a bit?'

'Not at all.' She finished smiling for the photos, then took her camera back and turned it to face them both. 'Smile,' she ordered, snapping them with the inside of the Colosseum behind them.

Without pausing, Arturo took his phone out too, taking an identical photo. He did it without thinking, knowing that he wanted to capture them both too. It suddenly seemed important to him.

'Can I pick the place for dinner tonight too?'

'Okay,' she said without a moment's hesitation.

They left the Colosseum, taking a few more pictures, then moving on to a café and sitting for a while drinking coffee, water, and eating cake.

'What time is the visit for the Sistine Chapel?'

She checked her phone. 'Five-thirty.'

'We have plenty of time. Do you mind if I visit a nearby antique store?'

Darcy looked momentarily surprised. 'Not at all. I'd love to look in an antique store.'

They finished at the coffee shop and Arturo took her hand again and led her down the streets until they reached a narrow alley with uneven stones. There was a variety of shops on the street, and Darcy looked in a few windows as they made their way down towards the green-canopied antique store.

Part of him wished he hadn't even mentioned this. It could be that Matteo only wanted a two-minute chat, but something in the pit of his stomach told him that it was so much more.

He pushed open the door and the bell sounded. Both of them blinked. The shop was much darker than the natural light outside and it took their sight a few seconds to adjust. A deep breath would let anyone know they'd just come into an antique shop. There was an odour of mustiness about the place but it wasn't unpleasant.

Darcy immediately made her way over to a glass cabinet to look at some jewellery.

A slightly rotund figure with spectacles perched on his nose emerged from the back of the shop. 'Arturo!' He couldn't hide the shock in his husky voice, and even Darcy started.

Arturo started speaking in rapid Italian in a low voice. 'You said you needed to talk.'

'Yes, but I didn't mean in person. I didn't think you were in Italy, let alone Rome.'

'Well, by coincidence I am. What is it you need to talk about?'

Matteo glanced over at Darcy. 'Who is she?'

'A friend. And don't worry, she can't speak Italian.'

'You're sure?' Matteo's glance was suspicious.

'Of course I'm sure,' snapped Arturo. He didn't even want Matteo to look in Darcy's direction.

'Come with me.' There was a flick of his head and a few moments later Matteo was showing him pictures he'd received of an artefact that Arturo, and his father before him, had been seeking for many years. It had been stolen from an old Italian count in New York eighty years before.

The beautiful painted sculpture was only the size of his hand, but the coloured paint on it looked as if it had only been done yesterday, even though it was apparently four hundred years old. Much of the artist's other work had been lost throughout the ages.

'Is it genuine?'

Matteo stared at him through his horn-rimmed spectacles. 'That's for you to say, not me.'

Arturo stayed silent, focusing on the pictures. 'Arrange a meeting,' he said, before glancing behind him to the shop. 'Let me know when. I have other business today.'

Matteo followed Arturo back out to the main shop. Darcy smiled when she saw them and nodded to Matteo. 'Would I be able to see this, please?'

Arturo was surprised, he hadn't expected her to be interested in anything in Matteo's shop. Matteo immediately moved into his charming proprietor routine, which Arturo had witnessed on many occasions. He pulled his key chain from his pocket, unlocked the glass cabinet and pulled out the item she was referring to with obvious pleasure.

He switched to English easily. 'Oh, yes. An ancient late Roman gold garnet ring. The flat band is made from a thick hammered sheet of high carat gold and the garnet cabochon is set in the centre in a closed back setting.'

He held out the yellow gold ring with its surprisingly bright red stone. It had a slightly orange tinge to it and the stone was set in the middle of the ring. 'The gold is twenty-two carat,' he added as Darcy slipped the stone on her finger.

The gold wasn't finished in the way that any jewellery made in the last few hundred years was. The rough working was clear. And it was small, though Darcy could slip it on her right-hand ring finger.

She held up her finger, obviously caught by the history. 'This is genuine?' she asked. 'And verified?'

Arturo tried his best not to smile. Matteo could occasionally be a charlatan in other respects, but with his antiques he was always above board.

'Of course,' Matteo blustered, a little offended.

'Can I see the paperwork?' she asked.

'It's in Italian,' he said dismissively as he walked over to a large cabinet.

'Luckily enough,' said Darcy astutely, 'I brought my own interpreter with me.'

Matteo shot Arturo a glance, fumbling through some files and producing the paperwork to verify the gold, setting and provenance of the ring. He gave Darcy a nod.

'I love it,' she announced. 'I'll take it.'

Arturo wasn't sure whether to be surprised or not. The price tag was a few thousand pounds. It wasn't that he thought Darcy couldn't afford it. He was more taken aback by the impulsiveness of her purchase. She handed over her credit card to Matteo, which Arturo quickly substituted for his own. She didn't notice, and shook her head when Matteo offered to package up the ring for her. She only took the receipt and a small box, which she put in her handbag.

Arturo exchanged a few more words with Matteo about the potential meeting before they walked back out into the now blistering sunshine. Darcy was still admiring her ring. 'I feel as if I have a part of the day now,' she said simply, then put her other hand on her heart. 'Something to always remember my sister by, and keep the memories of my visit to Rome alive.'

Arturo was instantly a little wounded by the words.

Wouldn't their ongoing friendship—or whatever it was— keep the memories alive?

But he could see by her face this wasn't about him. This was about her sister, and honouring her memory. He was wise enough not to say anything until Darcy turned to face him with a bright smile, holding her hand out towards him. 'Sistine Chapel?'

Then he slid his hand into hers and headed to hail a cab.

He wasn't quite sure what he would tell anyone about this day. His sister, although caught up in the last few whirlwind weeks before her wedding, would ask him a million questions in the way only a sister could.

In a strange way his heart ached a little that he couldn't have this conversation with his father. He'd been the wisest man that Arturo knew. Although he'd never interfered in his son's relationships, he'd been astute and full of good advice when it came to women. He wondered what his father would have thought of this Englishwoman.

Arturo knew that his mother had long expected him to marry an Italian woman, preferably from one of their peer group. She had been decidedly unhappy about his engagement to Faye. His father hadn't had the same expectations and had always told Arturo to follow his heart. He'd liked Faye and always been gracious to her. But— and it still made Arturo smile—he'd never given the follow your heart advice in front of his mother.

Darcy spun around as the taxi slowed beside them, almost tripping as both hands landed on his chest. 'Oops.' She smiled, the amber scent of her perfume assaulting his senses. She looked up, her pale blue eyes shining, energy emitting from every pore. Her happiness was infectious.

'This is the best day,' she said simply, staying still for a few seconds right under his nose.

The palms of her hands seemed electric through the fabric of his shirt. He wanted to stay there. He knew they were in a rush to reach the Sistine Chapel in time. But for the first time in as long as he could ever remember, Arturo Fabiano wanted to freeze-frame his life—capture this moment in time and keep it.

It had been so long since he'd felt like that. And he couldn't actually remember a time like that for him and Faye.

But Darcy? She was an entirely new person and all of a sudden he wanted to explore more, to push a little and see what might happen.

He knew that he would eventually let her know he'd been engaged before. But he still had a feeling Darcy had walls in place. It wasn't quite so apparent today. Today in Rome seemed to be a 'throw caution to the wind' kind of day. But back in Edinburgh she occasionally opened her mouth to say something, then clearly rethought and stopped.

He couldn't imagine what it might be, but one thing was for sure—he wanted to find out.

CHAPTER SEVEN

DARCY WAS FEELING as though she'd been swept off her feet. She wasn't sure how else to put it. It didn't matter that she'd actually swept herself off her feet by planning this whole twenty-four hours. She was consciously aware that while Rome was beautiful and fascinating, the same words could also be used to describe her companion.

Was now the time to mention meeting a handsome Italian to Libby and Fizz? She bit her bottom lip and quickly sent them the selfie of them both that Arturo had taken with her phone. As the taxi darted through the Rome streets, she typed two words: Loving Rome.

She tried not to look at herself too hard in the photo. One glance and she could see the glow coming from her, and exactly how happy she looked. She was sure her sister and friend would notice too. No doubt they would ask questions.

Her fingers twisted her new ring. There was something wondrous about owning a piece that had history and had belonged to generations of women before her. The price hadn't fazed her, but she had found Arturo's colleague a little…shifty? Was that the right word? It seemed irrelevant now as they sped through the city towards the almost final destination of the day.

As they pulled up outside the Vatican entrance to the

Sistine Chapel, the queue was still present. They climbed out of the taxi and Arturo guided her towards the entrance, where they showed their tickets.

'Do you know the way?' she asked Arturo, and he nodded and led them down a central corridor.

The walk to the chapel was long. History was all around them. If she'd been in Rome longer, she would have loved to spend a day on a whole Vatican tour, seeing the gardens, admiring all the tapestries and portraits and beautiful sculptures. As it was, she saw them all at breakneck speed since they knew the time of the last admission to the Sistine Chapel and she didn't want to miss it while admiring other parts of the museum. The inside of St Peter's Basilica would need to remain on her wish list.

As she walked along, Arturo by her side, interested in everything they were seeing and commenting on it all, it suddenly struck her that she might have been in a very different position.

At this point in her life, she could have been married to Damian for five years. And what struck her the most about that was just how much he would have hated this mad twenty-four-hour rush around Rome. He wouldn't have found enjoyment in this—in fact, he probably wouldn't have agreed to come. Museums, monuments and national buildings had never featured in Damian's plans. He just wasn't that kind of guy. She'd always known that while being stood up at the altar had been ultimately cruel, it had been the best thing for both of them.

The handsome man beside her was intelligent, gracious and the perfect companion. And the more hours she spent in his company, the more she realised it.

It was odd. Because she'd initially felt quite reserved around Arturo. But the more she got to know him, the more confident she became in being herself around him. He still didn't know everything about her—or she him— but gradually she could feel her walls and barriers beginning to come down.

It had been a moment of pure madness to invite him to join her. Some might infer she'd done it for convenience, and in a way she had. But that didn't stop the little hiccups she had inside her body when he smiled at her, or their skin came into contact. There was nothing convenient about that.

There were still moments to pause and admire some of the artefacts. By the time they reached the entrance to the Sistine Chapel she was dizzy with the beauty around her.

There was a sign telling visitors not to take pictures and not to talk in the chapel. Even though they were part of the last group to enter, the chapel was still busy. It seemed as if everyone in the world wanted to see the same place that she did.

Arturo spoke in low Italian to one of the security guards at the entrance, who murmured a few words to him. As soon as they stepped inside Darcy was struck first by the heat, and then by how thin the air seemed.

But all that disappeared as she lifted her head to stare at the ceiling and the frescoes on the walls. She could hear whispers all around her, but was reluctant to join in. She wanted to be respectful of her environment, and take everything in.

Her first surprise was how bright the colours were on the ceiling and, as she moved closer to the wall frescos, just how much detail was actually included. The clothing, the hairs, the skin wrinkles were all presented in a way that made her want to reach out and touch it. Of course she didn't. The security presence in the chapel was heavy, but she could understand people being overwhelmed by the sight in here.

The second thing that surprised her was how small the chapel was. In her head, she'd pictured it as much bigger, but now she was here she realised she could cross from the entrance to the exit in around forty steps. Not that she wanted to. But she could sense people around her being hurried along.

Arturo put his hand at her back and gently steered her to one side, out of the flow of traffic. It gave her a few moments to take some time and look properly. From her childhood in Sunday school in her home town of Bath, she recognised several of the biblical scenes, such as the creation of the sun and moon, Adam and Eve, the garden of Eden and the Last Judgement on the wall behind the altar, its brilliant blue tones standing out brightly to her.

Eventually, a guard signalled it was time to leave and they exited at the side of St Peter's Basilica, by the entrance to the stairs to the dome.

Although the air in Rome was still warm, the gentle breeze was a welcome relief from the stifling crush in the chapel.

'Too many people,' she sighed. 'I don't know why I expected anything else from Rome's most favourite tourist attraction.' She leaned back against the nearby wall, letting the cool stone penetrate through her white shirt. Her hair felt sticky and she really wanted to sit down again.

She couldn't help but stare up at the steps of the Basilica and wonder if she should try to cram that in too. Her stomach gave a loud rumble and she laughed and put her hand over her abdomen.

'How about a choice?' said Arturo good-naturedly.

'What do you mean?' She took a deep breath, trying to clear out her lungs.

He waved his hand towards the street down from St Peter's Square. 'We could do dinner at one of the restaurants that face the Basilica and admire the view here or...' He paused for a moment. 'Or I know another restaurant that looks across to the Colosseum. What would you prefer?'

The breeze was dancing across her skin and finally cooling her down now. 'How about a drink at one of the street places that look up to the Basilica, and then on to the restaurant near the Colosseum?' She grinned. 'And just so we're clear, I'm looking for a cocktail right now.'

He laughed and they walked amiably across St Peter's Square, stopping to take some photographs, and taking a few for some other tourists.

They stopped at a bar, drank some Rossinis then some Negronis and took some photos of the sun setting behind the gleaming white Basilica, before catching a taxi to the restaurant that Arturo had reserved for them.

Their table was on a rooftop terrace and, as they sat, lines of orange and violet were streaming behind the Colosseum. Their waiter took some photographs as Arturo ordered for them.

Darcy took the opportunity to drink some water as they waited for their food. 'I can't believe I've just had the chance to see the sun setting behind two of the most beautiful buildings in the world.' She held up her hands. 'It feels like magic.'

'Magic? Really?' Arturo was drinking a bottle of beer. He looked completely unfazed by their day.

Darcy held up her hand to admire her ring. 'When I tell people at work next week that this is what I spent twenty-four hours doing, I doubt if anyone will believe me.'

'You have the ring, and the photos to prove it. Why wouldn't they?'

She sighed and looked out across the Rome skyline. 'Because it's just not a very Darcy thing to do,' she admitted.

'But you're enjoying yourself?' His phone pinged, but he ignored it.

'Of course I'm enjoying myself,' she said. 'I just couldn't have imagined doing anything like this.' She gave a huge appreciative sigh as she looked at the elegant structure of the sunset-lit Colosseum again. 'And I definitely picked the right city and...' She hesitated, wondering if she should say it out loud. She raised her glass of water. 'And I definitely picked the right Italian to come along for the ride.'

His eyebrows raised. He was good at that—it was his signature move. 'Just the right Italian, not the right guy?'

'Oh...' She laughed. 'You're going to be like that then?'

'Like what?' he said with a gleam in his eye.

The waiter came over and set down their plates of salted cod, alongside courgette flowers with mozzarella. The portions looked small on the plate, but as soon as she started eating, Darcy realised how filling the dish was. The waiter also brought a bottle of chilled white wine and they ate in a leisurely fashion, taking their time, until the sun had completely set and a dark sky filled with a smattering of stars was above them.

'Did you order pasta?' she whispered across the table.

He nodded and she leaned back with her hand on her stomach. 'I'm not sure if I can.'

'How about I ask for a half portion?' He smiled. 'You really want to taste this pasta.'

'Can't be in Italy and not taste the pasta,' she said with a smile, taking a second to savour the moment.

She was unbelievably lucky. She knew she was. 'This day has been perfect.' She sighed. 'I think I'll still remember it when I'm old and grey.'

'You, grey? Never.'

She touched her hair. 'That's the thing about blonde. It hides the grey better.'

'You can't know that?' he joked.

She laughed as she took a small sip of wine. 'Not yet, but my mother told me.'

He raised his glass towards her. 'And our mothers know everything.'

She leaned forward. 'Tell me a bit about your family. They must be very proud of you.'

'Sometimes,' he said with a hint of humour. 'My mother both likes and dislikes that I do the same job as my father. She supported my studies, and the fact I travel so much for work, but the truth is, she would like me at home. There's much work to be done on the estate, and while I love the place...' he paused and took a deep breath '... I'm not ready to do that yet.'

'Could you work from home? Isn't that what everyone does now?'

He paused for a moment, clearly trying to find the right words. That made her instantly curious. 'My work is sometimes...intense. There are too many distractions at home. And that doesn't include my mother and my sister. Edinburgh gave me the change of scene that I needed.'

'I can relate to that,' she said with a smile, without explaining any further. 'What does your sister do?'

He smiled back. It was clear he had great affection for his younger sister. Darcy liked that. Even though her relationship with her sister was a little fractured now, family was important to her.

'Cara has done a number of things. She studied design and then started with one of the Italian fashion houses. She was doing well, but got into a certain rivalry with a colleague.'

'That sounds like a film or some kind of juicy novel.'

He gave a soft laugh and nodded. 'It could have been. Then things happened with my father, and she decided to leave. Right now, she helps my mother run the estate. She's excellent at it. Probably because she has a gift for systems, processes and, usually, people.'

'Is this a simple way of saying *Don't cross my sister*?'

There was a flicker of panic in his face, and for an instant she felt her cheeks flame. Of course she would never meet Arturo's sister. She hadn't meant to imply that.

Thankfully, the waiter appeared to set down their main courses. She thought he would leave it, and let the conversation naturally drift in another direction, but he didn't. He looked her straight in the eye.

'You would never need to worry about Cara. She would like you just as much as I do. My sister knows what's important to me.'

For a second she wondered if she'd heard right. One moment her heart had been plummeting, thinking she'd made a silly faux pas, but now...? Now, she was getting an entirely different message.

Her throat was instantly dry, even though her mouth should be watering with the aroma of pasta and meat sauce beneath it. She was kind of flabbergasted. Although they'd danced together, been up close and personal, even held hands today on a number of occasions, their friendship hadn't progressed any further. They still barely knew each other. But that didn't mean that the sparks weren't obvious. Of course he was attractive.

But Darcy wasn't sure she was ready to trust anyone again. Arturo had a distinct hint of mystery about him. She was sure there was much more to him than met the eye. Plus, there was the fact they moved in different circles. Arturo had never flung it in her face, but his casual comments about his office, where he was staying in Edinburgh, and the family estate in Verona made her know that money wasn't an issue for him.

Whilst she was financially independent and happy to be, she didn't have millions in the bank, and didn't aspire to either. She had an awful feeling that his sister might see someone like her as a potential money-grabber, and Darcy was too proud to let anyone treat her like that.

She gave a small smile. 'If we are talking about sisters, maybe I should warn you about mine.'

'Warn me? That doesn't sound good.'

Darcy held up her hand. 'Fizz is fabulous. But she can be intense.' She pulled out her phone and turned it round so he could see a range of texts. 'I sent her a picture earlier of us, saying that I loved Rome, and let's just say I've been inundated.'

'You never mentioned that we'd met?'

Darcy swallowed. Was he hurt? Finally, she came out with, 'I wasn't sure what to tell her.'

If he was offended at all, he didn't let it show. His voice was smooth. 'You could have told her you'd met a handsome Italian man at dance class, who waltzed you around the place as if you were floating on air.' He had a wide smile on his face.

'You're already taking this too far,' she said as she bent to sample some of the pasta.

'You could have said that we agreed to do a mad twenty-four hours together, and I was going to be your—what do you call it?—right-hand man?'

She thought he would stop but he continued. 'You could have told her we'd been for drinks, or that I'd seen your house.'

Darcy held up her hand. 'And if I'd told her all of these things there is a chance she would have demanded to meet you.'

'And that would be bad, how?'

Darcy laughed. 'She'd want to know name, age, place of birth, friends, family, job, intentions, past history, and even music and food tastes. Then,' she added with a wave of her fork, 'she would have asked for references.'

'Sounds a bit like Cara, to be honest,' he said easily.

'Then maybe they could be a good match. They could spark off each other, whilst we just got on with it.'

'And leave us alone?' he asked with a small rise of his eyebrows.

She licked her lips, taking a sip of her wine and saying playfully, 'If we wanted to be.'

The night was closing in around them. Darcy had thought she would be tired by this point—exhausted even. But she wasn't. Not while she was in Arturo's company. Something inside was keeping her going. A buzz. Biology told her it was pure adrenaline. But for Darcy it was about being around someone she felt a connection with.

He leaned forward. 'How do you feel about going to a club in Rome?'

Her eyes narrowed for a second. 'What kind of club?'

'A nightclub.' He smiled. 'There will be dancing, just not the ballroom kind.'

'Dubious dancing?' she asked cautiously.

Arturo laughed out loud. 'I think my sister would always call my dancing dubious.' But he clearly knew what she meant. 'Don't worry.' He reached over the table and touched her hand. 'All will be above board. You might even like it.'

There it was, that gleam in his eye again. The one that meant she found it really difficult to say no. She heard his phone ping but, as before, Arturo just ignored it. It seemed he knew who was messaging, and was in no hurry to reply.

They finished their wine, Arturo paid the bill and then he took her by the hand, leading her down some narrow streets. The walk was longer than expected, but the night was balmy and it was pleasant to see the streets of Rome while it wasn't so hot, and so busy.

There was a line outside the nightclub, but Arturo walked to the front and exchanged a few words with one of the stewards, who stood aside and gestured them both inside.

Even before they descended the stairs, Darcy could feel the music reverberate around them. She put her hand on the wall as it vibrated next to her. She grinned. 'This place is bouncing,' she said.

He nodded, smiling back. 'Best nightclub in Rome, best music, best DJs.'

The next few hours passed in a dark blur. The music was fantastic. Darcy had visited nightclubs when she'd been younger with her sisters and friends. But when Laura had become ill, all that had stopped. They'd all been worried because Laura was immunosuppressed. They didn't want to take a chance of bringing anything more serious than a cold home.

Because Darcy had been focused on work for the last few years, nightclubs hadn't been her thing. She didn't sit at home every night. She'd gone to the Edinburgh Festival Fringe a few times, and to the theatre to see various touring shows.

But here? Now? It was all about having fun with her handsome companion. Whilst neither of them was a self-confessed dance lover, in this environment they both came alive.

The beat of the music let them bounce when they had to bounce, groove a little when the tempo changed, and Arturo had hidden smooth moves when the music slowed to something more intimate.

As Darcy wrapped her hands around his neck, he put his hands at her waist, pulling her closer whilst whispering in her ear. 'So, what do you think of Rome?'

She tipped her head up towards his. 'Everything has been beyond my expectations so far.'

They'd been together all day. Not only had a nightclub been the last place she'd expected to be, she was still wearing her black capri pants, white tied shirt and flat shoes. It was hardly nightclub attire. But being with Arturo made her forget about the little things. Years ago, she would have spent hours picking an outfit for a nightclub. She would have spent even longer fixing her hair and make-up. She'd walked in here without even giving it a thought. Having Arturo's hand in hers, his skin touching hers was hypnotic, and made her not worry about things she would have considered before.

'We have one more thing to do before it's time to catch our flight home,' he said, his lips brushing against her ear. 'Are you ready for the next step?'

Her heart fluttered, her mind immediately going someplace else. It could just be his choice of words, but what did the next step mean to him? Because she could think of a million things it might mean to her.

They climbed the stairs, back out into the cooler night air. It was the early hours of the morning, but the streets weren't empty. It seemed that Rome was the city that never slept.

Hand in hand, they walked casually down a few streets to an open café. 'Coffee?' he suggested.

She gave a nod and he ordered them coffees and panettone, and they walked along the street nibbling their cake and sipping their coffees. It had been a good choice as the coffee warmed her again, and the panettone filled with fruit revived her a little.

As they disposed of their cups, Arturo gave her a sideways glance. 'Do you recognise where we are?'

Darcy looked around, scanning the street and shops and restaurants. With their shutters down it was hard to identify what part of the city they were in. She wanted to pull out her phone to try and get her bearings, but she trusted Arturo and just gave a shake of her head. 'Not a clue,' she admitted.

He took her hand again and stood in front of her. 'I wanted to bring you full circle,' he said.

'What does that mean?'

'Come on.' They walked along one more street and she was struck by the fact there were even more people around here. As they rounded the corner, she gave a little gasp.

They were back at the Trevi Fountain. At night, it looked very different. White and blue lights highlighted the whole space. The backdrop seemed brighter and more stark, the water in the fountains even more blue. It had a magical quality to it that hadn't quite been there in the heat of the day.

There were still some people around. The fountain in the middle of the night was obviously some kind of not so hidden secret in Rome. The constant trickle of running water was peaceful, almost hypnotic.

Arturo steered them over to a spot to sit, and as they settled he put his arm around her. A couple in front of them were throwing in their coins, lost in their own private moment.

Darcy relaxed into Arturo. She reached up to grasp his hand on her shoulder. 'This was a great final spot,' she said, then gave him a sceptical glance. 'You could have mentioned this before.'

'And spoil our happy ending?' he joked, and her stomach flipped. 'Anyhow, it was a good place to visit earlier, because then you could appreciate the contrast at this time of night.'

She heard him take a deep breath, and instantly her stomach clenched. 'So, I'm going to ask you something on the way home, and it's really important that I'm honest with you before I ask.'

'This sounds serious.'

He gave a sad kind of smile, but didn't actually give an answer. He took another deep breath. 'You know that I told you I was like Indiana Jones.'

She smiled instantly. 'Yes, it has kind of played on my mind.'

He pressed his lips together. 'I take it you've watched the movies?'

'Hasn't everyone?'

He gave the slightest of nods. 'In that case—' his eyes fixed over towards the fountain '—you'll remember that

Indiana Jones got into trouble sometimes. He got chased. People didn't like him.'

She almost laughed. 'Only the bad guys.'

He turned to look at her. 'Well, in my line of work, there can be bad guys.'

Her skin instantly chilled. 'What do you mean?'

'I mean that, on occasion, I get threatened. My job can make me unpopular—usually because I'm retrieving things that have been stolen, that don't belong to the people that currently own them. And sometimes, for me, and I think for my dad too, things can be a bit dangerous.'

'Like getting chased by a giant rock?' She was grasping at straws and it was the first thing she could think of.

He gave a soft laugh. 'No, I've never been chased by a giant rock. But I just want to be honest with you. I get threatened sometimes.' He ran his fingers through his dark hair. 'My family have never been threatened, I wouldn't let any of my friends get threatened, my fiancée was never threatened.'

'Your what?' Her heart had just stopped beating.

He winced. 'Faye,' he said without hesitation. 'She was in the same line of work. She died five years ago, in Japan. A road accident. Nothing to do with either of our jobs.'

'You were engaged?' She just had to say the words out loud to make herself process them.

To his credit, he didn't look abashed at all. 'Yes, I was. It's been five years since she died.'

It was Darcy's turn to suck in a deep breath. 'Oh, I'm so sorry.' She reached over and put her hand on his chest. She'd thought what had happened to her was bad. But this? It didn't bear thinking about. No wonder she'd thought Arturo seemed a little guarded around her. He'd had all this weight on his shoulders.

'There's never really a good time to say that, is there?' he asked.

Her stomach flip-flopped as she thought of what she hadn't told him. She gave him a sad smile. 'Not really, but you've done it. And I'm glad you have. I'm glad you told me.' She leaned back against him because she meant it. She was glad to know. It gave her a bigger picture to look at and consider.

But this news was huge. Maybe because she'd told him about Laura, he'd felt as if he should share about Faye. And he'd said it had been nothing to do with their jobs— but there had also been that other news that his job could be dangerous. How did a handsome Italian, with a partly dangerous job, end up at the same dance class as her in Edinburgh? Honestly, if she was writing a script for a film, she would never have thought of this.

Even though she wanted to ask a million questions, this beautiful setting was just not the time and place. She didn't want to put him on the spot. Indeed, she had no right to. She'd invited him here as someone to show her around a city in Italy. It had been convenient for her. And if she kept telling herself that, she could ignore that underlying pull towards him, and that obvious wave of attraction.

He held her gaze for a second, and she wondered if he was gauging her reaction. Was he happy she'd been accepting, or was he curious she hadn't bombarded him with questions? But Arturo seemed as unruffled as ever. He gave her a smile. One that danced down the nerves in her spine. So sexy…

Then he pointed over to the right side of the fountain. 'See that over there?'

She squinted as she followed his finger and nodded when she worked out where he was pointing. 'What is it?'

'It's called the Fountain of Love. Two simple water spouts that cross before landing together in the stone basin below.' His voice was deep and low. 'Legend has it that if two lovers drink from the crossing spouts together, they will remain in love for ever.'

It was as if someone froze the world around them. Their gazes were locked together. Darcy licked her lips. 'But we're not lovers.'

There was a soft smile on Arturo's lips. 'Not yet,' he said in a whisper. Darn, this man was sexy. 'But everyone has to start somewhere. How about with a kiss?'

A light breeze blew across her skin. She could have sworn it was just to make all the hairs on her skin stand on end.

She swallowed, then smiled. 'I think we could start there,' she said.

He bent his head towards her, his lips brushing against hers at first, before his hand moved gently behind her head and slid through her hair. Now he was kissing her, his lips firm but still gentle. She didn't even want to consider where Arturo had practised his technique—she just wanted to applaud anyone that had come before—and had helped him reach his current state of perfection. Because in this current state of perfection he was hers.

She angled her body more towards his, still sitting on the steps. Her hand slid up the front of his shirt and he gave a little groan.

Arturo pulled her closer, intensifying their kiss. His hand moved from the back of her head to the side of her face. His fingertip touch was butterfly-light, touching her cheek, her ear, then running down her neck and making her gasp for air.

For a few moments, nothing else mattered. Nothing bad had ever happened in her life, or in his. She was floating in a pink fluffy cloud, with the most gorgeous man focusing all his attention on her. Her lips were in heaven, other parts of her body were coming to life and urging for more. She couldn't remember a kiss ever doing this to her.

There was a shout to the side of them that sadly jolted her back to reality.

She laughed and leaned back. Another couple next to them—the one who must have shouted—gave a round of applause and Darcy could feel heat rush into her cheeks. Arturo gave them an amused nod and pulled her up, walking her over to the Fountain of Love, which was a little more secluded.

They paused above the two water spouts. 'Ready?' he asked.

'You're sure we can drink this?' she countered.

'Live a little,' was his wicked reply, and she flicked a little of the water at him, before they both bent to drink from the spouts.

'Remind me what this means?' she asked, wiping her chin.

'Apparently, it guarantees love and faithfulness.'

'Just for lovers?' She was teasing, but she couldn't help it.

'Who knows?' He gave a playful shrug. 'Guess we'll need to find out.'

He glanced at his watch, and she knew what would come next. Already she could sense the sky starting to lighten in gradual elements around them.

She stepped forward again and took his hands. 'Thank you. Thank you for coming with me and showing me all the best parts of Rome.'

He released one hand so he could put his arm around her, guiding her away from the Fountain of Love and back towards the main road, where they could hail a taxi.

'It's been my pleasure. But I did warn you that I might ask for something in return.'

'Oh, yes. What?' She was in a good mood and was relaxed, still recovering from that first kiss. Her lips still tingled.

'Come with me to my sister's wedding.'

Her footsteps faltered. 'What?'

'I need a partner for my sister's wedding. Who better than the person I'm dancing with? Who better than the person I've just spent twenty-four hours in Rome with?'

She wrinkled her nose. 'You've made your sister sound kind of terrifying.'

He laughed. 'Cara would love that you said that! But I refuse to tell her. Come with me. Meet my family. See the estate. I promise you, once you've seen an Italian wedding, nothing else will compare.'

She looked at him warily. 'Why do I think there's a little bit more to this?'

He gave the smallest shrug, but nodded. 'I've warned you about my family. They can be a little full-on. Now my sister's getting married, their attention will fully be on—' He lifted his hand to his chest, and Darcy finished the sentence for him.

'You.'

He nodded. 'I fear they may have a dozen lovely Italian daughters and nieces of friends lined up to try and pair me off with.'

'So, what am I? Your protection?'

He laughed out loud, his face breaking into a wide smile. 'Absolutely. If I'm there with you, then they won't try and pair me off with anyone else.'

A little part of her wondered if she should be offended by this ask. He was using her as a mechanism of convenience—just like she'd done when she'd asked him to come to Rome. Could she really say no, when he'd also opened up about other parts of his life too? Should she second-guess the kiss they'd just shared? Was it all just part of a bribe?

No. She pushed that out of her head. She wasn't going to let that perfect kiss be spoiled by her brain overthinking.

'When is it?' asked Darcy.

'It's in one week. Will you have problems getting time off work?'

'Oh, no.' She shook her head. 'I'm owed about a million holidays anyhow. Time off won't be the problem. Finding something to wear to your sister's wedding might be.'

'You can borrow something of hers,' he said nonchalantly.

She shook her head, laughing. 'You just don't get the girl thing, do you?'

'What?' he asked without a care in the world, waving to a taxi cab.

'I'll come,' she said, before she could change her mind, or talk herself out of it. 'But let me pick my own outfit.'

The taxi pulled up and Arturo opened the door for her. He bowed. 'Your wish is my command,' he joked as she climbed in.

Darcy sank into the seat, fatigue starting to come over

her in waves. By the time Arturo had climbed in beside her and put his arm around her again, her eyes wouldn't stay open.

'Sleep,' he said softly. And she leaned against him, wondering if this whole day had actually just been part of a dream.

CHAPTER EIGHT

'BUT WHO IS HE?' pressed Fizz.

'I told you. Arturo Fabiano. I met him at a dance class. He came to Rome with me. You've seen him. I sent you a picture.'

'But that's all you've sent. And you never mentioned him before you sent that picture. Now you're going to his sister's wedding with him at his estate in Verona? Who is this guy?'

Fizz said the words with such indignation that Darcy wanted to laugh out loud.

Darcy shrugged her shoulders. 'Don't read too much into things. It's kind of an arrangement of convenience. He helped me tick off something on my bucket list, and I'll help fend off all the Italian women his mother and sister will try and throw at him. He's just an Italian staying in Edinburgh. He's a sort of modern-day Indiana Jones.'

'That's the most dubious job description I've heard in a long time,' shot back Fizz. Then she frowned. 'Are you sure he's not making that up?'

Darcy leaned back and smiled. 'Well, if he is it's a great story.'

Fizz pointed her finger. 'There. You're doing that thing.'

'What thing?'

Fizz waved her hand. 'That thing you do when you get

all starry-eyed about someone.' She looked as if she was going to go further, but paused and clearly pulled herself back. 'I don't think this is a convenience thing for you. You've not done that for a long time.'

There was silence between them. They both knew the last time Darcy had been starry-eyed. It had ended in disaster.

'Anyway,' said Darcy quickly, 'I need something to wear to his sister's wedding. Any suggestions? Or where should I get something? It's been so long since I've bought an outfit like that I don't know where to shop any more.'

Fizz sat drumming her fingers on her desk for a few moments. She was clearly contemplating something. After a second, her eyes brightened. 'Actually, I've just thought of the perfect thing.'

'What?'

Fizz shook her head. 'I bought it last year. Never had a chance to wear it. It will look gorgeous on you, and it's perfect for a wedding.'

'Promise me it's not a bikini,' said Darcy cautiously. She knew how mischievous her sister could be.

But Fizz looked sincere. 'Honestly, it will be perfect. I'll pack it up and send it twenty-four-hour delivery.'

'Thanks. Are you going to give me a hint?'

Fizz's smile widened. 'Not at all.'

Darcy paused for a moment. 'Hey, how's Oli?' Fizz bristled. It was odd, she and Oli had been friends for ever. 'Didn't you two have plans for something?'

'Yeah, well, maybe. I'm not sure.'

Darcy was surprised. She'd always thought Oliver was secretly in love with Fizz and would do anything she asked. But maybe things had changed. They hadn't had a proper conversation about Oli in a while.

'I have a few things to sort out,' said Fizz, and Darcy wasn't sure if she was talking about life, the dress heading her way, or Oli.

'Hey.' Darcy smiled at her sister. 'Remember, we're the Bennetts—we can do anything.'

Fizz's face broke into a smile, slightly sad at first, then broadening. She gave a smile. 'You're right. Watch out for the post. Let me know what you think when it arrives, okay?'

Darcy nodded and signed off. Was everything all right with her sister? She didn't like to pry, and if something was wrong, Fizz would tell her, wouldn't she?

CHAPTER NINE

ARTURO'S PHONE HAD literally not stopped ringing since he'd finally arrived back from Rome and responded to the original message. Sleep hadn't been an option, and he'd spoken to discreet colleagues around the world in an attempt to authenticate the item he would soon try to retrieve.

In between this, he'd broken it to his mother and sister that he would be bringing a guest to the wedding. He didn't need to worry if Cara would attempt an internet search of Darcy, since she'd done it while they were on their video call and spun her tablet around to show him.

'Ooh, she's clever. And she's listed as working at a few major companies. That's good, isn't it?' Then Cara frowned, a suspicious gleam in her eye. 'Or does that mean she changes jobs before she's found out?'

'Found out for what?'

'Found out for not being able to do the job she actually got.'

'Cara—' his sister flinched at his warning tone, then was clearly amused '—I'm telling you right now, concentrate on your wedding. Leave my date alone.'

'Your date? Is that how you're describing her? Not your girlfriend. Or your new love interest.'

'Cara,' he warned again, 'don't you have a million

other details to worry about? Like the position of the sun in the sky? Or which way the wind might blow?'

His sister's face tightened. Yes, he knew her that well. She was an absolute perfectionist. Living in Edinburgh whilst she'd been planning her wedding had likely been a blessing in disguise.

His mother's face filled the frame and she pushed Cara from the chair. There was no malice in it. His mother had probably had her fill of Cara for the last few weeks, and when Arturo checked in she liked to give him her full attention.

'Well, I can't wait to meet your date. I'm sure she'll be absolutely charming.'

Arturo started to breathe a little easier. 'She may seem a little shy at first.'

'I thought all English girls were brash and outspoken.'

Arturo bristled instantly until he caught the amused glance on his mother's face. He took a breath. 'We've spent some time together. I like her. She lost a sister five years ago and...' He slowed. 'I suspect she's not quite over things.'

His mother gave an understanding nod. 'She might not be quite ready for a family like ours,' she said good-naturedly. Then, with more caution, 'Or a man like yourself.'

'What does that mean?'

'It means that it sounds like she may need some nurturing, some support.'

'And you think I can't do that?' He was wounded that his mother thought so little of him.

'I suspect—' her voice was even '—that your job might not allow for that. You leave at a moment's notice. You can be out of touch for days. Does she understand that yet?'

He swallowed. 'We haven't got that far. I did give her a little warning about my job.'

His mother gave a tiny bow of her head and put her hand on her heart. 'I loved your father dearly and he loved me, but he also loved his work.' She gave a gentle smile. 'You are your father's son. I don't think you ever really understood how much I hated the fact his job took him away, or that on occasion it put him, or even us, in danger.' She looked her son directly in the eye. 'And I would never have forgiven him if anything had happened to any of you.'

Arturo's skin prickled. His mother had never spoken like this. She'd never revealed this part of her marriage. And whilst it made him uncomfortable, he understood why she was doing it.

'Arturo,' she continued with a wave of her hand, 'you know that in my secret plans I have you settling down with the nice Italian girl and coming back to stay here for the rest of your life.' She gave him a warm smile. 'But I also know that the life I have in my head for you and the life you have in your head for yourself are two entirely different things.' She took a deep breath. 'I only want you to be happy. I am delighted you've found someone you want to bring to Cara's wedding. I only ask that you think carefully about the girl you've found, whether you are right for each other, and whether you can give her what she needs.'

He was glad he was sitting down because this was the most insightful conversation he'd ever had with his mother. They didn't talk about people and feelings—not even when Faye had died, or his father had died. They talked about business, other family and running the estate. But those conversations had been perfunctory. This was entirely different.

'You haven't mentioned what *I* might need,' he said, knowing exactly how his mother would react to that.

His mother gave a gentle laugh. 'And that's where our conversation ends. I don't need to know what you need. I'm sure you can work that out for yourself.' She gave a wave and the conversation finished, just as Arturo had predicted.

He stood and stretched his back, looking out over the city skyline. He still wondered how on earth he'd ended up in Edinburgh. Even though the city had captured his heart, he now wondered if something else had pulled him there. Was this just fate? Did he even believe in that?

His phone pinged again and he sighed. He still had work to complete, and a dance class to get to. He smiled. Margaret had better wave a magic wand at some point in the next few days or this could all get messy.

CHAPTER TEN

'I THOUGHT THERE would be other people here,' Darcy said as she stripped off her jacket and changed into her dance shoes.

Arturo smiled. 'There's another class in an hour. But I paid Margaret for some private tuition for us. I've still not got all the steps and I'm running out of time fast.'

Darcy put a hand on her hip. 'You could just sway around the dance floor. Other couples do that and...' she gave him a little smile '...you managed that the other night.'

He pulled a face, walked over and put his hand over hers, anchoring it on her hip. She automatically smiled and took a step closer as he spoke. 'That's okay for an actual couple. But for the guy playing Father of the Bride, it looks a bit stupid. I have to at least manage a few steps.'

'And how many have you actually mastered?' Margaret's voice made them both jump as she walked up behind them.

'The natural turn, the backward change with the left foot and the reverse turn.' Darcy jumped in quickly to save him.

He gave her a nod as Margaret rolled her eyes. 'Only halfway then? You still need to do the chasse change steps and the backward change with the left foot. Come on then, I'll help you master the rest.'

The next hour flew past. They only ended up on a heap on the floor once, when Arturo mistimed his steps a little too enthusiastically. But they were definitely getting better.

'You have improved,' said Margaret encouragingly. Then she winked at Darcy. 'He's gone from absolutely terrible to merely diabolical.'

Arturo opened his mouth to defend himself, but Margaret was laughing. 'We'll cover the Viennese waltz for the first half hour of the next class. Stay and practice. You're actually getting there.' She tapped Arturo's arm. 'We'll make a dancer of you yet.'

Once the rest of the participants filed in they continued dancing, concentrating on their steps until they'd mastered all the basics and things were starting to feel a bit smoother.

'I think we might have it,' whispered Darcy excitedly.

'But will I remember any of it tomorrow?' groaned Arturo.

'I think I know a way to imprint it on your brain so you don't forget,' joked Darcy.

'What?' He actually looked hopeful.

She nodded. 'Picture your sister's face if you get it wrong.'

He shuddered, and smiled. 'Yes, that will do it.'

'Hey,' he remarked, twirling her around. 'That's two items ticked off your bucket list. What's going to be your third?'

'I haven't had much of a chance to think about it yet.'

'Remind me what it is.' He had one hand resting on her hip and the other holding her hand. They were still up close and personal in the dance position and for the first time since they'd kissed she felt a little awkward.

The words seemed to stick in her throat as she said them out loud. 'The third thing was to make a commitment to someone or something—it has to be important, something that lasts a few years.'

He frowned. 'Your sister thought you had issues with making commitments?'

Darcy honestly wasn't sure how to answer that. There were still elements of her past that she hadn't shared with him, and she wasn't sure she wanted to.

He had the strangest look on his face, and did she imagine it or had his body just tensed a little?

A thought flooded into her brain. Oh, no. Did he think she was talking about them?

Her legs wobbled. What if he thought she was just making things up, and had thrown this bucket list item in for other reasons?

She pulled her hands away from his and wiped them on her skirt. 'I think we're done now. Margaret's getting ready to change the class onto the next dance.'

Arturo looked as if he had barely drawn a breath and she wasn't sure what to make of it. He blinked and then coughed, breaking his gaze from hers and turning to look around the room.

'Sure,' he murmured.

As they got their coats and made their way outside, Darcy reached inside her bag and pulled out the envelope that contained her bucket list. 'Here,' she said, not considering the handwritten notes that were there.

His brow wrinkled and he took the envelope from her hand and drew out the letter, unfolding it. His eyes widened as he realised what it was.

'The whole bucket list?' he asked.

'The whole bucket list,' she repeated.

His head tipped to the side by the tiniest angle. 'Why would you share this with me?' There was something about his words, and his tone.

'Because I told you the third item inside, and I wasn't sure if you believed me.'

It struck her that until that second she hadn't realised how important it was to her that Arturo *did* believe her. And that scared her.

'Of course I believed you.' His words were barely a whisper. She knew he was reading the rest of what was written on her letter. But he lifted his head with a clear expression on his face.

'Your sister gave you a bucket list. She gave you some hints and other comments. But you have to interpret this *your* way. Not hers. And if you can't do it in the time frame she gave you, so what? I get you want to honour your sister, and I think that's wonderful. But you have to remember to be you. You spent your life being one of three sisters—you might feel a bit awkward about being one of two now. But you will always be you. And the Darcy Bennett that I've met is pretty great.'

He reached up with his hand and pushed a strand of her hair behind her ear. 'I even invited her to a wedding,' he said, smiling.

'A very important wedding,' she replied as she stepped forward. Her heart had stopped racing now, and her stomach was unclenching. She still didn't know Arturo very well. But now she knew for sure that she wanted that to change.

Maybe going to the wedding and meeting the family would give her the background and history part that she needed to fill in some of his blanks. While she was nervous, she was also excited. So maybe it was time to be completely honest with him.

'I've booked our flights,' he said. 'Found a dress yet?'

She raised her eyebrows. 'Fizz found me a dress.'

'That sounds promising.' It sounded more like a question than a statement.

She pulled a face. 'It is. It's just a bit more daring than I would probably have picked myself.'

'But do you like it?'

Darcy took a few moments and then nodded slowly. 'Do you know, I do. It's a beautiful dress.'

'Then be daring.' He smiled at her.

He opened the passenger door of his car. 'Jump in, let's go for a drive.'

'Where to?'

He looked down the street. 'It's still light. We'll head to the beach. Might even see the sunset.'

She climbed in. 'This could be a bad decision. Think of the last sunset you showed me. Will this one compare?'

'Beauty is in the eye of the beholder,' he said, shifting his car into gear and taking off.

Fifteen minutes later they pulled up to Portobello Beach. The sky had dimmed, but the promenade still had people walking up and down.

As they got out of the car it was clear that the wind had picked up, and Darcy's hair flew in every direction. 'Need a thicker jacket?' he called as he walked around and opened the boot of the car.

'Sure.' She nodded, her denim jacket not quite up to the blustery breeze coming off the Firth of Forth.

There were a few other people around, mainly walking dogs, as they jumped down onto the sand.

'It's been a while since I visited a beach,' she said, enjoying the wind streaming through her hair, blinking her eyes at the tiny bits of gritty sand.

'Me too,' he admitted, slinging an arm around her shoulders as they walked down to the water's edge. The first part of the sand had been soft, spongy and difficult to walk on. But as they neared the waves the sand was much firmer.

'I wonder if the tide is coming in or out?' she asked.

'Let's take some time to find out,' said Arturo. It was one of his best traits. He was patient. He didn't try to rush things. They stood together, and after a few minutes worked out that the tide appeared to be going back out.

A little dog rushed past them, splashing them as it bounced and sprang through the waves with barks of pure enjoyment. Both of them laughed, not the least bothered by the splashing. A woman rushed up next to them, another dog on a lead in her hand. 'Scamp, come here. Sorry.' She gave them a rueful glance. 'He just gets so excited when he comes down here. He loves the beach.'

Darcy wrinkled her nose. 'What kind of dog is he?'

Arturo looked down at the other dog on the lead. It looked a bit older. It was white and shaggy, with short legs. 'Is that one a West Highland terrier?'

The woman looked at him in surprise as she picked the older dog up and tried to wrestle Scamp back onto a lead. Darcy dropped to her knees to help, trying to hold Scamp in place. He still wanted to dance in the waves.

'We have no idea what Scamp is, do we, gorgeous?' the woman said, staring fondly at her dog. 'I got them both from the dog rescue place just outside Edinburgh.'

'They're rescue?' Darcy was surprised. She didn't know that much about dogs and wasn't sure what kind of dogs ended up in a rescue centre.

The woman succeeded in getting Scamp back on the

lead and stood up, smiling. 'I've had five dogs—not all at once, of course—but all were rescue. I'd just lost my black Lab, and six months later the house felt empty so I went back along to the rescue centre. I went for one, and came home with two.'

'How did that happen?' asked Arturo.

The woman sighed and looked fondly at her dogs. 'They'd both been owned by an elderly man who'd passed away unexpectedly. When I took Scamp out of the kennels to see how he was with me, Hugo here started whining. They didn't like being apart. I couldn't take one without the other.'

'You weren't worried about taking on someone else's dogs?'

'Someone else's problem, you mean?' she asked.

Darcy nodded, embarrassed that she'd read her mind.

'The people at the rescue centre are always very honest about the dogs they have. These were probably two of the best trained in there. But most people don't want two dogs, so they'd been overlooked.' Her smile broadened. 'Or maybe they'd just been waiting for me.' She gave them a smile and a wave before heading off down the beach with her dogs.

As Darcy turned back, Arturo was watching her closely.

'What?' she asked.

'Nothing,' he said with a half-smile on his face.

The sun had dipped while they were talking, and he pointed at the darkening sky. 'Maybe we don't have shades of orange and the outline of the Colosseum, but I suspect Scotland's offer might be just as nice.'

'Nice?' Darcy put her hand on her hip. 'Just as well I'm an English girl and not a Scots, or I might be mortally offended by those words.'

He knew she was joking and gave her a smile. 'I can make amends.'

'How?'

He pointed to the few shops just parallel to the promenade. 'I can offer chips or ice cream.'

'They don't call it ice cream around here.'

'They don't? What do they call it?'

As they walked back up the beach, she gave him a sideways glance. 'A pokey hat.'

He almost choked. 'What?'

'It was one of the first things I learned when I got here. And I've got Arthur to thank for that.' She pulled a face. 'Although apparently the saying originated from the *other* big city in Scotland.'

'Glasgow?'

She nodded.

'I still don't get it—why on earth do they call it a pokey hat?'

'It's ice cream served in a cone, and if you turned the cone upside down it would be like a witch's hat.'

He wrinkled his nose for a few moments and shook his head. 'Does that mean you want ice cream?'

'Actually…' she grinned '… I'd rather have the chips. It's a bit cold around here.'

'Okay.'

They headed to the nearest fish and chip shop, then sat back at the beach, chips on their lap as they watched the sun finally dip in the sky.

'Hey,' she said, bumping him with her elbow. 'I've just realised that the two men I've been hanging around with most in Edinburgh are both called Arthur.'

He raised his eyebrows, but she laughed and continued. 'Arturo is the Italian form of Arthur, isn't it?'

He rolled his eyes. 'Yeah, I'll let you have that.'

She looked out across the view. 'I wonder what that means?'

'That both men you hang around with are called Arthur? Maybe their mothers just had good taste in names?'

Her eyes gleamed with mischief. 'Or maybe it's some kind of fate and I was destined to meet you both.'

Their gazes locked for a minute and neither of them spoke.

Darcy swallowed. It was now or never. Time for some honesty.

'You know how you told me about Faye, and your job?'

A wrinkle appeared in his forehead. He was surprised by the change in direction. 'Yes.'

Darcy licked her dry lips, blaming it on the wind. 'I haven't been to a wedding in five years,' she said quickly.

The wrinkle in his forehead deepened. 'None of your friends have got married?'

She shook her head. 'No—I mean yes. I've just made an excuse not to go.'

He still looked entirely baffled. 'Why?'

'Because the last wedding I went to was my own.' She said the words so quickly they all ran into each other.

His face dropped like a stone. 'You're married?'

'No.' The answer was emphatic. Then she dropped her voice. 'I went to my wedding, but my groom didn't.'

She hated these words. She hated saying them out loud. The humiliation still felt real.

'He what?' There was a change in tone from Arturo. He looked disbelieving.

Darcy turned her head, putting her face head-on to the oncoming brisk breeze from the sea. Hopefully, that would hide the tears that were threatening to spill.

'He stood me up.' Her voice was quiet now. But Arturo had moved closer, his hand around her waist. 'He phoned me to say he wasn't coming.'

After a moment he pulled her closer, sheltering her from the wind. 'He was a damn fool, Darcy. Please tell me you don't waste a second thinking about someone like that.'

Now she did blink back tears, but brushed them away. 'I just felt like I should tell you—be honest with you, before we reach Verona.'

'In case what?' It was as if he already understood.

'In case I wobble,' she admitted.

He put both arms around her, pulling her into his chest. It felt safe this way. It felt safe to say more.

'It all worked out for the best. Ultimately, we weren't right for each other. And after a few days away, I came back and spent the next three months with my family in Bath, helping to nurse Laura. It was where I needed to be.'

'Oh, Darcy,' was all he said, one hand reaching up and cradling the back of her head.

She'd told him. It was out there, and it felt more like a relief than a humiliation.

His voice was low and considerate. 'Are you sure you want to come? You don't need to. I don't want you to do something that might make you feel uncomfortable.'

She lifted her head. 'I've avoided weddings up until now. It's time that stopped. So where better to start than at a beautiful wedding at a fabulous estate in Verona?' She put a smile on her face. 'Where I will be on my best behaviour to keep the mother of the bride, and the bride, from attempting to marry you off to some random Italian woman.'

'You're sure you'll be okay?'

She gave a gentle smile, thankful he'd been so under-standing, and so kind. 'I'll be fine. A change of scenery again will be nice.' She stood up, ready to move from the breezy spot, scrunching the chip wrapper into a ball and lobbing it into a nearby bin.

His eyes widened.

'Who knows—' she grinned '—I might even surprise you.'

He stopped walking and put his hands on her shoulders. 'You do,' he said sincerely. 'Every single day.'

She stopped breathing for a second at the seriousness in his face. Was this about what she'd just told him? They'd had a few moments of sincerity. But mostly their time together had been fun and light-hearted. She knew that things might change once she met his family, and she was conjuring plans in her head about how she might introduce Arturo to Fizz, and then her mum and dad.

The fact that she was even considering those things made her know she was more hopeful about the possibil-ity of continuing this relationship. And that scared her.

Almost as if it was a sign from the universe, Arturo locked eyes with her. He bent down to whisper in her ear, 'You surprise me every single day,' he repeated. 'And sometimes—' he straightened up and looked at her again '—you downright scare me.' The expression on his face was soft, with the hint of a smile on his lips. She knew he was still talking light-heartedly, but something inside her was squirming.

She wanted to push on. She wanted this relationship to go somewhere. But could she really expose herself to the hurt she'd had before?

A guy with a job like Indiana Jones, who was from Italy, probably a secret billionaire, and had an air of mystery about him, was hardly the best candidate for her heart. She should look for someone who would want to set down roots here, who might seem like a safer prospect, work in tech or something similar to her, and be independent but not have enough money to buy a small nation.

That would be her ideal candidate, on paper, at least.

But none of those guys had sparked her interest in the last five years. None had made her heart beat faster. None had made her excited to want to see them again. None had made her skin tingle or her lips buzz like Arturo had.

Was she just destined for heartbreak again? Maybe she should call a halt to all this. Deep down was the familiar feeling of guilt. Why should she be able to move on and take a chance at happiness when Laura had never got that chance? Was that fair?

Maybe going to the family wedding was a very bad idea. Maybe she should just rock back up to her cottage and stop imagining what the royal suite might look like in that posh Edinburgh hotel, or what size of bed it had.

But as Arturo opened the car door for her and looked at her with those hypnotic dark brown eyes she knew she wanted to take this leap.

Even if it was a very bad idea.

Because if you didn't leap, how would you ever know where you could land?

CHAPTER ELEVEN

SHE COULD TELL Arturo was nervous. It was weird. It was not a term she'd ever associated with him. But as soon as they left Verona Airport and jumped in the sports car that was waiting for them, she could almost sense his jitters.

It could just be excitement at getting back to his home, and seeing his family again. It could be actual honest-to-goodness nerves about the upcoming wedding and his role in it. There had to be pressure on him, and she hadn't even asked if he needed to do a speech.

The Italian countryside was beautiful and the miles passed in a blur. When Arturo finally drove through a set of stone pillars with open gates, she got a real sense of what he meant by estate.

The house was not immediately visible and they continued along the curved red road for a few minutes. On one side there was open countryside, on the other, trees. Eventually the gleaming cream-coloured mansion emerged fully.

It had three floors, a fountain in front of the house and sweeping steps up to double doors. Surrounding the house were immaculate manicured gardens.

Darcy's first thought was it looked like it had been plucked from a luxury magazine. But the quiet look of the house was quickly dispelled by the number of people around. As they approached, she noticed multiple buildings on either side of the mansion, and other roads leading around the back.

A huge catering truck was parked off to one side, with another truck unloading what looked like hundreds of beautiful blooms.

Arturo didn't hesitate. He parked his sports car smack bang in front of the main door.

'Isn't there a garage?' Darcy asked dubiously.

'Serge will move it later,' he said, stepping out onto the driveway, putting his hands on his hips and taking a deep breath.

She watched with interest. After a few moments he ducked his head back down. 'Getting out, or have you changed your mind?'

'Is the air different here?'

He gave a smile. 'Everything is different here. Come on, let's embrace the chaos.'

Her nerves jangled, but she was excited too. She stepped out of the car just as the main doors opened and a man came down the steps. For some reason, she'd expected him to be in uniform. The place seemed grand enough for that. But he was wearing regular jeans and a T-shirt.

'Good to see you, Arturo,' he said easily. 'Bags in the trunk?'

Arturo's shoulders visibly relaxed. 'Nice to see you too—and yes, thanks, Serge.'

The guy gave a little nod to Darcy. 'I'll be Serge,' he joked, since Arturo had forgotten to make introductions.

'Darcy,' she said, holding out her hand, then realising that was ridiculously formal.

But Serge took it with good grace and gave her hand a

firm shake. 'Nice to meet you, Darcy. I'll take your bags up to your room. If Arturo doesn't remember to tell you where it is, come and find me later, and I'll show you.'

She gave a confused smile as Arturo cut in. 'And why wouldn't I remember?'

Serge popped the boot and started pulling out the bags. He looked at Darcy and smiled. 'You want to see the size of the list Cara has for him,' he joked.

Arturo groaned.

Serge lifted all three suitcases easily. 'They have actually made drinks for you coming. They're in the bar waiting for you both.'

Immediately, Darcy felt a little panicked and looked down at her travelling clothes. Beige cargo pants and a big white shirt. She would rather have had a chance to freshen up before she met the family.

She pushed her sunglasses up into her hair. Arturo had obviously read the panic in her face. He nodded to Serge. 'Give us two minutes.'

He walked her up the steps to the house and led her into the foyer. The floor was covered in tiny white and black tiles and a double staircase snaked up the curved interior walls. Doors left off in every direction.

Arturo took her down one corridor to a large bathroom, giving her a chance to wash her hands, tidy her hair and retouch her make-up. It only took a few minutes and he was waiting outside for her when she was done. She was already feeling swamped by the size and prestige of the place. How on earth could she fit in here? Arturo had tried to warn her that he had an 'estate', but she really hadn't grasped just *how* rich he was. She'd never mixed in this kind of circle before. The background thought that Arturo had brought her here as a convenience—to stop his family trying to pair him off with someone else—now seemed massively out of step.

'Ready?' He seemed steadier now. Maybe it was just the anticipation of being here that had made him seem nervous earlier.

She nodded, and pretended her heart wasn't pounding in her chest. He took her through another few rooms until they finally reached the room that Serge had referred to as the bar.

The Fabianos' bar was as big as any commercial bar, except it had a host of comfortable sofas and chaise longues, a few tables and chairs, a huge chandelier hanging from the ceiling and a whole wall of glass doors out to gardens with a wide array of colourful flowers.

Darcy had barely managed to take anything in before the noise erupted in the room. A woman in a coral-coloured dress with matching shoes and long dark hair stood up and flung her arms around Arturo. At first glance it was obvious they were siblings.

A graceful older woman with grey hair in a modern-cut bob and dark top and trousers came over to stand by them. She gave Darcy a kiss on the cheek. 'Delighted to meet you,' she said in perfect English. 'You must be Darcy. I'm Arturo's mother, but please call me Maria.'

'Thank you,' said Darcy, watching as Arturo's sister finally unravelled herself from her brother. She spun around towards Darcy.

Cara was stunning, with the same dark eyes as her brother and a warm complexion. She gave Darcy a slightly more chaste hug, then kissed both her cheeks. 'Cara,' she said. 'Welcome to our home.'

Darcy glanced around nervously. There was a handsome man standing behind Cara, and Cara pulled him forward. 'This is my fiancé, Dante.'

Dante stepped forward, shook her hand and kissed her cheek. 'How about a drink?' he said, as if he could sense her nerves.

The long bar had a variety of drinks already prepared. 'What do you like? A cocktail? Espresso martini? Strawberry daiquiri? Limoncello? Or some wine?'

Arturo walked over and helped himself to a chilled bottle of beer and Darcy picked up a strawberry daiquiri. The glass had condensation on it, and the first sip of the drink was pleasantly chilled.

Arturo led them over to a firm sofa to sit next to his family. As they started to chat, they drifted between a mixture of Italian and English. Clearly, they were speaking English for her benefit, but it was fascinating the way they all switched easily between languages. There were a few spirited exchanges between the siblings, but they were all in Italian and Darcy made a note to ask Arturo what they were sparring about later.

She relaxed into the sofa, her eyes occasionally caught by movement outside in the grounds. Off to the left, a large marquee had been set up in the garden. It was bigger than any she'd seen before and was already set with tables and chairs. A large archway of pink and white roses framed an arbour that made Darcy wonder if it was being set up for the photographs.

As the conversation slowed next to her, she turned towards Cara. 'Everything looks so beautiful. You are so lucky to be getting married in a place that you love.'

Cara tilted her elbow towards Darcy. 'Let me give you the full tour.'

Arturo shot her a worried glance, but his sister gave

him a look that only a sister could, and Darcy couldn't see any way out of this.

She smiled, slid her arm through Cara's and let her lead her around the house. Cara was charm itself, self-confident, intelligent, but with a definite hint of something else. Her coral silk dress was exquisite and clung to her perfect figure. She had long lashes, beautiful skin and even her nails were flawless. Darcy had never been the type of person to compare herself to someone else, but every now and then she sensed that Cara was looking at her clothes, her haircut, her nails... Or maybe she was just being entirely paranoid.

As they walked around the house, Darcy got a true feel for the extent of the property and land that the Fabiano family owned. She lost count of the number of bedrooms and bathrooms in the house. The larger suites had bedrooms, dressing rooms, sitting rooms and en suite bathrooms of their own. The kitchen that the staff worked in was a gleaming stainless-steel ensemble. The storage facilities for food seemed larger than any restaurant's.

There was a library, an honest-to-goodness ballroom, multiple sitting rooms and an orangery with a curved glass dome at the back of the house.

Cara pointed out parts of the grounds—the garages, stables, swimming pool and pool house, tennis courts and staff residences. All the while she gently plied Darcy with questions.

How had she met Arturo? How well did she know him? Had he told her about his job? What did Darcy do? What exactly was a cybersecurity job? Where did she live? Did she have children? Had she been married before?

The last question had thrown her, and she'd stumbled over it and been met with a tiny look of suspicion. Darcy should have expected it. She was twenty-nine. Lots of women of her age had been married before. It wasn't exactly an outrageous question. But she just hadn't expected it. Was it possible Arturo had said something about her to his family?

Cara spoke easily, her English had an Italian lilt to it that was hypnotic. But Darcy's stomach remained half clenched the whole time. Maybe she was a bit tired from the journey. If there had been a chance to wash and change she might have felt a bit brighter. Instead, she felt slightly under the microscope.

By the time they returned to the bar she was absolutely relieved to see Arturo again—and by the look on his face he was equally relieved to see her. He offered to take her up to her room and she accepted with a smile.

'Thought your sister had taken me captive somewhere?' she teased as they walked up the stairs.

'It crossed my mind,' he admitted.

'Are you okay?' she asked.

'Of course,' he said immediately, and it made her a tiny bit nervous.

Two minutes later he showed her to her room, with a large bed and bathroom and beautiful views of the impeccable gardens. From here, she could even see where the wedding festivities were being set up, and it was a real hive of activity.

'We're not sharing?' she asked, then wanted to slap herself for coming out with that.

It was forward, and ridiculous. Their relationship hadn't changed to that level yet. She was clearly tired or she would never have said that.

Arturo looked amused. 'You're welcome in my room any time you like. Even though my mother and sister will spot you on CCTV, or by the hidden alarms in the house, and likely make you meet our family lawyer on the spot.'

He must have recognised the horror on her face because he reached over and touched her arm. 'I'm joking. I didn't want to presume something, or make my mother ask questions you might not have wanted. I thought you might want some space to yourself once you meet the billion Italian relatives that will be attending tomorrow. Do you want me to move you?'

She shook her head. 'No, of course not, and thank you.'

He'd been courteous and gentlemanly. How would she have really felt if she'd just been shown into his rooms with no conversation about it? So why, oh, why did she feel the tiniest bit offended? She shook it off.

'Want some time to wash and change before dinner tonight?'

She raised her eyebrow. 'The dinner you forgot to tell me about?' She then gave a grateful smile. 'I'd love it.'

'Will I send you some food up meantime?'

Her smile widened. 'Go on then.' She patted her stomach. 'I think I'd better try and soak up the cocktails from downstairs.'

He paused for a moment then gave her a look. 'Everything will be fine,' he reassured. 'My family love you already.'

As he walked out and closed the door behind him Darcy swallowed nervously and sat down at the window seat. Strangely, she wasn't entirely reassured. And if she knew Arturo at all, from the expression on his face, neither was he.

Arturo was restless. He could already sense the vibe from his family. It wasn't that they didn't like Darcy. This was his fault. He'd sprung her on them at short notice. And while it had seemed like a good idea at the time, now, he wasn't so sure.

She'd looked nervy and jangly when she'd come back from the walk with his sister. He wondered what Cara had said. She had a gift for sometimes saying things without actually saying them. She also had a face that could express a thousand words. And he only hoped she hadn't made Darcy feel unwelcome, although he was certain she would never do that deliberately.

Or maybe it was the estate. He hadn't really gone into a lot of details with Darcy before they'd got here. Maybe the size of the place overwhelmed her. She had known about his office space, and about where he was staying in Edinburgh. Both places were clearly expensive, but he had never hinted at how much his family were worth. The cost of the office space, or hotel bill in Edinburgh, would easily be covered by the interest the family accounts made in only one day.

Tonight's meal would be a traditional sit-down family dinner, with several aunts, uncles and cousins from both sides, the groom's parents and brother, Arturo, his mother, Darcy, Cara and Dante. There would be around twenty people, which might seem a lot, but considering that another two hundred would arrive for the wedding on Sunday, it was actually minimal.

He'd forgotten to mention the dinner to Darcy at first—they'd been too busy talking about the wedding. So he'd made a few calls to ensure there would be something appropriate for her in the wardrobe to wear tonight. He'd gone for a few options and hoped she'd like something.

He walked through to the kitchen and found Rosa,

one of their staff, and asked her to take some food up to Darcy. Then he made his way back through to the bar to find his sister. She was sipping a negroni at the bar, her long legs swinging as she sat on a tall stool. She shot him a smile.

'Tell me you didn't bite her.'

Cara was momentarily amused. It was their own joke. She *had* actually bitten one of their mutual friends when she'd been three years old. 'That better not be in your speech,' she warned.

He smiled easily and tapped the side of his nose. 'I'll never tell.' He moved over to his sister, 'Where's Dante?'

'He's gone to meet his parents and brother. They'll be back in time for dinner.'

He gave a slow nod, wanting—but not wanting—to ask his sister a million questions about what she thought of Darcy.

'Would you like to dance?' he said with a hint of amusement in his voice as he held his hand out to her.

The expression on her face became serious and she downed her negroni rather quickly. 'I swear if you haven't practised I will kill you,' she said. And he knew she completely meant it.

They walked through to the ballroom. It was already dressed for the evening reception tomorrow night and looked impeccable. Arturo pulled out his phone and set it on the side, music filling the room. He led her into the middle of the dance floor and bowed. Cara looked at him in surprise and gave a prompt curtsey, then they both moved into position.

He started easily, listening to the music, following the beat and picturing the steps in his mind as he did them

with his feet. His sister followed smoothly. She'd probably learned the Viennese waltz in a day. Cara had always
been the type of person who made dance look effortless.

He was saying the steps in his head. *Forward turn,
reverse turn, forward change with left foot, backward
change with left foot, and chassé, change steps.*

As the music stopped Cara stepped back, an unbeliev-
ing expression on her face, and she raised her hands and
started clapping. 'I can't actually believe it. You managed it.'

'You have Margaret Scott to thank for that.' He leaned
forward and whispered in her ear, 'Former world cham-
pion for the Viennese waltz, and Darcy, of course, who's
been my partner.' He gave a soft smile. 'She has suffered
stood-on and bruised toes on your behalf.'

Cara studied him closely. 'You like her.' It was enough.
She wasn't going to ask a million questions of her brother.
She was just going to ask the most important one.

'I like her,' he agreed.

'Do you love her?'

He closed his eyes. He should have known she would
go there. How did he answer this question when he wasn't
sure of the answer himself?

'I think I could,' he said slowly, a sweeping realisation
coming over him.

Cara stepped forward and put her hand on her brother's chest. 'Have you told her?'

'About thinking I could love her, or about something
else?' he asked, momentarily confused.

'About Faye, you dummy,' she said, slapping him on
the chest.

He nodded. 'Yes, I've told her.'

Cara's eyebrows raised. She knew him better than he wanted to admit. 'If you've told her, does that mean you're ready to move on? Are you *ready* to love her?' Her voice was passionate, and he knew that his sister loved him fiercely and had his best interests at heart.

'I don't know,' he said, distinctly uncomfortable with this line of questioning now. 'There's something else. I know she lost her sister a few years ago. I know that was tough for her family. She revealed something else to me, just before she came here. The truth is, I'm not sure that she's ready. It feels like she might still have some walls up.'

'You'd know all about that.'

His eyes widened and he turned to his sister. She had one hand on her hip. 'What? I've been Team Arturo all my life. You've brought this girl to my wedding, Arturo. You're going to introduce her to around two hundred people tomorrow, half of whom are distant relatives of ours. You're effectively putting her under a microscope. Is she ready? You must know that as soon as I'm married, all our mother's attention will be on you.'

She shook her head and gave her brother a sympathetic look. 'I only hope you've done the right thing bringing her here. And I hope she's ready for tomorrow.'

He swallowed, knowing his sister was entirely right, and hating every second of that.

Cara shook her hair out—a terrible habit—and walked back over to him. 'Thank you for learning how to dance for my wedding,' she said with a grin. 'But promise me you won't keep mumbling the steps tomorrow night as you do them.'

'I was?' he asked in a shocked voice.

'You were—' she laughed '—just be glad I don't have video evidence!'

She gave a casual wave and walked out of the ballroom, leaving Arturo alone.

Alone to contemplate what she'd just said.

CHAPTER TWELVE

ROSA, THE MAID, was a dream. She'd come in with a tray of food as Darcy was unpacking her clothes. She'd taken one look at her outfit for the wedding tomorrow, which hadn't travelled quite as well as she'd hoped, and asked if she'd like Rosa to steam it for her.

She'd then directed Darcy to a walk-in cupboard where a few items were already hanging in covered sleeves.

'Mr Fabiano asked that some items were delivered for you for tonight. I believe he forgot to mention the family dinner.' Her eyes gleamed with amusement.

'He did,' said Darcy, staring at the items on the hangers, not sure if she liked Arturo buying clothes for her.

'Don't worry,' said Rosa conspiratorially. 'He has good taste, and said to pick whatever you like.' She turned to leave, but paused at the door. 'And if you don't like anything, come and find me. I'll be able to find you something to wear.'

She gave a wave and left the room.

How nice. Darcy's stomach growled, but she was too enticed now by the clothes in the walk-in closet. Her own things hanging there felt meagre in comparison, even though she was perfectly happy with them.

She unzipped the covers over the new clothes. The first was an elegant black jumpsuit with a black sequinned belt, the second a red dress by a popular Italian designer with matching red-soled shoes, the third another dress, this time in silver, with fine straps and a cowl neckline, and the last was a rose-pink dress with a square neck and ruched design that fell just below her knees.

All of these were gorgeous. She hesitated for around five seconds, then sent photos of them all to Fizz. As she sat down to eat, her table turned towards the display of clothes, Fizz gave her detailed thoughts on every dress. And whilst all of them were complimentary, they made her laugh out loud. It was almost as if her sister was in the room with her.

As she nibbled at the crusty bread, thin cut meat, cheese and olives she'd been brought, she walked into the grand bathroom and started running the shower. The truth was, she actually wanted to try all the outfits on. There was none she wanted to instantly dismiss. And that surprised her. Her initial indignation about Arturo buying her clothes had vanished. Granted, none of these clothes had price tags on them, and maybe if they did the indignation would return.

But, for now, she was just going to accept the gift with good grace. After all, if he'd warned her about a family dinner she would have brought something appropriate.

One hour later, showered, hair dried and make-up on, she stood in front of the full-length mirror admiring the black jumpsuit. She honestly liked it best, and when Rosa came back in the room with her crease-free dress for tomorrow she gave her an appreciative look.

'That's gorgeous. Is that the one you're going with?'

Darcy took one last look. The silver sandals matched impeccably and the black sequinned belt cinched the jumpsuit perfectly at her waist. 'It's the one I like best.'

'You look great.' Rosa hung up the dress Fizz had sent for her. 'As for tomorrow, your dress will look fantastic. What colour of wrist corsage would you like?'

'I think cream would be best.'

'No problem.'

There was a knock at the door, even though it was open, and she looked up to see Arturo standing in black trousers and a white shirt. He wore no tie, his dress shirt open at the neck and his jacket draped casually over his arm.

He walked in, not hiding the smile on his face at her choice of clothes. 'You look gorgeous.' He kissed her cheek and she gave a nervous laugh as Rosa was watching them.

He held out his arm for her and she joined him, walking down the curved staircase as he guided her to a room she'd only seen at a glance on the tour with Cara. His phone pinged and he pulled it from his pocket and silenced it without a word.

Some of the guests were already seated and she patiently let Arturo lead her around the room and introduce her to a host of aunts and uncles whose names she tried her best to remember.

As she settled in the chair next to him, a distinct feeling of unrest came over her. It wasn't the people, or the place. It was the wedding, and all the festivities around it, that were taking root in her brain and sparking memories she'd long since forgotten.

There was a round of applause and Dante and Cara entered, hand in hand, Dante in a smart suit and Cara in a spectacular green dress. Cara air kissed her way around the table, leaving no lipstick marks, her perfect smile never leaving her face. Instead of sitting at one end of the table, they sat together in the middle, giving themselves more opportunity to talk to their guests on either side.

'Cara looks beautiful,' Darcy murmured.

Arturo leaned a little closer. 'It's an Italian tradition. The bride wears green to the rehearsal dinner because it's supposed to bring good fortune for the happy couple's big day.'

'I hadn't thought about Italian traditions,' said Darcy softly, little pieces of panic taking seed in her brain.

Arturo didn't seem to notice. 'We have a few. I'll fill you in tomorrow.'

As drinks were served and food put in front of them, her skin prickled. She'd had a rehearsal dinner the night before her own wedding, with some of her relatives and Damian.

Hindsight was a wonderful thing, and whereas she'd thought him a bit jittery at the time, she hadn't paid attention to that. Laura had had a bad day at chemo a few days before and had tried her best to come for dinner, but lasted only a few minutes before going to lie down. The truth was, Darcy had been much more worried about her sister than any potential issues with her groom.

On reflection, Damian must have been feeling terrible. He'd drunk too much, not paid attention to the conversation around him and missed several jokes, clearly because he was thinking about other things. He'd asked to chat later, but Darcy had forgotten. Mainly because she'd been sitting at Laura's bedside, stroking her hair, as she wondered about the dark circles under Laura's eyes and the translucent appearance of her skin.

All of these things she'd pushed away. They'd been forgotten under the weight of actually being stood up at the altar. Warning signs she should have seen.

Warning signs that hadn't appeared in her brain much before now.

She'd been honest with Arturo and told him she hadn't attended a wedding since the disaster of her own. But somehow she'd totally underestimated how being here would make her feel. In truth, she hadn't expected it. And she hated the part of her brain that was allowing herself to dwell on the past, rather than focus on the present with this vivacious family and her gorgeous partner.

'You okay?' asked Arturo as she pushed her wine away.

'I'm fine,' she said automatically. 'Just decided to switch to water for now.'

He gave her an odd look, and she wondered if she'd just committed some cardinal sin by pushing Italian wine away whilst she was eating Italian food. But her stomach just couldn't cope.

The waiter filled her glass with water and she sipped as she nibbled at her food. It was delicious but her appetite had left her. A million things were catapulting around her brain, and she honestly couldn't believe she was being triggered by things five years on.

Even to her, it felt ridiculous. She'd reflected. She was adult enough to know it had been for the best. Yes, it had been upsetting at the time, but she'd got over it.

She wasn't even sure how much she'd actually loved Damian. She'd thought she had, but now wondered if it would ever have gone the distance.

'Something wrong with your food?' Arturo asked.

She put her hand on her abdomen. 'Nervous stomach,' she admitted. It wasn't a lie. It just wasn't entirely the truth either.

Many of the conversations around her were in Italian,

and she was kicking herself for not trying to pick up a few basic words. She hadn't done languages at school for exams, so only knew a few sentences in French and Spanish, as those had been the basics they'd covered in the first year of high school.

Of course she'd only known Arturo for a few weeks, and he'd only asked her to the wedding barely one week ago, but if she'd forward planned she would have asked him for a few hints. Too late now.

It made her feel quite ignorant, and awkward. A wave came over her. On the way here she'd been slightly nervous. But sitting here now she felt completely and utterly out of her depth.

She was in a strange country, with lots of people speaking their own language, being triggered by just about everything around her in a way she could never have imagined for herself.

She could hear the almost silent buzz from Arturo's phone. It was clearly ringing out and he was still ignoring it. She could ask him about it, but she was too swamped with what else was happening.

She'd subconsciously noticed all the wedding preparations but hadn't let her focus go there. The beautiful flowers being brought in earlier today, the aroma in the household, the white linen and table settings visible in the marquee outside.

Arturo's hand closed over hers. 'Darcy?'

It was just the way he said her name. She caught her breath, gave him a glance and said in a low voice, 'I need a moment.'

It must have been the look on her face. He stood up smoothly, but with no delay, and pulled her chair out for her.

She gave a brief smile and nod, muttering *Scusi* to those at the table, but didn't wait. She walked swiftly out the room, making a split-second decision. Did she want to be outside? Or somewhere inside?

Her legs made the decision for her, walking her quickly to the bathroom that Arturo had first shown her when they'd arrived at the house. She closed the door behind her with a click, then let herself slide down the cool tiled wall.

Black spots had entered her vision, but as soon as she reached the floor, her short sharp breathing started to slow.

She leaned forward, putting her head in her hands and concentrating on her breathing for a few moments, telling herself how ridiculous and pathetic this was.

She was a twenty-nine-year-old woman, and was sitting on some bathroom floor like a teenager. Shame flooded through her.

No. That wasn't helping. She lifted her head and leaned it back, letting the cold of the tile penetrate through to her scalp. Yes, that helped centre her a little.

Darcy closed her eyes, wishing she was miles away from this place right now and wouldn't have to make up some random excuse for her behaviour. She wasn't even sure how to explain what had just happened.

'Darcy?' The soft voice sounded at the door. 'Are you okay? Do you need me to get you anything?'

Darn it. Arturo. Of course it was. He was here for his sister's wedding. He should be concentrating on that. He should be enjoying himself.

This wasn't about her. *None* of this was about her. She took another few long breaths. Her mouth was so dry.

She pushed herself up from the floor, washed her

hands first, then splashed some water on her face. Apart from the red spots high on her cheeks, she didn't look too bad.

She swallowed then clicked the door open. Arturo was pacing outside, worry evident across his face. He moved to her instantly. 'Is it all too much?'

She gulped, hating how she was feeling. 'I don't want to spoil the evening. Would you mind if I went to bed? I think I'm just overtired.'

'If you can't do this—if it's all too much—you need to let me know.'

She swallowed, a huge lump in her throat at how understanding he was being, and how truly pathetic she felt right now. 'I'm sorry. I'll be fine tomorrow,' and even as she said the words, her brain told her that she had to be. She had to get past this. She had to move on with her life.

He put his arm gently behind her and walked her up the stairs to her room, giving her a soft kiss on the cheek at the door. 'Do you want me to stay with you?'

It was the first time she didn't want to say yes. She needed to sort her head out. She needed to understand why she felt so swamped.

'I'll be fine. Go, join your family. But thank you. I'll see you in the morning.'

She could see the tiny shards of regret in his eyes, but couldn't let herself be influenced by them.

He gave her a nod as she closed the door. She waited a moment before moving over to her bed. In the quickest change known to man, she slipped off the beautiful jumpsuit and her underwear, and pulled on her dark green shortie pyjamas, only noticing the colour at the last minute.

She still needed some air, so moved to the large windows and pulled one open, sitting on the window seat, with her back against the frame and her bent leg poised at the edge.

As the cool Italian air drifted in, she felt instantly better. It carried with it the aroma of the wedding flowers but, instead of distressing her, now she was alone, she just closed her eyes and let her body cool down.

She could call Fizz. She could call Libby. She could tell either one of them what had just happened, and that right now she felt as if she couldn't trust herself, or her own judgement.

But how did you explain something you didn't really understand yourself?

Tears glistened in her eyes. She had to hold things together. She had to keep her emotions in check—but then Arturo's face came into her head.

How was it for him? She'd been so focused on herself she hadn't considered him. His family home must be throwing up memories for him too, likely of his father.

He had to step into his father's shoes tomorrow and give his sister away. The pressure was real. They'd laughed and joked at the dance class, but now she'd had a glimpse of his family life and estate, she understood why he'd wanted things to be perfect for his sister.

Embarrassment swept over her again. He needed support right now, not a girlfriend who was crumbling.

Girlfriend? Was that what she was? She didn't even know that. What she did know was that she was glad to have a little space right now to try and sort her head out.

Tomorrow was another day.

And she only hoped she could get through it.

CHAPTER THIRTEEN

HE HADN'T SLEPT well last night, which was never a good idea when the next day would be so full-on.

He'd had breakfast at five, then again at six, with Dante, who was a mixture of nervous and excited all rolled into one. He was actually a joy to be around, and Arturo was delighted that he would be a full-time family member.

Cara had warned Arturo away from 'her half of the house' this morning. He hadn't even had the energy to laugh at her last night, and just agreed that he would pick her up at the last moment, to escort her down the stairs and out for the wedding. He could only imagine the chaos going on in those rooms today.

But even though today was all about his sister, the person whose room he was most curious about was Darcy.

She'd revealed part of herself before they came, and he accepted she might find some moments difficult. But other thoughts were circling in his head. If, five years on, weddings still affected her like this, was she really ready to move on? And if she wasn't ready—five years after the fact—would she ever be?

It wasn't the kind of conversation he wanted to have with her. Because then he would need to let her know that his feelings were developing into something so much stronger than he'd ever predicted. He'd seen her eyes yesterday when she'd taken in the vastness of the property. He didn't have a single worry that Darcy would be interested in his money, inheritance or family estate. The truth was, she'd looked downright terrified.

He moved across his room and touched the picture on his desk. It was from years before, him and his father together at a family ball, both in short-sleeved shirts and both laughing with their arms around each other. It hurt him with an ache he didn't like to acknowledge.

He brushed his finger across the glass. 'I'll do you proud today, Papà,' he said softly, then paused for a moment. 'I wish you could have met her. I brought her here, and now I wonder if I did the right thing.' He took a breath and looked out over the countryside stretching before him.

What he'd learned last night from his mother, and what he had to do today, had given him an insight into his current life he hadn't seen before. He had to take that into account today. Particularly when he'd finally answered the person last night who'd been desperate to get hold of him, and that conversation had been littered with innuendo and unspoken threats. He didn't take kindly to that kind of talk, and his phone was now in his bedside cabinet until this wedding was over.

The threats had never meant much to him. Since the death of Faye, and of his father, he hadn't really considered what might happen if someone decided to see a threat through. His mother and Cara would be taken care of. If he wasn't around any more, apart from his direct family, who would actually care?

The thought made him shudder. For the first time in five years, he considered someone other than his direct family—Darcy. It was like a little flower bud opening inside his brain. A chance again. A real chance at life. Perhaps the chance of love again? As the petals unfurled, he knew he had so much to consider. Maybe now was the time to reevaluate his future.

He knew today he had to concentrate on Cara. But once the wedding was over, he would be heading back to Edinburgh with Darcy. That made a warm feeling spread through him. He had to let her know that it was time to move their relationship on. Time to see where things could take them.

He only hoped that she would agree.

CHAPTER FOURTEEN

ROSA BROUGHT BREAKFAST to her room, and helped her fasten the tiny buttons on the back of her dress.

She turned around to get a good look in the full-length mirror. The lime-green satin dress was stunning, and was certainly something she wouldn't have picked herself.

It reached the floor but had a spectacular split, revealing some leg. It had tiny straps and a cowl neckline—similar to the silver dress that Arturo had picked for her. Maybe she should wear that, maybe the lime-green was too daring.

She held out her arm as Rosa fastened the corsage to her wrist. 'Maybe I should change? This dress is very fitted. It might be too much for a wedding.'

'Don't you dare,' scolded Rosa. 'You look fantastic, and remember I've seen some of the other guests. It's going to be a multitude of colours down there.' She looked up and down the length of Darcy. 'And while your dress is figure-hugging, there's nothing on show.' She winked. 'Just a bit of leg, and who doesn't like that?'

Darcy started to laugh. Rosa had been so nice since she'd arrived yesterday. She bit her lip and asked a nervous question. 'Is Arturo okay this morning? And the rest of the family?'

Rosa darted a glance at her. 'Arturo ate three breakfasts this morning. I don't know if it was nerves, or if he was covering every sitting to see if you would come down.' She looked at Darcy's wide eyes and shook her head. 'He's fine, as is Cara. In fact, I've been out of her range for nearly fifteen minutes. She'll have a list for me by now.'

Darcy took a few nervous steps. 'When should I go down?'

She could see other guests had arrived and were mixing in the garden. But since she didn't really know anyone and Arturo would clearly be with his sister, she didn't want to get in anyone's way.

'Give it another fifteen minutes,' advised Rosa, 'then go on down.' She disappeared out of the door.

Darcy moved to stand at the window. She wanted to focus on Arturo, and how he might be feeling today. She didn't want to think about herself in any way. That just seemed selfish. Today was Cara and Dante's wedding. They deserved the best day. And she would make sure that nothing she said or did would get in the way of that.

Thirty minutes later, the guests were still waiting. Dante looked handsome in his well-cut suit, his brother next to him. Their feet were starting to shuffle as they kept glancing towards the door of the house as they stood under the pink and white rose arch.

The man next to her had quickly realised she was English and had spoken to her a few times. He glanced at his watch. 'My bet was on thirty minutes, so I'm hoping she appears now.'

Darcy blinked. 'You bet on how late the bride would be?'

'You didn't?' He looked surprised. 'Of course, you're

Arturo's new girlfriend. You wouldn't have known about this.' He glanced around at the other guests occupying the white linen-backed chairs in the Italian sun. 'I think around fifty per cent of the guests put a bet on Cara being late.'

Darcy's mouth fell open, and he leaned forward and whispered, 'Remember, we're mainly family. We know this girl.'

There was some rustling, and the celebrant clapped their hands, bringing the guests to attention. The music started, and Darcy felt a little bit sick.

She turned her head and watched as Arturo and Cara walked down the aisle together. Cara's dress was beautiful, the top Italian lace with a white underlay, but her skin showing across her neckline and down her arms. The skirt was full, and she had a long veil that trailed magnificently behind her.

Arturo was wearing an immaculate dark suit, the same as Dante and his brother's. His bow tie and bright white shirt made his skin seem more tanned than usual. He caught her eye, and she saw the hint of a smile at the corners of his lips.

Then she turned back. It was an unexpected moment. If she'd thought things through last night, she might have pre-planned not to catch this second.

The second that Dante caught sight of his bride. There it was. The look on his face of pure and utter joy at seeing the woman he loved arrive for their wedding.

It was like a vice of steel clamping around her heart. Because she'd never had this moment. Her groom hadn't appeared.

Her breath caught in her throat as she blinked back some unexpected tears. She forced herself to turn back to look at Cara. The look was mirrored on Cara's face. She was overjoyed to be walking towards her groom. The love between these two was there for everyone to see.

The vice started to release on Darcy's heart, the gut-punch relieving itself from her clenched stomach.

Damian would never have looked like that at her, and she would never have looked like that at him.

She'd always known that the breakup had been for the best. But even though she'd told herself that all these years, she hadn't really faced up to what it meant.

It meant that she hadn't been paying attention to her relationship. She'd allowed things to drift on when they weren't right. She'd allowed herself to plan a wedding with the biggest thought in her head being that she wanted her sister still to be there for her wedding.

Her legs were momentarily like jelly and she gripped the back of the seat in front of her. The celebrant had started to talk, and the groom had presented the bride with her bouquet—another Italian tradition she hadn't known about.

There was such tenderness in the look between the bride and groom, and Darcy felt a pang in her heart. She wanted that. She wanted that moment between her and the man that she loved. She wanted someone to look at her the way Dante was currently looking at Cara.

A breeze blew across her skin and she remembered the occasions when Arturo had looked at her like that. A number of times when she couldn't wipe the smile off her face when she was in his company. The sensation of his lips on hers. His skin against hers.

The recognition made her catch her breath. Could he have looked at her that way because he loved her?

Her legs felt a bit weak as she recognised her strength

of feeling towards him. They'd been tiptoeing around the edges. Probably because things had moved so fast. But she'd never felt like this about someone. Never felt a connection like she currently did with him. Even the thought of Arturo filled her whole body with a warm glow. The glow of love. Her smile spread further. Should she be scared right now? Should she be panicking because she'd known him such a short space of time?

But she wasn't. She didn't feel like that at all. What she did know for sure was that she couldn't wait for him to be by her side again. Hand in hand, lips together. For the first time in a very long time everything felt just right.

Then other thoughts crowded her brain. He had family. He had family in Italy, and very clearly a place here. For now, in Edinburgh, Arturo seemed a bit rootless. He'd brought her here as 'protection' against his family. Maybe she was reading this all wrong. Maybe he didn't feel the same way about her at all. This guy had a dangerous job that he'd warned her about. If she continued a relationship with him, could she be putting herself in danger?

The seesawing of her emotions made her feel giddy. From one extreme to the other in virtually a few seconds. How could she trust herself right now?

Arturo shook hands with Dante and kissed his sister on the cheek. As he moved back to sit in the front row with his mother, his brown eyes met Darcy's, swiftly running up and down her body, then he winked at her and mouthed the word, 'Wow'.

And with that single word, her world catapulted yet again. Into a place where she might consider a future at his side.

Laura's face flashed into her brain, and for the first

time ever she took a breath and pushed it away. Today was about celebrating a gorgeous couple's wedding.

And as her face tilted into a smile for Arturo she let herself focus on only one thing—the here and now.

CHAPTER FIFTEEN

THE WEDDING WENT BEAUTIFULLY. Darcy—although not one of the immediate family—had sat by his side during the meal. He'd noticed a few eyes on them throughout the proceedings, and could tell that his more eager relatives were waiting to pounce and ask questions.

Cara hadn't quite been prepared for his father of the bride speech. He'd joked to her about it on several occasions. But when he'd broken it to his friends and family that his father had already written his father of the bride speech for Cara a few years before, silence had filled the room.

Those in the family knew why his father had done that. His mother's head was bowed, even though she'd been the person who had told Arturo. His father had written his speech when his life had been threatened ten years earlier over an artefact. He'd taken things *that* seriously. And the impact that had on Arturo couldn't be underestimated.

It hadn't mattered that he'd known that his father's death had not been related to his work in any form. What mattered was that for a time his father had believed the threat to be real. And in accordance with that he'd taken some steps, one of which was writing his father of the bride speech for Cara's potential future wedding.

Arturo held Cara's hand as he said his father's words,

his voice cracking in places. They'd only needed to be amended a little. Then he added some gracious words about Dante and what a wonderful addition to the family he would be.

By the time he finished the room erupted with applause. Cara's make-up was a mess and he might get into trouble at a later date, but the bear hug she'd given him let him know he'd be entirely forgiven.

As he looked next to him at Darcy in her stunning green dress, he could see tears flowing freely down her face and she looked as though she might be shaking.

He wanted to hug her too. But he had to support his sister first and foremost. So, in front of his family and friends, he reached down, took Darcy's hand and put it to his chest. It was a momentary gesture. And he was surprised by how many eyebrows raised at the intimacy of it.

Darcy blinked, leaving her hand on his chest, and blew him a little kiss with her other hand, the barest and most exposed of smiles on her face. And in that moment he knew. He knew that he loved her.

It had been there at the edges of his mind for the last few days. It didn't matter that it hadn't even been a month since they'd met. He'd never felt like this. Not with Faye. Not with anyone. Everything about this relationship had been out of step from the beginning. Their odd meeting. The bucket list. The fact he'd invited someone he'd only known for a short while to the most important family wedding he would ever attend. Deep down, he knew. He knew he had to ask her, because this just felt right. There were no other words for it. Darcy was the person he wanted to be with—despite all the other things he had to sort out—and he only hoped she might feel the same way.

The meal was finished, the toasts were made, and before they moved onto the evening reception, Dante and Cara broke the traditional glass, which shattered into a million pieces—the pieces signifying how many years they would have together.

The wedding guests cheered and raised their glasses in another toast.

As they moved from the marquee to the ballroom for the dancing, Arturo was caught with two elderly aunts for a few moments and bombarded with questions about Darcy, which he didn't completely answer. Once he saw them to their seats, he scanned the crowd for the lime-green dress. She should be easy to spot. But she wasn't.

He weaved his way through his family and friends, being stopped every few steps. It was difficult. Most of them wanted to talk about his father, and some, of course, about the potential of a 'new' family member. He couldn't walk away, even though the more the conversations grew, so did the lump in his throat.

Before he knew it, Cara was at his side, her face now immaculate once again. 'It's time to dance, dear brother,' she said.

He gave one last scan of the crowd for Darcy again. But he couldn't spot her, then accompanied his sister back to where his mother and Dante stood.

He knew the instructions for this part. Dante and Cara would dance first, followed by Arturo dancing with his sister, while Dante danced with his mother-in-law. After that, he would likely dance with a few more members of the wedding party, before hopefully, finding Darcy once again.

The first dance went like a dream. He could bet that Dante and Cara had also taken lessons, because their dance was smooth and elegant, followed by a little bit of fun funk at the end. He sent a silent prayer upwards that Cara wouldn't try anything impromptu like that with him.

On the music cue, he moved into place beside his sister, with a little bow of his head, before moving into position. As the Viennese waltz began he counted very loudly—in his head. But as they continued, he didn't need to count. It seemed that some of the things Margaret had told him were finally clicking into place. It became easier and smoother to dance, it felt more natural. Even with the layers of Cara's dress, it didn't throw him off balance, or accidentally step on her toes. And when they finally finished to a rousing applause, he was happy, relieved, and couldn't stop smiling.

He caught a glimpse of green. Darcy gave him a wide smile and a thumbs-up. As tradition dictated, the next dance was with his mother. By the time it was finished, he had only one thought on his mind.

He moved through the ballroom, then the bar area and the quieter room where some people were sitting, before finally making his way outside to the garden terrace. Darcy's silhouette was clear, her dress stunning. And as he walked up behind her, he could see the goosepimples on her flesh.

He slipped off his jacket and put it around her shoulders. She gave a little jolt, glanced over her shoulder, then shot him a wide smile as she pulled the jacket around her body.

'What are you doing out here?'

'Just contemplating the world,' she said in a faraway tone. 'It's been a beautiful day.'

He bent down and kissed the side of her neck. 'Since the meal, I've hardly seen you. I'm so sorry.'

'No, it's fine,' she said. 'There's been plenty to keep me occupied.'

'Please tell me you haven't been bombarded by my relatives.'

She held up one hand and counted on her fingers. 'Who am I? How old am I? Do we live together? Are we engaged? How long have we known each other? Can I cook? Do I like children? When am I moving to Italy?' She sighed and let her head hang down for a second.

'Oh, Darcy, I'm so sorry. If it's any help, I've had exactly the same questions.'

She hugged the jacket around her body. 'Let's just say, Italian families are...interesting,' she finished.

She spun around and wrapped her arms around his waist, leaning her head against his shoulder.

He was almost scared to ask. 'Are you okay?'

She looked back up at him and he could swear he saw something flicker behind her eyes. 'I am,' she said. 'When we get back to Edinburgh, we need to have a chat.'

It was like a stone settling in his stomach. He couldn't argue, because he knew he needed to be honest with her—about how he was feeling. He wanted to be, because he wanted, more than anything, to give this relationship a chance.

His mother hadn't presented him with the father of the bride speech until last night. She hadn't found it before then. It had been in an envelope tucked next to the diamond necklace that they'd always agreed would be Cara's on her wedding day. His mother hadn't had any reason to open the velvet jewellery case before then.

Darcy threaded her hands through his hair. 'How about I get a dance? I hate to think I've put in all these hours of practise with you, and then don't even dance with you on the day.' She had a soft smile on her face, but he could see an edge of sadness in it. Or was he imagining it? Was this a farewell dance? He couldn't find the words to ask.

'Of course,' he agreed, his mouth dry as he took her hand in his and led her to the ballroom dance floor.

As they took their positions he leaned forward and whispered in her ear, 'Have I told you how fantastic you look today?'

She gave a smile, which reached right up into her eyes. 'Not too shocking?'

'Not shocking at all,' he replied, his voice low and husky. 'Just entirely sexy.'

She laughed. 'I'll let Fizz know that you approve.'

The music had started and he spun her around. He didn't need to count this time. Dancing with Darcy had no pressure around it. They moved as one. After weeks of practice, it was as if they were meant to be in this position.

Due to the design of her dress, his hands were on bare skin at one point, and satin at the other. Although they both knew the frame and position Margaret had taught them, they were more relaxed and closer than normal.

It seemed easier that way. There were no missteps. No wrong timing. The music wasn't ideal for the Viennese waltz but neither of them seemed to notice, and as the music drew to a close, Arturo did one final spin, then bent Darcy backwards in a surprise move that they'd both seen professional dancers do.

She let her back arch and leg extend as he did it, and instead of a look of surprise she greeted him with a wide smile. Even whilst she was back in this position she whispered, 'Isn't this where you're supposed to kiss me?'

He supported her back and touched his lips to hers, gradually pulling her upwards as he did so.

Her arms changed position and entwined around his neck. Her body pressed against his as they both were fully upright. An elderly aunt and uncle next to them on the dance floor made some encouraging comments and Arturo let his lips reluctantly part from Darcy's to acknowledge them. She started to laugh. He bent his head so their foreheads rested together.

'Still can't speak Italian,' she murmured. 'Was it approval or disapproval?'

'I think we can safely say it was approval,' he replied with a smile on his face.

He felt her draw in a deep breath. 'Have you done all your duties this evening?' she asked.

'I hope so,' he said, sweeping a glance across the dance floor. 'I've done everything on the very long list that Cara sent me, except one.'

She tilted her head. 'What's the last one?'

'It's around the final dance at a wedding. Commonly known as La Tarantella. And it's usually guaranteed to make guests dizzy.'

She looked the tiniest bit sad. 'Then I guess we'd better wait.'

His heart clenched, and he absolutely wanted to ditch his sister's wedding at this point and just take Darcy upstairs. He wondered if Cara would even miss them. But a wave of responsibility swept over him. Of course she would miss them, and would likely be disappointed. If he knew Cara at all, she would spend the rest of her life telling him he'd missed the last dance at her wedding.

So he tightened his grip on Darcy's hand, got them

both some cocktails and took a comfortable seat and introduced her to some more family members.

He could see her concentrating hard, listening to the variety of accents. Most of his family spoke English well, a few stumbled over sentences, and after a while she turned to him, almost embarrassed. 'I should have made more of an effort. I should have learned some Italian before we came.'

He looked at her in surprise, because it had never even entered his mind. 'You hardly had the time. It's a nice thought though.' He swallowed before adding, 'Maybe next time.'

But his brain was whirring. Would he bring her back here? Would she want to come back, after he told her how he felt about her?

Things were taking on an entirely different perspective for Arturo now. Threats in the past he'd treated with disdain. Arturo was able enough to deal with anyone who decided to get physical. But he hadn't realised what kind of threats might have been made against his mother or sister in the past. Arturo didn't have a family—yet. Would he want to expose his future potential family to possible threats? Of course not.

His blood ran cold. Because there was only one person in his head right now. Darcy. And deep down to his core, he knew how he would react if anyone threatened her.

He'd known her for three weeks. If this was how he felt after three weeks, how would he feel in three months, three years, or three decades?

And how did he even start a conversation like that?

He ran his hand through his dark hair. These were his issues. All his. He had to deal with them, because the last thing he wanted was any consequences for the woman next to him.

She was talking again to his aunt. Her eyes were bright, her blonde hair shining, and her skin glowed under the soft lights in the room. She really was the most beautiful woman he'd ever seen. Without even thinking, he ran his finger down her arm and, without hesitation, she let his hand reach hers and threaded their fingers together.

The music changed and there was a variety of shouting. 'Time to join the final dance.' He smiled at her.

'Show me what to do,' she said simply.

The guests formed a circle around the bride and groom, joining hands together. There were too many for one circle, so some guests also formed an outer circle. The music started, the tempo quick and increasing with every beat. The guests began to rotate clockwise as the music speeded up, the circle on the outside going anti-clockwise. At one point, there was chaos as people came to a halt, then started to go in the reverse direction.

It didn't take long for Darcy to get the hang of things. She even kicked off her shoes as she stumbled a few times. The music reached a frenzied pitch as the guests shouted good wishes to the bride and groom in the middle of the circles and everyone almost collapsed in a heap at the crescendo of the music.

Arturo dropped hands and turned to pick up Darcy by the waist, spinning her around and kissing her on the lips as he set her back down.

'Can we lie down now?' she asked, looking up at him with those pale blue eyes.

He took her hand and led her through the crowd, still celebrating and coming down from the last dance. They made their way upstairs and along to Arturo's room.

Darcy leaned back against the door as it closed behind them, glanced downwards and flicked the lock.

He pulled off his tie, which was already loose around his neck, as she walked slowly towards him, before spinning around to show him the back of her dress.

'I think I'm going to need a little help with this,' she murmured over her shoulder in a low, husky voice.

He stared at the array of tiny buttons, wanting to wrench them apart, but instead taking his time to slowly, meticulously undo them one by one.

He got distracted, kissing her shoulders then her back as he released one after the other, before finally letting the thin straps drop down from her shoulders as she turned back around.

Her fingers were quicker than his, undoing the buttons on his shirt and trousers before her own dress dropped to the ground.

'You're sure?' he asked.

'Oh, I'm sure,' she breathed in response.

He walked her backwards to the bed and laughed as they fell on top of it.

And all talking stopped.

CHAPTER SIXTEEN

IT WAS FUNNY how some parts of her life seemed to move in slow motion, and others at breakneck speed.

After the perfect night in Arturo's bed, there hadn't been time for the chat they both knew they needed to have. Their flight was that day, and after she'd gone back to her own rooms to pack and had breakfast it was time to leave.

Cara, Dante and Arturo's mother had been gracious. If they'd noticed anything, or the change in sleeping arrangements, they were too polite to mention it.

From the moment they'd taken off from the airport, Darcy had found herself overtaken with tiredness and had slept most of the flight home. Arturo had wakened her with a smile, whilst she'd been leaning against him as the plane moved to descend.

He dropped her home with a kiss on the lips but made no indication he wanted to come in.

She wasn't quite sure what to tell either Fizz or Libby. So she messaged both with a few photos to say the wedding was wonderful, but not giving any indication of what had happened between her and Arturo. She knew she should have a conversation with one or both of them about how unexpectedly triggering she'd found the wedding, and the host of other emotions that had swept over her. But she just couldn't go there.

Instead, she focused on the bucket list. Because that was what had got her here.

The first two tasks had led to her attending the wedding. It had led to her facing up to part of the reason she'd built walls around herself, and also prompted her to examine why she hadn't felt able to start another relationship where she could invest herself totally.

Could Laura really have imagined any of this happening? Or had the message from Laura just given her the push to look at herself and the world around her in a different way?

She stared at number three on the list.

Make a lifetime commitment to something or someone.

She could remember the look on Arturo's face when she'd mentioned this one, and the fleeting glance had made her think that maybe—just maybe—he might have feelings developing for her, the way she had for him.

But Darcy didn't want to push. She didn't want Arturo to feel as if she was angling for more than he was willing to give. Their increased closeness gave her hope, but she wasn't naïve enough to think any further than that.

Instead, she needed to focus on herself. Making a commitment for the last few years *had* been tough on her—even though she hadn't recognised it at the time.

Signing her various work contracts had made her edgy. Signing for a mortgage on this beautiful property had actually made her feel quite sick, even though she loved it and the further renovations had worked out perfectly.

Now—a further commitment. What could that mean for her?

But there, at the back of her mind, was something. Something that had been nagging away at her, drifting into her head when she watched mindless TV, read a book that didn't completely capture her attention, or was just in that little spot between almost sleep and total sleep.

Could she really do something like this? She opened the browser on her computer—because the page had been bookmarked. Then she picked up the phone and dialled.

Arturo was furious with himself. He'd made contact again with the business associate who had been trying to warn him off an artefact. The bottom line was it had been stolen. And even though the current owners hadn't been the guilty party, they were still reluctant to relinquish their prize.

Arturo had been involved in many of these 'debates' over the years. Some people would prefer things were kept in dark cellars or basements than be allowed to be admired or enjoyed in a museum. Even when families didn't know they actually owned something, then discovered it through the gift of inheritance, they were still strangely reluctant to give up something that wasn't theirs to have. People had strange ideas about ownership. They had even stranger ideas about provenance.

He'd had a breakneck trip to Berlin. Then another to Sicily. He'd then received a phone call with a more explicit threat. And his mind had focused more completely than ever.

But Darcy had messaged and asked him if he would go somewhere today. She hadn't said where, but his response had been immediate. He would follow her just about anywhere these days, and he really, really wanted to sit down and talk to her.

As he pulled up outside her house, he noticed there was a different car parked outside. This one was a large four-by-four. Did she have another visitor?

She opened her door as he exited the car and gave him a broad smile. 'Like my new wheels? We'll have to take mine, as yours won't suit.'

He glanced at his low-slung sports car. There were a number of places it might not suit, so he smiled and climbed into the passenger seat of her new car.

'Mystery,' he said slowly. 'I think I like it, but where are we going?'

She gave him a smile, then took a slow breath. 'Since you've helped me with the first two things on my bucket list, I thought I'd invite you along to help with the third.'

His stomach squirmed. The commitment one. More or less what he wanted to talk to her about. He just didn't know where this one was going to go. But he had to be absolutely upfront with her before he could expect her to know whether she would consider a relationship with him.

'Where are we going?' he asked, not sure what the answer would be.

'Just watch and wait,' she said then tapped his leg. 'I think you'll be surprised.'

As they started along the road, he decided it was time to tackle the situation that had been on his mind since the wedding. Truthfully, it had probably been even longer than that.

'Do we have time to stop somewhere for coffee, or an early lunch? Just to have a chance to talk.'

She shot him a sideways glance. 'No,' she said, and it

seemed like an honest answer, which made him wonder if she was avoiding the topic of any kind of relationship between them. 'I've got a set time I need to be at the… this place.'

He frowned and she gave him a soft smile. 'Be patient. I'm a bit nervous about this one.'

He shot her a glance and she quickly added, 'I'm quite indecisive sometimes.'

'You are? Can't say I've noticed that about you,' he mentioned. 'But I have to warn you, I can be…what's that word Scots people use…crabbit, if I haven't had coffee.'

She laughed. 'Me too. But I promise we're going to endorphin city right now. Just be patient.'

Fifteen minutes later they pulled up in front of the last place he would have expected. 'Ready?' she asked.

'Not at all,' he said as they climbed out of the car.

The rescue centre was immaculate, and they were met at the reception desk by a woman named Jen, who shook Darcy's hand warmly.

'Hi Darcy. As you know from the email I sent, everything went very well with the home check. Probably because you'd already put a lot of safeguards in place. Now, it's time for me to find you the perfect match.' She held up one hand. 'But don't be disappointed if you don't find someone today. Sometimes it takes a few visits to find the perfect match.'

She looked over at Arturo, and Darcy quickly said, 'Jen, this is my friend Arturo. I'm hoping he'll help me choose.'

The noise of some dogs barking was clearly heard from the reception area, and they were led through the back to a whole row of inside kennels for the dogs in the rescue centre. Jen took them over to the nearest to show them a label. 'So, each dog has some information available. Their

name, age, breed if we know it, and some key facts about
what kind of home would be best for them. It mentions
if they can be housed with other dogs or cats, if children
can be in the home. It also mentions any special condi-
tions required for the dog, or any known issues. We are
scrupulously honest because we want to find the perfect
home for them all. One of the worst things we can do is
send a dog to a potential home then have them returned
because the new owner had unrealistic expectations.'

Darcy nodded solemnly. 'I understand.' She took a
deep breath, but she couldn't help but smile. 'I'm ready.'

Jen gave a nod. 'Take your time. If you want to spend
some time with a particular dog, let me know and I'll
open the kennel and take you through to our meeting
room.' She gave a final serious smile. 'Come and find
me when you're ready.' Then she walked down to an office and left them to it.

'You're adopting a dog?' Arturo was still a bit stunned.

'I'm adopting a dog,' she repeated, her smile widening.
'I've had my home assessment. I've talked to the farmer
next door, and he's repaired the hole in his fence. I've
bought some basics, and the rest I'll get once I know for
sure who picks me.'

'Who picks you?'

She licked her lips nervously. 'Apparently, my friends
who already have dogs have told me that really, they pick
you, instead of you picking them.'

'I'm going to pretend that makes sense,' said Arturo.

They started to walk along the row of kennels. Some of
the dogs were inquisitive and came to meet them. Some
of the dogs ignored them. Some barked or yapped. A
few growled. But Darcy stopped at every kennel, read
the card and bent down to see the dog.

After a few minutes, Arturo seemed to warm up, and got down to look at the dogs too. 'How long have you been considering this?' he asked. There was tension in the way he asked the question.

'Since we met that woman on the beach. It just made sense to me.'

They'd finished the length of the room and walked back down the other side. Some of the dogs were puppies, full of life and energy, others were clearly a bit older and more relaxed. She was glad of the identity cards since some of the breeds were unfamiliar to her.

'So, what size of dog do you want?' asked Arturo. 'Have you decided that much?' He was down on his knees, a Yorkshire terrier licking his fingers through the bars.

She laughed. 'I don't really have a preference. My house and land are big enough for any size of dog.'

She kept wandering along, stopping to talk to every dog, but eventually standing up and stretching her back.

Arturo came up beside her. 'No one pick you yet?'

She pressed her lips together and thought for a few moments. 'No, but I have an idea.'

She walked along to Jen's open office and stood in the doorway. Jen stood up, keys on her belt ready. 'Is there someone you'd like to meet?'

Darcy took a breath. 'Actually, I want you to help me. Show me the dog that no one else wants—the one that no one considers.'

Jen gave her a strange look, then bent her head. She was clearly thinking about something. After a few moments, she looked straight at Darcy, her eyes deadly serious.

She cleared her throat. 'I have an older dog. An absolute beauty. She's a former service dog.'

Arturo frowned. 'She sounds wonderful. Why does no one want her?'

Jen gave them both a nod to follow her and started down another corridor. 'Ruby is older. She's a red Lab. Labradors can be prone to joint problems. She has hip dysplasia. She had one hip replacement a few years ago, but is considered a risk for further anaesthetic.' Jen sighed and turned to face them both. It was clear she wanted to lay her cards on the table. 'Most people don't want to adopt a dog later in life, with complex health and care needs. She'll be impossible to insure, and her hydrotherapy costs eight hundred pounds a month alone. Your average person just doesn't have the finances to cover that.'

'I do.' The words were out of Darcy's mouth straight away. She looked at the expression on Jen's face, and Arturo's, and put her hand on her chest. 'No, honestly, I do. I work in cybersecurity. I've done well over the last few years. I can pay the expenses that will be needed. If Ruby likes me, of course.'

Jen seemed relieved. 'Okay,' she said and took them around a corner, where a red Labrador retriever lay on a comfortable bed. She had soft eyes and an adorable face. 'Hey Ruby,' said Jen, kneeling down beside her.

Ruby got to her feet. It wasn't quite a struggle. But it was clear she didn't weight bear evenly on all four paws. She still seemed good-natured and happy to be around people.

Darcy sat down next to her and talked to her. 'Hello Ruby. I'm here to see you today. You are the most handsome girl. What a beautiful colour. Everybody must just love you.' She rubbed Ruby's head, ears, and then started clapping her body as Ruby seemed to regard her carefully.

'So, you said Ruby was a service dog—what does that mean?' asked Arturo. 'Was she a guide dog?'

Jen shook her head, as she too clapped Ruby. 'No, nothing so simple. Ruby was trained to alert her owner to oncoming epileptic seizures. She was very good at her job. She would sense something and pull her owner's sleeve, letting her know to get down on the ground. Ruby would stay with her when she seized, watching over her and alerting assistance if required.'

'So, what happened?' Darcy asked.

Jen sighed. 'Her owner went to an event where the organisers didn't understand what a service dog was. They wouldn't let her enter. The owner went in, went to the toilet, had a seizure in the toilet area and fell and hit her head. Apparently, Ruby was going crazy outside and the staff called the police. They didn't even realise something had happened to the owner until the police entered to speak to her. Ruby was crying and whining. Her owner unfortunately died, and by then Ruby was too old to be matched as a service dog. She came to us instead, where we quickly realised she had joint issues. She's our longest resident. Three years.'

'Three years!' said Darcy, shocked that this beautiful dog hadn't managed to be rehomed. Ruby had lain down now and put her head on Darcy's lap. She was looking up at her with big brown eyes. Darcy leaned over and kissed her.

'Is this what it means when a dog chooses you?' Arturo said softly, his face only inches away from hers.

'How old is she?' asked Darcy, since there was no immediate card for Ruby.

'She's ten,' said Jen. 'The average age of a Labrador is around twelve.'

Darcy nodded. Jen had known exactly what she was asking. Darcy bent down and put her face next to Ruby's. 'Ruby,' she said in a soft voice, 'how would you like to spend the rest of your days with me?'

Something held Arturo's heart firmly and clamped hard. Those words. They touched him in a way that he was certain they shouldn't.

His head was spinning. After their connection at the wedding, Darcy had looked at her bucket list and decided her commitment was to...a dog.

While at heart he knew it was a good and kind gesture, he had to ask himself why the commitment hadn't been to him. To them. Being here today was compounding exactly how he felt about her. He'd asked to speak to her, and she'd made an excuse. Rightly, he should have tried to talk to her over the last few days, but work had been hectic.

Work had also been clarifying. He'd made a decision, one he wanted to sit down and talk to Darcy about. Had he got things all wrong? Had their closeness at the wedding not meant anything at all?

Maybe he was misjudging things completely. In his head, he'd been considering things. If they had a real chance at a relationship, he'd wondered if Darcy would think about moving to Italy. He knew that would be a huge step, but since she was just about to adopt a dog that step would be off the cards for the next few years.

He didn't want to have that conversation here. But it was clear when she'd been planning her future she'd not been considering leaving Scotland.

Things moved quickly. Darcy signed paperwork and took a note of particular things for Ruby, like her hydrotherapy appointments, her treatment plan and medication, what food suited her and what her normal routine was. Darcy was enthusiastic about every part of this.

Jen gave her a lead and collar for Ruby, then bent down herself to pat and kiss the dog. It was clear she was very fond of Ruby. 'You take her for four hours today as a trial, bring her back, and we'll do the same thing a few times this week, until we make sure she's settled and happy.'

Darcy nodded. 'Absolutely. I'll do everything I need to do.'

'If all goes well, in around ten days, Ruby will be yours.'

Darcy couldn't wipe the smile off her face.

She pulled out some things that were already stowed in the boot of the car, including a harness and dog seat belt and a comfortable blanket for Ruby to settle on for the journey home.

As they waved and drove away, she turned in an un- expected direction. 'Where are we going?' asked Arturo.

'A few places,' said Darcy. 'We're going to take her down to the beach for a few minutes. Apparently, she used to love going to the beach. Then we need to stop at a pet store to pick up her food, and although I have a bed I think I need a bigger one. Then—' she gave him a big smile '—we'll go to the drive-through and pick up some coffee for us and a pup cup for Ruby.'

'A pup cup?'

'What? I've seen people do it online. Let's see if Ruby likes them.'

Arturo hated himself for feeling agitated by a dog. He glanced over his shoulder. She was a beauty, and he needed to get his thoughts into some kind of perspec- tive. A dog. Something he'd never even thought about.

'Is Ruby going to be the most spoiled dog in the universe?'

'She's in her golden years,' said Darcy firmly. 'She deserves to be the happiest I can make her.'

An hour later, Ruby had paddled in the shallow waves with a little bounce in her step, they'd picked up her food and new bed, and she had shown them just how much she loved a pup cup.

'I never had a dog,' said Arturo, looking over his shoulder into the back seat. 'She seems very good.'

'I never had a dog either,' said Darcy. 'But when we were younger our gran had a dog, and we helped with the next-door neighbour's dog too. I'm not too sure I would have remembered everything about training a puppy.'

She started to look a bit nervous as they approached the cottage. 'Do you think she'll like it?'

He couldn't help but be amused by her worry. 'I think she'll love it. Do you think it's a good idea taking her back and forth between here and the kennel?'

Darcy frowned as they pulled up at her door. 'I'm not sure, but I *am* sure the rescue place know what they are doing. Maybe they're scared she'll be overwhelmed. Or maybe it's me they're actually keeping an eye on, and not Ruby.'

'I wouldn't be at all surprised,' he admitted, getting out of the car and walking around to help retrieve all the items from the boot. 'She's been in the shelter for three years. Maybe that's got something to do with it. Maybe it's a harder adjustment for a dog that's been there a while.'

Darcy opened the back driver's door and couldn't hide her smile as Ruby jumped down and sniffed the air around her.

'If it's possible,' murmured Arturo, 'I think she's a bit confused.'

'She will be, if she's always been a city dog,' said Darcy. 'She'll be smelling the sheep, cows and horses from the farm nearby. I did warn my neighbour I was getting a dog—just in case there were any issues.'

She'd told the farmer. She'd told her neighbour, but she hadn't managed to have that conversation with him.

'Dogs aren't supposed to be on farm land, are they?'

'Not unless they belong to the farmer, or are on a lead,' said Darcy, still watching Ruby smell the air.

She opened her front door as Arturo approached with the bed and food. 'C'mon Ruby, come and have a look inside to see what you think.'

Arturo watched in fascination as Darcy put out some food, just like Jen had told her to, and set up the bed for Ruby. He'd never imagined Darcy having a maternal side, but it seemed he'd completely missed it. Even if her maternal side only came out for dogs.

Ruby had a good sniff around the cottage, making herself at home, eating some food, drinking some water, then licking the glass wall.

Arturo had settled on the sofa, Darcy beside him as they watched Ruby. 'I can live with smears,' she said as she put her head on his shoulder. Ruby turned at her voice, came over, looked at them both, then jumped up on the sofa, sprawling herself across them.

They couldn't help but laugh, rubbing her head and patting her belly, and watching the dark red dog hairs coat the space around them.

'Going to need to get a better vacuum cleaner,' Darcy sighed, but the smile was still wide.

'So,' Arturo started gently, 'the commitment side—it doesn't bother you?'

She took a moment, opened her mouth and then just smiled. 'It's supposed to, isn't it?' Her eyes were wide as she turned to Arturo. 'But...' She shook her head. 'For the strangest reason, it just doesn't.' Her brow wrinkled, 'I mean, if you'd suggested this to me a few weeks ago— or put this down on paper for me—I would have been horrified.'

'So, what's changed?'

He had to ask, because it was clearer and clearer to him that he had to find out where he could fit into Darcy's life. *If* he could fit into Darcy's life.

She took in a shaky breath and looked at Arturo. 'I guess, in the space of a few weeks, a lot of things have changed.'

'Because of your sister's bucket list?'

'I guess so,' she said reluctantly. 'Or maybe it was just the right time.' She sighed. 'The right time for everything. To look at my life. To decide why I was where I was. To let something like a bucket list push me out of my comfort zone.'

'Am I out of your comfort zone?' He wasn't sure what he wanted the answer to this question to be. 'I have to be honest. I kind of hoped when you'd looked at the commitment thing on your bucket list, you might have considered something other than a dog.'

Her mouth dropped open. She continued stroking Ruby, almost using her as a comfort blanket. 'Honestly? You are? You terrify me.'

There. She'd said it. Was this his cue to make a graceful retreat and say nothing?

He shook his head. 'I'd hoped... I'd hoped that once

we got back home, we would have a chance to talk. To see what we wanted to happen next.'

Darcy closed her eyes for a second. 'But you've been gone the last few days.'

He cringed inwardly. 'I have. I was taking care of one last job.'

'What do you mean, one last job?'

He chose his words carefully. 'My job really isn't conducive to having a relationship with someone. I had one last thing to see through—something that my father had sought for many years. I've finally managed to return it to the rightful owners.'

She looked at him carefully. 'I would never ask you to give up a job that you love.'

'I know that.'

But the look in her gaze was panicked. 'We've only known each other a few weeks. How can you make a decision like that?' She put her hand to her chest. 'Based on me? Based on having a relationship with me that we've not even discussed yet?'

'Should I have waited?' Now he was feeling panicked. Maybe he hadn't thought this through.

She threw up her hands and Ruby jerked. So she placed them back carefully, and spoke in a low voice. 'I told you I hadn't been to a wedding in a while. It was...difficult.'

'It didn't seem difficult when we were in bed together, or did I miss something?'

As soon as the words were out of his mouth, he regretted them.

She flinched.

'Was it difficult because you realised you're still in love with your ex?' He was angry now, but kept it from his voice. He wanted to know why Darcy didn't seem as dedicated to this relationship as he was.

She shook her head. 'I'm not. But it gave me a chance to reconsider a number of things. Including the part I played in our wedding not taking place.' She kept shaking her head. 'I'd never done that before. I'd just moved on. Not wasted too much time thinking about it.' Now she met his gaze. 'Shouldn't that have partly told me what I needed to know?'

And now she'd started talking it seemed as if she didn't want to stop. 'You know the part that gripped me most about your sister's wedding?'

'What?'

'The way Dante and Cara looked at each other...' She brought her clenched hand up to her heart and shook her head. 'I would never have looked at Damian like that, nor he me.'

Tears were trickling down her face. Damian. Arturo even hated the name. 'Your sister's wedding was beautiful. But I probably shouldn't have come. The last thing I wanted to do was spoil things for you because I was facing up to what I should have, years ago.'

That made his heart clench further. The last thing he wanted was her to feel guilt.

'But it also made me face up to a whole lot more.'

'Like what?'

'Like I don't know if I'm ever going to be ready for a happy ever after. How can I, when I constantly think that my sister can't?' Her voice was shaky now. 'When all your relatives started talking to me, wanting to know everything about me, wanting to know if I'd be the next Mrs Fabiano, I just felt swamped. Just like when I saw your family home. I don't mix in those circles. I never have. How can I do it now? I don't even speak the language. How could we even contemplate having a relationship when we are so far apart?'

'Money isn't everything,' he said quietly.

She sucked in a deep breath. 'I know,' she agreed. 'But look at us, Arturo. Look at where we are. You have a job that's dangerous. You deliberately live far from home. I get the impression you haven't had much at stake in your life before this—' the tears were really flowing now '—and that's wrong. So wrong.'

'I didn't have anything to live for before,' he said quietly, and he realised that he actually meant it.

Another tear streaked down her cheek. 'You have so much to live for, Arturo. You're wonderful. But you need to realise that for yourself.'

She rested her hand on Ruby again, giving her a gentle pat. 'This?' she said. 'This is about as much as I can do right now. This is where I feel as if I can be safe. I know she'll break my heart in a few years, but I'll be ready for that.' She looked at him with tear-filled eyes. 'I'll make sure I am.'

This was all going so wrong for Arturo. He wanted to wind the clock back a few weeks—when they were sitting in the bar at the hotel, flirting, and everything was shiny and new.

There was silence for a few moments, then Arturo stood. It was the only thing he could do right now because his heart was breaking. 'Things have moved quickly between us,' he started.

'Too quickly,' she interrupted.

He hated the fact he was saying these words. He wished none of this was true. But if he really loved Darcy, if he really wanted what was best for her, he had to put her needs first, and put his own feelings aside.

'This isn't the way things are meant to be,' said Arturo softly. 'This isn't the way I want things to be between us. I love you, Darcy. I'm not sure when, or where, but at some point in the last few weeks I've met someone who's made me question choices in my life. Who has made me look at myself and let me know that I need to make changes to move on with my life.'

He took another breath. 'But I can't solve everything. You need to believe that you're worthy of a happy ever after, Darcy. You need to believe it, and reach out and grab it.'

When she didn't answer, he knew he had no other option available.

'I'm sorry it's come to this,' he said, hearing his own voice crack. He wanted to fix this. He wanted to make everything okay. He wanted more than anything to make his relationship with Darcy work.

But she didn't want that. And even though it was breaking his heart, he loved and respected her enough to put her wishes before his.

'Good luck with Ruby. She's found a wonderful owner.'

Darcy tilted her chin upwards. 'I think she's found me.'

And with a final nod he turned and headed out of the door. Out into his own car, away from the cottage in the country that held his person, and his heart.

CHAPTER SEVENTEEN

NOTHING HURT AS much as this. Not the acknowledgement that some of the things Arturo had said to her were true, and not the fact that she finally had to face up to her own truths. Her own life.

She'd been hiding away for the last five years.

The bucket list had been the kick in the butt that she'd needed badly. It had pushed her out of her comfort zone and made her examine her life. How could Laura have been so insightful five years ago?

Because at the end of the day, that was what all this came down to. Laura.

Darcy had shut herself off from the majority of her friends and family in an illusion of getting on with her new working life and buying and renovating a house.

All of it was the ultimate act of avoidance. While she avoided her parents and her sister, she was away from everything that reminded her of Laura. Part of the triggers of the wedding had been around the fact it was the last major event she'd attended with her sister.

It wasn't around Damian. It had never been about Damian. It was about remembering Laura in her bridesmaid dress. Remembering the paleness of her skin, and the way she'd trembled while they all waited. It was about the fact she'd fled for five days to Edinburgh and had felt horribly guilty about that ever since.

It didn't matter that Fizz and her parents had been with Laura those five days. It was because when she'd returned five days later Laura had looked worse than ever. And in those final two months she'd had to deal with putting a house on the market and packing it up, rather than spending every minute with her sister.

She knew that none of her family blamed her in any way. But she blamed herself. And even though she'd allowed that to beat herself up, and consume her with guilt, it meant that she didn't need to concentrate on the other part.

The part that told her Laura had contracted a horrible disease that couldn't be cured and there was nothing that she or anyone else could have done about it.

Accepting that would have meant eventually moving on. It would mean stopping thinking of every single thing Laura had missed out on. Accepting that would mean realising that she *was* worthy of a happy ever after. Arturo had seen it more clearly than she had.

And moving on was the plan that her sister had for her.

It seemed it was time to decide if that was the plan she had for herself.

CHAPTER EIGHTEEN

IT HAD BEEN five days, and Arturo couldn't bear it a second longer. The more he thought things through and processed, the more he came up with a million other ways he could have handled it and sorted things between them.

He wanted to see Darcy. He wanted to phone her or message her or go to her house, but he wasn't sure how she felt. And that made his heart ache.

After days of pacing, he finally decided to take the bull by the horns and try a neutral venue.

Jen looked up in surprise as he walked into the rescue centre. He gave her a cautious smile. 'I came to see if Darcy was here to pick up Ruby.'

She frowned slightly. 'She changed her day. She had her yesterday, and Ruby's going home day is on Sunday.'

He swallowed, thrown for a few seconds by the change of plan. 'Did she say why she had to change?' he ventured.

It seemed that Jen took pity on him. 'Something about a bucket list. The last thing on it.'

His skin prickled. The last instruction on the bucket list.

Find somewhere peaceful...to reflect on what you want out of life.

But where would Darcy go? Did she have somewhere in her home town of Bath that she'd consider a place to contemplate the world? Or maybe some place she'd gone with Laura? He tried to think of anywhere in Edinburgh. But there could be a million places. Up at Arthur's Seat with a view of the city. The Royal Botanic Gardens or the Princes Street Gardens. Maybe even a trip to Ross-lyn Chapel. It could be any of them.

He was feeling desperate now. 'Did she happen to say where she was going?'

Jen gave him a sympathetic look. 'Something about returning to a place. I think she said it was in Rome.'

He froze. 'Rome?'

She nodded. 'She said she'd definitely be back for Sunday and couldn't wait to take Ruby home permanently.'

Every beat of his heart was pumping the blood around his body more quickly, an adrenaline response for what he had to do next. There was no question about it. If he didn't do this, he would regret it for the rest of his life— because that would be a life without Darcy in it.

And he didn't want to accept that, not without taking that one final step.

CHAPTER NINETEEN

IT WAS A totally different experience being here alone.

It didn't help that it was the middle of the night. And while the Trevi Fountain wasn't exactly quiet, it wasn't busy either. It was two in the morning, and there were a few late-night stragglers, and some tourists who'd obviously heard of the best time to visit.

Once the taxi had dropped her, she'd taken a short walk to the place they'd bought carry-out coffee and cake, then taken it back along to the night-lit fountain, which was every bit as stunning as it had been a few weeks ago.

But her heart didn't sit quite right.

She settled on the steps and looked up at the star-filled sky. 'Okay then, Laura. You've got me questioning what I want out of life. Is there a right answer to this question, or can I sit here and tell you that I still don't know?'

She dropped her head as she said those words because she knew that wasn't true. Her heart was telling her exactly what she wanted. But the steps were just too far.

As a few more people moved away she stood up and went closer to the fountain, taking a coin from her pocket. She'd already made one wish here, and it seemed like she might have blown that one.

Was it really worth making another?

She closed her eyes and spun around, ready to throw

the coin over her shoulder, but her spinning was off-centre and she knocked right into someone.

'Sorry!' she exclaimed, opening her eyes then catching her breath in shock.

Arturo did not look his usual suave and calm self. His hair was out of place, his cheeks slightly red and his jacket and shirt crumpled. He was a bit out of breath. Had he been running?

'You weren't here,' he started. 'I thought I'd got it wrong. I was about to go to the Colosseum instead.' He caught sight of the paper coffee cup and bag sitting on the steps just in front of them, and he obviously realised where she'd been.

'Oh.'

'We must have crossed paths,' she said, her voice shaky.

'That could have been a disaster,' he replied, his brown eyes fixed on hers.

There was silence for a few moments then they both started at once.

'I needed to see you again.'

'I wanted to see you.'

They both paused, looking at each other in the pale light.

'You speak,' he said.

She took a breath. 'Arturo, this wasn't ever really about us. This was about me. And learning that I have to move on. I've spent so long thinking I don't really deserve to. That Laura was cheated out of so much. That so many of the experiences I'll have now should have been experienced by her too. I haven't been able to move on for fear of leaving my sister behind. I guess I've spent most of my time worrying about losing someone else.'

She put her hand up to her chest. 'I lost an ex—who wasn't worth much—then I lost my sister. Part of me thinks I must have deserved all this. Building the pieces of my heart back together has been the hardest thing I've ever done. And I don't know if I can put myself in a position where I might have to do that again. Trying to convince myself that I'm worthy of a second chance is hard.'

He gave a solemn nod. 'And us?'

She gave a gentle smile, reached up and touched the side of his cheek. 'We just got caught in the crossfire. My sister gave me a bucket list to teach me to live again. I got the pleasure of doing that with you.'

He caught her hand in his, holding it next to his cheek. 'I love you, Darcy. I never expected to. I don't even know if I'm supposed to. All I know is that, from the moment I met you, we've connected in a way I've never felt before.'

She blinked, feeling tears brim in her eyes. 'And I love you too, Arturo. I've never met anyone like you. I've learned to dance, had a whistlestop tour of Rome. I've been to an incredible family wedding and picked a wonderful dog. You've given me the best memories possible.'

'But...?' he asked, his voice wary.

'But,' she said as some tears started to fall, 'what if I lose you too? What if I take a chance on you, on us, and it doesn't work out? What if I get left again, and this time I don't have the strength to put the pieces of my heart back together?'

He gave her the gentlest smile as he reached up and cupped her cheek. 'We are more alike than you know.' He gave a shake of his head. 'When I lost my father, and my fiancée, I thought that was it. My life didn't mean much any more. Of course I love my mother and sister, but I've always known that, deep down, they would survive if I wasn't around. I never found anyone else to invest in—to take a chance on. Until I met you.'

He smiled at her. 'How could I have a proper relationship when I moved around all the time? I thought if I didn't tread the same path as my father I would be letting him down.' His brow furrowed. 'But now I try and be reflective about it, I realise that the man I loved was actually selfish. He put my mother through heartache. He put his family at risk. I need to get over that. I need to move beyond that.'

Something inside her twisted. 'You said that you were changing your job. I didn't want you to do that for me.'

He moved his flat hand to his chest. 'And I'm not. I'm doing it for *me*. I'll still do what I love. Archaeology. I may have spells where I need to be away on digs. I'll likely work with museums around the world. But nothing that could bring anyone harm. I needed to see the big picture. Cara's wedding helped me do that. I'm sorry you were overwhelmed by my relatives. They love you. They want me to be happy—and they could see that I was happy—with you.'

He moved her over to the steps, where they could both sit down. 'But changing my job is only a tiny part of this,' he said seriously.

'Okay,' she agreed, wondering what would come next.

'It's about you and me. Are we both ready for this? Are we both ready for a relationship? Are we ready to take a second chance—on each other?'

He put one hand on his heart. 'I love you. I know I love you. But I think, in different ways, both of us have been in a bubble of grief for the last few years, processing differently, and dealing with things in our own way. I want this to work. I want *us* to work. And I think we might stand the best chance if we maybe ask for some help.'

She blinked as a huge lump appeared at the back of

her throat. He saw her. He knew her. And he still wanted to be here.

'I love you too,' she said. 'I didn't expect to. But the connection? I feel it too, more than anything. And whilst I hate what you're saying, in a way, I know it needs to be said. Our family were all offered counselling just after Laura died. My mum and dad went, but Fizz and I didn't. I think it's time for me to take up the offer. To learn how to move on without her, and not to feel guilty about it. And to learn how to have a relationship with my sister without feeling as though something is missing. To know that I am worthy of being happy. To learn that we can be enough on our own. And, most of all—' she took the biggest breath '—to take a chance on someone else. To reach out and grab the happiness that's right in front of me. To learn to not be afraid.'

He leaned forward and kissed her head. 'I don't ever want you to be afraid, Darcy. I promise you that your heart is safe with me.'

She mirrored his pose and put her hand up to her heart. 'How do you feel about agreeing that while we work on it we can still be together?'

He slid his hand into hers. 'I can't think of anything I want more. Your bucket list was fate, Darcy. For you, and for me. We can do this—we can do this together.'

She tilted her mouth up towards his. 'There's nothing I want more.'

He grinned and whispered in her ear, 'Then maybe we can create our own bucket list.'

'That will be negotiable,' she agreed. And then she kissed him at the most magical fountain in the world, tossing a coin over both their shoulders, because she wanted to start the way she meant to continue.

EPILOGUE

One year later

'READY?' FIZZ ASKED her sister.

'Absolutely.' Darcy grinned, picking up her colourful wedding bouquet and heading to the top of the stairs.

Although it would have been lovely to get married at Arturo's Italian estate, the complications involved in taking Ruby with them were more than either wanted. Ruby was getting older, and neither wanted to put strain on their guest of honour at their wedding.

Arturo, with the help of his sister, had found a beautiful Scottish castle to hire for the event and, from the sounds outside, the guests were already having a ball.

'Okay?' checked Fizz one more time.

Darcy nodded, and picked up the skirts of her wedding dress to start down the stairs. Her relationship with her sister was so much more solid now. In the last year they'd talked every day and seen each other a dozen times.

Her dad was waiting for her at the bottom of the stairs. He looked totally relaxed, and she knew he wouldn't have been able to resist checking that Arturo was already in place.

She'd never had a single doubt about her and Arturo. They'd spent the last year doing some individual counselling, then some together. Grief was a journey. And they were walking the path together.

As Darcy and her father stepped outside, the bright Scottish sun was high in the air. The temperature was every bit as warm in Scotland today as it was in Italy. 'This is clearly our one week of summer,' whispered her dad in her ear as he gave a little tug at his collar.

The ceremony was being held in the grounds of the castle, and as she looked down the aisle she could see her gorgeous groom waiting for her. Arturo was so handsome in his wedding suit and bow tie, and her heart swelled in her chest.

She practically wanted to skip down the aisle, but she let Fizz walk in front of her, nodding at her own beau as she went, then Darcy and her father walked down the rose-strewn aisle.

Whilst her father nodded at their guests, Darcy only had eyes for her groom. As they reached the front he bent forward and whispered in her ear. 'You look stunning.'

She couldn't stop smiling. Her dress had incorporated some Italian lace to pay homage to her new family and she'd had fun choosing it with her mum, sister, Cara and Arturo's mother.

They both turned to watch Ruby, with the rings tied around her neck, come towards them. Her joints had been giving her issues and she had developed a limp, but to Darcy and Arturo she just represented love. Arturo bent down, gave her a treat, a kiss on her head, and untied the rings. Ruby sat proudly at their feet.

The celebrant started the ceremony and it passed in a blur for Darcy, as they sang some songs of celebration and exchanged rings.

As the celebrant announced them man and wife, Arturo settled his hands on his hips. He couldn't stop smiling. 'Well, my Bucket List Bride,' he said, 'how about we seal this with a kiss?'

Then he caught her and tipped her backwards, recreating their kiss from a year before as their guests shouted and Ruby barked in celebration.

* * * * *

A FAKE BRIDE'S GUIDE TO FOREVER

KATE HARDY

MILLS & BOON

For Scarlet—always a joy to work with you! xxx

CHAPTER ONE

FIZZ GLANCED AT her phone for the umpteenth time. All of twelve seconds had passed since she'd last checked, even though it felt more like several minutes.

Oliver was nearly twenty minutes late.

It wasn't like him: her best friend was the epitome of organised, taking everything in his stride with a smile on his face and never being late for anything. Had something awful happened? Her nerves, already taut from wondering just what her sister Laura had written in her last letter, stretched that little bit tighter.

Then she saw the heads turning, looked in the same direction and let out the breath she hadn't even realised she was holding as she saw him walking into the wine bar. Oliver Harrison was the archetypal tall, dark and handsome man. Add eyes as blue as a spring sky and a ready smile that reached his eyes, and it was no wonder that women turned to stare at him as he passed. He had the same kind of stage presence as a movie star or rock hero.

He lifted a hand to acknowledge her; she mirrored the gesture, noting the disappointment on several female faces around him as they realised that he was meeting someone. Two minutes later, he slid into the booth opposite her and replaced her empty glass with a glass of chilled white wine. 'I assumed you'd like your usual,' he said.

A crisp and fruity New Zealand Sauvignon Blanc: her favourite. 'Thank you. Is everything OK, Oli?' she asked, concerned about that look of strain in his eyes— or was she projecting her own anxieties onto him?

'Just something I needed to sort out in the office that took a bit longer than I expected,' he said. 'Sorry. I should've texted you so you didn't worry. I thought I could make the time up, but then there was a delay on the Tube.'

Oliver's loveliness wasn't only in his looks: he was kind, thoughtful and paid attention. Yet more reasons why Fizz valued him so much. Her best friend was the most important person in her life outside her sisters and her parents.

'I was a bit surprised you asked me to meet you tonight. I thought you'd be with your family after you'd seen the solicitor—or at least with Darcy,' he said.

Her oldest sister. The one who'd met the solicitor with her…and then left. Fizz lifted a shoulder with a casualness she didn't feel. 'Mum and Dad are in the south of France.' Not because they'd forgotten Laura's anniversary, but because they still couldn't bear it. They'd gone to Provence to put distance between themselves and their home in Bath where her other sister Laura had taken her last breath. 'And Darcy had to go back to Edinburgh. Work.'

It was five hours between London and Edinburgh by train, and seven and a half by car: of course Darcy had needed to leave straight after their quick cocktail in the bar next door to the solicitor's office. But Fizz had hoped that Darcy might stay a bit longer. Just long enough to open Laura's letters to them together, rather than tackling them alone. Especially as today was the fifth anniversary of Laura's death from leukaemia. She usually kept Laura's anniversary as a quiet day, missing her middle sister's sunny nature; but the day felt heavier than usual, today.

Darcy had suggested they could text each other about the letters, instead. Fizz didn't suggest a phone or video call because *she* wouldn't want to have that kind of conversation in the corridor of a train so she wasn't going to make Darcy do that. Faced with behaving like the needy, annoying little sister who demanded attention—and that wasn't who she wanted to be—Fizz had forced a smile she didn't feel and agreed that texting would be fine.

It seemed that the distance between herself and Darcy wasn't just physical any more; it was becoming emotional as well.

And that *really* hurt.

It was bad enough that the 'Trouble Trio', as their parents had always called them when they were tiny, were a duo now that Laura was gone. Did Darcy want them to become the Sad Singles? Or was she just overreacting on a day she always found difficult? Fizz didn't really trust her judgement where Laura was concerned. Or Darcy. All she knew was that she missed her sisters.

Both of them.

Oliver reached across the table and squeezed her hand briefly. 'Are you OK, Fizz?'

'Yes,' she fibbed.

He raised both eyebrows and stared at her. She caved. Of course he knew her well enough to realise that she wasn't OK. He'd been her best friend for seven years, since they'd met at a mutual friend's birthday party in her first year at art school while he'd been in the first term of doing his Master's in Arts and Cultural Management. They'd talked all night, to the point of grabbing a mug of coffee from the kitchen and going to the top of Primrose Hill to watch the sunrise together, and they'd never looked back.

'No, I'm not all right,' she admitted, and lifted her chin. 'But I will be.'

'What did the solicitor have to say?' Oliver asked.

Fizz drew the envelope from her bag. Even seeing Laura's familiar handwriting looping across it made her catch her breath. Laura had even sketched a tiny champagne bottle with the cork flying out and bubbles cascading everywhere. Felicity Bennett, the youngest of the three sisters, had been known to everyone as 'Fizz' ever since she'd pronounced her name that way as a toddler, and turned out to have an effervescent personality to match. 'Laura.' The name came out as a wobble.

'Take a gulp of wine, breathe, then tell me,' he said gently.

The wine didn't help. Neither did breathing. But the concern in Oliver's eyes did the trick. 'OK. Mr Cochrane—the solicitor—gave us a letter.' Fizz had been the one to read it aloud in the office, and the tears had slid down her face with every word. 'Laura was worried about us. Darcy and me.' She blinked back the tears, refusing to let them overwhelm her again. 'She left the solicitor something to give us today if we weren't settled…happy.'

Of course their clear-sighted middle sister would've worked out what was likely to happen and planned for it.

A few months before Laura's death, Darcy had been jilted at the altar and fled to Edinburgh. Fizz had been torn between going with her oldest sister, who she knew was heartbroken and needed someone to help her through it, and supporting her middle sister, who she knew was dying. Darcy had made the decision for her: Laura's next round of chemo was in two days' time, so in Darcy's view Laura was the one who needed the most support. Darcy had told Fizz to stay put and look after their sister.

So Fizz had stayed in Bath, and texted Darcy regularly to check she was OK.

Darcy had returned five days later, her head clear and knowing what she wanted to do next. And she'd stayed in Bath in the dark days when they knew Laura was dying. Fizz had rearranged a couple of her classes so she could spend long weekends at home, and she and Darcy had taken it in turns with their mum and dad to look after Laura, bringing their sister little treats to make her smile and making sure she got to see everyone she wanted to say goodbye to, in between resting.

After Laura's funeral, Darcy had gone back to Edinburgh. Damian had broken her trust, and since then she hadn't dated much, if at all. She worked too hard; although her immaculate make-up could hide the shad-

ows under her eyes, it couldn't hide the ones in them.
Fizz didn't even know where to start dealing with those
shadows. Not when Darcy refused to let her help and
claimed that she was absolutely fine.

Fizz herself had gone back to art college in London.
And she hadn't told a soul about the day after Laura's
death. She'd gone back to London briefly to see her
tutors and arrange a couple of weeks of compassion-
ate leave from her course, plus pick up her sketchbook
and the project she'd been working on as part of her
second-year degree assessment. That night, something
had happened. She'd kept it locked away in a box ever
since and buried it as deep in her heart as she could.
It was the reason why she never let a relationship go
past the third date, any more.

Shame burned through her. What would Darcy say,
if she knew? What would Laura have said?

But Fizz would never tell her secret. Not to anyone. Not even Oliver, who'd been in New York when
it happened.

Oliver, who'd just asked her what the solicitor had
said. If she didn't tell him something, and fast, he'd
start asking questions that she might not want to answer. 'She left us a task. And some money.'

'What type of task?'

'It's a bucket list.' The words from the letter she'd
read out loud in the solicitor's office, holding Darcy's
hand, were practically engraved on her heart. 'She said,
"I want to push you both to maybe do something you
haven't. I want my sisters to have fun. Have fun in my
memory. Know that I am right by your side when you
do all these things. I love you girls."'

Typical Laura. She'd always been the sunniest of the three sisters; and it was because of Laura that Fizz's signature jewellery range was based on sunflowers. Not just because they'd been Laura's favourite flowers; Fizz saw her work as something to brighten someone's day, just as Laura had always brightened everyone's day around her. Of course Laura would always be there with them both, in spirit—and she'd be there with them as they carried out her bucket list.

'A bucket list where you have fun is a really nice way to celebrate someone as special as your sister,' Oliver said. 'I assume you and Darcy are doing it together?'

'Apparently we're supposed to do it on our own.' Maybe that was why Darcy had wanted to open the envelopes separately. Fizz lifted one shoulder in another shrug that she hoped looked casual. 'We might not even have the same list.'

He frowned. 'Don't you know that already?'

'I haven't opened mine yet.'

His frown deepened. 'Why didn't you and Darcy open the envelopes together?'

'Darcy thought it'd be better to wait and do it separately.' Fizz aimed for toneless, but of course Oliver knew her too well. He'd know exactly how much that stung.

'And the meeting was this morning?' he asked.

'Lunchtime. Darcy caught the first train from Edinburgh this morning. I met her at King's Cross.' And she'd tried not to feel hurt that Darcy hadn't wanted to spend the whole of today with her. Her sister had a demanding job; and they both dealt with things in different ways. Darcy buried herself in work, and Fizz… Fizz had spent the rest of the day walking, lost in her memories and trying not to let the sadness overwhelm her.

Clearly guessing what was in her head, Oliver reached over to squeeze her hand briefly. 'You could open the envelope with me, if you like?'

She nodded, not trusting the lump in her throat to let the words out and knowing he'd realise how grateful she was for that offer.

She turned the envelope over, slid her little finger into the gap where the flap of the envelope wasn't stuck to the back, and eased the flap open. Then she took out the folded piece of paper and placed it on the table between herself and Oliver, so they both had to turn slightly to read it.

'"Fizz's bucket list,"' she read. Laura had doodled a bucket containing an uncorked bottle of champagne, with little bubbles popping out of the top.

Oliver smiled and gestured to the doodle. 'That's lovely. I can almost see her sketching that.'

'It feels like a hug,' Fizz admitted. 'She must've doodled something on Darcy's, too.' But so far her oldest sister hadn't shared much: just that Laura had left little personal messages all over the bucket list.

'"It's up to you how you do this,"' Fizz read, returning to the letter. '"On your own, or with someone else. And it's up to you what order you do them in. Just do them within six weeks. Most of all, have fun. Love you, L."'

'Six weeks. Four items—that works out at one every ten days or so, which is doable,' Oliver said. 'Unless

she's asking you to climb a mountain or run a mara-
thon, in which case you need to train properly first.'

'She wouldn't ask me to climb a mountain. She
knows I'd worry about damaging my hands and not
being able to work,' Fizz said.

She glanced back at the list. Each item was written
in capitals and bullet-pointed with a sunflower.

Do something that scares you.

Fizz blew out a breath. 'Laura said she wanted to
push me. She wasn't kidding: the first one is to do
something that scares me. But, hey, nothing scares me.'
Well. One thing did. But she'd never admit that to a
living soul, not even Oliver—because then she'd have
to follow through. And she wanted to keep that bit of
her life buried. 'Something that scares me,' she mused.
'What exactly do I do with that?'

The one thing Oliver was pretty sure his best friend
was scared of was losing her other sister. But, given that
Darcy hadn't stayed for long in London after the meeting
with the solicitor, that was a bit too close to the bone right
now. Saying it out loud and ripping open her wounds
wasn't going to help, and it certainly wouldn't persuade
Fizz to talk. With his best friend, he'd learned to take
the oblique approach. She was always full of smiles, but
since Laura's death she'd used that smile as a shield, not
letting anyone see what was really in her heart. Even he
got the super-glittery smile from her, from time to time.

Instead of pushing her, he suggested, 'You could start

with people's most common fears. Did you know the top three in the UK are heights, spiders, and small spaces?'

He could see the relief in Fizz's eyes that he wasn't going to put any pressure on her to talk, right now, and knew he'd done the right thing.

'How do you know that?' she demanded.

'It was in an article I read last week on an in-flight magazine.' He smiled. 'Which probably isn't *quite* the most tactful place to bring up a fear of small spaces.'

'I'm fine with heights and spiders,' Fizz said. 'And I'm not scared of small spaces.' She looked at him, her blue eyes narrowing, clearly not willing to admit what really scared her. 'You're right—other people's fears could be a good place to start. Can you remember anything else from that article?'

'Public speaking and clowns, I think. Hang on. I'll see if I can find it.' He took his phone from his pocket and tapped into a search engine. Within a few seconds, he'd found the article. 'Here we go. Oh, you'll love this one. How about pteromerhanophobia?' Teasing Fizz might give her the chance to ground herself and feel less vulnerable. The alternative was wrapping his arms round her and telling her he'd fight every single dragon for her: single-handedly, without a scrap of armour and while walking barefoot over a path of molten lava. But he didn't think she was ready to hear that. Not right now, and maybe not ever. So he'd keep it light, the way he always did.

'Obviously the last bit means "fear of",' she said, 'but the first?'

'Think of something that starts with "ptero",' he said.

'Pterodactyl,' she said promptly.

'Strictly speaking, that should be ptero*saur*,' he said.

She rolled her eyes. 'You're *such* a pedant, Oliver Harrison.'

'It goes with my job, as well as yours. Attention to detail is important,' he retorted. If she was insulting him, that meant she wasn't going to cry. Which was a good thing. 'And a pterosaur is?'

'A flying dinosaur. OK. Fear of flying. Though you of course had to find the long word for it.'

She smiled at him, and his heart rate kicked up a notch. Oliver just hoped it didn't show in his expression. He knew Fizz saw him as her best friend, not as a potential life partner. Definitely not as a lover. Apart from that moment when she'd told him about her middle sister's prognosis and he'd wrapped his arms round her, wanting to comfort her, and somehow they'd ended up sharing a kiss: a kiss that had melted his bones and made him want so much more. But he'd pulled back, knowing that Fizz was vulnerable and refusing to take advantage of that. He'd wanted her; but he wanted her to want him for *himself*, not for comfort. Back then he'd decided until Fizz was ready to give her heart to him, he wasn't going to tell her how he felt about her. But she never had. So he'd buried those feelings, determined to protect their friendship. She didn't need the pressure. But she did need him—as a friend. And if she thought he was a workaholic: well, that was a good enough cover for why he didn't date much. For now, anyway.

She steepled her fingers. 'What else are people scared of?'

'There's a new kid on the block: nomophobia. That's the fear of not having a mobile phone,' he said.

'Utterly ridiculous,' she said, dismissing it with a roll of her eyes. 'You can always borrow a phone from someone if your battery dies. And our parents and grandparents managed just fine without a mobile phone when they were our age. Any more?'

'Dentists, needles, dogs, balloons…oh, wait, here's one for you. Garlic.'

To his relief, this time she laughed. 'I love garlic dough balls. I'm not scared of garlic—or vampires, if that's what you were implying.' She raised her eyebrow at him. 'What are you scared of?'

I used to be afraid that you'd never fall in love with me, the way I fell in love with you.

He definitely wasn't sharing that one. 'Making a monumental cock-up at work when I'm valuing a painting—or losing my head at an auction and going way beyond Dad's maximum bid.'

She laughed. 'That's never going to happen. Not with your attention to detail.' She wrinkled her nose. 'And that wouldn't happen for me, either. I always check with my clients if I can't find the perfect stone within their budget, to see whether they'd be prepared to compromise on colour, clarity or size instead. I should've been working on a commission, this afternoon, but wrapping silver around really fragile gems isn't a good idea on a day when you can't concentrate properly. I didn't want to end up with a pile of fragments, so I'll catch up with myself tomorrow.' She shrugged. 'Better doing a super-long day than ruining my stock and having to start all over again.'

'What did you do after Darcy left?' he asked.

'A bit of urban hiking,' she said. 'I went to Primrose Hill.'

Where they'd watched the sunrise together, the first day they'd met. Had she gone there because it was a happy place for her, filled with good memories? He hoped so.

'I stopped for coffee, a couple of times. And I stuffed my face with cake, to the point where I definitely don't want dinner tonight.' She rolled her eyes. 'And, yes, I know cake isn't great nutrition.'

'Some days you just need cake. Tomorrow you can make up for it with a wheatgrass smoothie,' he said with a smile.

She grimaced. 'That's the worst thing I've ever tasted! I'll pass on the smoothie, but I promise I'll eat proper food tomorrow.' She paused. 'Something I'm scared of needs a bit more thought. I'll put that at the end of the list.' She looked at the paper in front of them. '"*Go somewhere nice and quiet, take time to reflect on what you want out of life.*"' She wrinkled her nose. 'That probably needs to be a later task, too.'

'How would you define "nice and quiet"?' he asked.

'A beach,' she said instantly. 'Not a tropical one—I want a big, wide, sandy one where you can watch the sun rise. Where the sea swishes on the shore.'

He wasn't surprised. Fizz was a sunrise rather than a sunset person. 'The east coast of England, then. Norfolk or Northumbria?'

'Or a garden. The sort you get at a stately home, but when it's not open. Something stuffed with colour and scent and loveliness.' She smiled. 'You know me and flowers.'

'Half the time, you're thinking about what kind of jewellery they put in your mind,' he said.

'Are you calling me a workaholic?' she asked. 'Because it takes one to know one.'

'I know.' A garden not open to the public, he could definitely offer her. But he wouldn't push her just yet. She needed time to work out what she wanted. 'What's next?'

'"*Make a commitment to someone or something.*"'

That would make her run a mile, Oliver knew. Apart from her career, Darcy and her parents—and himself, in terms of being her best friend—Fizz was very careful not to commit to anything or anyone. She'd practically stopped dating ever since Laura's death.

'She's added a note,' Fizz said. 'She says it has to be something that lasts a few years.'

'So, what? Do a qualification? Join some kind of club?'

Or commit to someone...

Oliver thought about the news he'd received before coming here. He needed to make a commitment himself. But he couldn't ask Fizz to do that with him. Not without risking losing the relationship he valued most, and he wasn't prepared to do that.

'I don't know.' She sighed. 'There's another note here to say it has to be something important.'

'Mentor someone?' he suggested.

She shrugged. 'Maybe. I think the easiest one is going to be the last one. *"Have a wild twenty-four hours in a European city you've always wanted to go to.'* And apparently I can take someone with me.'

'Darcy?' he asked.

She shook her head. 'I don't think that's an option.'

He frowned. 'Surely Laura suggested it to help the two of you get close again?'

'Darcy's theory,' Fizz said, 'is that Laura wanted us to work things out for ourselves instead of leaning on each other.' She sighed. 'I have no idea which order to do them in. Do I do the easiest task first—or leave it until last, as a kind of reward?'

'What do you really want, Fizz?' he asked gently.

'A magic wand and a time-travelling device,' she said promptly. 'Neither of which exist.'

'Maybe they do—only not in the form you expect. Maybe this is both,' he said, indicating Laura's bucket list. 'A way of getting you to a place where it's easier to deal with things.'

'Maybe.' She gave him a tight smile. 'How do you fancy going to Paris, Oli?'

'I thought it was supposed to be somewhere you've always wanted to go to?' He looked at her, surprised. 'Wait a second—are you *seriously* telling me you've never been to Paris?'

'I've been to France, skiing and seeing the sunflower fields in Provence. But never the capital,' she confirmed.

'You went to art school for three years. *How* have you never visited Paris?' he asked.

'Because I went to Florence, Amsterdam and Vienna instead,' she said. 'With Paris being only a couple of hours from London by train, I thought it was somewhere I could go at any time.'

'But you've always been too busy?'

'Building a business means putting the hours in,' she said. 'And don't nag me. You work silly hours, too.'

For his dad's business.

Where everything was about to change. Not that he was planning to talk about that. Today, Laura's anniversary, was a day when Fizz needed him to support her, not lean on her. 'Uh-huh,' he said.

'You haven't answered the question, Oli. Will you come with me?'

Go with her to Paris. One of the most romantic cities in the world. The city of light, of wide boulevards and pretty little parks, of cafés where you could watch the world go by as you enjoyed amazing pastries. Paris in the spring, at its most romantic, full of blossom and wisteria and lovers strolling with their arms wrapped round each other.

It was probably the worst place he could go to with Fizz. Yes, he'd forced himself to move on; but that involved protecting himself from further hurt, pain that would surely be caused by dancing with her on the banks of the Seine, or kissing her at the top of the Eiffel Tower! And yet, how was he supposed to resist doing those things in Paris? It was the City of Love!

On the other hand, right now she wasn't in a place where he could turn her down, even if he did it gently.

'Sure,' he said. 'When did you have in mind?'

'When do you have a space in your diary?'

He could move meetings easily enough. For her. He spread his hands. 'Whenever.'

'Let's go on Friday.'

'*This* Friday?' he asked, shocked.

'You did just say you could go at any time. Why wait?' She gave him her trademark impulsive smile, and his heart—annoyingly—did a backflip.

'All right. I'll book us somewhere,' he said. Somewhere to make her first trip to Paris special. He knew a gorgeous hotel just off the Champs-élysées, with tall windows, elegant awnings, pretty wrought-iron balconies and a stunning Art Deco interior. She'd love it. And he knew some excellent restaurants, too. Fizz loved good food with good presentation. He could make sure she'd always remember her first time in Paris. *With him.*

'No,' she said. 'This is all part of the bucket list stuff, so it's on me.' She grinned. 'Which means I'm afraid it's not going to be whatever Paris's equivalent is of Kensington or Knightsbridge.'

He winced. 'I'm not *that* much of a snob.' Though Oliver's background had attracted a few women who were more interested in his bank balance than they were in him; he'd learned to spot the type early and avoid them.

'You're not any sort of snob. I was teasing.' She patted his arm. 'What I'm saying is, don't expect something swanky. It's going to be wild and impulsive.'

Which was her all over, he thought.

'Cheap, cheerful and *very* Parisian,' she continued. 'And we'll go by Eurostar.'

'More eco than a plane,' he said, approvingly, 'and a lot more convenient for getting to wherever we stay in the city.'

'Great. I'll book something tonight and text you the details,' she said.

He nodded his agreement. 'Is there anything in particular you want to see in Paris?'

'The Musée d'Orsay, and I know it'll be a good idea to book tickets for that before we go,' she said. 'But the idea is to have a good time for twenty-four hours. Unplanned. Apart from seeing the clock and the Van Goghs at the gallery, we can go wherever the mood takes us.'

Oliver would rather plan the whole thing in advance, especially if they were limited to only twenty-four hours; without planning, how could they possibly fit in the gorgeous buildings of the Marais, the art at Montmartre, the narrow streets of the Latin Quarter, the Louvre and the Eiffel Tower? And he'd much rather buy skip-the-line tickets than waste half their time in Paris stuck in a queue.

But this was Fizz's list, so they needed to do it her way, not his. 'OK,' he said.

'So now it's your turn to spill,' she said. 'Tell me what's really wrong.'

'Nothing,' he said quickly. Too quickly, because she raised her eyebrows at him, and he caved just as fast as she had. 'Dad had a hospital appointment, this morning. I think it scared him.'

She reached across the table and squeezed his hand, letting him know that she was on his side no matter what.

At her touch, all Oliver's good intentions of not leaning on her went straight out of the window. 'It scared him to the point where he's decided it's time to retire.' He took a deep breath. 'And he wants me to take over. To be the managing director of Harrison's Fine Art.'

'That's a good thing all round, isn't it?' she asked.

Yes—and no. He didn't know where to start with that one.

'You love your job, and you'll be the third generation of Harrisons to run the company. Plus it means your dad will take life a bit easier, so you won't have to worry about him quite so much,' Fizz said. 'OK, so you're only twenty-eight, and that's pretty young to take over a family business: but he's been training you for the role practically since you were a toddler. You've worked at the gallery since you were fifteen and you've spent the last six years doing a stint in every single part of the business. You know the business inside out; you've done everything from restoration and conservation through to curating exhibitions, preparing catalogues and dealing with artists and auctions.'

If it was only that, Oliver would be fine about it. He knew there wouldn't be any mutterings at the gallery about the boss's son taking over, because everyone was well aware that he put in the hours, he listened to other people's ideas and he wouldn't ask anyone to do anything he wasn't prepared to do himself. He'd earned the job.

It was the rest of his dad's requirements that bothered him.

Now Fizz knew there was something wrong. Oliver wasn't paying attention. But it wasn't a dream that was distracting him; from the expression in his eyes, it was a nightmare. 'Oli?'

He gave her a bright smile that didn't reach his eyes at all. 'I'm fine.'

No, he wasn't. 'Just because today is—well, what it is,' she said, 'it doesn't mean you can't talk to me.' At the sceptical look on his face, she added, 'Think of it this way: telling me what's wrong will distract me and help me stop brooding about how much I miss Laura. It's always easier to fix someone else's problems than it is your own. Tell me what's wrong, and we both win.'

He grimaced. 'There are...' He looked as if he was trying to find the right word. 'Strings,' he finished lamely.

'What sort of strings?'

He took a deep breath. 'Dad wants me to get married and have kids.'

'And that's a condition of you getting the job?' She winced. 'Oli, that's really not fair. Not to mention going against just about every bit of employment law there is. He wouldn't be able to make that demand of anybody else.'

'I know,' he said. 'But I'm not anybody else, am I? I'm his only child.'

'Surely he realises that it's better for you to marry someone because you want to spend the rest of your life with them, not because you want to please him?' Fizz asked. 'It's not OK to tell someone else to have kids for your sake, either. What if it turns out that you or your future wife can't have kids?' She frowned. 'I know you said he had a hospital appointment today that shook him up a bit, but what he wants from you is completely unreasonable.'

'I know,' Oliver acknowledged. 'But it's not because he's a control freak. It's because he's scared. He wants to see me settled before he dies.'

The worry in his eyes flickered again, and she re-alised what Oliver wasn't saying. That he thought he was going to lose his dad much, much earlier than he'd ever expected. And she knew how bad it felt, to watch someone you loved die and not be able to do a thing to save them. She'd been there herself, five years ago. 'Sorry. Ignore what I just said. If he's that sick, of course it changes things.' She bit her lip. 'And you know I'll support you. Is it...?' She caught her breath. She couldn't face using *that* word today, but she knew Oliver would understand what she meant. And she'd be there for him.

'No. It's not what Laura had,' Oliver said gently. 'It's his heart. Apparently it's developed an abnormal rhythm. Considering he doesn't eat meat, he drinks decaf coffee and he has no more than one glass of red wine a day, he's pretty upset,' he added. 'Dad thought he was doing everything right to keep himself healthy.'

'You haven't mentioned exercise,' she said. 'Sitting at your desk is meant to be the killer.'

'That's what really shocked him—suddenly being out of breath on a short walk, as if he'd been running up a hill instead of strolling through the park. He's scared of taking Poppy out for a walk now, in case he collapses and drops the lead and she ends up in the road and gets run over.' He grimaced. 'Which I know is catastrophising, but he can't see past the fear.'

'When did it all happen?' she asked.

'It started a couple of months ago. He's been keep-ing it from me because he didn't want to make a fuss over nothing, but he admitted he saw the GP. The doctor gave him some medication, but it hasn't made Dad's heart rate normal again so the GP referred him. And he's tired all the time. As of this morning, the specialist was talking about surgery.' He took a deep breath. 'Dad's really, really scared he'll die before he gets the chance to see me settle down and have a family of my own.'

And she'd just told him his dad was being unreasonable.

Mark Harrison wasn't trying to be a control freak and organise his son's life, the way she'd assumed; instead, he was scared that he wouldn't see his beloved only child settle down with someone who'd make him happy and feel supported for the rest of his life. Hadn't Laura worried about precisely the same thing where Fizz and Darcy were concerned? She'd given the instructions to the solicitor.

'Considering my sister sent me a message from the grave for a very similar reason,' Fizz said, 'I should probably take back most of what I said. Though I do think your dad's gone a bit too far. Laura didn't say I had to get married and have kids. She just wanted me to…' She paused, trying to think how to put it. 'Stop grieving so much and start living, I suppose.'

'She could probably have written that bucket list for me,' Oliver said. 'Do something that scares me—that'd be taking over Harrison's Fine Art, because I didn't think I'd be doing that for at least another five years, and what if I mess it up?'

'Of course you won't. You're way too organised and capable to do that,' she said.

'Thank you.' He blew out a breath. 'And I have to make a commitment.'

'To the firm, yes; but you don't have to make the commitment your dad wants you to make, to someone else,' she said. 'That's where I think one of the other things on the list comes in. You need to find a quiet place to think and reflect on what *you* want from life, Oli. If that's the same as what your dad wants, then go right ahead. If it isn't, then don't get married to the first suitable woman you find, because you'll just make yourself miserable—not to mention your bride. And then your dad will feel guilty that he's ruined your life and it'll affect his health. It's a vicious circle.' She lifted a shoulder. 'You can come in with my beach-or-garden reflection trip, if you want.'

'I might just take you up on that,' he said. 'I'm happy to drive us both, any time you choose. And maybe your twenty-four hours of fun in Paris will help me chill out enough to come to terms with the rest of it.'

'Good. Given what you've just told me, are you really sure you can fit in going to Paris this week?'

He gave her a wry smile. 'I'm sure.'

'Then I'll book everything and let you know what time you need to be at St Pancras on Friday morning.' She squeezed his hand again. 'I'm sorry your dad's ill, Oli. I'm here whenever you need me. If you want to talk at three in the morning, that's fine. Just call me. And if I can do anything to help—drop in and distract him, and challenge him to a game of chess or something, just let me know.'

'Thank you. And I hope you know I'm here for you,'

he said, raising his own glass. 'To us. And to Laura's bucket list.'

'To us,' she echoed. 'And to Laura's bucket list.'

Later that evening, Fizz adopted the nearest she could get to a yoga lotus pose in the middle of her living room, and thought about what Oliver had told her.

Married, with children.

That would change everything between them. They wouldn't be able to spend as much time together as they did now; of course his partner would want him to spend more of his time with her and their children.

And it really should've occurred to her before now that Oliver would settle down with someone, one day. Just because she'd learned the hard way that love ruined things—she'd never forget how her sister Darcy's heart had been broken by Damian jilting her, and how deep the hurt had gone—and Oliver had fended off more than his fair share of gold-diggers in the past, it didn't mean that he wouldn't want to try and find love in the future.

Though, now she thought about it, he didn't actually date very much. She could probably count the number of women he'd dated during the last couple of years on the fingers of one hand. And none of his relationships had lasted very long, either. She'd assumed that it was because Oliver had been focused on making sure he knew every part of his family's business, knowing that one day he'd be taking it over, and his girlfriends hadn't been prepared to wait for him.

Though the timescale on Oliver taking over Harrison's Fine Art seemed to have changed from 'sometime' to 'right now', in the space of two seconds. And if he was serious about finding a bride...

It suddenly felt as if someone had strapped her into a G-force simulation rig and turned the velocity up to full.

She blew out a breath. Maybe Paris would be the last real time she and Oliver would spend together. Who was it who'd said about them always having Paris? It was a film, she was sure; Laura the film buff would've known, but she couldn't ask Laura any more.

Fizz unpeeled herself from the not-quite-there lotus pose, grabbed her laptop and flicked into the internet to check it out. Of course. Bogart to Bergman, in *Casablanca*. Not that her situation or Oliver's had anything in common with the movie.

Paris. A wild twenty-four hours they'd always have to look back on.

They'd have fun. Eat flaky croissants and glossy *macarons*, baguettes and good cheese. People-watch while they sipped espressos or red wine. Maybe they'd hop on a bus or a boat to see some of the famous sights, then lose themselves in the narrow back streets to find a different side of the city.

'Yeah. We'll always have Paris,' she said, and started looking for an apartment to stay in.

CHAPTER TWO

ON FRIDAY MORNING, eyes gritty from lack of sleep and half wishing he'd never agreed to this, Oliver met Fizz at the Eurostar check-in.

'Five minutes past six. I mean, I know you're all about the sunrise instead of the sunset, but this is a completely uncivilised time of the morning,' he grumbled.

She handed him a bamboo cup with a silicone lid and rolled her eyes at him. 'Don't say another word to me, Oliver Harrison, until you've drunk at least half of this. Our train's at seven, which means we'll be in Paris at twenty past nine. We'll drop off our stuff, and then we get to explore the City of Light for twenty-four glorious hours.'

'We'll hardly scratch the surface in twen—'

'Shh.' She pressed one fingertip against his lips, and his entire body felt as if it were tingling. 'No more talking until the caffeine's kicked in.' She grinned. 'I bet at work they've learned to greet you with coffee at the door.'

'I'm not that bad,' he muttered.

'Yes, you are. Being a night owl, you're only reasonable at this time of the morning if you've stayed up.'

He could happily work until two in the morning,

whereas Fizz normally fell asleep before half-past ten. Oliver was never sure how she'd managed to come by her reputation as a party girl. Maybe it was because she usually found a way to snatch some sleep in the middle of a party and then be awake again at four in the morning, fresh as a daisy. Though she'd stay up all night if it meant catching a meteor shower or a lunar eclipse. Just as he'd drag himself out of bed at a ridiculous hour to watch the sunrise with her.

'Come on. Let's check in and find our seats. And I've already sorted breakfast, before you ask. We have carbs.' She held up a large paper bag bearing the logo of one of the shops on the concourse.

This was the Fizz he was used to. Irrepressibly cheerful, full of smiles and bright ideas, rather than the woman he'd met in a bar earlier this week, on the edge of tears. He knew that Fizz and her sisters had their own tagline—*We're the Bennett sisters: we can do anything*—and usually she lived up to it.

Today she was wearing jeans and canvas shoes, teamed with a bright flowery shirt, a pair of dark glasses and a straw sunhat; she looked incredibly pretty. He was glad he'd asked her what the dress code was for their trip, because he too was wearing jeans, a light shirt and canvas shoes—a far cry from the beautifully cut suit and handmade Italian shoes he'd normally wear at the gallery on a Friday morning. Her backpack was small; he knew she'd learned the art of travelling light a long time ago. His own luggage was equally minimal, for the same reason; he'd rather spend his time doing something than queuing for baggage.

Once they were settled in their seats, she unpacked the contents of the paper bag. 'Warm brioche bun filled with brie, bacon and cranberry—there are two for you; *pain au chocolat*, also warm; a punnet of raspberries; and freshly squeezed orange juice.' She looked gleeful. 'I was first in the queue. That's how I managed to pick up this lot *and* the coffee before I met you.'

'I hate to think what time you arrived here.' The coffee was just starting to unscramble his brain cells.

'Probably about the time you might consider going to bed. Eat,' she said. 'And then I'll tell you the sort-of schedule.' Her blue eyes sparkled with excitement. 'I can't wait to explore Paris with you.'

Was she excited about Paris, or about exploring it with *him*? Though he wasn't going to ask; until he was fully awake, the words would come out garbled—or, worse still, reveal things he'd buried long ago, which would be a complete disaster. Instead, he did what she'd suggested, and worked his way through the breakfast she'd bought them. A few minutes later, the carbs had done their work and he felt human again.

'Thank you,' he said. 'That was the perfect breakfast.'

'De rien, mon nounours,' she said with a smile.

'Your *what*?'

'Nounours. It means "teddy bear".' She sang a couple of lines of Elvis at him, swapping *'nounours'* for 'teddy bear'.

He couldn't help laughing. 'I hate to think what website you picked that up from.'

'Oh, it was a good one.' Her grin widened. *'Mon petit nounours en sucre.'*

'I'm not even going to try topping that one. Unless,' he said, 'you're *ma petite minette en sucre avec une cerise sur le dessus.*'

He waited while she worked it out, enjoying that little pleat just above her nose when she was concentrating, followed by the infectious laugh when she'd finished. 'Double pun—topped it with a topping. OK. You win. And your reward is...'

A kiss?

He pushed the thought back. Where was this even coming from? He'd put away those feelings years ago. Maybe it was everything with his father, the idea that marriage was so much closer than he'd planned, and that Fizz, for the first time in a long time, was being vulnerable with him again? Besides, that wasn't what the wild twenty-four hours was about.

'...finding me a seriously good *macaron*. A violet one.'

'I can do that,' he said, and went hot all over at the idea of lounging on the grass of a Parisian park with her, making her reach up to take a bite of *macaron*. He really needed to stop daydreaming! To give him breathing space to get his wayward thoughts back in control, he asked, 'So is there a plan?'

'Of course there's a plan. Actually, I'm bending Laura's rules a little bit, because I got this fabulous deal on an apartment in the north of the city—they'd had a very last-minute cancellation—so we're actually staying for two nights.'

'Two nights is good,' he said. 'Though I wish you'd told me, because then I could've booked somewhere for dinner tomorrow night.'

'That's precisely why I didn't tell you. This is my bill,' she reminded him. 'We're going for "cheap and cheerful" and having *fun*. We don't have to worry about dress codes or anything else. I booked tickets for the Musée d'Orsay this afternoon, but the rest of the time we're just going to wing it. I arranged with Eloise, the owner of the apartment, that I could drop our bags as soon as we arrive in Paris, so we're not going to waste a single second.'

'You don't want to think about which sights you'd like to see while we're on the train, and plot them on a map so we concentrate on one area at a time—rather than zig-zag all over the place and use up half our time in Paris on the Métro?' he checked.

'I know that's how you'd do it, but no.' She gave him an over-the-top wink. 'We have rules to follow. Laura wanted me to have a wild twenty-four hours, which means no real plans.'

'You're already breaking her rules by making it two nights instead of twenty-four hours,' he pointed out.

'Nope. That's merely a bit of creative interpretation. My sisters would both expect me to take advantage of a good deal,' she shot back.

He loved bickering with Fizz. She had an answer for everything.

'But, since you clearly want to sort-of plan things… where would a dealer in fine art and a jewellery designer *possibly* want to visit in Paris, apart from the Musée d'Orsay?' she asked, her blue eyes sparkling.

'You tell me.' He batted it back to her.

'I suppose it ought to be the Louvre and Montmartre,' she said. 'And the flea market—actually, as that's near our apartment, I thought we could do that one first thing tomorrow morning. I'll put an alarm on my phone so I don't drag you about all day rummaging for bargains.'

'Sounds good.' Relentless shopping definitely wasn't his idea of fun, and he was pretty sure it wasn't hers, either. 'What about the Eiffel Tower?' he asked.

'Absolutely.' She grinned. 'I want to do all of the touristy things—you know, pose as if I'm holding the Eiffel Tower in the palm of my hand, and dangling the Louvre pyramid from my finger and thumb.'

'I know just the spots where you can do that, and I'll take the photos for you,' he promised.

'What do you want to do?'

He shook his head. 'This is your trip. Your first time in Paris. So it's what *you* want to see that matters.'

'You've been to Paris before. What's your favourite thing?' she asked.

'The clock in the Musée d'Orsay,' he said. 'Which is touristy—so I'd say you need to take a photo there—but it's gorgeous and I like the art there more than anywhere else. And I like the Marais. It'd be fun to *flâner* there, even if it's only for a little while.'

'*Flâner?*' she asked, looking slightly confused.

'Wander around and people-watch,' he explained. 'Drink good coffee. Maybe persuade someone to let us look through one of the archways into the courtyards that aren't really open to the public.'

She beamed. 'I'm definitely up for that. And this is spring, so I want to see all the flowers.'

'The cherry blossom will be near the Eiffel Tower and in the gardens near the Louvre—the Tuileries and the Palais Royale. You might even get the end of the magnolias, and the beginnings of the wisteria and the roses as well,' he said.

'Wisteria. Hmm. That'd make interesting jewellery,' she said thoughtfully. 'Glass, enamel and seed beads. Definitely earrings; maybe even a necklace and bracelet set.'

'Hang on—do Laura's rules allow you to work while you're having a wild twenty-four hours in Paris?' he asked.

'I'm not actually *working*, just thinking,' she said. 'Just like you'll be doing in Montmartre.'

He was more likely to find the kind of art that his family's gallery dealt with in the Marais than in Montmartre, though he wasn't going to be snooty about it and make her feel bad. 'If you want to do classic touristy things, you need to have your portrait sketched in charcoal at Montmartre,' he said instead.

'Only if you have yours done as well,' she said. 'Actually, better than that, we should have a joint portrait.'

As friends, he reminded himself. 'Sure.'

The rest of the journey to the Gare du Nord whizzed by. Once they were through to the Métro, Oliver wasn't surprised to find that Fizz had their destination saved in the map on her phone. Although she was way more spontaneous than he was, he knew she wanted to make the most of their time in Paris, so she would've worked out how to get to their apartment from the train station, as well as how long it would take to get from the apartment to the city centre.

Once they left the underground, they emerged onto a busy Parisian street under a bright blue spring sky, then after a two-minute walk she led him through an archway that opened into a paved courtyard with buildings curved round it. The three-storey white townhouses had grey slate roofs, tall narrow windows and wrought-iron balconies; there were zinc tubs and huge terracotta pots bursting with flowers by all the back doors, little round bistro tables with two wrought-iron chairs set around the courtyard, and lush greenery looking as if someone had just draped it casually round the doorways.

'It's hard to believe we're in the middle of the city, isn't it?' she asked. 'But Eloise says we're ten minutes from the Champs-élysées and fifteen minutes from Montmartre on the Métro.'

'It's not what I expected,' he said with a smile. When she'd told him she'd booked a budget apartment in the north of the city, he'd expected the building to be in the middle of an industrial area rather than anywhere like this hidden paradise.

There was a key safe set discreetly by the side of the door. Fizz tapped in the code, retrieved the door keys, and opened the door to let them into the atrium. The floor was polished wood planks; the walls were painted cream; and there was an old-fashioned radiator under the window, painted a dark green. The stairs were also plain wood, with a polished wooden banister and wrought-iron balustrades painted the same dark green as the radiator.

So far, so good, Oliver thought.

He followed her up the stairs, and then had to blink when she unlocked the door to reveal a tiny, tiny room. 'I thought you said you'd booked an apartment?'

'It's more like a studio,' she said. 'A bedroom, living room and kitchen in one.'

Only one bed.

He forced himself not to think about that. 'Fizz, am I being dense? Only I can't see a kitchen. There's a kettle on top of that cupboard, but a kettle doesn't really count as a kitchen.'

'Hang on.' She opened the door of the small cupboard. There was a mini fridge; the curtain on the other side of the cupboard door pulled back to reveal shelves containing a microwave, glasses and crockery. 'Ta-da! One kitchen.'

Just as well they were only in Paris for the weekend and would hardly be in the apartment long enough to drink coffee, he thought. The bed took up most of the rest of the space in the room; there were two tiny chairs and a bistro table by the window, which he assumed was meant to be the 'living room' section of the studio.

His expression must've said it all for him, because she winced. 'Sorry, Oli. I assumed there would be a bed and a sofa, and I would've taken the sofa because you're taller than me. But at least it's a *big* double bed. And I'm fairly sure I don't snore. We can cope with sharing a bed for two nights, can't we?'

'Yes.' Just as long as he didn't do anything stupid, like kiss her good morning because his brain hadn't switched on properly.

He couldn't even avoid the risk by offering to sleep on the floor, because there just wasn't enough space to do that. 'But don't complain if I snore,' he said.

'I promise. We can argue later over who sleeps on which side,' she said, and deposited her backpack on one of the chairs. He followed suit, putting his own luggage on the other chair.

'Let's go and explore,' she said.

Oliver wasn't going to let himself think about that bed. Or about what Fizz would look like, all sleepy and with her corn-coloured hair loose and spread across the pillow instead of being in a braid. 'Paris in the spring. We have flowers to find,' he said.

Oliver wasn't a snob, but he came from a wealthy background. He was used to space, Fizz reminded herself. His reaction to their weekend apartment had been a bit on the grumpy side, but she rather thought that owed more to the fact he was worried sick about his dad's health—not to mention the fact that he was supposed to be finding himself someone to settle down with.

But he seemed happy enough to walk beside her right now.

'Look—*muguet*,' she said, gesturing to the little pots of lily-of-the-valley outside the local florists. 'They're so pretty. And they smell divine. I'd love to take a pot home.'

'You'd need a lot of paperwork, first,' Oliver reminded her.

One of her friends was a florist, and Fizz remembered her talking about the certificates and licence she needed for any stock she brought in from outside England. 'Sadly, you're right.' She took a snap on her phone. 'I'll have to content myself with photos.'

They took the underground out to the Champ de Mars, and she caught her breath when she saw all the trees; the fat, fluffy clumps of bright pink flowers were the perfect counterpoint to the blue spring sky. 'I love this,' she said.

He seemed to have lost his grumpiness, now, his expression showing that he was enjoying the cherry blossom as much as she was. He took photos of her under the blossom, so she could send them to Darcy and her parents, and then the touristy shot she'd wanted of herself 'lifting' the Eiffel Tower in the palm of her hand. 'That's such a terrible cliché,' he said, his eyes crinkling at the corners. 'But I admit, it's cute.'

'Now you,' she insisted.

He groaned, but went along with it.

'I don't think we're going to climb the Tower just yet,' she said, grimacing at the long queues.

'Later is definitely a good idea,' he said. 'And maybe buying a skip-the-line ticket. Because there isn't enough time to queue to see everything in Paris in twenty-four hours. Or even forty-eight.'

'Hmm. We'll discuss that later,' she said. 'More blossom, now.'

To her delight, they found more cherry blossom in the Tuileries, and a last bit of fuchsia-coloured magnolia in the Jardin du Palais-Royal; plus they were able to take the shots she wanted of herself pretending to grasp the top of the Louvre pyramid as if she were holding a bell.

'That queue's enormous,' she said, disappointed.

'I have a suggestion,' he said. 'How about we do the spontaneous twenty-four hours thing this weekend—but we come back at the end of the summer and do Paris my way?'

'Everything planned in advance with skip-the-line tickets?' she said.

'And a boutique hotel. And tables booked at good restaurants.'

'Which will be lovely,' she said. 'And I accept, as long as we go halves. But the whole point of Laura's list was to push me out of my comfort zone. Remind me how to have fun. Even though I like fancy restaurants as much as you do, I think Laura meant this to be about finding the unexpected. Looking for joy in simple things—good bread and cheese from a market stall, eaten in a park with flowers all around. And what you were saying earlier about persuading people to let us have a sneak peek at courtyards that aren't open to the public.'

He put his arm round his shoulders and squeezed. 'You're absolutely right, and I apologise. We'll do this your way. No reservations or skip-the-line.'

'Apart from the Musée d'Orsay,' she said. 'Though I haven't forgotten that you promised to find me a violet *macaron*.'

'I will.' He laughed. 'I know better than to deprive you of cake.'

'You're just as much of a cake fiend as I am,' she reminded him.

'As long as it's more cake than frosting. I hate sickly frosting. Where next?' he asked.

'Over there.' She gestured to a wrought-iron railing which had purple wisteria cascading down it. 'This is heavenly. And very Instagrammable.'

He took more photographs, and they wandered through the streets, enjoying the blooms.

'I thought you were teasing about roses. I really didn't expect to find any here at this time of year,' she said, spotting delicate pink damask roses climbing up a railing.

'These are Pierre de Ronsard roses,' he said. 'Paris is famous for them. You'll see them in gardens, on balconies in terracotta pots, climbing up arbours.'

She walked over to them and sniffed one. 'That's the most glorious scent. Who were they named after? The horticulturalist who bred the rose?'

'No—de Ronsard was a French Renaissance poet. I did some of his poems for A level, and I still remember the first bit of his *Ode à Cassandre*.' He smiled at her. *"'Mignonne, allons voir si la rose/Qui ce matin avait déclose/Sa robe de pourpre au Soleil...'"*

She translated mentally: *Sweetheart, let's go see if the rose/Which this morning has disclosed/Her purple dress to the sun...*

It was a lovely image, but what surprised her was her reaction to Oliver's voice. Speaking in French, he sounded slightly husky and incredibly sexy.

But this was her best friend.

Sex didn't come into their relationship.

She loved him dearly, but she'd never really thought of him as a lover. Not even that one time they'd shared a kiss... And she'd better not start letting her thoughts go in that direction! Not now, when they were sharing a bed tonight in a very tiny apartment indeed...

What the hell had possessed him to quote that poem? Oliver thought. The next lines were about the rose petals falling, which the poet described as the rose losing her dress. And now he couldn't get the image out of his head: Fizz wearing a pretty sundress the same colour as the de Ronsard rose, peeling the spaghetti straps from her shoulders and the dress floating to the ground like the petals of a rose...

He went hot all over.

This was impossible. He needed to get things back on an even keel before she guessed at what was going on in his head. 'It's actually about how beauty fades quickly. I guess it's the French equivalent to Herrick's *"Gather ye rosebuds"*.'

'Carpe diem,' she said. 'The posh guy's attempt at seduction.'

'Hey. Shakespeare did it, too, and he wasn't posh. "Come kiss me, sweet and twenty."' He stopped, aware that he was digging himself into a deeper and deeper hole, here. Fizz had been sweet and twenty when she'd kissed him and ruined him for all other women. 'The roses are pretty, anyway,' he said gruffly.

'They are,' she said.

'And what you said earlier about eating good bread and cheese in the park...' He glanced at his watch. 'Let's go and find some.' Food was safe, at least.

They found a little street market where they bought bread, cheese and a pot of olives; they were passing a fruit stall when Fizz stopped. 'I thought strawberries were *fraises*?'

'They are.'

She pointed to the sign. 'Why are they listed as *gariguettes*?'

'I'll buy some and ask,' he said.

The stallholder selected a punnet for him and explained; Oliver headed back to Fizz. 'Apparently it's a really old variety—they're very early, and it's something to do with the elongated shape that makes them taste very sweet and juicy.'

'Perfect,' she said with a smile.

They walked back to the Tuileries, where people were gathered round the fountains in the park, sitting on the slatted green metal benches and enjoying the sun and the scent of the flowers. They managed to find a bench to enjoy their bread and cheese; and the *gariguettes* lived up to their promise, too.

After a wander through the Musée d'Orsay—where they both found favourite paintings, and Oliver snapped pictures of Fizz doing the tourist pose by the clock— they headed for the Marais.

'According to the internet, this used to be marshland,' Fizz said, checking her phone. 'Though I guess you already knew that.'

He nodded. 'A lot of the mansions were built in the seventeenth and eighteenth centuries. I think you'll love the architecture round here, and it's worth having a wander round the Place des Vosges. It's the oldest public park in Paris.' It was a place he particularly liked, and he was pretty sure Fizz would love it, too: a gorgeous square with a fountain, edged with perfectly manicured trees, in the middle of houses with slate roofs, tall windows and arched passageways. 'You'll definitely get good photos here for your parents and Darcy.'

They explored the shops and galleries, people-watched and drank coffee; and he found a shop selling *macarons* in all different colours. 'I know this is meant to be on Laura's budget, but I promised you a violet *macaron*. Wait here.'

He came back with a whole rainbow of *macarons* for her.

'Oh, now this is clever,' she said. 'I should've guessed you'd do this.'

He took a snap of her with the rainbow of *macarons* in front of her. 'One for your album,' he said.

'I'll make Darcy, Mum and Dad guess the flavours,' she said with a grin.

'Actually, that's a good idea. I challenge you to guess the flavours before you try them,' he said, and had to suppress the sudden mental image of Fizz leaning against the bench with her eyes closed while he fed her bite by bite. What was wrong with him?

'It's very obvious. Strawberry, orange, lemon, pistachio, blueberry, blackcurrant, violet,' she said, pointing to each one in turn.

'You are so wrong,' he said. 'I should've put a forfeit in there for every one you get wrong.' *A kiss.* Oh, for pity's sake. He had to stop this. It seemed that food wasn't a safe subject, after all. In fact, no subject felt safe. He was going to have to keep a rein on his tongue.

'Forfeits are fine by me. I'll cook you dinner one evening when we're back in London for every one I get wrong,' she said. 'And you cook me dinner for every one I get right.'

'Deal.'

'And you have to share them with me,' she said, lifting up the red *macaron*. 'I'd say this is strawberry. Unless you've been very clever and bought rose instead, given that the last one is very obviously violet.'

'One *macaron*, one guess,' he said reprovingly. 'No cheating or ever so slightly bending the rules, Felicity Bennett.'

'Strawberry.' She bit into it, and he had to stop himself watching her mouth. 'It's raspberry—well, that's near enough to strawberry, isn't it?'

'No, it isn't. First point to me,' he said, accepting the half a macaron from her. 'Oh, this is good. Nice and tart. I hate the super-sweet ones.'

'Orange,' she said, taking the second. 'Oh, it's passionfruit! I love this. I think this might be the best flavour ever. And we need to have passionfruit martinis tonight. Can we find a rooftop bar, somewhere to watch the sun set?'

'Can't you have the cocktails and I can have a glass of decent red wine instead?' he asked plaintively.

'Nope. Laura's rules, I'm afraid. She even sketched a martini glass next to the task. I bet she did on Darcy's, too. Passionfruit martini was our sisterly drink. And you're with me, this weekend, so you're on the passionfruit martinis as well.'

He thought Fizz might be bluffing; but she was smiling and clearly having fun, which made him happy, so he went along with it. 'Cocktails it is,' he said.

The yellow *macaron* was pineapple rather than lemon; the green one was pistachio and orange blossom, which made her crow in triumph and amused him highly; and the blue one stumped her.

'It's a Marie Antoinette,' he said.

'And I was supposed to guess that *how*, exactly?' she asked indignantly, her hands on her hips as she gave him a mock glare. 'That's rampant cheating, Oliver Harrison, and you know it.' She took another nibble. 'I can't work out what's in the ganache. Honey, I think.'

'It's the Marie Antoinette tea, so it's meant to be tea and roses as well.' He tried it gingerly. 'Hmm. I still think the raspberry one's the best one,' he said.

'Nope. *This* one is,' she said after biting into the violet *macaron*. 'I'm afraid I don't think I can share this one with you, Oli.'

'Fair enough. Be greedy,' he teased.

She closed her eyes in bliss, clearly enjoying every morsel, and he couldn't resist snapping a picture that he most definitely wasn't going to share with her.

'That was a really lovely thing to do, Oli,' she said when she'd finished. 'Thank you for spoiling me.'

'That's what best friends are supposed to do,' he said with a smile. 'And you're the one spoiling me, whisking me off to Paris for the weekend.'

'In the smallest flat in the world, with a micro-kitchen,' she chuckled.

'And there isn't anyone else I'd rather share it with,' he said.

She beamed at him. 'Me, neither. Now, while you were buying macarons and coffee, I looked up good places to see cherry blossom. The Jardin des Plantes isn't far from here, is it?'

'No.'

'Apparently it has the biggest cherry tree in Paris.'

He stood up and held out his arm to her. 'Come with me, *mademoiselle*. Let's go and find you some more cherry blossom.'

She laughed and took his arm.

How could something be so perfect and such torture, all at the same time? He loved having her close; yet he wanted her closer still, and he couldn't find the words to tell her. It was madness to even contemplate it.

They found the enormous cherry tree Fizz had seen on the internet, and she insisted on taking selfies of them together under it. A slight breeze sent a cascade of petals over them, and for a crazy moment it felt as if someone was throwing confetti over them. He caught her eye, and it felt as if all the breath had been knocked out of his body. Had she thought it, too?

But he couldn't risk the best friendship he'd ever had. Particularly now, when she was doing the first task on Laura's bucket list and her emotions were all over the place. She needed this to be wonderful.

So he kept it light; although they didn't manage to get a ticket for a boat trip, he found a tiny restaurant with a view of the Eiffel Tower and made sure that she had the view, so she could see the Tower sparkling on the hour. The food was wonderful—a perfectly spiced veggie tagine served with flatbreads, followed by tiny sweet pastries with good coffee.

But he wasn't ready to go back to their apartment, just yet.

'I've been thinking,' he said. 'I know you wanted to do cocktails, but could this trip include dancing beside the Seine?'

'Seriously? That's a real thing, not just an urban myth?'

'It's real a thing,' he said. 'Tango and salsa.'

She looked at her canvas shoes. 'I really ought to be wearing strappy heels for dancing.'

'You can dance in anything,' he said. 'Do anything: isn't that what the Bennett sisters do?'

She met his gaze for a long, long moment, then smiled. 'Yeah. All right. Let's do the cocktails tomorrow and go dancing tonight.'

They walked along the Seine until they found the little semi-circular dance areas around the Jardin Tino Rossi. People were dancing in the centre to sensual tango music, while others sat on the steps and watched.

'Can you tango?' he asked.

'No. Laura loved that film with Antonio Banderas dancing the tango,' she said. 'So I kind of know what it's meant to look like, but I've never done it.' She smiled. 'Darcy said she's thinking about taking ballroom dance lessons as part of her bucket list thing.'

'Is that the committing to something task?'

She shook her head. 'Apparently, it's the thing she's scared of.'

'Well, if she's got two left feet,' Oliver said, 'I kind of get it. It's daunting when everyone else can do something and you can't.'

'People are too busy having fun to notice someone getting a few steps wrong,' she said. 'If Darcy had been in London, I would've gone to the class with her, for moral support. But I'll text her.' She gestured to the dancers. 'They're amazing. I guess we could always grab a drink and just watch them.'

'Or you could follow my lead and we'll join them,' he said. 'Or let's find somewhere with something a bit less complicated like a waltz.'

'You can tango and waltz?' She looked at him in surprise. The way he'd talked earlier about dancing being daunting, it had sounded as if he had two left feet. 'Since when?' She knew everything about her best friend—or so she'd thought. She'd had no idea that he could do formal dancing.

'My first year at uni.'

Three years before she'd met him.

'There was a charity thing. A local dance school was giving lessons, and it seemed like a good idea at the time. I haven't done it for years, though, so expect me to be a bit rusty,' he warned.

The sudden shyness in his smile made her heart skip a beat. Which was absurd, because this was Oliver Harrison, her best friend. She wasn't meant to feel like that about him.

'OK. What do we do?' she asked, striving to sound normal.

'Let's find the place where they're waltzing.' In the

next semicircle, she could see dancers spinning round, and it looked gorgeous; at the same time, the footwork looked a bit daunting. For the first time, she realised why her oldest sister might have been scared of dancing.

But Fizz didn't have to be scared. She had Oli.

He talked her through the dance hold and walked her through the steps, keeping them out of the dance floor so she didn't feel pressured.

Two songs later, any suggestion of rustiness on his part was completely gone. And she trusted him not to let her mess this up. 'Let's do it,' she said.

Somehow, the tinny taped music had been replaced by someone playing an accordion and someone else playing a violin. And it felt very different, dancing under the lights and the stars on the flat paved semicircle, the river swishing gently next to them. Even though they were in the middle of a crowd, Oli was the only person she was aware of. His strength, the way he led her round the floor, the unexpected whooshy feel when he spun her round—as if he'd swept her off her feet, yet at the same time he managed to keep her safely grounded. His gracefulness as they moved around the floor, his steps effortless and sure.

It made her breathless, something she wasn't used to where Oli was concerned. Sensual. Close. Her pulse throbbed with the violin, staccato and much quicker than usual, but it wasn't the physical effort of dancing. With shock, she realised it was the dance itself. With Oliver. Cheek to cheek, their bodies pressed close, the rise and fall of the dance.

If he could have this effect on her when they were both dressed casually, what would it be like to dance with him in proper ballroom clothing? A dark suit and a crisp white shirt, with herself in heels and a red silk dress that billowed out when he spun her round...

And he was so close. She could feel the warmth of his body against hers, feel the drumming of his own heartbeat. And his cheek was against hers. If both of them moved just the tiniest fraction, their lips would be touching.

Her mouth tingled.

A kiss...

She was only aware that the song had ended because of the applause from the other dancers.

Dear God. She'd never forgotten herself like that before when she'd been out dancing. Never been swept away in the moment. Never felt suddenly head over heels.

Maybe it was starting the bucket list that had stirred up her emotions, but she was seeing Oliver with very different eyes right now—and it was scary. Way out of her comfort zone. He wasn't just the geek with a passion for art who could make you see all the things you'd never noticed before in a painting, or the man with an eye for detail who seemed to just snap his fingers and turn a logistical mess into something smoothly organised with the minimum of effort. Right now, he was all male. The thing she'd never really let herself see before.

And she had no idea where this was going to lead.

CHAPTER THREE

IT HAD BEEN a while since Oliver had danced like this, and it made him feel giddy to be this close to Fizz. He'd forgotten just how sexy a waltz could feel. And then there was the rest of it: the last remnants of the sunset fading into the night, the lights sparkling and reflecting on the water as it darkened to reflect the sky, the romance of the music...and her nearness. It would be oh, so easy to kiss her right now; but they were sharing a room tonight. *Sharing a bed.* It wouldn't be fair to put that kind of pressure on her.

So he kept himself under strict control.

They'd been dancing for nearly an hour when he noticed that she was starting to droop.

'Come on, Sleeping Beauty. I'll call us a cab,' he said.

She shook her head. 'I'll be fine on the underground.'

He stroked her cheek. 'You were up ridiculously early this morning. I know you want to do everything on your budget, and I respect that, but will you let me take you back to the apartment by taxi? Because I worry about you, Fizz. You can't burn the candle at both ends and be OK. And I'm sure Laura would bend her rules so you get to see the city all lit up.'

He could see the indecision on her face, but eventually she nodded. 'All right. Thank you.'

When their cab arrived, he asked the driver to take them through the city rather than on the ring road, even though it would take a few minutes longer, because he wanted to give Fizz the chance to see some of the famous buildings lit up at night. They drove along the quayside, where the lights were reflected on the Seine; across the Pont de la Concorde, where the obelisk was lit up in front of them; past the Louvre and the Palais Garnier, the buildings looking stunning in the spotlights; and past Sacré-Coeur shining like a white beacon on its hill.

'I can see why they call Paris the City of Light,' Fizz said. 'It's so beautiful at night.'

Oliver took her hand. 'This is a bit slower than the underground, but I thought you'd enjoy this. It's kind of making up for not being able to get tickets for a river trip.'

'And how,' she said. 'You've made Paris special for me, Oli.'

'Good.'

Back at their flat, he said, 'You have the bathroom first. Do you want me to make you a hot drink—a chamomile tea or something?'

'No. I'm all right,' she said. 'But thank you for the offer. And I'm sorry I'm cramping your style a bit. You could probably have danced until midnight and not even noticed the time.'

'It's fine. You can remind me of that tomorrow morning when you have to wake me up and I'm grumpy,'

sible to put some distance between them and get her head straight, so she could face him again on their usual best-friend terms. Very gently, without waking him, she wriggled out of his arms and slipped on her clothes.

The last time she'd woken in bed with someone, he'd been a stranger rather than someone who knew her almost better than she knew herself. Shame and guilt had piled on top of her grief, that morning. The whole thing had been a mess, tangled up with the worst moments of her life. She'd never spoken about it to anyone, and she wasn't going to start now. She shoved the memories aside, scribbled a note for Oliver saying that she'd gone to pick up breakfast, and headed out in search of buttery croissants.

The *boulangerie* that the owner of the apartment had recommended sold a variety of pastries as well as croissants and bread, plus *macarons* made with bitter chocolate that she knew were Oliver's favourite. She bought a small box of *macarons* to give him once they were back in London and a selection of pastries, then headed to a nearby café to have her water bottle filled with freshly squeezed orange juice and the two reusable cups with good coffee.

Oliver was still asleep when she got back. She set everything on the small bistro table, then tapped him gently on the shoulder. 'Hey, Sleeping Beauty. Time for breakfast.'

'Uh…' He squeezed his eyes shut, then sighed. 'OK. Thank you. I don't expect you to wait on me hand and foot.'

'I know. See you at the table when you're ready.'

He dragged himself out to the table; they'd break-fasted together in pyjamas a few times, when one of them had stayed in the other's spare room, but today felt different. Which was utterly ridiculous. She gulped orange juice to hide her confusion.

'The pastries look nice,' he said. He took a sip of the coffee. 'Oh, that's *good*.'

It didn't take long for the coffee to kick in. Oliver insisted on doing the washing up before he had a quick shower and dressed in the bathroom; meanwhile, Fizz sent a selection of the photographs she'd taken yesterday to Darcy and her parents.

Enjoying Laura's bucket list in Paris. Raising a cocktail to her tonight. Have stuffed face with a rainbow of macarons, seen some of the sights, seen the Eiffel Tower sparkling at night and tangoed next to the Seine.

Darcy replied almost immediately.

You took Oliver to Paris?

Well, it was a bit late for her to be upset about it now. If they'd opened their lists together, maybe they could've done some of it together. She pushed down the flash of irritation. Darcy was as messed up as she was.

She texted back, trying to be conciliatory.

Sorry. If you want to do Paris with me, we can go when you're free.

Might be going to Rome for Laura's list.

Darcy wasn't asking Fizz to go with her?

She damped down the twinge of hurt, typing back.

That's a bit cryptic. Going with...?

The ensuing radio silence made her narrow her eyes. If Darcy wanted to be cagey, there wasn't a lot she could do about it. 'Laura, I wish you were here. I think we need you to glue us back together. We can't do it ourselves,' she said with a sigh.

'Can't do what yourselves?' Oliver asked, walking back into the main room and clearly overhearing the last sentence.

In response, Fizz handed him her phone.

'Fizz, you can't really tell someone's tone from a text message,' Oliver said gently. 'She's not necessarily upset that you asked me to go with you instead of her. And she's not knocking you back. Maybe she's met someone and she's not ready to talk about it yet, in case she jinxes it. I've never met anyone else who was jilted at the altar, but it must really make it hard to trust anyone again once it's happened to you.'

'She barely dates,' Fizz agreed.

'The two of you need to sit down and talk,' Oliver said. 'But not now. Right this minute, you're in Paris, on Laura's orders—and I believe the flea market awaits.'

'Proper bargain hunting,' she said. 'You might even find an undiscovered Modigliani.'

He laughed. 'I doubt that, not even a sketch—but

you might find some interesting jewellery you can take apart and reset.'

They left the apartment to discover that the famous flea market really was right on their doorstep. The stalls displayed their wares to the browsers, everything from stands of copper pans to stalls of little tables. There were gilt chairs with striped pastel chintz upholstery, shelves of gleaming silverware and glass, and walls filled with mirrors and paintings and framed sketches—though not one of the originals she'd teased Oliver about—and stacks of empty frames. Old-fashioned suitcases opened to reveal vintage toys and battered teddy bears; other stalls had baskets to rummage through.

Fizz couldn't resist buying an old-fashioned manual coffee grinder shaped like a box with a handle on the top and drawer to collect the grounds. Then her alarm rang on her phone.

'Two hours. That's enough flea market shopping,' she said.

'What do you want to do now?' Oliver asked.

'Let's drop this back at the apartment, so we don't have to carry it all round the city,' she said, gesturing to her coffee grinder. 'And then I think we'll look for street art.'

'La Butte aux Cailles is meant to be amazing,' he said.

'Then that's where we'll go.'

There turned out to be lots of street art, from a prowling tiger with turquoise eyes to a child skipping and looking as if her knees had vanished through the wall, seeming almost three-dimensional with the 'shadow' of the skipping rope. Fizz was drawn by a wall of sunflowers, and Oliver spotted a balloon. 'Which is fitting,' he said, 'because this was where the Montgolfier brothers' first hot air balloon landed.'

'It doesn't feel anything like the wide boulevards in the middle of Paris,' Fizz said. 'It's more like a village.' The streets were narrower and cobbled, the small front gardens of the terraced houses filled with greenery or bursting with spring flowers.

'It's more like parts of Notting Hill than Paris,' Oliver agreed.

Further on, it felt even more like a village, with beautiful old-fashioned streetlamps and pastel wooden shutters against the cream-painted walls.

'The Canal Saint-Martin's meant to be lovely, too,' she said. 'We can stop for lunch at a café, walk a bit under the chestnut trees, and then head for Montmartre.'

'Fine by me,' he said.

They found a patisserie with wide canvas awnings and fancy lettering; the queue for the takeaway section told them just how good the food was. Fortified by a traditional croque monsieur served with a rocket and baby plum tomato salad, they wandered along the banks of the Canal Saint-Martin, her arm tucked through his. She was glad the scratchy awkwardness of this morning had gone, and she had her best friend back, to tease and laugh with.

'Alfred Sisley painted along here,' Oliver said. 'The invisible Impressionist.'

'Didn't we see some of his paintings yesterday at the Musée d'Orsay?' Fizz asked.

'Yes. What I mean is he's a bit overshadowed by Monet and Renoir—they were friends of his, and he was one of the founding members of the Impressionists, but they had a lot more success. The last few years of his life were pretty rough.'

'Pretty standard for painters in Paris,' she said. 'Think about Van Gogh, Picasso, Modigliani.'

'Some of Sisley's paintings were gorgeous, though,' Oliver said. 'There's one in the National, a view of the Thames at Charing Cross Bridge—I love the sky in that one.'

'Maybe we can go and see it when we're back in London,' she said.

'I'd like that,' he said.

They caught the Métro to Montmartre and climbed the steps all the way up to the Sacré-Coeur. They wandered towards the Place du Tertre; the pretty square at the top of the hill was stuffed with stalls showcasing the work of artists, everything from postcard-sized pencil sketches through to oil landscapes.

'Apparently there's a ten-year waiting list to get a pitch here, and the pitches are shared by artists on alternate days,' Oliver said.

There were buskers, too—a violinist playing Fauré, a man with an accordion playing Aznavour, and a guitarist playing Satie.

'I love it,' Fizz said. 'I can imagine living and working here.'

'It's even lovely in the rain,' Oliver said. 'Come and see Utrillo's pink house.'

On the corner of two cobbled streets, La Maison Rose lived up to its name: bright pink, with green shutters and doors.

'That's charming,' Fizz said. 'And, oh, the wisteria! That's glorious.'

Oliver took some snaps of her along the cobbled street with the wisteria in the background.

'I think this is my favourite bit of Paris,' she said. 'And I'm guessing it's yours, too.'

'Pretty much on a par with the Marais. That timer you had on your phone—you'd *definitely* need that if you let me browse those stalls back in the Place du Tertre,' he said.

She grinned. 'More likely, we'd laugh and ignore it because I'd be right there with you.'

'We need coffee,' he said. 'And a pastry. And a sketch.'

'In that order,' Fizz said.

There was a nearby patisserie with an enormous display in a glass cabinet; Fizz found it hard to choose, but eventually picked a Paris Brest: choux pastry shaped like a bicycle wheel and filled with piped praline cream, topped with flaked almonds and icing sugar. 'This is wonderful,' she said after her first mouthful. 'Want to try some?'

'No, and you can keep your beady eyes off my *tarte au citron*,' Oliver retorted with a teasing grin.

'Spoilsport,' she pouted.

He loaded up a forkful. 'Actually, this is probably

the best lemon tart I've ever tasted. So I'll be nice. You can try it.'

And there it was again as he held the forkful of lemon tart out to her: that little flash of sensualism. As if he were a lover, feeding her treats…

She really needed to get a grip. Especially as she could feel the betraying colour flushing through her cheeks. Would he notice? Did she *want* him to notice?

'Fabulous,' she said, and hoped that he'd put her blush down to a sugar rush or something similar. The last thing she wanted to do right now was admit to this weird feeling; though, at the same time, it intrigued her. It was something she didn't think she'd ever feel.

They found an artist to sketch them together in charcoal, and sat smiling at each other as the artist worked; he rolled the drawing and slotted it into a cardboard tube to keep it safe from damage. And then they wandered through Montmartre, exploring the gorgeous cobbled streets and stopping to take photographs of places where the famous painters had lived and worked, loved and laughed and despaired, a hundred or so years before.

After dinner of chicken chasseur with bulgar wheat and buttery, garlicky spinach in a traditional little bistro with red and white checked tablecloths, bentwood chairs and raffia-covered bottles used as candleholders, they found a rooftop bar with an amazing view over the city. On one side was the Sacré-Coeur; on the other, they could see the Eiffel Tower.

'This is just *perfect*,' Fizz said, settling into one of the wicker chairs.

'I believe *mademoiselle* was insisting that we should both have passionfruit martinis tonight?' Oliver asked.

'We're in Paris, so I suppose we really ought to drink something that's properly Parisian, instead,' she said.

'Pernod or pastis? Or maybe absinthe,' he suggested.

'Isn't absinthe banned?' she asked.

'No, that's a myth. And it's not hallucinogenic, either,' he said. 'It's just a really high proof, so people get drunk more quickly on it.'

She couldn't help smiling. 'Oli, you're such a geek. How do you know all this stuff?'

'In-flight magazines can be surprisingly interesting,' he said. 'Hemingway apparently invented a cocktail in Paris named after his book, *Death in the Afternoon*—absinthe and champagne.'

'What's actually in absinthe?' she asked.

'Hang on, and I'll tell you.' He looked it up. 'Wormwood, fennel and star anise. I've never actually drunk it, but apparently it's quite bitter, which is why it's served with a sugar lump.'

'Well, this is meant to be a wild time in Paris—let's try absinthe,' she said. 'Both of us.'

Oliver had a word with the barman, who brought over a tray and set up the drink for them. There was a clear green liquid in the bottom of the two glasses; he balanced a flat spoon with a slatted bowl on the glasses, and a sugar lump on top of that.

'This is the absinthe fountain,' the barman said, putting a contraption between their glasses that looked a bit like an old-fashioned lantern glass, filled with ice cubes and water. There were four tiny taps running from it. 'You drip the water really slowly onto the sugar cube until it dissolves,' he explained. 'It goes cloudy, like Pastis or Pernod. And then, when the sugar is dissolved, it will be ready to drink.'

'*Merci beaucoup,*' Oliver said.

'So this is *la fée verte,*' Fizz said. 'OK.'

Oliver took photographs of her with the absinthe fountain working, and then took a photograph of her as she was about to taste the drink.

She almost choked on her first mouthful. 'How could the artists possibly have drunk this stuff?' she asked, grimacing.

'It's that bad?' Oliver asked.

'Uh. Try it and tell me.'

He did so. 'That's possibly not my favourite,' he said.

'It's absolutely revolting, Oli. Admit it,' she demanded.

'An acquired taste, maybe.' He returned her grimace. 'I'll ask the barman if there's a sweeter Parisian cocktail you might like—if not, do you want your usual?'

She smiled. 'Yes, please.'

He sent the photographs over to her and took the drinks and the fountain back to the barman. Fizz forwarded the pictures to her parents and Darcy.

Absinthe sounds much, much nicer than it tastes! More like la fée bleugh than la fée verte! xx

Oliver came back a few moments later with two martini glasses. One held an amber liquid, garnished with strips of orange peel, and the other was pink with a foamy top, garnished with a raspberry.

'A 1789,' he said, nodding at the amber one, 'and a French martini. I'm assuming you'll try both, so start with the 1789 because it's the less sweet one.'

Even a small sip made her catch her breath. 'What's in it?'

'French whisky, white wine and a French citrus aperitif,' he said.

'It's a lot better than the absinthe, but still not *quite* my thing,' she said.

'That's why I suggested you try that one first.' He smiled. 'You'll love the other one.'

'I'm sure my gran used to drink something she said was a French martini,' Fizz said pensively, 'and it was vile. Though it wasn't frothy.'

'I know the stuff you mean,' he said. 'I had an aunt who loved it, too. She used to mix it with lemonade.'

'So did my gran.' Gingerly, she tasted the cocktail. 'Oh, my God. That's definitely *not* what she used to drink. This is fantastic! It's even better than a passionfruit martini. I need to know what's in this so I can make one for Darcy.'

'Vodka, pineapple juice and black raspberry liqueur, shaken over big lumps of ice—that's what gives the frothy bit at the top,' he said. 'Give me your phone. I need to take a picture of you smiling like that, before your sister hunts me down and kills me for letting you drink absinthe. Because I'm assuming you told her how bad it tastes.'

She laughed, and he took the snap.

'"French martini,"' she read aloud as she typed in the caption. '"Better even than passionfruit. Oli's suggestion.'" She pressed 'send'. 'You're safe from her wrath, now,' she said with a smile.

'Good. Darcy's scary.'

'She's a pussycat,' Fizz protested.

'Not where her baby sister's happiness is concerned,' Oliver said. 'I know you worry that you've drifted apart, but deep down I don't think you have.'

She trusted his judgement—Oliver had always been astute—and it took a lot of the sting out of how she'd felt after seeing the solicitor with Darcy on Laura's anniversary.

He stuck to wine, after that, and she tried several more different cocktails. And she was glad she was wearing canvas shoes rather than heels when she almost tripped on the way back to the Métro.

Oliver put his arm round her. 'Let's make sure you stay upright.'

'Sure,' she said, and grinned at him. It didn't feel like it usually did when Oliver gave her a hug, but it was a new kind of nice. She found herself sliding her arm round his waist in return; and, even on the Métro, he didn't let go of her. She couldn't remember the last time she'd felt this cherished, and it warmed her all the way through. It made her want to dance through the streets.

'I do love you, you know, Oli,' she said, when they got back to the apartment.

'Love you, too, Fizzikins. Though in the morning I'm pretty sure you won't remember telling me this, so I promise you now that I'm not going to embarrass you by bringing it up.'

'I think the cocktails might have gone a bit to my head,' she said. That, or maybe Oliver had. Not that she was going to tell him.

'Just a little bit.' He dropped a kiss on her forehead. 'You have the bathroom first. And then I'll get you a big glass of water and you can drink it all tonight before you go to sleep, to stop you having a monstrous hangover tomorrow morning.'

'I love you,' she said again. 'And I love Paris. And I really, *really* love French martinis.'

'I know.' He laughed. 'Go get your PJs on.'

Just as he'd promised, Oliver brought Fizz a big glass of water. And, just as he'd suggested, she drank the lot. But, unlike the previous night, she was still awake when he came to bed—even though she closed her eyes and pretended to be asleep.

Since they'd been in Paris, she'd started to feel differently towards her best friend. She'd seen him in a different light: dancing sensuously with her by the river, feeding her tastes of things, and walking through the most romantic city in the world with their arms round each other.

And now he was lying next to her. In a big bed, admittedly—but it wasn't that big. They'd woken in each other's arms, this morning. What if...?

But the water had started to sober her up. He'd just told her he loved her, but she was pretty sure he meant it platonically. She didn't want to risk wrecking their friendship by making a move on him, particularly if he turned her down. And he would turn her down, she knew; he'd never take advantage of a woman who was even slightly tipsy.

All the same, she couldn't help wondering. What if she and Oliver…?

Oliver woke ridiculously early, the next morning. Fizz was snoring gently, so he knew it was safe to open his eyes; he wouldn't have to talk to her until he was properly awake and could marshal his words into a coherent order.

Last night, she'd told him that she loved him.

This morning, would she remember that? Would she remember him telling her that he loved her, too?

Though he rather thought they had different definitions of love. Fizz had always made it clear that he was her best friend and—apart from that one kiss, when he'd turned her down because she was vulnerable and he absolutely wasn't going to take advantage of her— she'd always treated him like a brother.

Maybe he was being a coward, not raising the issue. But the way he saw it, he had too much to lose. If they had *that* conversation and she turned him down, things would be awkward between them. She'd start to avoid him, and the distance between them would grow until they were nothing more than acquaintances. His life would be much flatter and duller without her. If the choice was between having her as his best friend and nothing, it was a no-brainer. He'd keep his mouth shut—and keep her in his life.

He glanced at his watch. It was still early, but it was late for Fizz to be asleep. Which probably meant that, despite the water he'd persuaded her to drink last night, she'd have a bit of a hangover. He climbed out of bed without disturbing her, dressed, left her a note to say he was fetching breakfast and crept out of the flat.

As soon as he left the courtyard, he could smell coffee and fresh-baked bread. He followed his nose and bought a baguette, on the grounds that Fizz could do with something more substantial than a croissant to mop up last night's cocktails, along with jam from a market stall, some handmade chocolates that his parents would enjoy, two takeout coffees and some paracetamol.

Fizz was awake when he got back and had clearly showered and dressed; her bag was packed, and she was sitting on the bed, using her knees as a desk for a small sketchpad.

'Working?' he asked.

'Only a teensy-tiny bit,' she said. 'I wanted to make some notes about the wisteria earrings. And I think cherry blossom earrings in pink enamel, maybe with a matching ring.'

He smiled. 'I expected you to have a hangover.'

'From mixing those cocktails, last night? I probably deserve one,' she said, 'but, actually, I feel wonderful.'

'If that changes, I bought paracetamol,' he said. 'Plus coffee, a baguette and jam.'

'Perfect,' she said with a smile.

After they'd had breakfast at the little table overlooking the courtyard, he showered, changed and packed. They tidied the tiny apartment, put the key back in its safe box by the back door, and headed for the centre of Paris for a last look at the cherry blossom and an ice cream, before catching the train back to London.

Back at St Pancras, Fizz said, 'Thank you for coming with me to Paris, Oli. For helping me start Laura's bucket list.'

'I'm glad you asked me,' he said. 'And if I can do anything to help with the other three tasks, just tell me.'

She nodded. 'I'll call you later in the week.' And then, to his surprise, she handed him a box. 'They're the bitter chocolate ones because weirdly, for a cake fiend, you hate sweet things.'

'You really didn't need to do that, especially as you treated me to Paris and only let me buy you a couple of drinks and some *macarons*, but thank you.' He kissed her cheek. 'Check your diary for September and let me know when you're free, because we're going back to Paris and next time we're doing it my way, all planned. My treat. No arguments.'

'All right. Thank you.' She smiled at him. 'Catch you later.'

At ten o'clock on Monday morning, Fizz was interrupted by the doorbell. A delivery driver handed her a glorious arrangement of sunflowers. She recognised the writing on the envelope, and the card that came with it confirmed it.

Thank you for Paris. Love, Oli x

She knew why he'd sent her sunflowers, too. They were Laura's favourite flower, the ones that always made Fizz smile with their brightness. The flowers that made up her signature jewellery collection.

He'd be busy at work now, so she'd call him later. In the meantime, she texted him.

Flowers gorgeous. Thank you. F xx

His reply came when he was clearly taking a break.

Least I can do. Speak soon, O xx

And it left her smiling for the rest of the day.

CHAPTER FOUR

ON TUESDAY, Fizz sat at her jeweller's bench, putting the final polish on the engagement ring she'd been working on: a central round diamond, with smaller diamonds set round it, and then a row of spaced diamonds in three-pronged claws. The overall effect was of an Art Deco sunflower. Pleased with it, she slipped it onto her left hand to see how it would look being worn; luckily, her finger was the same size as the bride's. It felt comfortable against the skin and moved easily. She turned her hand so the diamonds caught the light, and was in the middle of examining the ring critically under her loupe for anything that needed a final tweak when her phone shrilled.

She frowned as she saw Oliver's name on the screen. At this time he'd be busy at work—even more than usual, right now, as he was gearing up to take over from his father. If he was ringing her, something must be up. 'Oli? Is everything all right?' she asked.

'No,' he said. 'Mum rang me. Dad's been rushed into hospital.' He swallowed hard. 'I've called a taxi and I'm leaving the gallery now. I just wanted to let you...' His voice tailed off.

She knew that feeling. She'd been there. He was panicking that his dad might not make it, and he needed her support. Which of course she'd give him. Even if she'd been in the middle of a meeting with a client when he'd called, she would've apologised to the client and rearranged the meeting so she could be at the hospital with him. 'I'll meet you at the hospital, Oli. Which one?'

'Hampstead. The Emergency Department.'

'Got it. I'm leaving now,' she said. 'Ring me if you need me. I'll text you as soon as I know my ETA.'

She grabbed her bag, locked the front door and headed straight for the Tube station.

She was held up on the street by a mass of pedestrians moving at the slowest pace in the world. The train was just disappearing into the tunnel when she arrived on the platform, so she had to wait another three minutes; she texted Oliver to let him know that she would be there in less than twenty minutes. She checked her watch every few seconds; time seemed to be moving like treacle. But at last the train arrived and whizzed her through to Belsize Park. She'd already tapped in the hospital's address on her phone while she was waiting on the platform, so the directions were ready and she power-walked to the hospital.

Oliver hadn't texted her back, so Fizz assumed that he'd switched his phone to silent—at least, she hoped it was that and not because Mark had taken a sudden turn for the worse.

'How can I help?' the receptionist asked when Fizz got to the Emergency Department.

'I'd like to see Mark Harrison, please. He was

brought here by ambulance—I think it was about an hour ago?'

'Are you family?'

Not strictly, but Fizz didn't want to risk being told to wait somewhere; Oliver needed her support. 'His son's my other half,' she fibbed. And then, wanting to back up the fib with some truth, because she didn't like lying, she added, 'He called me at work to let me know his dad's been brought in, and I said I'd meet him here.'

'All right, love. I'll just check where he is.' The receptionist checked her computer system. 'He's been moved to the cardiac care unit.' She gave Fizz the directions.

'Thank you,' Fizz said gratefully, and went to find the Harrisons.

The receptionist at the cardiac care unit directed her to the waiting room, where Oliver was pacing up and down, and his mother, Juliet, was sitting staring numbly at a paper cup of something brown with a bit of scum on the top that was probably meant to be coffee.

'Fizz.' He wrapped his arms round her. 'Thank you for coming. I appreciate...' His voice caught, but she knew what he was trying to tell her.

'I know.' She hugged him back. When he released her, she went over to his mother and hugged her, too. 'Hi, Juliet. How are you doing? And how's Mark?'

'They're doing tests.' Juliet's breathing was shallow, and Fizz could see that the older woman was only just managing to contain her emotions. 'That's why they sent us out to wait here. But he's talking and he's making sense. Downstairs, they said they didn't think he'd had a stroke.'

'What happened?' Fizz asked.

Juliet bit her lip. 'One minute he was talking to me, and then next minute he said he felt a bit weird—and then he passed out. He'd come round again by the time the ambulance arrived, and they brought him straight here.'

'That must've been so scary for you.' Fizz sat down beside her and took one hand. 'What have they said so far?'

'Just that they think it's his heart. They can't tell us anything more until they've run the tests,' Oliver said.

'Can I go to the kiosk downstairs and get you both a decent cup of coffee?' Fizz asked.

Juliet shook her head. 'Thanks, love, but I don't really want any. I don't even know why I accepted this one.' She put the paper cup down on the table in the waiting room.

'Have you had anything to eat?' Fizz asked.

'I'm not hungry,' Juliet said.

'Same here,' Oliver agreed.

'But I *could* do with the loo,' Juliet said. 'I haven't dared leave, just in case. Will you come and get me, Fizz, if the nurse says we can go back in to see him?'

'Of course I will,' Fizz promised.

When Juliet had left the room, Fizz looked at Oliver. 'OK. What didn't you want to say in front of your mum?'

His eyes widened. 'How did you know that?'

'Because I know *you*,' she said quietly. 'Though she's

in too much of a flap to have picked it up. You've got away with it.'

A muscle flickered in his jaw, betraying his tension. 'I'm scared that Dad won't get through this.'

'He's in the right place,' she said gently. 'This is a specialist ward. They're the best ones to fix whatever the problem is.'

'I know. But I can't stop thinking the worst. Even when he was first diagnosed with the cardiac arrhythmia, he was still Dad. Still strong and in control. I've never known him be anything else. I don't think I've ever even seen him cry, not even when we lost Wilf the Westie ten years ago. And now...' He closed his eyes briefly. 'Sorry. After everything you went through with Laura, I'm being self-indulgent.'

'No, you're not. He's your dad, and he collapsed. Of course you're worried,' Fizz said.

'Sorry for dragging you away from work.'

She smiled. 'Oliver Harrison, you could ring me at stupid o'clock in the morning and I wouldn't have a hissy fit on you. You're important to me. Of course I'll be there when you need me—just as you supported me when Laura was ill, and you've been there for me for the bucket list stuff. I would've been a lot more upset with you if you hadn't called me.'

'Thank you.' He gave her a wry smile. 'Sorry, I'm all over the place.'

'Which is perfectly natural. I'd be the same, in your shoes,' she said, giving him another hug. 'When did you last eat?'

'Breakfast.' He blew out a breath. 'I can't face any-thing now.'

She glanced at her watch. 'It might make you feel better. And you need to look after yourself if you want to be able to look after your dad.'

Just as Juliet joined them again, one of the nursing team came in. 'We've finished doing our tests on your husband, now, so you can go back to see him whenever you like. We're going to keep him in overnight and do an ablation tomorrow—that's where we use radio waves to block off the electrical circuits in his heart that aren't working properly, and that should restore his heart to a normal rhythm. No driving for at least two days, and no lifting for at least two weeks, but he should be able to go home the day after tomorrow.'

Juliet's eyes filled with tears. 'So he's going to be all right?'

'We'll do our best to make sure of it,' the nurse said with a smile. 'It'll take him a little while to recover, but we can support him through that, too. Would you like to come and see him?'

'Definitely,' Juliet said. 'You come, too, Fizz. It'll do him good to see you.'

Mark was leaning back against the pillows, wearing a hospital gown and looking tired and drawn, but he smiled when he saw them. 'Sorry to have worried you all. Fizz, how lovely to see you. Come and sit down.'

She did so, and he took her hand. 'Did you enjoy Paris? Oliver said you'd never been before. I thought he was teasing me—how could an art student never have visited the Louvre?—but...' Then he did a double-take and stared at her left hand. 'Oh, my God. Is that an *engagement* ring?'

Oh, no. Since Oliver's call, it had completely slipped her mind that she'd been checking the ring. Before she could explain that it was a commission and she was working on it for someone else, Juliet had taken her hand and inspected the ring, too. 'Oh, that's gorgeous—it looks like a sunflower. Is it one of your own designs?' At Fizz's shocked nod, Juliet added, 'Oh, so now we know why you two *really* sneaked off to Paris for the weekend. Oliver told us a story about it being part of a bucket list thing—when you actually went there to get engaged.' She looked delighted.

'Well, that's the best news ever,' Mark said, smiling broadly. 'And if that isn't an incentive to get well soon, I don't know what is! Our boy getting married—and, best of all, getting married to someone we already love.'

Fizz looked at Oliver; his mouth was hanging open slightly.

'Over the years, we always hoped this was on the cards,' Juliet said. 'You've been such good friends for such a long time—and you fit right in with our family, Fizz.'

Oh, help.

'We really ought to have champagne to toast your news,' Mark said, 'though I'm not allowed alcohol at the moment.'

Oliver cleared his throat, seemingly coming out of his shock. 'Fizz and I will go and get some sparkling water, as the next best thing,' Oliver said, tipping his head towards the door of his dad's room and widening his eyes at Fizz.

'Good idea,' Fizz said, filled with panic and realising that Oliver was trying to get her out of the situation before his parents got completely carried away. 'We'll be back in a minute.'

'No rush,' Mark said. 'We might be ancient, but we remember what it was like to be young and in love—don't we, Jools?'

'We certainly do. Take your time,' Juliet said. Her blue eyes, so like Oliver's, were filled with joy.

As soon as they were outside the doors of the cardiac care unit, and were unlikely to be overheard by Juliet or Mark, Fizz burst out, 'Oli, I'm *so* sorry. I was working on the ring and I'd just put it on my finger for a last inspection to see if I was happy with it or if anything needed tweaking. Then you called, and I—well, I dropped everything so I could come straight out to you. I didn't even *think* about the ring.' She bit her lip. 'I'm so, so sorry. It's all my fault, so I'll explain the mistake to your parents when we get back.'

'Mum and Dad were so thrilled,' Oliver said. 'But they're going to be really upset when we tell them the truth.' He looked awkward, his mind clearly working something through. 'Fizz, I know this is a big ask, but do you think we could hold off telling them until after Dad's operation? Maybe even until he's recovered?'

She felt her eyes widen. 'You mean, pretend we really *are* engaged?'

'I know it's lying, and neither of us is in the habit of doing that; but my parents are at a really low ebb right now. Mum's only just holding it together. And you heard what Dad said about it being an incentive to him getting well. The engagement will give them both something else to focus on and help stop them worrying so much about Dad's heart.'

'The longer we leave it before we tell them, the harder it'll be to admit the truth—and the more hurt your parents will be that we lied to them,' Fizz warned.

'I know.' Oliver raked a hand through his hair, looking vulnerable. 'But they'll be in a better place to deal with it then than they are right now. It's his *heart*, Fizz. I'd never say this in front of Mum, but if he doesn't pull through the operation tomorrow...what then? Who knows how long he didn't tell us about the symptoms before he first went to see the doctor, and if being untreated for so long has weakened his heart? If we tell him the truth before the operation and the shock kills him, I'll never forgive myself. If we wait until after the operation, then if he doesn't...' He swallowed hard, and whispered, 'If he doesn't make it, at least he'll die happy.'

Even though Fizz thought this might be the worst idea in the world—and it was all her own fault—she could understand Oliver's point of view. In his shoes, wouldn't she feel the same?

'All right,' she said. 'Until he's recovered, as far as your parents are concerned, we're engaged. But then we need to tell them the truth. And I have a bride-to-be who needs this ring on Friday afternoon. That's not negotiable.'

'Could you make another one? I'll buy the materials,' he said.

To do this properly, she'd need to spend a while in Hatton Garden, matching gems and negotiating. And that would take up way too much time. 'It'd probably be quickest if I made it in silver and zircona—and I have both of those back at the flat. I can make the ring and collets fairly quickly.'

'Collets?' Oliver asked, looking confused.

'The bits of the setting that hold the jewels in place,' she said. 'Though actually it's the filing and sanding that takes the time, rather than making the initial shapes.'

'But you could do it before you have to give the ring back to its real owner?'

Given the circumstances, she'd move everything else on her list to make sure she could do it. 'Sure.'

'Thanks, Fizz.' He hugged her. 'I couldn't ask for a better fake fiancée.'

'Same here,' she said.

They headed to the hospital canteen to buy sparkling water and four blueberry muffins, then went back to the cardiac care unit.

One of the doctors was talking to Mark when they walked into his room.

'Sorry for interrupting. Do you want us to come back later, when you've finished talking to Mum and Dad?' Oliver asked the doctor.

'No, it's fine. I've gone through everything with your parents,' the doctor said. 'By the way, congratulations on your engagement.'

Fizz exchanged a glance with Oliver. This was snow-balling already. But she didn't know how to stop it without causing the kind of stress and drama that might be too much for Mark. 'Thank you. We bought healthy bubbles to celebrate,' she said, holding up the bottle of sparkling water, 'and I hope it's OK for Mark to have cake?'

'Of course,' the doctor said with a smile. 'Though he'll be nil by mouth later today, to prepare for tomorrow's operation,' she warned. She looked at Oliver. 'I've given your parents some leaflets and some website links that might help answer any questions—there's a lot to take in—but if you're worried about anything, come and grab one of us and we'll do our best to answer.'

'Thank you,' Oliver said. 'Would you like some sparkling water or cake?'

'I'm afraid I have patients still to see, so I'll have to say no, but thank you for asking,' the doctor said, patting his arm. 'Congratulations again.' She smiled. 'You make a lovely couple.'

'So what happens with the operation?' Oliver asked when the doctor had left the room and they'd all raised a glass of sparkling water to toast the 'engagement'.

'They're going to do an ablation,' Mark said. 'That means they're going to put some wires through my veins, use radio frequencies to take out the electrical pathways that aren't working properly, and then everything should be back to normal and I'll stop feeling so terrible. I'll stay in overnight, and then I can come home.'

'And you have to rest, Mark. The doctor said he'd be tired for a few days afterwards—weeks, even,' Juliet told Oliver.

'Yes, so *please* don't tell me you're whisking us off to Venice to get married next week,' Mark said, 'because I won't be able to travel.'

Fizz exchanged a glance with Oliver. 'Don't worry, we haven't set a date yet. There's no rush. Just concentrate on getting better, Mark.'

'I suppose you're right,' he said. 'But I'm so glad you're getting married.'

'You need to rest, Dad,' Oliver said. 'I'm going back to the gallery to sort out some things so I can be here tomorrow with Mum during your operation, and then I'll stay with you both and work from your place for the rest of the week, but I'll call in again tonight. Mum, do you want to stay with me, tonight? Or I can come and stay with you, if you'd rather.'

'It'd be nice to have you both at our place,' Juliet said wistfully.

Oliver glanced at Fizz, who nodded. 'I can do that. I'll cook dinner so you don't have to worry about a thing,' she added. 'See you later, Mark. Do what the medics tell you.' She kissed his cheek, and then Juliet's. 'You've got my number, Juliet. Ring me if you need anything at all.'

'Thank you, sweetheart,' Juliet said.

'I can make an excuse if you'd rather not stay at Mum and Dad's tonight,' Oliver said when they were walking out of the hospital towards the Tube. 'And don't worry about dinner. I'll pick up something from the supermarket, or we can get something delivered.'

'It's fine. I think you could both do with the company, and I don't mind cooking,' Fizz said. She paused.

'It looks as if your parents think that we stay over at each other's flats.'

'Well, we do, sometimes, if we've been out somewhere—but not in the way they obviously think we do.' He winced. 'I didn't think about that. Mum will probably assume that, as my fiancée, you'll expect to sleep in my room rather than wanting a guest room. Don't worry, I'll take the floor.'

'And what if she decides to bring us a cup of tea in the morning?' Fizz asked. 'Then we'll have to explain and ask her to keep it secret from your dad, and she doesn't need that kind of stress. Look, we managed in Paris.' Then she remembered waking up in his arms, and how much she'd wanted him; she felt her face heat. This really wasn't appropriate.

'In a month, six weeks tops, we can tell them the truth,' Oliver said.

'We can manage, for now. I'd better start making a replacement for this.' She gestured to the ring on her finger. 'If they notice I'm not wearing it, I can always say I don't wear rings when I'm working, and I forgot to put the ring back on because it's still so new to me.'

'I feel horrible that I'm making you do all that extra work for nothing,' he said.

'It's not a problem. I can use it in publicity material. But we'd better start practising whatever engaged couples do. Hold hands, giggle...'

Just as she hoped, he rolled his eyes. 'I'm not a giggler, and neither are you. For which I am unspeakably glad.'

But he held her hand on the Tube to Camden, and he

kissed her lightly on the cheek before she got up—his own stop was three further on the Northern line and then he had a ten-minute walk to the gallery. 'I'll pick you up tonight on my way to the hospital.'

'Ring me before you leave, so I know what time to be ready and outside, waiting for you,' she said.

'Thank you, Fizz. I owe you.'

'No problems. It's what best friends are for,' she said.

Though her head was in a whirl as she walked from the station back to her small flat.

A fake engagement, until Oliver's dad was better. Holding hands and...kissing? Her cheek was still tingling from that little brush of his lips. A full-on kiss on the lips would definitely turn her knees to jelly.

This was probably the worst idea they'd ever had between them.

She shook herself. There was no time to mull it over. She needed to make a replica of the engagement ring she'd just finished, and work out what she was going to cook for dinner for Oliver and his mum, this evening. Gnocchi with caponata sauce, perhaps, a green salad and good bread. That would be quick and easy.

And she wasn't going to let herself think about sharing a bed with Oliver tonight...

A fake engagement.

To Fizz, his best friend. The woman he'd loved for years, always as a friend—once as more than that, but he'd supressed it when he'd realised that she hadn't loved him in the same way.

Was he foolish?

Probably, Oliver thought ruefully. He was worried sick about his parents. Although Fizz had reassured him that his dad was in the right place, he still wondered what would happen if the operation didn't work. Or, even worse, if his dad didn't survive it?

He called a quick staff meeting when he got back to the gallery, explaining that he'd be away tomorrow and working from his parents' house for the next few days. And he had to blink away the stinging in his eyes when Ashley, his father's PA, gave him a 'get well soon' card that everyone in the gallery had signed. 'We'll send him a care package when he's home,' she said. 'Something to keep him occupied. We thought we'd send him a couple of biographies, some good decaf coffee and those biscuits he likes from the Italian deli—if he's allowed them?'

'That would be lovely,' Oliver said. 'Thank you all. It means a lot to know...' The lump in his throat stopped him saying any more.

She patted his arm. 'We know, love. Nobody ever leaves Harrison's Fine Art, except to retire. It's like a family. And it goes without saying that we're here for you, too. If you need any one of us, just call me and I'll sort it out.'

'I really appreciate that,' Oliver said. 'I appreciate all of *you*.'

He sorted out what needed to be done and when; then he made a couple of phone calls to move meetings, and took a pile of paperwork back to his flat to add to his overnight things. Then he called Fizz. 'I'm leaving my flat in ten minutes.'

'OK. How did it go at the gallery?'

'They all signed a card for Dad. They're planning to send him a care package when he's home. Things to keep him occupied and stop him worrying about work.'

'That's lovely,' Fizz said. 'OK, I'll get my things together. See you soon.'

As he pulled up outside the Victorian terrace where she lived in the ground floor flat, he saw her waiting for him. How ridiculous that his heart did a backflip.

She put her bags in the back of the car and climbed in beside him. 'Any news?'

'I spoke to Mum a few minutes ago and she says Dad's the same as when we left him. He's starting to get a bit nervous about tomorrow.'

'I'm not surprised. How are you holding up?'

'Fine.'

'It's me you're talking to,' she reminded him. 'And I'm not going to say a word to your mum.'

'I'm worried,' he said. 'But you were right when you said he's in the best place.' He took a deep breath. 'And I'm really glad you're going to be here tonight.'

'I'll stay for as long as you need me,' she said. 'I can stay at the hospital with you tomorrow, if that would help.'

'It would help a lot,' he said, and reached across to squeeze her hand briefly.

At the hospital, they stayed for a chat with his father, then drove his mum back to the house in Belsize Park. Juliet went to collect Poppy, the family's Westie, from the next-door neighbour while Fizz busied herself in the kitchen, boiling potatoes to make the gnocchi and chopping ingredients for the sauce, with Oliver helping here and there.

'It feels odd to be here without Dad,' Oliver said.

'He'll be back home, the day after tomorrow,' she reminded him. 'And you can stop scoffing those red peppers or there won't be enough for the sauce.'

'Sorry,' he said.

'Sure you are,' she teased.

How good it felt, having her around.

At dinner, Juliet picked at the gnocchi. 'I'm sorry, love,' she said to Fizz. 'It's not your fault—the food's lovely. I'm just not very hungry.'

'Because you're worried about Mark. Even though you know he's in the best place,' Fizz said. 'Why don't you go and put your feet up, Juliet? I'll make you a mug of chamomile tea and honey.'

'While I clear up in the kitchen,' Oliver said.

'And so you should, as sous-chef,' Fizz said, dropping a kiss on his forehead. It was odd how natural it felt to do something so affectionate.

'You two make such a good team,' Juliet said. 'I did wonder earlier if you were pretending to be engaged, just to keep your dad's spirits up.'

Oliver exchanged a glance with Fizz. Maybe this fake engagement hadn't been his best suggestion. He'd been panicking at the time and it was the first thing he'd thought of. His mum had just given him an opportunity to tell the truth; perhaps he ought to come clean?

But Fizz smiled before he could say anything. 'I love Oli, Juliet. Never doubt that.'

How could he contradict her now?

Sharing a room with her tonight was going to be so awkward.

Except he found it wasn't. Once Fizz had changed into her pyjamas and climbed into bed, she simply patted the mattress beside her. 'Come and talk to me about your favourite painting. It'll take your mind off your worries.'

Weirdly, lying there in the dark with her and talking about art made him feel calmer. As if the world had stopped spinning madly; with Fizz, he felt as if there was a still place, somewhere he could just *be*.

Being here with her felt so right.

Maybe, once his dad was better, he could persuade her to take a chance on him for real...

CHAPTER FIVE

THE NEXT MORNING, Fizz woke first. Oliver looked worn out, so she left him sleeping and went downstairs to let Poppy out. She could hear Juliet moving about upstairs, so she put the kettle on and shook coffee grounds into the cafetiere. Having stayed at Oliver's parents' house before, she knew how Juliet took her coffee and she knew her way round the kitchen well enough to get everything prepped for breakfast.

'Morning,' she said when Juliet came into the kitchen. 'Coffee's just ready.'

'Oh, Fizz, you are a darling. Thank you,' the older woman said gratefully, accepting the mug Fizz handed her. 'I can't believe how lucky we are. You hear all these horror stories about people ending up with the daughter-in-law from hell, and instead we have you—the daughter-in-law we've always wanted. You're perfect for Oliver.'

'I have my faults, you know,' Fizz said. 'I'm impulsive and I can go off into a daydream. Ask Oli how many times he has to tell me to pay attention when he's talking to me.'

Juliet chuckled. 'You're a breath of fresh air, love.'

Fizz inclined her head and smiled in acknowledgement of the compliment. 'How's Mark this morning? I assume you've already called him.'

'I have. He's nervous. And hungry,' Juliet said.

'Ah. If he's like Oli in the morning, he needs coffee and carbs before you can even speak to him.'

'Like father, like son,' Juliet agreed.

'I'll go and prod Oli awake,' Fizz said. 'The toast will be ready in a moment. Oh, and I let Poppy out earlier.'

The Westie, hearing her name, wagged her tail, but sat where she was with her gaze fixed on Juliet, waiting for her share of toast crusts.

'Thank you,' Juliet said.

Oliver, predictably, grunted at her when she tried to wake him. She ignored him. 'Breakfast is ready downstairs. Go and join your mum while I have a shower.'

Oliver grumbled, but hauled himself out of bed and headed down to the kitchen.

Fizz smiled to herself. For a moment, she could see herself in twenty years' time, with a grumpy husband and an equally grumpy teenage son, neither of whom were fit for conversation until they'd had breakfast, and a daughter who was wide awake and teasing them both.

She shook herself. Where on earth had that come from? Apart from the fact that her engagement to Oliver was completely fake, she'd never thought about having children. Well. Not since those weeks after Laura's death, when everything was grim and she was full of panic about what her future held. When she'd walked for miles and miles, but nothing had been able to clear her head or help her decide what to do.

She tamped it down, determined not to dwell on it

as she finished showering and changing. Knowing that it was going to be a very long day with a lot of waiting around, she'd brought playing cards and a travel Scrabble from her flat to take to the hospital. Even if they were reduced to playing Snap because they couldn't concentrate on anything more complicated, it would at least be a distraction.

'I'll take Poppy for her w-a-l-k while you get dressed, Juliet,' she said, spelling out the word so the little Westie didn't get overexcited.

'Thank you, love.'

'Are you human yet, Oli?' she teased, kissing him on the cheek. Warmth bloomed in her chest when he leaned into her. She knew they needed these little moments of affection if they were going to keep up their ruse until Mark was better. But she hadn't expected them to play havoc with her real emotions too.

'Nearly,' he grouched. Poppy woofed, and Oli sighed. 'All right. Sit, paw, and then you can have this crust.'

Poppy sat obediently with a paw raised, and deftly caught the bit of toast that Oliver threw to her. Fizz attached the lead to Poppy's collar. 'See you in a bit.'

By the time she got back with Poppy, Juliet and Oliver were ready to go to the hospital. Juliet took the Westie to her neighbour's house, and then Oliver drove them in. Mark was delighted to see them all. Although Fizz could see that he had the same tension 'tell' as Oliver did—a tightening around his eyes—he hid his nervousness with a stream of terrible dad jokes until he had to say goodbye to Juliet at the door to the operating theatre.

Fizz was very aware of Oliver's worries about

whether his father would survive the operation, and she was pretty sure that Juliet thought the same, even though she hadn't voiced them to Fizz. Both of them were surreptitiously looking at their watches every couple of minutes, and the hours seemed to go by so very slowly. But somehow she kept them going throughout the operation, playing games, making sure they were drinking water and eating properly.

Finally one of the nursing team came into the relatives' room to see them. 'I'm pleased to say Mark's come round from the anaesthetic and is properly awake now,' she said. 'The ablation looks as if it's been successful, and you can go in to see him. Though he must keep lying flat for the next few hours.'

'Thank you.' Juliet was almost in tears with relief.

Oliver's voice sounded equally wobbly as he thanked the nurse; he held Fizz's hand tightly as he followed his mother out of the waiting room and into his father's room.

'They're letting me home tomorrow,' Mark said, 'but there are so many rules. No driving, no lifting or strenuous exercise, no alcohol, *still* no coffee...and I have to lie flat for the rest of the afternoon.' He rolled his eyes. 'It's going to drive me mad.'

'You follow every single one of those rules to the letter, Mark Harrison,' Juliet said fiercely, 'because I don't want to be without you for a single second more than I have to.'

'I don't want to be without you, either, Jools,' Mark said.

Fizz swallowed the lump in her throat and glanced

at Oliver, who was looking straight at her. What would it be like to have someone feel that way about her?

She realised that was the way she felt about Oliver. It wasn't just uncomplicated friendship, any more. It was turning into something else, something she hadn't expected. Or was this whole fake fiancée thing just messing with her head?

'We'll let you rest, Dad,' Oliver said. 'Mum, I'll come and pick you up later.'

'I've got client appointments first thing tomorrow,' Fizz said, 'so I'm going back home tonight, Juliet, but if you need anything just ring me. And I'll come over tomorrow evening to see you—let me know if you need anything from the shop.'

'You're such a sweetheart, Fizz,' Mark said, squeezing her hand. 'I'm so glad you're officially going to be part of our family.'

What could she do but smile and say, 'So am I.'

Oliver insisted on driving Fizz back to his parents' house and then, once she'd collected her bags, dropping her back at her flat.

'Thank you for everything you've done.' He held her tightly. 'I'll call you tomorrow.'

Now wasn't the time to tell him of her misgivings about them getting in too deep with this fake engagement thing, Fizz thought. Or how she was starting to feel about him. Right now, he was as vulnerable as she'd been the night they'd ended up kissing—and she understood now why he'd called a halt. 'All right. And call me if you can't sleep,' she said instead.

He didn't call her. She got through her meetings the

next morning and then spent the rest of the day working on the fake engagement ring. In the middle of the afternoon, her doorbell rang. Odd: she wasn't expecting a delivery, and she knew Oliver was in Belsize Park, taking care of his parents.

She was taken aback by the gorgeous arrangement of white roses, stocks and delphiniums. 'Are you sure they're for me?' she asked the driver.

'If you're Felicity Bennett, yes,' he said.

She put the flowers on the table and opened the card that came with it.

Congratulations on your engagement to Oliver, with love from all at Harrison's Fine Art.

Oh, no.

How had his company found out? This engagement business was starting to get out of control, and she didn't know how to calm things down.

She called Oliver.

'Everything OK?' he asked.

'Uh-huh. Are your parents nearby?'

'In the living room.'

'Go upstairs, and video-call me back with the door closed.'

'All right.' He sounded surprised, but hung up and then video-called her a couple of minutes later. 'What's wrong?'

'I just got these.' She moved the screen briefly so he could see the flowers.

'Very flashy. Who are they from?'

'All the team at Harrison's Fine Art. Congratulating me on our engagement.'

He blew out a breath. 'Ah. Ashley—Dad's PA—popped in to see him this afternoon, with a care package from the team. He must have told her the news. And she must've sorted out the flowers locally, since you got them that fast.'

'What are we going to do, Oli?' she asked. 'We can't keep lying to the whole world.'

'I know, but Dad's going to take a few weeks to recover.' He grimaced.

She sighed. 'All right. I'll send a thank-you card to the gallery tomorrow. And I'll send an excited photo to you and your parents.'

'Actually, I was going to call you anyway—Mum wanted to invite you to dinner tonight.'

Did he want her to make an excuse? Or did he need the moral support? She didn't have a clue, so she asked him outright.

'Both,' he said. 'I'll make an excuse because it's not fair to lean on you. I'm old enough to handle this stuff myself.'

'I'll be there,' she said. 'Princess Fizz to the rescue.'

To her relief, he laughed. 'I thought the princes were supposed to be the rescuers?'

'Nope. Princesses can do—'

'—anything princes can do,' he finished, 'particularly because you're one of the Bennett sisters, which gives you extra superpowers. OK. Does half-past seven work for you?'

'It does,' she said. 'See you then.'

She ended the call, and sat staring at the ring on her desk. This whole thing had started with a mistake, and then continued with the best of intentions. But she hadn't thought about it spreading further than his parents. Right now it seemed in danger of getting out of control.

Maybe Darcy would have a good idea how to fix this.

Fizz rang her sister, but Darcy didn't answer her phone.

This wasn't something she wanted to talk about by text. Maybe some fresh air would sort her head out. She went out to the shops; on the way to the florists, she noticed a new display in the bookshop on the corner. There was a book of historical-based puzzles. It was the sort of thing Mark would enjoy, and it might keep him occupied and sitting still, she thought, rather than being restless and worrying Juliet. She went inside to buy a copy, then picked up the rest of the things on her list before heading back to her flat and making the collets for the smaller gems on the outside of the ring.

The alarm on her phone warned her when it was time to pack everything away on her jeweller's bench. Armed with the book for Mark, some roses for Juliet, dog treats for Poppy and a tub of Oliver's favourite artisan ice cream from the deli on her road, she caught the Tube to Belsize Park.

Juliet was thrilled with the roses, Mark loved the book, Poppy wagged her tail madly at the crinkle of the bag of treats, and Oliver kissed her. On the lips. 'Best treat ever,' he said. 'Dad fancied something Indian for dinner, so I've made the heart-healthy version—plain rice, tandoori chicken, dhal and veggie dhansak.' He smiled. 'Go and sit down. I'll bring everything in.'

Fizz headed to the table, her lips still tingling from Oliver's kiss. Was he as affected as she was? He didn't seem to be. She needed to get her head on straight and remind herself this was for show. Oliver was just playing the part and she needed to do the same—for her friend's sake. Real emotions had no place here.

She made the effort to pull herself together. She couldn't risk their friendship, not when she couldn't give Oliver what he really deserved—she was too broken. But she could be there for her *friend*.

The food was wonderful, perfectly cooked and full of flavour.

'Did you get the photograph I sent you of the flowers from the gallery, Mark?' Fizz asked. 'They were so gorgeous.'

Mark looked pleased. 'I hope you don't mind that I told Ashley. My staff at the gallery are more like family anyway, and they wanted to celebrate with you and Oliver.'

Fizz felt a flush of guilt at the fib she and Oliver were telling—but it was in a good cause, she reminded herself. The best cause.

'And, what with everything that's happened, we haven't asked you about Paris,' Juliet said. 'Where did Oliver propose to you?'

Help. How did she answer that?

To her relief, Oliver swept in. 'By the clock in the Musée d'Orsay. It's the perfect place,' he said.

'What did your parents say when you told them?' Mark asked. 'And your sister must be thrilled at the idea of being a bridesmaid.'

Fizz shuffled in her seat. 'I haven't told them yet.' At Mark's look of concern, she added quietly, 'They're still in Provence. It was Laura's anniversary a few days ago. They need some quiet time before they'll have the headspace to celebrate.'

'Oh, of course,' Juliet said. 'I'm sorry, love. You must miss your sister.'

'Hugely,' Fizz said.

'And your oldest sister lives somewhere up north, doesn't she?' Mark asked.

'Edinburgh,' Fizz said. 'She fell in love with the place after university.' It was true, up to a point. Although she knew they'd assume Darcy had been a student there, it was better to tell the small fib than to give them the whole horrible story about how Darcy had fled there after Damian dumped her at the altar.

'I'll clear the table,' Mark said, standing up.

Fizz noticed that he was still a bit breathless. 'Sit down, Mark. You're meant to be resting. I'll do this—and I count as family rather than a guest, now, so it's OK for me to help out,' she said.

'I suppose you're right,' Mark said. He frowned. 'But I do feel a bit like a spare part.'

'Dad, you had a four-hour operation yesterday,' Oliver reminded him. 'The surgeon said that you need to pace yourself. You're not a spare part at all—and we want you around for a *lot* longer. I know it's frustrating for you, but can you please just do what they told you and rest?'

Mark nodded. 'Still, at least we have a wedding to plan.'

'That's mine and Fizz's job,' Oliver cut in swiftly, to her relief. 'We're still thinking about what we want.'

'But you've known each other for nearly a decade!'

'Bit of an exaggeration, Dad,' Oliver said mildly.

'I just hope you don't take as long to decide where you'll get married as you did to get engaged in the first place,' Mark grumbled.

'We won't,' Fizz said with the sweetest of smiles.

'Let's see the ring again,' Juliet said.

Fizz winced. 'Sorry, Juliet—it's back at my flat. I was working earlier, and I never wear anything on my hands or wrists when I'm working. It's still so new that I forgot to put it back on my finger.'

Juliet looked disappointed. 'Oh, well. Another time.'

'Another time,' Fizz promised.

After they'd cleared up in the kitchen, played a board game and Mark had finally admitted that perhaps he could do with an early night, Oliver drove Fizz home.

'Your parents will expect you to dally a bit,' Fizz said, 'so you might as well come in for a drink. Chamomile tea?'

Oliver groaned. 'Is this my fiancée trying to reform my coffee habit?'

She laughed. 'I thought I'd try it on. All right, I'll make you coffee.'

She was just pouring hot water into the mugs when

her phone pinged. Glancing at the screen, she saw that finally Darcy was returning her call.

Well, not actually *calling* her. Instead, her sister had sent a selfie from the Colosseum. Standing next to her was a good-looking dark-haired man Fizz had never seen before. The only words with the photo were Loving Rome.

What?

OK, Laura had told them to go and have a wild twenty-four hours; and the guy was gorgeous. Darcy was more than overdue some fun. But what worried Fizz most was that her sister looked starry-eyed.

She sent Darcy a barrage of questions.

Who is he?

How long have you known him?

How are you? How's Rome?

And Darcy didn't answer a single one.

'I recognise that frown,' Oliver said. 'What's up?'

'Darcy. I'm worried about her. She's doing her bucket list city trip.'

'Darcy will be fine,' Oliver said. 'She's the oldest, and she's used to doing things her way. She can look after herself.'

'I still worry about who this guy is next to her.' She showed him the photo. 'I don't even know his name. And she didn't tell me she was going to Rome. She only said it was a maybe on her list.'

'Did you tell her you were going to Paris, before we went?'

'Yes. And I sent photos to her, Mum and Dad while I was there. You took some of the photos for me,' she reminded him.

'Perhaps she forgot to tell you because she was being spontaneous,' Oliver suggested.

'You mean, Laura meant she should be more Fizz?' she asked wryly. 'And I should be more Darcy. She's on her second task, and I haven't even thought about which one I'm going to do next. Laura wanted us to do it all within six weeks, and at this rate I'm going to end up panicking and doing everything else on the very last day.'

'I kind of derailed you because of Dad, so I'll help you.' He paused. 'Have you told Darcy about our, um, "engagement"?'

'No. I was going to, but she hasn't returned my calls. She just sent me this instead.' She stared at the photograph. 'It's obvious that she's busy.'

'This is Darcy we're talking about. She's not going to do anything rash,' Oliver said. 'Chill. What are you going to do next on Laura's list?'

She had three things left. Commitment, facing a fear, and taking time to think. It was becoming clearer to her now that thinking should be the last thing on the list, the thing that would help her ease into the rest of her life. Facing her fear... No, not yet. Which left her with one thing. 'Making a commitment,' she said. 'I don't suppose a fake engagement would count?'

'No, it wouldn't.' Oliver gave her a wry smile.

'Laura said it has to be something important. I would consider adopting a dog—I think, from what Darcy's said, that's what she's going to do—but my flat's completely the wrong environment for a dog.'

'It doesn't have to be a pet,' Oliver said. 'What about committing to something that will connect you to people?'

'Such as?'

'Joining a choir?' he suggested.

'Not with my flat singing,' she said wryly. 'Once they'd heard me, they'd politely suggest that I stuck to being their biscuit monitor or something.'

'Mentoring a young jeweller? Teaching a class once a week? Volunteering?'

'I'll have a think about it,' she said. 'Sorry, I don't mean to shut you down—you've actually been really helpful because you're making me think about what I can do.' She hugged him. It was the same hug she'd given him a thousand times. And yet, something about it felt different. It wasn't like their old, easy friendship. There was something else, something she couldn't quite put her finger on. Something that scared her and thrilled her at the same time.

He kissed the top of her head. 'Any time.'

She knew he meant it. He'd always been there for her. But what if things changed while they were pretending to be more? Would he still be her friend then?

CHAPTER SIX

THE NEXT DAY, Fizz went out to pick up some milk and spied a gorgeous red jug with white polka dots in the window of the charity shop next to the supermarket.

When she paid for it, she noticed the ginger cat sitting on a cushion in a patch of sunlight. 'What a gorgeous cat,' she said to the woman at the cash desk. 'Can I make a fuss of them, or would they rather be left alone?'

'She'd enjoy the fuss. Her name's Tilly,' the cashier said.

'Hello, Tilly.' Fizz held out her hand, and the cat rubbed her face against it to signal acceptance. Fizz stroked her, and the cat purred.

'Is she yours?' Fizz asked.

'Yes and no. It's tricky.' The cashier bit her lip. 'Tilly's actually my neighbour's cat. I promised to look after her while he was in hospital—except he died, last week.'

'Oh, dear. I'm sorry,' Fizz said.

'He was a nice old man. Sadly, he didn't have any family, so there isn't anyone who could take her in. I'm looking after her for the moment, but I can't keep her because my partner has asthma and since Tilly's been staying with us he's been struggling quite a bit.' The

cashier sighed. 'I know I ought to take her to the rescue centre down the road, but I just haven't been able
to bring myself to do it yet. She's thirteen, and people
tend to prefer kittens who'll play for hours to elderly
cats who just want a quiet life. It might be a long time
before they can find someone suitable, and I don't think
she'd enjoy being in a rescue centre. She's used to a
home.' She shook her head. 'I've been bringing her
here during the day and crossing my fingers that the
area manager won't turn up unexpectedly and tell me
I can't keep her here.'

'Why would he do that?' Fizz asked. 'Surely all the
customers like her?'

'Yes, and she's no trouble—all she wants is a patch
of sunlight to snooze in and the odd cuddle—but he's
a bit of a stickler for regulations,' the cashier said. 'If
there's a health and safety issue, he'll bring it up in the
first five seconds.'

In Fizz's student days, her landlady had lived on
the top floor of their house and had a cat who used to
enjoy spending time with the students. On nights in,
Fizz had enjoyed curling up on the sofa with Bubbles
the calico cat snoozing on her lap.

This was an absurd idea.

But, if it worked, she'd be making a commitment that
would benefit someone else. Doing something important. Giving an elderly cat a comfortable, happy home
for the rest of her days.

'I know I'm a stranger, and of course you're not going
to give a cat to just anyone, but maybe I could give her a
home,' Fizz said. 'If we get the rescue centre involved,

then Tilly gets a proper safeguard. Maybe someone could foster her—or maybe you could keep her for a few more days—just until the rescue centre has a meeting with me and decides whether I'm a suitable owner.'

'Maybe,' the cashier said, looking doubtful.

'I work from home, so Tilly would have company all day, most of the time,' Fizz added. 'Guaranteed cuddles and a comfy bed.'

Tilly looked up from her cushion and miaowed softly, as if she knew they were talking about her.

'Give me your number, and I'll talk to my partner tonight,' the cashier said. 'I'm Trisha, by the way.'

'Felicity, but everyone calls me Fizz,' Fizz said, shaking her hand.

They exchanged phone numbers, and Fizz sent Trisha the link to her website and social media accounts. 'You can look me up, just to reassure yourself and the rescue centre that I'm not some random weird person,' she said.

Tilly miaowed again, as if in agreement.

'All right. I'll be in touch,' Trisha said.

Fizz's bride-to-be was thrilled with the sunflower ring when Fizz dropped it off at her office at lunchtime. 'It's absolutely perfect,' she said, nudging her fiancé. 'I'm just going to smile and smile every time I look at it.'

He stowed it safely in his pocket. 'I can't wait for you to be officially my fiancée, Aleisha.'

'And the engagement's tomorrow night?' Fizz asked.

'The party's tomorrow night,' Aleisha said. 'But we're getting engaged tomorrow morning. Just the two of us.'

'As soon as the National Gallery opens,' her fiancé said. 'When it'll still be quiet. And I'm going to ask her to marry me in front of her favourite painting in the world.'

'Van Gogh's *Sunflowers*,' Aleisha said. 'And obviously I'm going to say yes. We're going to ask the gallery staff to take a picture—not for social media, but for *us*.'

'That's lovely. I'm sure they'll help. I wish you both every happiness,' Fizz said, smiling. 'And it's been a privilege to make this for you.' Even if it had ended up landing her in a situation she really hadn't expected.

She headed back home and worked on the silver and zircona replica, soldering the collets to the ring. What would it be like if she and Oliver were engaged for real? Would he think of somewhere special to propose and slide the ring onto her finger? Stupid question: of course he would. Except he wasn't going to propose to her for real, and this whole thing was messing with her head.

She was still thinking about Oliver when he called her. 'Are you busy tonight?'

'I don't have anything planned,' she admitted. 'Why?'

'Would you like to come to the theatre with me? My parents had tickets for the first night of *A Midsummer Night's Dream* in Covent Garden, but Dad doesn't feel quite up to it and Mum doesn't want to leave him home alone, so she's offered us their tickets.'

'Yes, please—that's my favourite Shakespeare,' Fizz said. 'Can I get a nice dinner delivered to your parents in return?'

'Way ahead of you. I've already booked it,' he said. 'I've got a meeting at the gallery, this afternoon. I know we'll both be going in on the Northern Line, but I think it's probably easier if we meet outside Leicester Square Tube station.'

It was a sensible suggestion; in the rush hour of commuters, they wouldn't have a hope of finding each other on the platform at Goodge Street, the closest station to the gallery, let alone on the Tube itself. 'OK. What time?'

'Quarter to six,' he said. 'Because we've also got Mum and Dad's reservation for a pre-theatre dinner in Covent Garden. We'll walk there from Leicester Square, and I'll buy you dinner.'

'Thank you—that'd be great,' she said. 'See you later.'

She set an alarm on her phone to make sure she had enough time to get ready before the theatre, and continued working on the ring, gradually sanding down the silver to perfect smoothness.

When her alarm buzzed, she chose her favourite little black dress—a V-necked crepe slip dress with spaghetti straps—and teamed it with a silver and enamel sunflower choker on a black velvet ribbon, a sunflower silver and enamel bracelet, and red court shoes that looked like killer heels but were actually really comfortable to walk in. She left her hair loose and wore the minimum of make-up, just enough to emphasise her lips and her eyelashes.

Oliver was already waiting when she arrived at Leicester Square—dead on time.

'You look stunning,' he said.

She inclined her head in acknowledgement of the compliment. 'You don't scrub up too badly yourself,' she said. He was wearing a navy suit with a crisp white shirt and an understated tie, clearly his office suit. 'Good meeting?'

'Very,' he said, and tucked her arm through his.

At the restaurant, they chose different mains and starters, so they could taste each other's; it was a joy having a best friend who liked food as much as she did, and liked trying new things. She swapped a mouthful of her bruschetta with cannellini beans and pancetta for his agrodolce summer squash, and a taste of her gnocchi with chicken and chilli pesto for his risotto primavera. They finished with cheese, fennel crackers and fig jam, washed down with a good Venetian valpolicella.

'The food here is fantastic,' Oliver said, leaning back against his chair with a sigh of pleasure. 'We'll have to come back here.'

'Definitely,' she said. 'Next time, it's my treat.'

Somehow they ended up walking with their arms round each other between the restaurant and the theatre, and Oliver held her hand throughout the play. They were just practising for their public role as an engaged couple, she told herself; though it felt surprisingly good to sit beside him with his fingers tangled with hers. She actually felt a tingle in her knees, as if they'd gone all weak on her—something she hadn't expected to happen with Oliver.

Then again, since Paris, everything had felt different. It had changed her awareness of him; had it changed his awareness of her?

He held her hand when they left the theatre, too. Neither of them commented on it, and she kept the conversation light all the way back to Camden, chatting about the play.

'I really regret not being part of the drama society, as a student,' she said. 'They did *A Midsummer Night's Dream* in my last year, and I would've loved to play Puck.'

'Because of his impetuous streak?' Oliver teased.

'Because he gets to fix things when they go wrong,' she corrected.

'But they go wrong in the first place because of him,' Oliver said. 'Plus Oberon didn't actually order him to turn Bottom into an ass. Puck did that himself, out of pure mischief.'

She grinned. 'But we all know someone like Bottom—someone who's just too much and needs taking down a peg or two. Wouldn't it be fun to be able to give them an ass's head for a day? Though my absolute favourite bit in the play is when the Mechanicals perform Pyramus and Thisbe. Written down, it's dull. On stage, it's *hilarious*.' She raised an eyebrow. 'Who would you be?'

He laughed. 'Oberon, so I could boss everyone around.'

'That's so not you,' she said, shaking her head. 'Oberon's a bully. He's the epitome of the malevolent fae. I'd design him a crown of spikes and tangles, all shadowy and sharp.'

'All right. Who do *you* think I'd be, then?' he asked.

'Peter Quince,' she said.

He raised an eyebrow. 'Ambitious but lacking talent?'

'Not at all,' she said. 'You're clear-sighted and you direct people for the good of the company. You know your team, you know what they're good at, and you can see where they'd get something out of being stretched.'

'That,' he said, 'is a lovely thing to say. And it's how I want to run Harrison's. Like Dad did, but maybe broadening things out a bit.'

'And that,' she said, 'is why he picked the perfect person to take over from him.'

He squeezed her hand. 'Thank you.'

Oliver got off at her Tube stop so he could walk her back to her flat.

'Do you want to come in for a glass of wine?' she asked.

'That'd be nice,' he said.

She connected her phone to her speaker in the living room and found some slow blues they both liked on her streaming service. Then she pulled the curtains, switched on a lamp, poured them both a glass of red and sat on the sofa next to him.

'My bride-to-be and her fiancé picked up their sunflower ring today.' She smiled. 'It's so romantic. They're getting officially engaged tomorrow morning as soon as the National Gallery's open, in front of the *Sunflowers* because it's her favourite painting in the world. Well, that's why they chose me as their designer, because she's already got some of my earrings and loves them.'

'That's special,' he agreed. 'Something they'll always remember.'

She took a deep breath. 'I'm sorry I've deprived you of a proper engagement.'

'You mean our fake one at the Musée d'Orsay, with no pictures?' he asked. 'That's not a big deal.'

Wasn't it? 'Your mum and dad must think it's odd, though,' she mused. 'That we didn't even take a photograph of something so momentous, I mean.'

'We could always have a quiet private engagement when you've finished making the replica ring,' he said.

'That'll be tomorrow. Though, actually, I have plans for tomorrow—with any luck, it's my next bucket list thing. Commitment.'

He looked intrigued. 'What did you decide to go for in the end? Mentoring or teaching?'

'Neither,' she said. 'It's the weirdest coincidence. I went out for some milk and I saw this jug I really liked in the window of the charity shop round the corner.' She told him about the ginger cat and what she'd learned of Tilly's plight. 'Trisha's talking it over with her partner. Hopefully she'll be happy for me to take Tilly, and then we'll go to the cat rescue place and formalise me adopting Tilly. That way everyone gets a safeguard and everybody wins. And I'm fulfilling Laura's list—because it's a commitment, it's long term, and I'll be making a difference to the life of an elderly cat who's just lost her owner.'

'Didn't the landlady in your second-year digs have

a cat who spent a lot of her time draped round your neck?' he asked. 'A pretty cat, black and white and ginger.'

'Bubbles,' she confirmed. 'She liked cuddles. Obviously it's hard to sketch with a cat on your lap, and that's why she ended up draped round my neck so often. The art student's answer to a pirate's parrot,' she added with a grin. 'Actually, I think I'd like to have a cat. She'd fit into my lifestyle without me worrying about getting her enough exercise, as I would with a dog. Keep your fingers crossed for me that I can adopt Tilly.'

'I will. I have to admit, that's one of the things I've enjoyed about staying with my parents to keep an eye on them, this week—it's been nice having a dog around,' he said.

'Poppy's a sweetheart,' she agreed. 'I was thinking: if your dad's feeling up to it, the weather's meant to be nice on Sunday. Maybe we could take your parents for a gentle walk round the garden of a stately home, and I can treat them to afternoon tea as a thank you for the theatre tickets.'

'I'll ask them tomorrow and let you know,' he said. He finished his wine and stood up. 'Thanks for the wine. Keep me posted on your commitment situation tomorrow.'

'I will,' she said. Part of her was tempted to ask him to join her; though she didn't want to put pressure on him. He had enough on his plate, worrying about his parents. 'Thanks for this evening, Oli. I had a really lovely time.'

'Me, too.' He bent his head to kiss her cheek, and somehow his lips ended up brushing the corner of her mouth. She wasn't sure which of them turned their head—maybe both of them—but then they were really kissing, his arms wrapped round her and holding her close, and her hands in his hair and urging him on.

Everything around them was forgotten. The soft lights, the music, whatever they'd been talking about—everything vanished in the whirlwind of that kiss.

When he finally pulled away from her, both of them were shaking. His pupils were so huge that his eyes looked black. And he looked as dazed as she felt.

'That wasn't…'

'I didn't…'

They both stopped, not wanting to talk over each other.

'That wasn't meant to happen,' he said. 'Sorry.'

'My fault completely,' she said. 'Sorry.'

And she could see he knew she wasn't sorry at all—just as she knew he wasn't, either.

This had been going to happen ever since Paris. Ever since they'd danced together by the side of the Seine and she'd thought he was going to kiss her then. Ever since they'd agreed on this ridiculous fake engagement. And especially ever since they'd wandered through Covent Garden this evening, holding hands.

But what now? If they turned their fake engagement into a real relationship, what if everything went wrong? She didn't want to lose him from her life. But at the same time she knew they couldn't stay like this, either.

Was he panicking about this as much as she was?

But he seemed to get his head together more quickly than she did.

'We need to talk,' he said. 'But not right now, when we're both a bit shell-shocked. Maybe tomorrow.'

'When we've had time to think everything through,' she agreed.

'Goodnight,' he said, and this time he didn't kiss her, not even on the cheek. Which was probably just as well, even though at the same time it made her feel miserable.

Knowing she was being a coward in not facing up to the situation, Fizz spent Saturday morning immersed in work, and at lunchtime she had a call from Trisha. 'I've spoken to the rescue centre. If you're free on Monday lunchtime, we can go together and sort out the paperwork.'

'That's wonderful news,' she said. 'Thank you. And I should add that you're always welcome to pop round and see her any time.'

She sent a text to Oliver.

Busy working today. Seeing rescue centre people about Tilly on Monday.

He texted back.

Good news.

The ball appeared to be very much in her court. Well, she'd just leave it there for now, because she wasn't ready to talk about that kiss.

Did you ask your parents about tomorrow?

Yes. Can they decide tomorrow?

Of course—if your dad doesn't feel up to it, I understand. Will wait to hear from you.

On Sunday morning, Oliver texted her.

Sorry. Dad's still feeling a bit rough. Maybe next Sunday?

Absolutely, she responded. Give your parents my love.

Will do. Let me know how you get on with the rescue centre.

He'd let her off the hook; it gave her another couple of days' breathing space to decide how to react to that kiss. How to react to him. And what she was going to do next.

On Monday, Fizz saw the rescue centre people, who wanted to visit her flat before they made the final decision.

On Tuesday morning, she made sure she had good biscuits to offer with the tea and coffee, and gave Nadira, the assessor, a tour of her flat.

'I thought Tilly could have a bed in my bedroom as well as a bed in the living room,' she said. 'Plus a litter tray in the bathroom, and her water bowl and food bowl in the kitchen. Trisha told me she's an indoor cat, and she's used to company because her previous owner was elderly; I work from home, so she'll have me around most of the time.' She gestured to the jeweller's bench and worktop in her living room. 'Not that much of my work is noisy—for those bits, maybe she can go and nap in my bedroom.'

Nadira made notes. 'That's good. She'll need a snug place to hide away while she settles in. It can be an igloo-type bed or even just a cardboard box with holes cut into it and a blanket inside.'

Fizz smiled. 'Trisha has Tilly's bed from her previous home, so that should help her settle in. I'll get her a second bed, and I'll keep her with the same vet so she has continuity of care.'

'I think this is going to be a good home for her,' Nadira said. 'Congratulations.' She was able to give advice on which food to get, and how to help Tilly to settle in with a cat pheromone spray. 'If you don't have a carrier from her previous owner, you'll need a carrier when you pick her up.'

Fizz nodded. 'I'm going to check things with Trisha, then head to the pet shop. I'll get her a scratching post and some toys, too.'

'Sounds perfect,' Nadira said with a smile.

On Wednesday, Fizz called in on Trisha to pick up Tilly, brought the cat back to her flat, and in a ridiculously short space of time Tilly had investigated the flat, decided on her favourite spot in the living room, and was happily snoozing in a patch of sunlight.

Unable to resist the impulse, she took a photograph and sent it to Oliver.

Tilly says hello and would you like to come and meet her tonight?

The reply was almost immediate.

Love to. What time?

Seven? Thought we could order a Chinese takeaway. Usual?

Yes, please. See you then.

Next, she sent the pic to Darcy.

My name's Tilly, I love sleeping in the sun, and I live with your sister as of today.

To her relief, Darcy responded quickly.

OMG! You got a rescue cat?

Sort of. She's elderly and her owner died. We made friends in the charity shop where she was staying temporarily. Tilly's my commitment.

She's gorgeous.

A picture of a fox-red Labrador appeared on Fizz's screen.

I might have a new friend, too. Going back for a second visit at the weekend.

A dog would really suit Darcy, Fizz thought.

That's lovely!

She was itching to know if there was any more news about the guy in the photo, but she didn't want to make her sister back off.

Everything going OK? she asked instead, giving Darcy the opportunity to tell her more.

Yep. You?

No, it wasn't. It was getting complicated. And Fizz was fully aware that she was using Tilly as an excuse not to have the discussion with Oliver about that kiss.

Yep, she fibbed.

At seven precisely, her doorbell rang. Oliver came in with a brown paper bag. 'I brought a couple of house-warming gifts for Tilly.'

They turned out to be a catnip mouse and a 'fishing rod' toy with a feathery bundle on the end. Tilly loved them. She also took to Oliver immediately, sitting on his lap and purring loudly.

'I think she's just taken over chairmanship of your fan club,' Fizz said with a grin.

'It's mutual. She's lovely,' he said, smiling back.

And their mutual admiration of her new commitment made things much easier for her to manage. She could still avoid talking about that kiss. She wasn't going to bring up the subject unless he did.

A few minutes later, their Chinese food arrived. She'd already put bowls and cutlery on the small bistro table in her kitchen, and she slotted the cartons in the spaces between them with extra spoons for serving. 'Kung Pao chicken, veggie chow mein, crispy duck with pancakes, and mushroom fried rice.' She took a bottle of soy sauce from the cupboard.

'It smells wonderful,' he said.

Tilly looked hopeful and gave a single plaintive miaow when Oliver shredded the crispy duck for the pancakes, but Fizz shook her head. 'Sorry, puss. The spice and sauces aren't good for you. But I did buy a bit of cold poached salmon yesterday to help you settle in. You can have some of that while we eat.' She went to the fridge to get the salmon and chopped it up in Tilly's bowl.

'I think you've fallen on all four paws here, Tilly,' Oliver said, rubbing the top of the cat's head.

'She's helping me, too,' Fizz said. 'If it wasn't for her, I'd still be a bit stuck on task two of the bucket list.' She put the cat's bowl on the floor and Tilly ate daintily.

'Halfway there. So that leaves doing something that scares you and thinking about what you want,' Oliver said.

Her eyes caught his. She was beginning to think that the two things were actually one and the same; she certainly couldn't have one without the other. 'I still have a bit of time,' she said.

At the weekend, Mark was feeling a lot more himself, so Fizz and Oliver found a seventeenth-century house with a gorgeous walled garden and plenty of seating where he and Juliet could have a gentle stroll to enjoy the late spring flowers and stop for a rest whenever Mark needed to. Fizz took photographs of flowers that she thought had potential for a jewellery collection, and Oliver found a wisteria tunnel.

'To inspire your seed pearl earrings,' he said.

'Oh, yes. And you can look decorative for me.' She grinned, and took various shots of Oliver with the wisteria in the background.

'Mum and Dad are coming,' he murmured. 'So I'm going to kiss you, OK?'

The warning wasn't quite enough to stop her knees turning to jelly when he rested his hands on her waist and brushed his mouth against hers. His sunglasses hid his eyes, so she couldn't tell if the kiss had had the same effect on him as it had on her.

'Oh, you two,' Juliet sighed, clearly delighted to have caught them kissing. 'What it is to be young.'

'I can still kiss my wife,' Mark said, proving it. 'And hold her hand.'

'Let me take a picture of you together,' Fizz said, and snapped away. 'I'll Bluetooth them across to you over tea.'

Juliet produced her phone from her bag. 'Let me take a picture of you together, too.'

Oliver draped his arm casually round her shoulders, and her skin tingled where his bare arm touched hers. Though she had a feeling that even if she'd worn a thick coat instead of a strappy summery dress, and he'd had long sleeves instead of a T-shirt, she would still have been just as aware of him.

What was she going to do about this?

The question ticked round and round her brain as they headed for the café and found a table for a full-blown afternoon tea. Trying to push it into the background, she smiled and laughed at Juliet's anecdotes of Oliver as a toddler. But she was very aware of Oliver's arm across the back of her chair, and how easy it would be to shuffle her chair just that little bit closer and lean into him.

Today was meant to be an afternoon out to give Mark a change of scenery and Juliet a bit of a break. And it was working; the strain had lessened on both their faces.

But it was also crystallising for Fizz what she wanted.

A partner with a family background like her own, close and loving.

Scratch that. What she wanted was Oliver.

But.

How did she know this wasn't going to go wrong? She'd never told anyone about that awful night, five years ago. She'd tried to keep it boxed in and shut away, so it wouldn't hurt anyone else.

If she told him what she'd done, would he think less of her? Would he change his mind about her?

The longer you kept a secret, the more dangerous it became.

And she had a nasty feeling this could all blow apart.

CHAPTER SEVEN

'YOU'RE LOOKING WORRIED,' Oliver said, when she met him for a drink in the middle of the week. 'Spill.'

'Darcy's going to Verona, to this Arturo guy's sister's wedding.' Darcy had texted her with the mystery man's name and her plans.

'And?'

'He's a guy she met at dance class—the one she went to Rome with.'

He coughed. 'You went to Paris with me.'

She flapped a dismissive hand. 'I've known you for ever, and she barely knows this guy! She says he's a modern-day Indiana Jones.'

'What's the problem?'

She frowned. 'Don't you think it's all a bit…impulsive? Rash?'

'Coming from you, Fizz…'

She brushed the teasing aside. 'Yeah. I know, but I've been like that since I was a toddler. Darcy's not.'

'You said it earlier, maybe Laura's list was to try to make Darcy more like you and you more like Darcy—balance you both out,' Oliver suggested.

'Maybe. Anyway, she was worrying about what to wear, so I sent her a dress. One I bought last year but never got round to wearing.' She sighed. 'At least she'll look and feel fabulous. Just as long as she doesn't end up with a broken heart.'

'Why are you so convinced that she'll end up with a broken heart?'

'I was there when Damian dumped her at the altar. I saw what it did to her,' Fizz said.

'That was a long time ago. She's older and wiser now.' He paused. 'Is that why you hardly ever date? Because you're worried it'll turn out like that for you, too?'

'Mm,' Fizz said. It wasn't a complete fib, but it was only a partial answer.

A full answer was the thing that scared her most. The thing she'd never shared with anyone. She already judged herself and found herself wanting. But if Oli, whose opinion mattered to her, despised her if she told him the truth...

'Fizz, your parents have been married for ever. So have mine. Yes, there are more break-ups nowadays than there were thirty years ago, but it doesn't mean that your relationship won't stay the course. How are you ever going to find the right person for you if you never give anyone a chance?'

That was just it. She was beginning to think that maybe Oliver was the right one for her. But would her past—the bits she'd kept from him—mean that she was the wrong one for him?

'You know,' he said, 'when I kissed you by the wisteria, it felt like you kissed me back.'

Panic flooded through her. She didn't want to discuss this. 'We were acting for your parents,' she said. Which was true... up to a point. But even thinking about it made her feel as if all the air had been sucked out of the room. Why was he bringing it up *now*?

She mumbled something else anodyne to brush it off and changed the subject.

But as the days went by, the thought wouldn't go away. It was like having a leaky tap in the kitchen and hearing every drip more loudly than the last. *Tell. Him. The. Truth.*

The longer she left it, the more insistent the voice in her head became. Like a waterfall instead of a drip.

And time was running out to fulfil Laura's bucket list.

Task three: *Do something that scares you.*

If she didn't face her demons and tell Oliver the truth, she wouldn't be able to move forward.

In the end, she messaged him.

Can we talk? Somewhere private, just you and me?

Sure. I'll meet you outside Goodge Street Tube station. I know somewhere nearby. Text me when you're at Camden station.

She was grateful that he didn't ask questions.

She made a fuss of Tilly. 'I won't be long,' she promised. 'I just need to talk to Oli. Tell him the truth.'

She texted him from the platform to let him know that her train was due in two minutes. As he'd promised, he was waiting for her outside Goodge Street station.

'Are you OK?' he asked.

'I'm not sure,' she admitted.

'Let's walk,' he said.

She was glad that he didn't take her arm. She needed to be strong for this. Self-contained.

He led her through a couple of back streets and then into what looked like a Victorian building from the outside but a modern open-plan office inside. He went over to the receptionist, who gave him a key, and he beckoned Fizz to follow him round the corner.

He opened the door onto a tiny courtyard. In the centre was a small knot garden made from box hedges and stuffed with lavender and herbs, and placed casually round the knot garden were several wrought-iron benches. There were a couple of wrought-iron frames, too, with roses planted in their centre; no doubt by the middle of the summer the roses would have climbed all over the frames and be scenting the air.

'This is an amazing space,' she said. 'How did you find out about it?'

'Do you remember my friend Sanjay from uni?' he asked. 'He's a senior account exec at the ad agency here. The agency's a big believer in holistic spaces, and they set up this courtyard a couple of years ago. I asked if I could borrow it for an hour or so.'

'This is beautiful. Butterflies flitting everywhere, birds singing—you'd never believe you were right in the middle of London.'

'And it's private, like you wanted. Just you and me,' he said. 'I can ask Sanjay for some coffee, if you want.'

She shook her head. 'It's fine. I don't need coffee. I just...' She blew out a breath. 'I don't know where to start, Oli.'

'The beginning's good,' he said. 'Or anywhere that feels comfortable.'

Nothing would feel comfortable about this. 'The third task in my bucket list. Do something that scares me.'

He looked at her, his blue eyes kind. 'That's losing your other sister, isn't it? I know things aren't quite the way you want them to be with you and Darcy at the moment, but I'm sure you can talk it over and work something out.'

'It's not that—though you're right, I do worry about that.' She took a deep breath. Right now, it felt as if she were about to leap off a precipice and she wasn't sure the bungee rope was properly attached. 'I'm going to take a risk. Tell you something I've never told anyone else.'

Oliver had a bad feeling about this. He could see the seriousness in Fizz's expression. Whatever she was going to tell him had clearly hurt her badly. And he didn't have a clue what it was.

She was his best friend, as well as the woman he'd fallen in love with. He'd known her for years. Why didn't he have the remotest clue what was wrong?

'OK,' he said. 'Just so it's clear, I'll treat whatever you tell me as completely confidential.'

'I already know that. I didn't need to ask.'

It warmed him to know that she trusted him that much. 'Sorry for interrupting. I'm listening,' he said gently.

'It happened just after Laura died.'

Five years ago. He'd been in New York at the time, on business for his father. He'd known that Laura was fading, but he'd hoped he'd be finished in New York and back to support Fizz before Laura actually died.

'A couple of days afterwards, I came back to London to see my tutors and sort out my work. I had a project I knew I needed to work on—something that counted towards my degree, so I couldn't just ignore it—but I didn't want to leave Mum and Dad unsupported before the funeral. They were barely able to put one foot in front of another.'

Understandable. Having to bury your child was any parent's worst nightmare.

'Darcy agreed to stay in Bath for a couple of days, while I sorted out things in London and rearranged my deadline, and then she was going to go back to Edinburgh for a few days and come back for the funeral,' Fizz continued.

Which all sounded fair enough, to him. What was he missing?

'One of my tutors couldn't see me until the day after I got back to London. My housemates weren't around and my head really wasn't in a good place,' she said. 'I went out that night. I intended to get very, *very* drunk, dance my feet off, and maybe snog someone to make myself feel better.' She closed her eyes. 'Except, the next morning, I woke up in this guy's flat. A place I didn't recognise.'

Now he was starting to understand what the problem was.

'I don't actually remember anything between snogging him on the dance floor and waking up the next morning.' She shook her head. 'I didn't even know his name.'

Fizz clearly felt guilty about having a one-night stand. But that wasn't fair. These things happened. He took her hand. 'Fizz, right then you needed comfort—and sometimes only physical comfort will do.

You were free to choose someone to do that for you.'
Or was that what he was missing? 'Unless he hurt you
or pressured you into it?'

'I don't *think* so. I did wonder if he'd slipped something into my drink, because I couldn't remember very
much the next day. Or maybe I'd just drunk more than I
thought I had.' She bit her lip. 'Or maybe I just blocked
everything out of my head, because I was so ashamed
of what I did.'

'Fizz, you have absolutely nothing to be ashamed of.
This isn't the Victorian era. You were twenty years old
and you were single. If you wanted to sleep with someone, that was your choice and it's nobody else's business.'

Her eyes narrowed. 'You don't think any differently
about me?'

'No.' He stroked her hair. 'Of course I don't. Darcy
and your parents wouldn't, either. Or any of your friends.
I'm sorry you never told me about this before. I could've
maybe reassured you that it's nothing to feel bad about.
A one-night stand isn't a big deal.' Or was there more
to it than that, something that was so subtle it'd gone
over his head? He folded his fingers round hers. 'I wish
I'd been there, that night, instead of in New York. I
knew how ill Laura was and there wasn't much time. I'm
sorry. I should've stayed in London to be there for you.'

'Your dad wanted you to go. It was your first time
of doing something for the gallery on your own. You
needed to go,' she said. 'And I'm not sure you could've
rescued me from what happened.'

'If you'd been with me, nobody would've spiked your
drink or anything else,' he said.

She dragged in a breath. 'Thank you. But I could've said no.'

'If you don't remember what happened, then you weren't in a position to say no—or to give consent,' he said. 'Any decent guy would've either made sure you got home to your own place safely and had someone to look after you, or taken you back to his place and kept an eye on you himself, sleeping on the floor instead of taking advantage of you. This isn't on you, Fizz. Please don't beat yourself up about something that wasn't your fault.'

Oh, but the next bit was definitely her fault. She should've predicted it. Done something about it. At least gone to the pharmacy and asked for help, the morning after, instead of blocking it out and refusing to deal with it.

He kept looking at her, his eyes kind, and that gave her the courage to say more.

'That's just the beginning,' she said. 'I guess I wasn't thinking straight. I went back to my place without waking the guy from the night before, because I didn't want to be late for the meeting with my tutor. I showered and changed, then had my meeting. And then I packed everything I needed and I took the train back to Bath. I put everything out of my head. Pretended it hadn't happened.'

Oliver had made it clear he didn't despise her for the one-night stand. But the next bit… How could he not despise her? She closed her eyes again. 'Two weeks later, I realised my period was late. I convinced myself it was because I was upset about Laura.'

He rubbed the pad of his thumb against the back of her hand, still keeping his fingers wrapped round hers. 'It could've been,' he said. 'You were grieving. Stressed.'

'True, but I knew deep down it wasn't that. I felt different,' she said. 'It took me another three days to work up the courage to do a pregnancy test.' She dragged in a breath. 'I went to the supermarket furthest away from home, and just hoped I wouldn't bump into anyone I'd been to school with or who knew my parents. Anyone who might see what I was buying and start gossiping. I put a magazine over the top of the test in my basket to hide it while I was in the shop, and I went through a self-checkout so I wouldn't have to have the test on show for more than a couple of seconds before I stuffed it in my bag. And then I went to the supermarket's toilets and I did the test. I just stared and stared at the test stick in the cubicle, wanting that first line to come up so I knew it was working. And then it seemed to take for ever for the test results to show. I'd just about convinced myself that I was panicking over nothing, and feeling a bit different was just psychological. Obviously it was negative and I had nothing to worry about. I looked away.' She swallowed hard. 'And then I looked back again and the second line was there, out of nowhere. Really dark. There was no chance I could be mistaken. I was definitely pregnant.'

He said nothing, so she risked a glance at him. He looked concerned, but not as if she'd shocked him. 'You're quiet,' she said, a slight edge to her voice.

'I'm listening,' he said, and squeezed her hand briefly. 'Not judging.'

'Thank you,' she said raspily. Her throat felt constricted, as if something was blocking it. The words she didn't want to say. The words that scared her. The words that needed to come out.

'Keep talking,' he said gently, when she still said nothing. 'It's not going any further than me. Keeping it locked inside you is hurting you. Telling me might make it lose its power.'

His faith in her was enough to make her push on. 'I didn't know what to do, Oli. I wandered round in a bit of a daze. God knows how I managed to find the right bus home. I was in the middle of my degree, I'd just lost my sister, and my life was in enough of a mess as it was. The idea of bringing an unplanned baby into the middle of all that—especially as I didn't even remember the guy's name and I had no way of getting in touch with him...'

'It must've been terrifying,' he said. 'And there was nobody you could talk to? Darcy?'

'She was hurting as much as I was. So were Mum and Dad. I couldn't dump my worries on them.'

'You could have talked to me,' he said. 'I wouldn't have judged you.'

'I felt too guilty. The mess was all of my own making. If I hadn't gone out that night, or if I'd kept an eye on what I was drinking and not gone home with that guy, or if I'd seen a pharmacist the next day and got the morning after pill—any one of those things would've meant I hadn't screwed up completely.'

'I'm sorry I wasn't there for you,' he said. 'If I'd had any idea, I would've done my best to support you. I hope you know I'll always listen.'

'I'm sorry I shut you out, back then,' she said. 'I think I shut everyone out. I had a bit of a meltdown at home. Everyone thought it was because of Laura's death, and it was easier to let them believe that than to tell the truth. And then…two weeks later, I was on the train, on my way back to London, when I started getting cramps. I went to the loo and realised I was bleeding. I didn't have any sanitary protection with me, and there was no way of buying anything on the train. The only people in my carriage were men, and a couple of women who looked as if they were older than my mum and probably didn't need to carry anything with them any more—nobody I could ask for emergency help. I just had to make do with stuffing toilet roll in my knickers and hoping I wasn't going to leak everywhere. I think that was the worst train journey of my life.'

'Oh, Fizz. That must've been so hard to deal with.'

'I made it to Paddington, and I went straight to the shops so I had something a bit better to help me get back to my flat. And then I stood in the shower and cried until the water went cold.'

Then he moved, scooping her onto his lap. 'If this is the wrong thing, tell me and I'll back off,' he said. 'But right now I'm guessing you could do with a hug.'

'I could.' She squeezed her eyelids shut, willing the tears to stay back, but one slid out anyway. 'Sorry. I'm messing up your shirt.'

'I don't care.' He kept his arms round her. 'It's not important.'

'I feel so guilty.' She could hear the shudder in her own voice. 'I'd messed everything up. And then I lost the baby—I should've been relieved, because it solved my problems, but I felt even worse. I was sure it was my fault because the baby knew it wasn't wanted.'

His arms were warm and comforting round her. 'It wasn't your fault. A lot of babies don't make it through the first three months of pregnancy, and there are all sorts of reasons why. It really *wasn't* your fault,' he repeated. 'You'd already lost Laura; even though the baby wasn't planned, losing it must've been hard.'

She nodded. 'I tried to tell myself I was lucky, because it meant I didn't have to make any difficult choices or even face up to what I'd done. But I was just miserable. I still am, deep down. I couldn't tell Mum, Dad or Darcy, because they were already in bits and they didn't need me dumping an extra load on top of them.'

'What about your personal tutor?'

'He wasn't the most sympathetic of people,' she said. 'And I didn't want any of the tutors I liked thinking as badly of me as I thought of myself.'

He held her a little bit more tightly. 'Any tutor worth their salt would've given you a hug, made you a cup of tea, fed you cake and made you talk. What about one of your housemates?'

She leaned against him. 'It was easier just to let everyone think I was upset because of Laura. And that felt wrong, too—my sister deserved better than that from me. I shouldn't have used her as an excuse to cover up what I did.'

'Laura,' he said, 'would've understood. And I can say that because I met her.'

'I buried myself in work, a bit.' She lifted her head and gave him a wry smile. 'You were good about that. Even though you were busy at the gallery, you always made me feel you had time for me. And you took me to the sea for long walks.'

'I knew you were upset, and I thought it was because of Laura,' he said. 'I worried that you were working too hard because that was the best way to block out your feelings.'

'It was,' she said. 'It helped me cope. Work, and you.'

'When I feel low, walking by water always helps me. Being a bloke, I'm not great at talking about emotional stuff—so I tried to do for you what I knew would help me, and hoped it helped you as well.'

'It did.' She bit her lip. 'I've buried it, Oli. To the point where I can't tell my family now because they'll be hurt that I didn't confide in them years ago. And I'm stuck. Until I've dealt with how it makes me feel, I can't move on.'

'I get that,' he said.

'This is what scares me,' she said softly. 'Talking about it. What I did. The consequences.'

He stroked her hair. 'Everyone makes mistakes, or looks back and wishes they'd done something differently. You were only twenty. You'd handle things differently now because you're older and you've had more life experience. If one of your friends came to you and told you a similar story, you'd support her rather than judging her harshly, wouldn't you?'

'Yes,' she admitted.

'So be kinder to yourself.' He paused. 'Fizz, did you get any kind of medical advice at the time?'

She nodded. 'I went to the student health centre. They did some tests. Whoever he was, he'd taken proper care of his physical health, and I'm beyond grateful for that.'

'That's not what I meant, but I'm glad you didn't have that worry on top of everything else.' He stroked her hair. 'I meant, did they talk to you about why you lost the baby, and how you might feel in the future?'

'Not really,' she said.

'Then maybe it would help you to talk to someone about it.'

'Like who?' she asked.

'A counsellor, a helpline, or someone in a support group—someone who can help you work it through and teach you the tools to deal with how you feel. Obviously you can always tell me anything, and I'll always listen,' he said. 'But I don't know how to make you feel differently about what happened to you. You need to talk to someone professional, someone who knows how to do that.'

'So you don't despise me?'

'Of course I don't despise you. You make my world a much better place. Nothing's going to change that. And, just so you know, that'll be the same for anyone else who knows you.'

'I just felt so ashamed. And guilty. I still do.'

'I think that a lot of people in your shoes would feel like that, even though you've done nothing wrong.' He stroked held her close. 'What do you need, Fizz?'

'I don't know,' she said.

'I want to support you,' he said. 'Right now, I'm terrified that I'm going to say the wrong thing and hurt you. But it's what *you* need that's important right now. So help me out here, a little?'

She blew out a breath. 'I just wanted to be honest with you.'

'I get that,' he said. 'I wish you'd told me before, because I would've been there for you. I hate to think of you carrying all that pain on your own. If you want me to go with you for moral support and wait outside when you do see someone, I'll be there.'

'I think,' she said, 'you're right. That's what I need to do. It scares the hell out of me, opening up like that to a complete stranger...but I need to do it.'

'Whatever you need, tell me and it's yours,' he said. 'If you want me to help you find a counsellor, or just sit in your flat and play with Tilly and keep you company while you're looking, I'm in. No judgements, no telling you what to do.'

'Thank you,' she said. 'For listening. For understanding.'

'Any time,' he said.

And she knew he meant it. Regardless of what happened in their relationship, Oliver Harrison would always be her friend.

But did she want him to be so much more...?

CHAPTER EIGHT

A FEW DAYS LATER, Fizz went to her first counselling
session. Oliver accompanied her for moral support, and
while she was in her session he sat in the waiting room
reading a magazine on his phone. When she came out,
her eyes were red, but she looked lighter of spirit than
he'd seen her in a while.

'How did you get on?' he asked.

'It helped.' She gave him a slightly wobbly smile.
'I've got a way to go, but I'm heading in the right di-
rection. And thank you for your support. I'm not sure
I would've had the courage to come on my own.'

'Yes, you would,' he corrected. 'And I got some
much-needed reading time, so I have a lot of nerdy
stuff to regale you with. Did you know that the pattern
on top of custard cream biscuits is meant to be ferns—
because of the Victorian pteridomania?'

Just as he'd hoped, she laughed and tucked her hand
through his arm. 'Oh, Oli. You're *such* a nerd. What's
pteridomania? If *ptero* is flying and mania's a craze,
then maybe something to do with ballooning?'

'Not even close. It's fern fever,' he said. 'Pterido-
phytes—ferns—hadn't been studied as much as flowers, so amateur botanists had more of a chance of

finding something new.' He grinned. 'They were really popular in decorative arts. You could always add them as a range of jewellery and start the craze going again.'

She shook her head, but she was smiling. 'Where do you get this stuff?'

'It was yet another article in a magazine,' he said. 'My guilty pleasure.'

'Custard creams and fern patterns.' She smiled. 'I think that's our cue to go for a cup of tea and—well, you can have a custard cream, if you like, but I'm thinking warm scones. And it's my shout, because you've been a star.' She hugged into him feeling more content than she ever had before.

The next day, things went in completely the opposite direction. Oliver was just about to leave the gallery for his flat when his mum texted.

Can you call in to see us tonight?

She hadn't mentioned why. His first thought was that his father was ill and she was downplaying it.

He rang her back rather than texting. 'Mum? Is Dad all right?'

'Yes.' But she sounded subdued. Upset, even.

'What's happened?' he asked.

'I'd rather talk about it face to face.'

His hot date tonight was only with some paperwork, and it didn't matter if he got to it later than he'd planned. 'I'm on my way,' he said.

Given that it was rush hour, the Tube was more of

a squash than usual, but it was still quicker than driving. He didn't pause to pick up flowers for his mum or a magazine for his dad, the way he usually would; the tone of her voice had alerted him that it'd be better to go straight there.

Juliet Harrison wasn't the needy sort who made a fuss over nothing. If his dad hadn't taken a turn for the worse, what could have upset her?

He rang the doorbell to signal his arrival, then used his key; Poppy the Westie came scampering through to the hallway to welcome him, wagging her tail madly. Oliver stooped to make a fuss of her, then went in search of his parents.

He found his mother in the living room on the sofa. 'Hi, Mum.' He frowned. 'Where's Dad?'

'Having a lie-down.'

That raised a red flag. His father hated resting. Oliver caught his breath. 'Is he having symptoms again?'

'No.'

'Then what's wrong?'

'I had a text from my friend Tamsin this afternoon.' His mother's voice was toneless. 'She sent me a story she thought I'd like. She said it was really romantic and sweet. Which, I suppose, it was.'

'OK.' He was still none the wiser.

Juliet handed her phone to him with the message open. He duly clicked on the link and read the news story.

The article was about a couple who'd recently got engaged in front of Van Gogh's *Sunflowers* in the National Gallery. The bride-to-be's love of sunflowers had inspired what she wanted for an engagement ring—and a brilliant up-and-coming jeweller had designed and made it for them.

Oliver winced as he saw the close-up photograph.

Fizz's borrowed engagement ring.

The ring she'd designed for someone else.

It looked as if he was going to have to come clean about their fake engagement a bit sooner than he'd expected.

'Mum. I can explain.'

'Can you?' Her eyes narrowed. 'You lied to us, Oliver. The pair of you.'

'We didn't mean to hurt anyone,' he said.

'But Fizz made that ring for someone else,' Juliet said quietly. 'And you let us believe it was an engagement ring from you. And we've seen her wearing it since this article came out. What did she do—borrow it from that poor girl every time she saw us?'

'No. She made a replica,' Oliver said. He sighed. 'Mum, will you let me explain?'

She frowned. 'I'm so disappointed in you, Oliver. You lied to us.'

'It wasn't meant to hurt you.' He blew out a breath. 'Mum, you know Dad wants me to settle down and get married before he's happy for me to take over the gallery fully. At my age, you were already married.'

Juliet nodded. 'He just wants to see you settled. We both do.'

'And I will settle down. When I'm ready,' he said. 'When you called me to say Dad had collapsed, I called Fizz. She came straight to the hospital from work—and she was worried enough about you both that she didn't even think about the ring. She'd put it on to check for any last-minute tweaks. Dad saw it, and you both assumed I'd given it to her as an engagement ring.'

'But you didn't correct us. You let us believe it. Both of you.'

'Because,' he said quietly, 'I asked her to. I didn't know if Dad was going to make it or not. In case he didn't pull through that operation, I wanted him to be happy before he went under the anaesthetic. And the idea of us getting married distracted you from worrying quite so much about Dad. That was a good thing.'

She shook her head. 'I'm not a child, needing to be humoured. Neither's your dad. You could have told us the truth at any time since the operation.'

'We were going to tell you,' he said. 'Soon. When Dad was stronger and you were less stressed.'

She ignored the comment. 'Everything you said about your relationship was a lie. She said she loved you.'

Oliver winced. 'I'm her best friend. Of course she loves me.'

'You *behaved* like an engaged couple,' Juliet continued. 'You were kissing by the wisteria—or was that all an act, too?'

He'd meant the kiss. He had a feeling that Fizz might have meant it, too; but when he'd tackled her about it, she'd brushed it aside. Then she'd told him the secrets she'd buried, and he'd dropped the subject because he didn't want to put any pressure on her until she was ready to move forward. And he wasn't going to break his promise about keeping what she'd told him confidential. 'I'm sorry we upset you,' Oliver said. 'Look, let me call Fizz. I'll do it on speaker so you can hear everything I say to her and everything she says to me.'

'I don't think there's any point. Right now, I don't want to talk to her. I'm too hurt and angry,' Juliet said. 'And as for wanting your father to be happy—did you not think about how he'd react when you told him the truth?'

'No,' he admitted. 'I panicked, and I focused on the moment.'

'That's what he said,' Juliet said. 'So how can he trust you with the business? What if something happens and you panic at work? Are you going to tell a pack of lies, get found out, and ruin the gallery's reputation?'

Oliver stared at his mother, horrified. 'Is that what he really thinks I'd do?'

'To the point where he's planning to go back to the office next week.'

'He *can't*. He's supposed to be resting,' Oliver said.

'How can he rest, when he's worrying what you might be doing to the gallery? At least if he's in the office, he can see what's going on and he won't be so worried.'

'I'm running it exactly the same way he would. With integrity,' Oliver said. 'I know you're both hurt and angry, and you have every right to be, but think about it logically, Mum. If anyone at the gallery was concerned about my performance over the last few weeks, they would've had a quiet word with Dad about it long before now.'

'Try convincing your father of that,' Juliet said. 'The way he sees it, if you can lie about being engaged, what else could you lie about? And I can completely see his point.'

It was stress, Oliver told himself. His mum had been worried sick about his dad; right now she was lashing out at him because he was an easy target. She didn't mean it. He needed to calm things down rather than react, even though he was really hurt they seemed to think so little of him. 'I'm sorry,' he said again. 'Yes, I lied, but it was with the best of intentions.'

'Lying isn't a good basis for any kind of relationship,' Juliet said.

'I know,' he said quietly. 'I did what I thought was the right thing, and I was wrong. I'm sorry I've let you down. I'll go and apologise to Dad, and then I'll talk to Fizz.' He bit his lip. 'If Dad has a setback on his health, because of me, I'll never forgive myself.'

When he knocked gently on his parents' bedroom door, there was no answer. He opened the door quietly and could see that his dad was asleep. Rather than waking him, Oliver retreated to his own room and called Fizz.

'You know your couple in the National Gallery? There was a news article about them. Mum's best friend sent it to her.' He paused. 'There was a close-up of the ring.'

'Oh, no.' She sounded horrified. 'I take it your parents worked the truth out for themselves?'

'Yes. They're pretty upset,' he said. 'You were right. All I did by not being honest with them was to push the reckoning further down the line.'

'I'll come over and explain it's my fault,' she said immediately.

'It *wasn't* your fault,' he said. 'I was the one who asked you to pretend.'

'The least I can do is take half the blame. I should've told them the truth tactfully, there and then, and I didn't.'

He blew out a breath. 'Fizz, please don't come over. They, um, need some distance.'

'Ah.' There was a pause. 'I understand,' she said.

But he'd heard that note of hurt in her voice. Rejection, from a couple who'd always liked her so much and made her welcome. Now she was *persona non grata*. None of this was fair, because it wasn't her fault. He'd fix it, but it would take time. And in the meantime she was hurting.

And his worst nightmare was coming true.

He'd always known that Fizz had had issues about relationships, that she was leery about settling down. He'd thought it was because of seeing her oldest sister jilted at the altar, until she'd told him about what had happened after Laura's death. Fizz didn't believe in love. Friendship she could deal with, but not love. If she knew how he really felt about her, she'd back away—and he'd lose her completely. It was why he'd held back in the past; and telling her now that she was the love of his life would make her back away even faster.

Right at this moment he needed to put his feelings on hold, so he could sort things out with his dad and the gallery; and then he'd have time to sort things out between the two of them. She'd been his best friend for long enough to understand that he needed a little space, right now... hadn't she?

'Fizz. I'll still be there for you. Of course I will. I'll go with you to your appointments. But right now I need to support my parents. Dad's worrying that I'm going to make as much of a mess of the gallery as I have of my personal life—and I need to take the strain off him before it makes him ill again. I haven't worked out how I'll fix things, yet, but I will. It's not you. It's me.' And how horrible he felt, saying that. As if he were dumping her. Which he wasn't, because they weren't really together at all. Even though he wished they were. This was rapidly becoming a horrible mess. And all because he'd wanted to protect his dad, to keep him happy before that life-saving operation... 'It's me being a bloke and not being able to multi-task,' he said, frantically willing her to understand him the way she always had.

'If there's anything I can do, just let me know,' she said.

'Thanks. I will,' he said, knowing that he had no intention of leaning on her—and knowing that she knew it, too. 'And if you need anything, ring me.'

'Of course,' she said, and he knew that she wouldn't. She'd agreed to give him the space he needed to fix things with his family, but at the same time he was pretty sure that she was already backing away from him. He had a nasty feeling that she'd slide quietly out of his life before he could do anything about it, and he didn't have a clue what to say to stop that happening. If he told her he loved her, she'd panic and he'd ruin things between them for ever. If he didn't tell her, he'd lose her. Whatever he did, he lost.

'Take care,' she said. 'And tell your parents I'm sorry.'

Fizz knew Oliver was right to ask her for some space. He was under enough strain; he didn't need her to add to it.

Just she hadn't expected it to hurt so much.

She'd always called and messaged Oliver as often as she'd called both her sisters: when she heard a joke she thought he'd enjoy or a piece of music he'd love, or came across a painting he'd adore. With Darcy being so far away, Oliver was her go-to person if she wanted to see a film or a play. He was the one she went with if she was trying a restaurant for the first time. He was the one she guinea-pigged when she found an interesting recipe.

Stepping back from him felt *weird*. As if there was an Oliver-shaped space in her life that wasn't going to be filled again. Which was ridiculous: of course she'd see him again. He was her best friend, for pity's sake.

But she knew it wouldn't be quite the same. There would be a new awkwardness between them, thanks to their ridiculous fake engagement. And as for the way she'd thought their relationship was going, after Paris—that was completely out of the question. Hadn't she learned from her sister's example that love didn't last? Hadn't she learned from that dark space after Laura's death that reaching out for love just spelled disaster? Wishing that things were different was just setting herself up for more heartbreak.

She and Oli weren't together. There wasn't going to be a happy ending. She wasn't even sure that their friendship was going to survive this, and she'd been closer to Oli than to anyone else outside her parents and her sisters. And it broke her heart to think that she'd lost his friendship—as well as the chance to make that friendship something deeper.

How, just how, was she going to fix this?

She didn't have a clue. Especially as the person she wanted to talk to about this was the very person she couldn't talk to, right now.

'I have an apology to sort out,' she said to Tilly, stroking the cat's head.

Flowers and an anodyne message written by somebody else weren't enough. She couldn't deliver anything personally; but she could at least give the florist a personal card to go with the flowers.

She sat down at the kitchen table with art paper that she'd folded in half, and did a pen and ink drawing of Poppy the Westie from memory. While it was drying, she drafted a letter.

Dear Juliet and Mark,
I'm so sorry.

I understand why you don't want to see me at the moment, but I can't just ignore the hurt I've caused you or pretend nothing's happened.

I want to apologise for not being honest with you right at the start about the ring. I really didn't mean to hurt you. I also don't want to come be-

*tween you and Oliver. He loves you very much
and you're so important to him. He's a good man.*

*I misdirected you with the very best of inten-
tions. I'm sorry I got it so wrong, and I hope that
you'll find a way to forgive me.*

*With love and very best wishes for Mark's con-
tinued recovery,*

She stopped and read it. How did she sign it? They'd
always called her Fizz. But would the more formal Felicity be more appropriate?

It wasn't exactly a great letter. Too many of the
sentences started with 'I'. Her primary school teacher
would've written a red note in the margin: *Try to vary
the beginnings of your sentences, Felicity.*

The problem was, she couldn't vary them. Unless she
wrote 'we'—and it wasn't fair to drag Oliver into this.
That comment about him being a good man could go;
his parents already knew that, plus it sounded like suck-
ing up—even though it wasn't and she really meant it.
The rest of her message was heartfelt, and she hoped
they'd take it in the spirit with which she'd written it.

She held the card she'd drawn at an angle to the
light to check that the ink was dry, then opened it and
wrote up her draft in her neatest handwriting. In the
end, she signed it 'Fizz'. She found an envelope for it,
then made a fuss of Tilly. 'I'll take this to the florists
as soon as they open tomorrow.'

In the meantime, she was glad of some routine accounts work to take her mind off things, and then re-runs
of a favourite comedy with Tilly curled up in her lap.

* * *

The next morning, Fizz called in to her local florists for a chat; they promised to arrange a nice summery bouquet and deliver it to Juliet along with Fizz's card in the early afternoon. Then she headed to Covent Garden to drop off some more stock at the shop that sold her flower earrings—including the first wisteria ones.

She loved the buzz of the market: the turquoise-painted wrought-iron arches and glass panes of the roof, the ancient paving stones in the piazza, the stalls crammed with arts and crafts, the scent of freshly baked cookies and coffee, the old-fashioned shop fronts with their hanging signs outside, the opera singer in the corner downstairs whose voice soared above the hub-bub of the tourists' chatter, and the jugglers and poets entertaining everyone with street theatre in between the market and the Roman temple-like façade of the church. Just as it had been for hundreds of years; the first Punch and Judy show in England had been per-formed near here, witnessed by Samuel Pepys and re-corded in his diary.

But there were quiet spots in Covent Garden, too: only a few steps from the bustle of the Apple Market and Jubilee Market were the gardens behind St Paul's church. The wooden benches with their brass memo-rial plaques, interspersed with old-fashioned lamps, lined the alley between the two stretches of garden. The trees were in full leaf and the gardens themselves were full of early summer flowers. At this time of day, in the half-hour before lunchtime, the gardens were almost empty; just the occasional bench was occupied by somebody reading a book.

A quiet space to think about what she wanted...

The last task of her bucket list.

This would fit the bill perfectly.

Fizz walked over to the Diamond Jubilee Memorial on the south side of the church, an oversized cast-iron replica of a penny surrounded by a maze of red and yellow bricks. Walking a maze was meant to be like a meditation, wasn't it? And maybe that would help her think. So she duly walked it.

What did she want?

Before Paris, she would've said that she already had everything she wanted. A family she loved, a job she loved, and good friends.

Laura's bucket list and Paris had changed everything.

She'd gone to Paris with Oliver, and seen him in a different light—as a man, rather than just as her best friend.

She'd made a commitment, and now she had an elderly ginger cat who'd adapted to her routines and just liked being with her.

She'd done something that scared her: she'd finally faced up to what had happened, five years ago. Her badly managed one-night stand. The unplanned pregnancy that had sent her into a spiral of panic—and then the miscarriage that had made her feel so horribly guilty. It would still take a while for her to work it through, but she realised that it was time to stop beating herself up about it. To let herself move on.

So what did she want now?

The more she thought about it, the more she realised.

What she wanted was Oliver. Not just as her best friend, but as her partner. A man who'd always have her back, but who was also strong enough to let himself lean on her when he needed support. A man who loved her family, and they loved him right back. A man whose family loved her, too—well, they *had* loved her, she amended silently. If she could persuade them to accept her apology, maybe they'd find their way back to a warm, easy relationship, in time.

But the question was: did Oliver want her?

His dad wanted him to settle down and get married; but Oliver hadn't asked her to marry him. He hadn't even suggested it as a remote possibility. So all the stuff in Paris: had they both just been carried away by the romantic atmosphere in the City of Love? And those kisses since their fake engagement: had he felt anything at all for her, beyond their friendship?

Plus she'd told him the worst about herself. Things she'd kept secret for years and years. He'd been supportive and kind: but had he started having second thoughts about her? Now he knew what a mess she was beneath the surface, would he quietly back away? Had he used his dad's health as an excuse to put another barrier between them—the whole 'it's not you, it's me' routine?

Walking round a tiny, easy-to-solve maze wasn't the relaxing, meditative experience it was meant to be. Instead, it raised more questions and made her feel even more mixed-up. Miserable. Wishing things were different and not knowing how to change them.

She needed to talk this through with someone. Oliver would be her go-to whenever she wanted to tease out a knotty problem; but she could hardly talk to him about himself, could she?

She texted Darcy.

Are you free to talk some time today? Could do with some advice xx

The reply was almost immediate.

In wall-to-wall meetings. Will ring you tonight xx

In the meantime, maybe she ought to do the same: go back to her flat, make a fuss of Tilly, and get on with her work. Suppressing the ache in her heart, and hating the fact that she missed Oli so much—how, how, *how* hadn't she realised before what she really felt about him?—she texted back,

Thanks xx

Later that evening, Darcy video-called her. 'Are you all right, Fizz?'

'Yes.' She sighed. What was the point in pretending? She'd wanted to talk to her sister about this. 'No, actually, I'm not. I've made a huge mess of things.'

'How?'

'I don't even know where to start.' She blew out a breath. 'I think the only thing I did right was the commitment bit—I've got Tilly, and she's settled in really well.' She angled the camera so Darcy could see the ginger cat snoozing happily on Fizz's lap, her paws tucked neatly under her.

'Good. So has Ruby. And I'm enjoying the walks.'

'Good. And the wedding in Verona went all right?'

'Yes. Thank you for the dress. It wasn't what I'd have picked for me, but you were right. I felt amazing in it.'

'That's brilliant.'

'Tell me what's wrong, Fizz,' Darcy said softly. 'I can see it in your face.'

'Oliver,' Fizz said. 'When we went to Paris, I thought I was being clever in booking an Airbnb, and getting a good deal that meant we could stay for two nights instead of one.'

'A wild twenty-four hours and then a bit more. I'd have done that, too,' Darcy agreed. 'What happened?'

'It was tiny. I had no idea that a "studio" would mean a double bed that took up most of the space, a bistro table and two chairs, and a microwave.'

Darcy laughed. 'It isn't as if you were going to cook anything. Not with all those bistros around.'

'No, but I did expect the apartment to have a sofa as well as a bed.'

'So you slept with Oli?'

'Sleeping only as in snoozing, not sex. But I could've done. And waking up in his arms… I started seeing him in a different way, Darcy. And we danced together by the Seine. Drank cocktails—well, I did, after that first disgusting mouthful of absinthe. He stuck to wine.'

'I could've told you that absinthe tastes pants.' Darcy laughed. 'You only ever do it once.'

'Never again,' Fizz agreed. And it felt so good to laugh with her sister. As if the distance she'd felt between them had snapped short again.

'OK. So you thought about having sex with your best friend.'

'I didn't actually have sex with him,' Fizz said. 'But then it got complicated. His dad's been having heart trouble, and he collapsed. Oli rang me, so of course I went to support them.' She sucked in a breath. 'I'd been working on an engagement ring. I was just doing the final "squint and see if anything needs fixing" bit when Oli rang. I could hear how upset he was, so I just dropped everything to go to the hospital, and I kind of forgot I was wearing the ring. And his parents...they thought Oli and I had sneaked off to Paris to get engaged. They were so happy.'

'But that's good, isn't it?'

'No. Because we lied to them,' Fizz said. 'We were going to tell them the truth when Mark was feeling better. But I liked being engaged. I liked doing all the family stuff, and walking hand in hand, and stealing kisses. No, I more than liked it—I *loved* it, Darcy. It's what I never realised I always wanted.'

'Oli's always been in love with you, Fizz so what's the problem?'

'Oli isn't in love with me,' Fizz corrected. Because he wasn't, was he? Or he would've asked her to marry him when his dad had first given him the ultimatum. Or at any time since. Or at least told her how he felt about her—and he hadn't. 'And my client's story was in an online magazine about getting engaged in front of the *Sunflowers* in the National Gallery. The magazine featured a picture of the ring, and Juliet saw it. And Oli's parents are really upset with us.'

'They'll get over it. It's not as if you did it to cheat them out of anything. You just didn't want to tell them the truth while they were already so worried over Mark's heart,' Darcy said. 'Or is there more to this than what you're telling me?'

Caught by sisterly intuition. But she'd promised herself that she'd tell Darcy. 'There's something more,' Fizz said. 'Like I said, I finished the bucket list. I did something that scared me. I told Oli something I've never told anyone else. And I want to tell you in advance that I'm sorry I kept you out of the loop.' She clenched her fists for a moment, and then told Darcy about the one-night stand, the pregnancy and the miscarriage.

'Oh, Fizz. I'm so sorry you went through all that—and even sorrier that you went through it on your own. Why didn't you tell me, honey?'

'Because you, Mum and Dad were already in bits,' Fizz said, feeling miserable. 'You didn't need me making things worse.'

'You're my little sister. You can *always* tell me anything,' Darcy said fiercely, 'no matter what else is going on in my life. Oh, honey. I'm so sorry.'

'I'm telling you now,' Fizz said. 'And I'm OK. Really, I am. Because Oli talked me into going for counselling, and it's helping.'

'Good.'

'The counsellor said I needed to talk to you about it. To Mum and Dad.'

'It's your place to tell them, not mine. But I'll be there when you tell them, if you want me to support you,' Darcy said. 'And I'm proud of you. What you did is a *lot* scarier than going to ballroom dancing lessons.'

'You would've been brave enough to tell us, in my shoes,' Fizz said.

'And you wouldn't be scared by something as pathetic as ballroom dancing,' Darcy said. 'You'd just throw yourself in and have fun.'

'I think,' Fizz said, 'Laura gave us those lists to make us balance out. Be more like each other. Me more of a planner, and you more spontaneous.'

'Maybe you're right.' Darcy paused. 'And that means you've done the fourth thing—the thinking about what you want.'

Fizz nodded. 'Today. In the gardens behind St Paul's in Covent Garden.'

'And what do you want, Fizz?' Darcy asked, her voice gentle.

'Oli,' Fizz said simply. 'Except, in the circumstances...' She shook her head. 'He said we needed some space. And I'm scared he's going to back away from me for ever, now he knows what a mess I am. I mean—love doesn't really work, does it?'

'If you mean what Damian did when he dumped me at the altar, he actually did us both a favour. We weren't right together. It would've been a mistake. But love— love really exists, Fizz,' Darcy said urgently. 'And Oli loves you as more than just a friend—I'm sure of it. He asked you for space because of his parents. But if you talk to them, open up to them, they'll see you didn't mean any harm,' Darcy paused. 'You need to talk to Oli. Properly. Tell him how you really feel about him. And, you know, there's nothing in the rulebook that says he has to be the one to propose. There's no reason why you can't make him an engagement ring and ask him.'

Fizz blinked. 'You do know how long it takes to make a properly nice ring?'

'You're one of the Bennett sisters. You can do anything,' Darcy reminded her. 'Improvise. Use a bit of tinfoil and put a sticker on it or something!'

Fizz couldn't help laughing. 'That's silly.'

'But you'll both always remember it. It'll be one of those stories you bring up and smile about, year after year.'

Her sister had a valid point. 'What about you and Arturo?' Fizz asked.

Darcy smiled. 'I'll tell you more when you've talked to Oli and reported back to me. Not a word before that.'

'That's *cheating*.' But Fizz was smiling when she ended the call.

Proposing to Oli.

That would be taking a huge, huge risk. All her doubts came back. What if he said no?

On the other hand, what if he said yes?

She hadn't spoken to or texted him for a day. That barely counted as space. Then again, they talked and texted all the time, so a whole day probably did count as space. It was a lot longer than she was used to.

And, if she was honest with herself, she missed him. Bone-deep missed him. Without him, her life felt flat. Miserable. Full of shadows. 'I'm Felicity Bennett, and I can do anything,' Fizz told Tilly, stroking the sleeping cat. If Oli said no, at least her proposal would make him realise that she didn't see him as a just a friend—and maybe, if he thought about it a bit more, that no might turn to a yes. All she had to do was be brave enough to carry this through. Reach out for what she wanted. Believe that love could really be hers.

She typed a message to Oliver.

Meet me at Shakespeare's Tree, Primrose Hill, in an hour?

It took him a while to answer, but eventually he sent a message back.

OK.

So far, so good, Fizz thought. Now to sort out the ring.

CHAPTER NINE

As she crossed the road and started to walk up Primrose Hill, Fizz's heart was thudding—and not from the exertion of walking up the slope.

Was Darcy right, and Oliver had been in love with her for years? Or had her sister mistaken deep friendship for something else?

What if he said no?

What if she ruined their friendship? Then again, their fake engagement might already have done most of the work for her when it came to wrecking their friendship.

What if…?

And then she stopped thinking as she saw Oli. Casually dressed, in jeans and a T-shirt, sitting under the tree and reading something on his phone.

'Hey,' she said.

He looked up and gave her a slow smile. 'Hey, yourself.'

What now? Would he kiss her cheek, the way he usually did? Give her a hug? Stay at a distance?

And why on earth did she feel so ridiculously shy around him?

He stood up in one lithe, graceful movement, and

slid his phone into his pocket. How had she never noticed until these last few weeks just how gorgeous he was? 'Any particular reason why you wanted to meet under Shakespeare's Tree?' he asked.

'*"Shall I compare thee to a summer's day?"*' she quoted.

'*"Thou art more lovely and more temperate,"*' he quoted back. 'Are we really trying to out-sonnet each other, Fizz?'

'No,' she admitted. 'I just thought this was an easier place to meet, and it might be quieter than the viewpoint at the top.'

'You're right.' He smiled. 'Mum loved your flowers, by the way. She cried when she read your card. And she wants to frame that sketch of Poppy.'

'Good tears or bad tears?'

'Probably a bit of both,' he said. 'She's going to ring you tomorrow. I'm pretty sure she wants to make things up with you.'

Fizz dipped her head in acknowledgement. 'How's your dad doing?'

'OK. Better than yesterday. He's calmed down and being reasonable, and he's stopped saying that he has to go back to the office.' He raised an eyebrow. 'So. You wanted to talk?'

'I do. I…um…spoke to Darcy this evening. I told her about what happened when I came back to London. And the baby.'

'Good,' he said. 'How did she take it?'

'Pretty much the same as you did,' Fizz admitted. 'And I've done the fourth thing on Laura's bucket list.'

'Did you go to the beach?'

'No. To the garden behind St Paul's in Covent Garden. It's a good space.'

'Uh-huh.'

'I did a lot of thinking,' she said. 'About you, mainly.'

'Should I be worried?'

'I don't know,' she admitted. And it was crazy. She knew him so well, her best friend of years and years and years—but she didn't have a clue how he was going to react to this. Whether the world was going to feel full of sunshine afterwards or full of freezing rain. 'Darcy says you've been in love with me for years.'

'Does she, now?' he asked coolly.

What did that mean? That Darcy was wrong? Or that she was right? He hadn't admitted it. He hadn't denied it. He hadn't asked why she wanted to know.

All her ability to assess a situation seemed to have deserted her.

And since when had Oliver had a perfect poker face? Since when had she been unable to read his mood? It worried her even more, but she needed to ask.

'Is she right?'

'Why?' he riposted.

She narrowed her eyes at him. 'It's rude to answer a question with a question.'

'It's rude to ask someone if they've been in love with you for years,' he shot back.

She raked a hand through her hair, wishing she'd tied it back. Stupid to think that he might be swayed by a pretty dress and canvas shoes; Oliver was a lot deeper than that. And all this verbal sparring with him, much as she normally enjoyed it, really wasn't helping her nerves. This was too important to get wrong.

Maybe she should try another way. Being honest.

'I followed Laura's instructions. I found a quiet place to think, and I walked the Jubilee Memorial. You know, the little brick maze with the huge penny in the middle.'

'Using the maze as a meditation rather than a puzzle?' he asked.

She nodded. 'And I thought about what I really wanted. I've already got most of it: a family I love, a job I love, a flat I love. A cat.' She sucked in a breath. 'It might be considered greedy to want something more.'

'It might,' he agreed.

'But I do. I want more. I want…' Her throat dried.

'What do you want, Fizz?' he asked softly.

'I want a partner. Someone who'll always have my back but will let me take care of him when he needs it. Someone who doesn't mind that I'm a scatty daydreamer, and will even dream with me if I ask. Someone who brings out my nerd tendencies. Someone I can laugh with and feel safe enough to cry with.'

'And do you have anyone in mind?' he asked.

'I do,' she said. 'I think I've always known, deep down. Except I didn't think he thought of me in that way. I assumed he saw me as a kind of little sister. We kissed, once, but he was the one who called a halt, so I thought I'd got it wrong.'

He was very still, and his eyes were very, very blue. Like a fathomless ocean.

'After that, I think subconsciously I measured everyone I dated against him. They weren't even close, so they never lasted more than three dates. Everyone thought I was being a flaky party girl, but I wasn't,' she said. 'I just didn't connect it up properly. I didn't realise what was right in front of my eyes. That everything I wanted was in reach and I didn't have to go looking and discarding.'

'Go on.' There was a slight raspiness to his voice that told her this was important to him, too. That he felt it as intensely as she did. It gave her the courage to go on.

'He kissed me again,' she said, 'and then I knew. I knew he was the one I'd been looking for all along. The one who makes me feel complete.'

When he didn't say anything, it gave her hope. He wasn't pushing her away. She could do this. Follow through with her plan.

She dropped to one knee, fumbled in her bag, and brought out a small plastic box. 'Oliver Harrison, will you marry me?'

He blinked. 'You're offering me a ring?'

This was where he'd either laugh, or he'd reject her. And she really, really wasn't sure which it would be. 'Yes,' she said.

'An engagement ring,' he checked.

'A *temporary* engagement ring.' She had to be honest.

'Temporary?' He removed the lid to reveal the neatly made tinfoil ring with its heart-shaped honeycomb 'gem'.

'Ah. I think I understand "temporary",' he remarked.

'Limited shelf life,' she said, spreading her hands. Was that amusement in his eyes? Or horror?

'Representing a yellow gem,' he said. 'Now, what would that be?'

This was Oli. She was pretty sure he was expecting her to give him the nerdy answer. 'It could be amber, or a citrine, or a topaz, if you're looking at a budget option. Tourmaline. Danburite.'

The corner of his mouth quirked. '*Danburite?* Is that something you just made up?'

She shook her head. 'It's a silicate, similar to topaz.'

'I see.'

'At the top end of gems, it could be a yellow sapphire or a fancy yellow diamond. Heat-treated, lab-grown or natural.'

He nodded and gestured to the ring. 'And this is?'

'Honeycomb,' she admitted. 'I cut it myself. With a kitchen knife, not my jeweller's saw.'

'I should hope so. And you attached it to the tinfoil with…?'

'Melted chocolate. And I hope it hasn't melted again, or it'll fall off the tinfoil before you can put it on.'

He grinned, peeled the honeycomb off the tinfoil, and ate it.

'Oli! You were supposed to treat that with reverence, not eat it!' she said indignantly. 'Look at me, Oliver Harrison. I'm down on one knee, asking you to marry me. And what do you do? Instead of answering, you eat the engagement ring I just made for you.'

'Just the gem,' he said. 'The ring's still here.' He dangled the tinfoil off his little finger.

'How can I get engaged to you with a bit of crumpled tinfoil?' she asked.

'Don't forget the honeycomb. Which, I admit, was quite inventive,' he said. He took her hand and drew her to her feet.

'You didn't answer my question,' she said. 'So I take it that was a no to my proposal.' Except he hadn't let go of her hand. She had no idea what was going on in his head.

'I asked you to tell me what you wanted, Fizz.' He paused. 'Are you going to ask me what *I* want?'

Hope quickened in her veins. 'What do you want, Oliver?'

'A long time ago,' he said, 'I was a hardworking student, doing a Master's in Arts and Cultural Management. One night, I went to a party. I started talking to a girl, and we ended up talking all night. We watched the sun rise together, here on Primrose Hill. And it felt as if I'd known her for my entire life. She just *fitted*. But she was eighteen and I was twenty-one, and I could hardly tell her that I wanted to marry her right there and then. She still had a world to conquer. But I could be her best friend. So that's what I was.'

Then Darcy was right and Oliver *had* been in love with her for years?

'One day, she told me she'd had the worst news in the world. She was crying. I wanted to wave a magic wand and make everything all right, though I knew that wasn't possible. All I could do was to hold her close. And then she kissed me. It was amazing. Like fireworks going off in my head. I wanted more, but I knew she was vulnerable and I wasn't going to take advantage of that. I wanted her to want me for myself, not for comfort. So I called a halt, and I told myself I needed to stay in the friend zone.'

All that time they'd wasted, Fizz thought. But she didn't interrupt. Oliver still hadn't actually told her what he wanted.

'And then,' he said, 'she took me to Paris. On a budget, to fit in with her sister's bucket list. Which was possibly the worst place in the world I could go with her: how could I keep telling myself that we were just good friends, when there was all that romance around us? How was I going to resist kissing her, or telling her I loved her?'

She looked at him. 'But you *did* resist it. You didn't kiss me, and you didn't tell me you loved me.'

'I didn't kiss you,' he said. 'Because I was scared that, if I did, it'd make you back off. But I told you I loved you. You might've been too tipsy to remember.'

'The night we had cocktails?' She looked at him. 'But I felt it, the night before. When you took me dancing. You swept me off my feet. I didn't have a clue you could dance like that. But you made me feel special, as if I were floating on air. You weren't my best friend any more. You were this incredibly sexy, funny guy who made my heart do a backflip when you smiled. You quoted romantic French poetry at me—and instead of making me tease you, it made me feel all gooey and mushy. And it was thrilling—as well as scaring the hell out of me.'

'It made me feel all over the place, too,' he said. 'But it wasn't just Paris. It was the way, back in England, when the bottom dropped out of my world and you were there. Supporting me. Making things better.' He shook his head. 'That fake engagement stuff—part of me wanted it to be real, right from the start, but I knew you had issues about love, after seeing that guy break your sister's heart at the altar.'

'But I realise now that wasn't love. He was self-centred and utterly wrong for my sister,' she said. 'And I think now I used it as an excuse. I was scared of what love could do when it went wrong, and it was safer not to give it the chance to go right. Except it was right under my nose, all the time. It took me long enough to work it out.' His eyes were deep, deep cornflower blue. Like a midsummer night. It would be so easy to lose herself there. She caught her breath. 'And Laura's bucket list made me face it head-on. Made me work out what I wanted from life.' She swallowed hard. 'You. That's what I want. That's why I asked you to marry me.'

'With a ring made from a piece of honeycomb stuck to tinfoil with chocolate.' His mouth quirked again.

'Which you *ate*,' she reminded him. 'You were supposed to say yes, not seize the chance to stuff your face with sweeties.'

He grinned. 'I think we need to take a rain check and reframe this.'

Fizz stared at him. 'Are you going to be sexist about it and insist on being the one to propose?'

'Sweet as your honeycomb gesture was…'

He paused long enough for her to laugh and say, 'Yes, I saw what you did there.'

He swirled his free hand in acknowledgement. 'I

want to be the one doing the flashy proposal stuff. I've waited a lot of years to do it. It's not being sexist. I just really, really want to be the one who says the words. If you'll humour me.'

'Of course.' She waited expectantly, but he didn't drop to one knee.

'Not here,' he said softly. 'Primrose Hill has different memories for me. Of the night I discovered it really was possible to fall in love with someone, the first time you met them.'

'Why didn't you say anything to me before?' she asked.

'Wrong time, wrong place. And I'm not going to say the words yet either,' he said. 'I'm a planner. I have a particular time and place in mind. Oh, and I have a commission for you. I need an engagement ring. That is, unless you'd rather I asked someone else to make it?'

'No way am I letting someone else make my engagement ring,' she said. 'What do you have in mind?'

'Something that sparkles, like the way you make me feel,' he said. 'Unless you don't like sparkly rings?'

'I admit I'm not keen on pavé rings, but I do like a well-cut gem,' she said.

'It's your choice what you make. Just as long as you wear it for me.'

She smiled. 'I already know what I'll design.'

He smiled back. 'A sunflower?'

'No. That's Laura's flower. For me, I was thinking a forget-me-not: a round brilliant-cut yellow diamond in the centre, with five pear-cut sapphires the same colour as your eyes,' she corrected.

'Do forget-me-nots have five petals?' he checked.

'Oh, you pedant.'

'Details specialist,' he corrected.

She laughed. 'Actually, they do. But, even if they didn't, I'd still make an uneven number of petals.'

He tipped his head slightly to one side. 'Why?'

'Think about it. *"He loves me, he loves me not,"*' she said. 'Even is bad. Odd is good.'

'Hmm,' he said. *"'Doubt thou the stars are fire:/ Doubt that the sun doth move;/ Doubt truth to be liar;/ But never doubt I love."'*

'Would it be pedantic to point out that we know the stars aren't fire, now?' she asked.

'And incorrect. Because, when those lines were written, people believed the stars were fire,' he said.

'You're such a nerd, Oli.'

'Takes one to appreciate one,' he said, and leaned forward to kiss her.

It was a long, slow, sweet kiss, full of promise and pent-up longing. The sort of kiss that could break a heart and stick it back together with sunshine. And it made her knees go weak.

'How quickly can you make that ring?' he asked when he broke the kiss.

'I need to source the gems. And I'll need a hallmark on the ring—I can cut down on the time that takes if I take it to the Assay Office myself and get it done priority.'

'Are we talking days, weeks, months?' he checked.

'Days, if I can get hold of the right gems,' she said.

'I'll check in with my usual dealer first thing tomorrow. And you can come with me, if you like.'

'I'd like that.' He nodded. 'Days. All right. So if I book something for Friday, perhaps we can finish this conversation then.'

'This Friday?' she asked, and thought about it. 'It'll be a bit of a squeeze, but I'll rise to the challenge.'

'Of course you will. You're Fizz Bennett. I'll let you know details as soon as I've sorted it,' he said.

From the way he'd suggested it—using the same words she had when booking their wild twenty-four hours in Paris—she was pretty sure that was where he was going to propose. And she had a feeling that he was going to be inventive about it.

In answer, she kissed him. Together, they walked back down the hill, their arms wrapped round each other. Even though the sun was setting and it was starting to get the tiniest bit chilly, the world felt bright and full of sunshine.

They hadn't said the words, but she knew it. She knew it in her heart. Oli loved her, and she loved him. And everything was going to be OK.

'I assume you're coming back to mine?' she asked. 'Much as I love your parents, I don't want to...' Her voice faded with embarrassment.

He nibbled her earlobe. 'You don't want to make love with me for the first time with anyone else in the house?'

Her cheeks flamed. 'Yeah.'

'God, you're pretty when you blush.' He spun her

round into his arms. 'You know what? I'm seriously thinking about being old-fashioned.'

'You mean, no sex until we're married? No *way*,' she said.

'Waiting until we're engaged,' he corrected. 'I've waited seven years for you, Fizz. I can wait until Friday.'

Was he teasing her? But then she saw the seriousness in his face. 'Oli.' She pressed her palm lightly against his cheek. 'You've waited seven years for me to come to my senses and realise that you're the love of my life. I've worked it out, now. So why wait any longer?'

'Because I want it to be special,' he said.

'Being spontaneous now doesn't mean that our engagement night won't be special,' she said.

'I want to have the fun of wooing you. An old-fashioned courtship. Concentrated into one evening.' He caught her lower lip briefly between his. 'And then, just you and me. A wide, wide bed.'

She went hot all over. 'All right,' she agreed huskily.

'I'm going to see you home, kiss you chastely at the door—and on Friday…'

The promise and the look in his eyes were delicious.

It was strange, working on your own engagement ring, Fizz thought. Technically, it was the second time, because she'd made the replica ring for her fake engagement; but this felt different.

And she thought of Oliver with every moment she spent crafting the ring.

He still hadn't actually *said* the three little words to

her. That declaration from *Hamlet* wasn't quite enough. And even though she knew how he felt, she wanted to hear the actual words so she could be absolutely certain that he, Oliver Harrison, loved her, Felicity Bennett, and wanted to spend the rest of his days with her. Clearly he was going to wait until he asked her to marry him before saying it.

On Friday.

When they'd be in Paris, which was all that he'd told her.

And she had absolutely no idea what he'd planned, because he'd flatly refused to be drawn into giving her any more details.

Would he ask her to marry him by the clock in the Musée d'Orsay, his favourite place in Paris? By the banks of the Seine, where they'd danced together under the stars? Had he booked the tiny studio apartment in St Ouen and he'd put the ring in the mini-fridge under a pastry to tease her? Or maybe he'd ask her to marry him underneath the huge cherry tree in the Jardin des Plantes, with blossom falling like confetti? The café in the Marais where he'd fed her a rainbow of *macarons*—perhaps with the ring hidden in the middle of a pyramid of her favourite flavours? Or somewhere she hadn't even thought of?

Oliver wasn't as predictable as he seemed. And she liked that, too: it meant he was reliable, but he was also flexible. The perfect combination.

Once satisfied with the ring, she took it for hallmarking; and she gave him a crimson velvet-covered box with the finished product on Thursday evening.

He opened the box and looked at it. 'I loved that sunflower you made—but this is definitely more you,' he said. 'It's beautiful.'

'Thank you.' She smiled at him.

'Ready for tomorrow?' he asked.

'All packed and ready. And I bet I'm at the station before you are,' she said.

She was wrong. He was already there when she walked into St Pancras, waiting for her by the check-in desk. 'I have coffee,' he said. 'And lunch. Which is a lot more civilised than having to be here at six o'clock in the morning.'

'You've already missed the best part of the day,' she said.

He kissed her, then whispered in her ear, 'Tell me that tomorrow morning.'

And she went hot all over as the possibilities bloomed in her head.

He'd booked them on the train, on the grounds that it was better for the environment—but, unlike their first trip to Paris, he'd booked them in business class. He'd bought them a wonderful picnic for lunch with salads, herbed chicken and flatbreads, followed by lemon tart. And at the Gare du Nord in Paris they were met by a car that took them to a very plush hotel that had been renovated from one of the old Parisian mansions, all cream-coloured walls and huge windows and wrought-iron Juliet balconies. Their suite had an enormous bed, the kind of carpet you sank into, and a stunning view of the Eiffel Tower. And the bathroom alone was bigger than the whole apartment they'd shared a few weeks ago.

'So you're going for the opposite of what we had in St Ouen, then?' She tutted. 'What on earth are we going to do without that micro-kitchen?'

'Room service,' he retorted with a grin. 'Right now, we're dropping our bags, and we have a date at the Louvre.'

She was dressed casually, with comfortable shoes for walking and a sunhat; but she'd brought a dress with her at his request, and hung it up in the wardrobe so any creases would fall out while they were exploring the city. She noticed that he, too, hung up a suit and shirt.

Their hotel wasn't far from the Louvre; he'd arranged skip-the-line tickets, and Fizz thoroughly enjoyed wandering round the galleries hand in hand with him. He took her to the Egyptian gallery to see the Sphinx of Tanis and the incredible painted statue of the Seated Scribe; and she loved the jewellery, from the gold bangle made from two intertwined serpents to the incredible detail on the tiny ducks sitting on a ring.

Every corner seemed to bring a new and famous masterpiece: the *Venus de Milo*, Canova's incredibly romantic *Psyche Revived by Cupid's Kiss*, the *Mona Lisa*. Though Vermeer's *The Lacemaker* was the painting that took her breath away. 'It's the light,' she said to Oliver. 'And I can't believe he managed to squeeze all that detail into such a tiny painting.'

He'd booked skip-the-line tickets for the Eiffel Tower, too, and they zoomed up to the very pinnacle in the glass-sided elevator to drink pink champagne and gaze over stunning views of Paris.

Oliver, Paris and art. It didn't get any better than that, she thought.

Except it did. Because the dinner reservation he'd made for them was at their own private terrace at the hotel. There was a table with a white starched table-cloth, and all around it were white pillar candles and arrangements of deep red roses. A cascade of the de Ronsard roses wound round the wrought-iron railings, and a piano piece she recognised as Debussy played softly from a hidden speaker. In front of them was the Eiffel Tower, and the sky was a riot of colour.

Oliver looked incredible in a dark suit, crisp white shirt, and a blue silk tie with tiny forget-me-nots on it. She'd dressed up, too, in a simple sleeveless round-necked navy dress with a flared skirt and an overlay of chiffon embroidered with tiny white flowers, teamed with her favourite red court shoes.

'You look amazing,' he said.

'So do you,' she said.

Because tonight was special.

Not a surprise engagement, but one that had been a long time in the making. Seven years. Seven years when the most patient man in the universe had been by her side, her best friend.

The food was exquisite and beautifully presented. Scallops with sage butter, spiced squash risotto with greens, and then a *café gourmand*: a beautifully bitter espresso served with four tiny desserts.

'This is perfect. I would never have been able to choose between a tarte tatin, a crème brûlée, a passion-fruit *macaron* and raspberries with Chantilly cream,' she said in delight.

'I know. This is the best of all worlds,' he said.

When they'd finished and the table had been cleared, he glanced at his watch. 'Right this very second, I feel more nervous than if I was having a *viva*, a driving test and a really important job interview, all at the same time. Oh, not to mention being a client's proxy at an auction when it was their favourite painting in the world and someone was bidding against us and I was getting near the agreed limit.'

'It's four little words, Oli. And you were the one who insisted on saying them,' she reminded him. 'If you'd accepted my beautifully carved honeycomb ring instead of scoffing it...'

He laughed. 'Yeah. But I'm still nervous. Because this is the most important question I'll ever ask in my entire life.' He took a deep breath. 'Fizz. I fell in love with you the day I met you. You're like a ripple of champagne in the sunshine, spreading light and brightness wherever you go. And I love everything about you. I love the way you can't suppress a smile when you're supposed to be serious. I love the way you focus when you're making something delicate out of what looks to everyone else like little lumps of stone and bits of wire—but in your head you've already seen what their potential really is. I love the way you find joy, that you follow your impulses even when they land you in trouble, and that your heart's big enough to take on an elderly cat whose owner died, so she can enjoy her sunset years with you.' He glanced at his watch again. 'I'm running out of time. Felicity Bennett, I love you so much. You really are my best friend. My soulmate.

I want to spend the rest of my life with you, make babies with you if we're lucky, and have a house full of love and laughter.' He stood up, walked round the table to her chair, and dropped down on one knee. 'Will you marry me?' He opened the crimson velvet box to display the gorgeous forget-me-not sapphire and diamond engagement ring she'd made.

She leaned forward to kiss him. 'I love you, too, Oliver Harrison. Yes, I'll marry you.'

There was a perfectly timed burst of sparkling in front of them as the Eiffel Tower lit up.

He slid the ring onto her finger, then stood up and drew her to her feet. 'So we're officially engaged.'

She remembered what he'd said, the night she'd proposed to him: he'd wait for her until they got engaged.

Suddenly there wasn't enough air—which was ridiculous, considering they were outside.

'We need a selfie for the parents,' she said, suddenly panicking.

'You have a point. And we have about four minutes to get a good shot.' He stood behind her with his arms round her, and she held her left hand up, displaying the ring.

He held his phone out. 'Smile—three, two, one...' He snapped the photograph of them together, with the Eiffel Tower sparkling in the background. 'And now just the hands.' He slid one hand under hers and she curled her fingers round his hand, displaying the ring.

'Perfect,' he said, and spun her round so he could kiss her. 'We'll send this to your parents, mine, and Darcy, later tonight. But first I want to dance with my new fiancée.' He flicked into his music app, and she recognised the song immediately: George Michael's version of 'The First Time Ever I Saw Your Face'.

'It's a song that was written way before both of us were born,' he said. 'But it says everything I want to say to you. I love you, Fizz.'

'I love you, too, Oli,' she said. She stepped into his arms, closed her eyes, and as they began to dance she kissed him.

She wasn't sure which of them moved off the terrace first, or which of them closed the door and the curtains behind them. But then he'd swept her off her feet and was carrying her to that beautiful wide bed.

And, as he set her back on her feet, seven years of waiting was finally over.

EPILOGUE

One year later

DARCY ADJUSTED FIZZ'S veil when she'd climbed out
of the car and handed her bouquet to her, ready for the
photographer to take the traditional photographs of the
bride, the matron of honour and their father.

The empire line wedding dress covered her bump—
the little bit of news that Fizz and Oliver weren't quite
ready to share with their family, until Fizz had reached
the twelve-week point and stopped worrying quite so
much.

Darcy smiled. 'You look amazing.'

'So do you.' Darcy was also wearing an empire line
dress, except hers was in sapphire blue rather than
ivory, and there were small sunflowers threaded into
her updo to go with the sunflowers in Fizz's bouquet.

'The sun's out,' their father remarked. 'And it's warm
for December.'

'That's our Laura making sure my hair stays nice
until after the photos are done,' Fizz said. 'I think she'd
be pleased with the result of her bucket list.' She looked
at Darcy. 'You married to Arturo, me about to marry
Oli—both of us settled and happy, the way she wanted

us to be.' Fizz and Oliver had sold their flats and had moved into a terraced house in Chalk Farm, the previous month; Tilly the cat had settled happily into her new abode, either people-watching from the back of the sofa in the living room, or curled on a cushion next to Fizz in her workroom.

'She would,' Darcy agreed. 'She'd have loved Ruby and Tilly, too. And she'd be pleased that you chose her favourite flower for your theme. That cake your friend made with the cascade of sunflowers down it is *incredible*!'

Fizz blinked back the prick of tears. She'd always miss Laura—always—but today was a day for smiles. The day that she and Oliver pledged their love in front of their family and friends.

'Ready to go, love?' her father asked. 'Or do you want to be traditionally late?'

Fizz smiled. 'I think I've kept Oli waiting for long enough.'

'Agreed.' Darcy laughed, and made a last adjustment to Fizz's veil. 'All set.'

'All set,' Fizz said, and her father pushed the church door fully open.

Oliver heard the creaking of the church door as he stood at the altar. Then the usher had clearly alerted the organist, who started to play Pachelbel's Canon. And Oliver found his pulse rate rocketing at the idea of his bride walking down the altar to him.

Sanjay, his best man, nudged him. 'You can look

now. Actually, you should *definitely* look. She's the definition of a radiant bride.'

Oliver turned round, and he couldn't help smiling as the woman he loved walked down the aisle of the Victorian church towards him, carrying a bouquet of sunflowers softened with gypsophila, holding on to her father's arm and with Darcy bringing up the rear.

I love you, he mouthed as Fizz handed her bouquet to Darcy and came to stand beside him.

Love you, too, she mouthed back.

Everything was perfect. The music, the weather, the smiles on all the guests' faces. Fizz's father reading from Corinthians about love being patient, and the mischief on Fizz's face when she squeezed his fingers and mouthed, *You were beyond patient. Seven years!*

His mother reading Shakespeare's *Sonnet 116.*

The vicar asking if Felicity Bennett would take Oliver Harrison as her lawful wedded husband, and the love in her eyes as she said, 'I will.'

The two of them exchanging the rings she'd made, simple bands of gold engraved inside with their initials and the date.

The vicar declaring them man and wife, and finally the words he'd been looking forward to: 'You may kiss the bride.'

Maybe he lingered a little too much over the kiss, because their guests all cheered, and when he broke the kiss Fizz was laughing.

The guests showered them with delphinium petals as they left the church; he helped Fizz into the old-fashioned Rolls-Royce, then climbed in beside her. They posed for a couple of photographs before Sanjay closed the car door, and the Rolls-Royce drove slowly down the gravelled track.

'Well, Mrs Bennett-Harrison.' He savoured the words.

'Indeed, Mr Bennett-Harrison,' she said with a grin.

'Ready to start the rest of our lives?' he asked.

'Now and for always,' she said.

And this time he took his time kissing his new bride, all the way to the gorgeous Queen Anne building just down the road in Hampstead, which housed an art gallery and music room where they were holding the reception.

Once they'd greeted their guests and made sure that everyone had a glass of passionfruit martini or champagne in the music room, the wedding breakfast was served in the art gallery section of the house. The tables were in a horseshoe shape, covered with starched white tablecloths, and the arrangements of tiny sunflowers brought a touch of extra brightness to the room.

'Trust you to hold your reception in an art gallery,' Darcy teased.

'I was an art student and my new husband's a fine art dealer. Of course we'd celebrate in an art gallery,' Fizz answered with a grin.

Oliver chuckled. 'We did think about hiring the middle of the Eiffel Tower.'

'Except dancing isn't allowed on their glass floor. So that's a no. Because this is a party,' Fizz said, 'and I want dancing.'

Darcy smiled. 'I'm not scared of dancing any more. Thanks to Arturo.'

'Good. Because you're dancing with me, later. All of you.' Fizz hugged her brother-in-law.

The food was wonderful—a wild mushroom and thyme tart garnished with edible petals, chicken marinaded in lime and served with sweet potato mash and green beans, and a *café gourmand* at Fizz's special request with a mini crème brûlée, lemon curd tart and a blueberry Eton mess. Fizz had also arranged a special bottle for herself, which looked like champagne from the outside but was actually sparkling elderflower, and the bar staff had all been quietly briefed that if anyone bought Fizz a cocktail they should mix her a special version of a passionfruit martini without the vodka and with sparkling water in place of prosecco.

After the meal, everyone's drinks were topped up and Fizz's dad made a short but very sweet speech, Sanjay enjoyed telling terrible stories about Oliver's student days.

And then it was Oliver's turn.

'I think everyone knows I fell in love with Fizz the very day I met her, but it was never the right time to tell her—until she had to do Laura's bucket list, and asked me to go to Paris with her.' He bent down to steal a kiss from his new bride. 'Maybe if I'd taken her there years ago, we wouldn't have wasted all that time being just best friends. Maybe I'm just a bit slow on the uptake. Or maybe she would've turned me down and this year was exactly the right time for me to tell her how I really felt about her.' He smiled. 'And now I'm going to shut up. Thank you all for coming to celebrate with us, but most of all thank you to Fizz for marrying me and making me the happiest man in the universe.' He raised his glass. 'I give you my bride. It's taken me seven years to get her to the altar, but she's worth the wait. Fizz Bennett-Harrison.'

'Fizz,' everyone echoed, raising their glasses.

And then it was time to go into the music room, with its gorgeous light wood panelling and elegant sconces. A baby grand piano was installed at one end, flanked by enormous ferns; they'd hired a pianist and singer to perform a mixture of songs, from slow jazz-based numbers through to dance-floor fillers, so there was something for everyone for their guests.

But the first dance was theirs alone.

And, after Paris, there was only one song it could be.

Oliver looked at Fizz as the first notes of 'The First Time Ever I Saw Your Face' floated into the room. She smiled, slipped into his arms, and began to waltz with him.

Halfway through, their parents, Darcy and Arturo, and Sanjay and his partner Ruby joined them on the dance floor.

'Happy?' Oliver asked, looking into Fizz's eyes.

She smiled. 'With you? Always.'

* * * * *

MILLS & BOON MODERN IS
HAVING A MAKEOVER!

The same great stories you love,
a stylish new look!

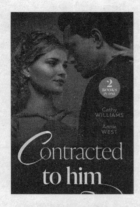

Look out for our brand new look
COMING JUNE 2024

MILLS & BOON

COMING SOON!

We really hope you enjoyed reading this book.
If you're looking for more romance
be sure to head to the shops when
new books are available on

Thursday 4th July

To see which titles are coming soon, please visit
millsandboon.co.uk/nextmonth

MILLS & BOON

MILLS & BOON®

Coming next month

UNEXPECTED FAMILY FOR THE
REBEL TYCOON
Rachael Stewart

'Where's Fin?'

'He's in the front room, doing his summer project for school.'

'He's doing *what*?'

Matteo flicked Porsha a look to find her staring at him, and grinned. 'I know, wonders never cease, right?'

She shook her head and fisted her hips, her blouse pulling taut across her front, not that he was noticing or reacting in any way, shape, or form—*Neighbour. Friend. Fin's parental figure*!

The mental mantra was getting tired. Stepping in as Fin's manny for the summer had been an easy offering, one that Porsha had eventually accepted and one that was going swimmingly in all ways but one…*this*.

The incessant pull he felt towards her, the attraction, the chemistry…

Experience told him it should have eased by now.

Instead it was doing the opposite.

Maybe that was denial for you…evil.

But seeking out a fling right on one's doorstep was

never a good idea. Especially when he had no interest in commitment. Short term, long term, any kind of term.

And then there was Fin to consider, a boy who'd already been through enough upheaval to last a lifetime.

No, denial was the only option.

Continue reading
UNEXPECTED FAMILY FOR THE
REBEL TYCOON
Rachael Stewart

Available next month
millsandboon.co.uk

LET'S TALK
Romance

Follow us:

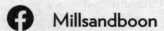 Millsandboon

 @MillsandBoon

 @MillsandBoonUK

 @MillsandBoonUK

For all the latest titles and special offers, sign up to our newsletter:

Millsandboon.co.uk

afterglow BOOKS

Afterglow Books is a trend-led, trope-filled list of books with diverse, authentic and relatable characters, a wide array of voices and representations, plus real world trials and tribulations. Featuring all the tropes you could possibly want (think small-town settings, fake relationships, grumpy vs sunshine, enemies to lovers) and all with a generous dose of spice in every story.

♪ @millsandboonuk
📷 @millsandboonuk
afterglowbooks.co.uk
#AfterglowBooks

For all the latest book news, exclusive content and giveaways scan the QR code below to sign up to the Afterglow newsletter:

SCAN ME

Never Date A Roommate
PBO 9780263322897 £8.99
Ebook 9780008938420 | Audio 9780263324860
For publicity enquiries please contact
millsandboonpressoffice@harpercollins.co.uk

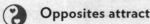
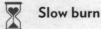
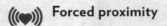
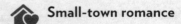
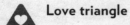
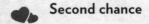